Born in a small town in Rajasthan, India, Vijaya spent her childhood in Wales and then moved to Delhi with her family. After completing her Masters in Psychology from Delhi University, she got married and shifted to Kolkata.

She has been teaching and working with differently-abled children and adolescents for more than 20 years. While working at the Indian Institute of Cerebral Palsy, Kolkata, she completed her M.Phil. in Special Education from Manchester University, UK.

Vijaya lives in Delhi. She is a counsellor, corporate trainer and special educator; and heads the Special Education Needs Department in a renowned inclusive school in Noida.

Passionate about her work, Vijaya is a romantic at heart. She enjoys listening to music and loves to read.

With deep gratitude for the two angels in my life:

My princess, Neha, the light of my life and my biggest fan and critic

&

My Guardian Angel
You and I are in complete and rare harmony
But the symphony is unfinished
Its haunting melody will transcend the silvered wings of time
Into the unknown eternity

And for my hero – Rattan: "I think a hero is an ordinary individual who finds the strength to persevere and endure in spite of overwhelming obstacles. They are the real heroes and so are the families and friends who have stood by them" *Christopher Reeves*

Vijaya Dutt

IT HAPPENS ALL THE TIME

AUSTIN MACAULEY
PUBLISHERS LTD.

A CIP catalogue record for this title is available from the British Library.

ISBN 9781786120687 (Paperback)
ISBN 9781786120694 (Hardback)
ISBN 9781786120700 (E-Book)

www.austinmacauley.com

First Published (2016)
Austin Macauley Publishers Ltd.
25 Canada Square
Canary Wharf
London
E14 5LQ

ACKNOWLEDGEMENTS

The first draft of this book, based on my life, was less than 50 pages long. "It's a great beginning," Jaya, my sister, said cautiously, knowing how irrationally and fiercely possessive I am of my writing. "Each sentence has an entire story to tell." She advised, criticised and deleted so skilfully that I did not even feel the pain!

Special thanks to my brother, Ashim, for his creative insights.

I am especially grateful to Mum, Dad & Ma. Their unstinted support and faith in my abilities kept me on track.

Heartfelt gratitude to my dear friend Radha, for her constant encouragement. She took me to book launches to keep my faltering flame of "publishing hopes" burning bright!

Thanks to my friend Anu, for her unshakeable belief in me. I think I will appoint her as my PR Manager!

Gratitude to all my friends for their constant encouragement and enthusiasm.

I would also like to acknowledge the tremendous unconditional support I received from my dear friend Sanjay.

It is difficult to find enough words to thank all the people who have come into my life - stayed there, moved on, taught me and made me who I am today.

I am blessed to have Neha, my daughter. She stood by me, encouraged me to carry on writing and never gave up on me. Without her constant push this book would have never seen the light of a publisher's office! She is my inspiration...my joy! Thank you darling.

I have been fortunate to have Austin Macauley as my publisher. Vinh, my Production Manager, and his team have been so encouraging and patient in responding to all my queries. It has been a wonderful experience.

Selection of the title was fun! I decided on 'Just Another Life…' "That sounds so depressing," said my brother. "That's too trite," said a friend "It needs to be something more poetic to do justice to your story."
"An Unfinished Symphony…" and "Life is a plate of Burmese Pakodas" were close contenders but finally I decided on -
It Happens All The time

So here it is….

Tonight I'm gonna break away
Just you wait and see
I've never been imprisoned by
A faded memory

It happens all the time
This crazy love of mine
Wrapped around my heart
Refusing to unwind
Ooh-ooh, crazy love, ah

Count the stars in the southern sky
That fall without a sound
And then pretend that you can't hear
These teardrops coming down

(Excerpts from 'Crazy Love' – Poco, 1978)

2006... A Silver Wedding Anniversary

A sonorous, long and drawn-out "Om", pushes through the smoky air saturated with the religious heady scent of incense. The pandit's rich baritone lifts a notch. "Shanti, Shanti, Shanti..." he continues, his pitch getting progressively lower. A long bunch of hair fountains from a small, tightly wound knot at the top of his closely cropped head. A glistening oily tail that tassels flaccidly. An oily Brahmin's knot of supposed superior lineage. Menhuin-like, he raises his right hand − a signal for everyone to join in. A multi-pitched chorus of "Oms" follows. Divya chants softly with the other people gathered around Asha and Gautam as they shower rose petals on them. The bright yellow canopy flutters gaily in the early winter breeze. A fragrant cascade of rose gently floats down, peppering their shoulders, settling at their feet in a velvet carpet of pink and red. The sweet perfume of crushed rose fills the air.

Realising the ceremony is soon to end, everyone moves closer to the couple, like iron filings to a magnet. With an expert flick of his wrist, the pandit pours the last few spoonfuls of ghee in the fire, energising the flames into a mesmerising serpentine dance. The havan is over. Asha's face glows happily as she and Gautam stand and accept blessings and good wishes for their silver anniversary.

Dressed in the heavy, vermillion and gold brocade sari that she had worn when she married him, Asha lowers her eyes coyly like a bride. Apart from a few strands of silver shining through the golden veil covering her head, she looks as beautiful as she had in her youth. Divya's thoughts yoyo back to their college days and the fun they had together and then to the present again. *She has aged so gracefully*, she thinks smiling at Gautam, who looks debonair with his salt and pepper hair, which he refuses to colour. "They look so good together." The years have been kind to them. In the tight embrace of their son and daughter they form an island of love in the sea of people surrounding them. A bright green twinge of envy rears its ugly head in Divya's heart. She quashes it fiercely with a mental menhir! No! She didn't want to go down that treacherous road of self-pity again.

Friends and relatives surge forward, elbowing each other, pushing gently to reach the silver couple who has just renewed their marriage vows. Each one wants to be the first to congratulate them. As the crowd ebbs before the next flow, Divya watches Asha and Gautam bend to touch the feet of all their elders, receiving their blessings as they bend and rise. "Sada suhagan raho," "May you have many more happy years together," "May silver turn to gold," "Happy Anniversary." The music of wishes fills the air, expanding into a placid hum. Loving hugs and warm wishes envelope them. It is their day of glory. They are the epicentre of attention.

Thanks to her five-feet-nothing height, Divya can only see heads and hair after a while. Heads of different ages and genders bob up and down in front of her. Brown hair, black hair, grey hair, no hair, streaked hair, hair decorated with flowers and ornate pins. *That woman must have spent hours and lots money at a beauty parlour to get that done*, she thinks inanely, as a head with hundreds of thin plaits each woven with gold and silver threads, pops up before her. An intricate work of art that blocks her view.

Divya's thoughts turn elsewhere. Moving aside, she gives way to the jostling crowd. Her good wishes can wait.

Like a Kamikaze pilot, her mind zeroes in to what is really bothering her. Her knees buckle and she leans against a wobbling bamboo pillar supporting the canopy. Her silver wedding anniversary is just two days away. She should be ecstatic and glowing too. Inviting friends, planning celebrations, unveiling her deep maroon wedding sari from its protective muslin wrap, airing it after 25 years to wear for the occasion. Staring down at the havan kund still alive with flames she inhales deeply, trying to cleanse her soul with the sacred sweet fragrance of incense.

Her thoughts drift like wisps of smoke spiralling upwards... to Ravi lying bed-ridden, thousands of miles away. *What kind of a wife am I?* she thinks guiltily. *Shouldn't I be there by his side, fulfilling all the promises made at the time we got married? All those '... for better or for worse... till death do us part' vows??*

His face fills her mind. A gaunt, pain-lined face staring at her with sunken eyes ravaged with despair.

How could I have left him at a time when he needed me the most?

Familiar waves of guilt flood her again. And what about the deep sadness? The remorse? The impotent rage she had lived with for so many years? Were they to be unspoken burdens she was to carry for as long as she lived? This is not the way it was meant to be. What had gone wrong? Why was God constantly testing her? What was the deeper meaning behind all this? She feels despondent and lost… Tears threaten to well up, spill and ruin her makeup. She blinks them back, suddenly remembering where she is and self-consciously looks at the people around her.

I hope they think it's the smoke in my eyes or that I am just terribly moved by the ceremony.

Patting her wet eyes with the edge of her sari pallav, she tries to shake off the ominous cloak of depression, its folds clinging to her not wanting to let go, like the lizard that had fallen off the mango tree onto her arm, many years ago… its claws sinking in. She can feel the ominous approach of a panic attack, as her heart starts galloping. *Breathe deeply. One, two three… Focus on each breath. Calm down.* November breeze cools the beads of sweat on her flushed face.

The havan kund splutters crackling flames in a swan song. She stares entranced, at the hypnotic glowing embers. Her mind accelerates in reverse, as she retraces her life in the flickering fire. Fire… they were old adversaries…

A Birth, and a Trial by Fire

1959. A cold, dark January night in a house in Fatehpur Shekhawati, a small village in the deserts of Rajasthan. Barely a few days old, Divya lay secure and snug against her weary mother, Tara's warm breast. A thick cotton quilt immobilised them with its weight. Following norms laid down by her widowed mother-in-law, Tara and her new-born daughter slept in a back room, segregated from the world for forty days. The white, windowless room was so small that the wooden bed they slept on filled it up, leaving just enough space for a person to walk around it. Apart from a rickety aluminium table squeezed into the corner, it was bare. The bright red roses splotched on the yellow quilt cover lent their colour to the stark room. A faded green curtain hanging in the opening where a door should have been, separated the tiny confinement room from a bigger front room. Tara's husband, Varun slept here with his mother and Jyoti, their one-and-a-half-year-old daughter.

The small room glowed an orange-gold with the warmth of the angithee... a bucket of burning coal was kept at the foot of the bed to protect the weary mother and baby from the harsh desert winter of Rajasthan. But it also ended up ensuring that Divya's new born life was tempered with fire.

A storm raged outside. Its restless cold hands relentlessly rattled the rickety rafters, demanding to be let in. Suddenly, a window swung open, its latch loosened by the wily fingers of the desert wind. The wind rushed in with a victorious howl. A spark from the angithee, energised by the current of air, leapt up and settled on the quilt, in a smouldering circle of burnt orange. Smoke started billowing from the foot of the quilt and it burst into flames. Tara, still weak from a prolonged labour, could hardly move, let alone jump out of bed with her newly-born babe in arms.

"Raja! Raja!" she screamed weakly, as the heat and smoke engulfed them. *Varun was her raja, her god, the "king" of her life. She worshipped the ground he walked on.* Overcome with fear, Tara struggled to push away the heavy quilt and stood on the burning bed, clutching Divya protectively in her arms. Horrified, she watched the fire quietly work its way round the edge of the quilt, the smell of burning cotton and smoke stinging her eyes and nose. One red rose after another vanished in quick succession off the yellow quilt, as the hungry flames greedily got too close for comfort.

"Help! Raja! Wake up! Help!"

Tara's feeble screams finally penetrated Varun's sleep and he woke up, startled, to the strong acrid smell of burning cotton. Jumping out of bed, he rushed into the room horrified by the sight of his frail wife standing in a bed of fire clutching their scrawny new-born daughter! Phoenix rising from a sea of flames.

"I'm coming, Tara!" he shouted, twisting his lungi into a knot around his waist. "I am here!"

Without a moment's hesitation, in true 'Hindi-filmi' style, he strode through the thick wall of smoke and fire and just plucked both of them off the bed carrying them to the safety of his room before he tackled the burning bed.

Tara's knight in shining armour, her Raja had saved them from a grisly death. Shaken by the incident, Varun ensured that from then onwards, they slept in his room, by his side. That fire ended the forty-day isolation very dramatically and prematurely.

He had been devastated when, just a couple of days ago, he'd heard the news of Divya's birth. "You have another little baby girl, Guha," the mid-wife, Sona Bai had announced drawing aside the green curtain. Her words rang loudly above the protesting wails of the baby, not happy to leave her fluid world. Yes, a daughter – his second. This new life, created with love and passion… and hope, had just shattered his dreams.

As the cold wind whistled through the naked trees, rearranging the desert sands into dynamic dunes, he sat down on the cold floor contemplating his fate. The shadow of this skinny young Bengali doctor danced on the bare cement wall in the flickering light of the lantern. A picture of palpable disappointment, he was curled up, foetus-like, palm against forehead, in mourning.

"Sorry, Doctor Sahib, no son this time… better luck next time!" Sona Bai continued in a matter-of-fact voice. "Mark my words, your next child will definitely be a boy." Her empathetic heart went out to this young man. Though he was a Bengali and an outsider in the neighbourhood, his healing touch and affable manners had endeared him to the proud Rajputs. He was the respected and much loved village doctor. Having another daughter was tough. She consoled him in her own straightforward, religious way. "So what if she's a girl. Just accept her as God's gift to you. She is divine." Explaining difficult situations as God's will always helped.

Conscious of the doctor's disappointment, but helpless in the hands of fate, Sona Bai dropped the curtain and hurried back to Tara. She had no time to waste sympathising. Duty called. Efficiently wrapping up the baby into a white bundle of soft, clean cloth she placed her in the secure warmth of her exhausted mother's arms. She still had a lot of cleaning up to do before she could leave for her next patient, who lived more than a mile away in the next village. And anyway, there was no point in waiting after the birth of a girl, she thought forlornly as she folded the towels. There would be no celebrations or the heavy baksheesh that she had hoped to get if she had delivered a boy. The New Year had begun badly for her. She prayed for better luck at the next house where the village pradhan's daughter-in-law was going to have her first baby. "Please, God, let her have a boy. I could do with some extra money." She thought of the hole in her roof that needed to be repaired and the cow that she'd wanted to buy for a long time.

Varun had yearned for a son. Prayed so hard... as never before. But God had not heard him. First came Jyoti and now he had another daughter! Wearily rising to his feet, he stared dispassionately at the green curtain. It still fluttered gently behind the retreating white back of Sona Bai, the bearer of such frustrating tidings. With leaden feet he pushed the curtain aside and walked into the small room. Tara watched him approach the cot wishing she could wipe away the disappointment from his face... feeling guilty to be the cause of his distress. She clutched the innocent infant to her breast as if to get strength from that tiny body. Swallowing the lump in his throat, Varun wiped the sweat of exertion from the face of the woman he dearly loved. No matter how upset he was he could not shirk his responsibilities to this helpless bundle. Reluctantly he reached down and picked her up as she demonstrated her lung power and screamed angrily at the injustice of being dragged out of the warm comfort of her mother's arms. Staring at her misshapen, glistening bald head, he held her tiny body close to his, as if to protect her from his chauvinistic thoughts. "Divya," he whispered, Sona Bai's words still fresh in his mind. "She is God's gift to us, Tara." He told Tara, "She is divine." His words were balm to her exhausted body and distraught mind. Tara fell into a deep sleep.

Divine or not, Divya had survived her first trial by fire, her 'agni pariksha', saved by the scrawny arms of her father, wielding strength borne out of fear, out of protecting his loved ones... However, there were to be many times during Divya's life when she wished that those flames had consumed her.

Tara

Divya was hardly a few months old, when Varun left for England to study to be a surgeon. As they were not very well-off, Tara willingly sold whatever little jewellery she had to help him along his way. She stayed back in Delhi with the apple of his eye (Jyoti) and his shattered dream (Divya)!

With Varun away, they had to live with Tara's family… all of them squished into a smallish room, on the first floor of a house in Sita Ram Bazaar, in old Delhi. Tara's childhood home. She was a middle child, sandwiched between two elder sisters and two younger brothers. Born in Amritsar, most of her early years were spent away from her family home. She lived in a different part of town with her mother's family where her only companion was a young, unmarried aunt, Urmila, who was not much older than her. Often, after school, Tara would go home to see Chaiji, her mother, but would promptly be sent back. Weak and weary due to many pregnancies, Chaiji was overworked and simply relieved that with Tara in Urmila's care, she had one less child to look after.

After the historic Partition of India, Tara's family decided to move to Delhi but they left her behind with Urmila. Though she was fond of Urmila and well cared for, Tara obviously wanted to go with her mother. She was young and needed her family around her. But Chaiji was firm – Tara should stay in Amritsar and continue her education.

"Your sisters have not had the opportunity that you are getting to study in such a good school. Study hard beti. It is important. Education is something no one can take away from you. You can come and visit us during school holidays."

A sad and tearful Tara bid them a reluctant farewell. She loved going to school but she was jealous of her sisters and brothers who were living together in one big happy family. And she missed Chaiji tremendously. Affected deeply by this separation, Tara wilted like a rose plucked from its bush. Seeing her so unhappy Urmila promised to send her to Delhi after her exams during her summer holidays. She was in class six.

The days crawled by in agonising slow motion. Finally Tara's exams were over. True to her word, Urmila organised for her to go to Delhi. Travelling by train, in the custody of a family friend, she was soon on her way. The excitement of the journey and anticipation of being reunited with her family made her skin tingle with goose bumps. Soon she would be home. She couldn't wait to feel her mother's arms around her again.

For want of anything better to do, Tara opened the plastic bag of food that Urmila had packed for her. Two aloo parathas with a small piece of mango pickle, a banana and a barfi. The pungent smell of raw mango pickled in mustard oil filled the compartment, making her mouth water. She ate hungrily as she stared out of the window at the fields of maize dancing in the breeze. The meeting and parting dance of the telegraph lines fascinated her in a hypnotic sort of way. The journey was long and the train painfully slow. Finally it chugged into Delhi station. Scanning the crowd through the bars of the grimy window, Tara saw her father standing on the crowded platform.

"Pappaji!" she shouted waving happily at him from the window. This was the day she had circled in red on her calendar. Yes, she would now be with her family again.

Her father was a serious man of few words. Very rarely did Pappaji display his emotions. Patting her head, he silently held her hand, picked up her small suitcase and led her out of the station. At last she was going home.

Tara jumped off the rickshaw and ran all the way up the steep stone stairs. She ran straight into Chaiji's arms. Tears of the joy of being reunited streamed down her face. It was this loving embrace that she had missed during those lonely months in Amritsar. Happy and secure, she wished she could hold on to this moment forever. It was at this point, with her face hidden among the folds of her mother's sari and her thin arms wrapped around her in a tight circle of love that Tara made up her mind. She would not go back to Amritsar.

"But what about your school?" Chaiji said, alarmed at this decision. "You are such a good student, beti. You are doing so well in your studies there."

"I'll go to a school here," Tara said adamantly. "There are good schools in Delhi." Her fourteen-year-old mind was made up – she would not go back.

She was ready to do anything to stay with her family. With true grit born out of sheer desperation, she went to a local school for admission. She went all by herself. She met the principal and explained her situation. Amazed at the sheer gumption of such a young child, the principal agreed to admit Tara in the school. Not wasting any time, Tara rushed home, took the money for fees from her mother and went back to the school to complete the admission procedure. She could not believe her luck. She would live with her family again. Her joy was boundless.

Eagerly she started going to her new school and picked up where she had left off. She was a diligent student. After completing her daily homework she would voraciously read not only her textbooks but also newspapers and magazines, anything that came her way. The other members of the family shared the housework, leaving her to her books. Life couldn't have been better for Tara.

A few months later, Tara fell ill in school. Feverish and out of sorts she decided to go to her aunt Bimla's house which was close by. She did not want to bother her mother who after recovering from two miscarriages, was heavily pregnant once again. Her eighth pregnancy.

Bimla was Tara's tai ji... Pappaji's elder brother – Pitaji's wife. She was childless and always looked forward to Tara's visits. That day, lugging her school bag that seemed to get heavier with each step, Tara somehow made it to her aunt's house. Banging feebly on the door she called out to her aunt. "Aaeee, aaeee," she heard Bimla's voice in the haze of her fever. As soon as the door opened, Tara collapsed on the doorstep, into a surprised Bimla's arms. She was shivering uncontrollably and had high fever. The doctor was called. It was typhoid. Together with a whole heap of medicines and injections, complete bed rest was prescribed. Bimla felt it was better if Tara just stayed with her till she recovered.

Since Chaiji was unwell, Tara's parents could not come to see her immediately. They came two days later. Too weak to get up, Tara lay on her bed and watched her mother ease down her hugely pregnant body awkwardly on a chair next to her.

"Please take me home with you, Chaiji. Please," wept Tara. "I want to go home."

But she was still not fit enough to leave the house.

"We'll come and pick you up in another week or ten days," promised her mother hugging her. "By then you will be stronger."

That was the last time Tara saw her mother.

A week later Chaiji died giving birth to a premature stillborn baby. Unaware of her great loss, Tara, in the throes of Typhoid, nearly died herself. It was unanimously decided that she was in no condition to hear the traumatic news of her mother's death. Every time Tara asked about Chaiji, Bimla made up some excuse or the other. One month later, though still weak from the ravaging disease, she was on the mend. Her sisters came to visit her. It was only then she learnt that her mother had died.

"Chaiji is no more," they wept. Tara fainted. Her sisters splashed cold water on her face to revive her. Revive her for what? A future without her most precious mother?

"You were so ill yourself that we couldn't tell you."

"We did not want to lose you too."

Tara stared at them in stunned disbelieving silence as they tried to console her. Their words floated in and out of the penumbra of her consciousness. No, how could it be true? Her mother had promised to come back and take her home. She didn't bother to ask about the fate of the baby. She was not interested. If it had not been for that baby her Chaiji would still be alive. If only she hadn't fallen ill, she would have been with her mother. An unreasonable, impotent rage swept through her young body. She was heartbroken. For days she wept. Silent tears of anger and sorrow drenched her pillow. She wished that she had spent more time with her mother. That she could get one more hug from her. That she could hear her soft, loving voice once again. But it was not meant to be.

A new widower, Pappaji was completely lost without his wife. How would he bring up so many children all by himself? He was clueless. He had never really played an active role in their upbringing. He did not know what to do. Luckily for him, and the children, Bimla, took charge. She picked up the reins that were dangling loose since her sister-in-law's untimely and sudden tragic death. Bimla and her husband shifted house to stay with Tara's family. Though inexperienced in the art of child rearing, Bimla took it on her able, plump shoulders to care for the five motherless children. Taiji took on the role of 'Mataji' in their lives... and though she was not their biological mother, she loved and cared for them as any mother would.

Life slowly limped back to normal in their household and soon Tara was fit enough to go to school again. But she was in for a shock. Pappaji refused to send her back to school.

"You have missed so many classes already. You will definitely fail in your exams," said the man of few words firmly. "And anyway, I have no money to spare for a girl's education. Focus on cooking and keeping the house clean."

Tara couldn't believe what she was hearing. Hadn't she stayed back in Amritsar, away from her family, so that she could continue with her schooling there? Chaiji had always put her education before anything else. Now here was her father contradicting it all. Her younger brothers were going to school, why couldn't she? Anger and resentment bubbled inside her. She begged and pleaded. But his mind was made. No more school... it was a waste of his money to educate a girl who would soon marry.

"But, Pappaji, I love studying," Tara pleaded. "I promise I won't fail."

"Your sisters haven't gone to school so why should you? And anyway, what use is all this school and studies? Go to the kitchen and learn something more useful like cooking." The argument was sealed with the stamp of patriarchal power. "I will not spend any more money for your school," he reiterated vehemently.

But Tara was not willing to give up her mother's dream. Her own dream. She wished that her mother were alive... that she had more money... that she had been born a boy. But soon Tara realised the futility of such thoughts. She needed to be rational and practical. Taking matters in her young hands, she decided a concrete plan of action. Once again, armed with her courage and fortitude, Tara went to a school of well repute. Once again, she went alone. She met the principal and put forth her case.

"Please, madam," she pleaded, "I am a good student and am very keen to study but my father will not pay my fees."

The benevolent principal not only admitted Tara to her school, but also exempted her from paying fees. Happy and victorious at her achievement, Tara prepared to go to school again. Even though she missed Chaiji tremendously, deep down in her heart Tara knew that she done her proud.

Life without Varun

So what did Tara do while her 'raja' sailed the high seas to foreign shores? Life was not easy for her. Together with Jyoti and Divya, a total of nine people living under that one-roomed roof. The Bhatia clan. Papaji, Tara's brothers – Manoj, Pappu and Pinku, and Mataji and Pitaji. It was a tight squeeze. At night they slept on cotton mattresses, unrolled to cover the cracked, grey cement floor. Everyone had to wake up early so that these mattresses could then be rolled up and heaped at one end of the room, like sand bags around trenches. Only then could breakfast be served to the hungry men who had to leave for work. All meals were eaten in shining steel thalis, sitting cross-legged on the freshly swabbed floor.

The one-roomed house was in Neela Wali Gali, one of the lanes of Bazaar Sita Ram. Halfway up the narrow and steep stone staircase, to the left, was a tiny and rather dark, grubby toilet with a broken, two-panelled, rusting metal door. The lower end of one of the panels had corroded into jagged crevices. The stench of the much-used toilet followed people as they held their breath and hurried up into a small open space flanked by a kitchen, a tiny bathroom (gusalkhana) and the door to the one and only room they all lived in. A black wooden staircase, against the wall opposite the kitchen led up to the roof. The four white lime walls of the room had different identities. The wall facing the entrance to the room was

27

lined with folding wooden doors, painted a bilious green that opened out into a narrow balcony overlooking the lane. The wall on the left, covered with pictures of Ram, Sita, Durga, Krishna and Hanuman, was the 'prayer wall'. Incense sticks, wedged into the frames of the Gods and Goddesses were lit morning and evening by Mataji. The family faced this wall when they prayed in silent monologue with the divine powers. The wall opposite the prayer wall had a wooden cupboard built into the wall and a long shelf. On one end of this shelf rested a mirror, a few combs, a bottle of Afghan Snow cream, a tin of Cuticura talcum powder and a bottle of coconut hair oil that would freeze white in winter. At the other end was a big box-like HMV radio that was switched on for the major part of their waking hours, churning out news, Hindi film songs or religious songs – depending on who was in charge of the controls at that time. The central pride of place, on that shelf, resting on a white, lacy mat crocheted by Tara, was a framed photograph of Varun. Below this was a narrow wooden couch, which served as a divan during the day and a bed at night.

Apart from helping Mataji, with the housework, Tara struggled with her two bawling brats, who became hysterical if she moved out of their audio-visual range. Insecure at the thought of 'losing' another parent, Jyoti clung to her and became uncontrollable if she could not see her. Too young to understand the situation, Divya would just mimic Jyoti's behaviour and add to the furore. Jyoti was her role model. The puller of her emotional strings. She often sat and wept in front of their father's framed photograph.

"Daddy! Daddy! I want my Daddy!" Jyoti would howl, her young mind trying to fathom the cause of his sudden absence from her life. How could he have just left her and gone off like that? Was it something that she had said or done? Staring at the photo on the shelf, of a strange scrawny man with a thin pencil moustache, Divya would join her, tears of empathy rolling down her cheeks, upset because Jyoti was. In fact, at times she even cried louder than Jyoti. Once she started crying, Divya would get so involved in it that there was no stopping her! Hearing their sorrowful duet, Tara would rush to hug them and end up crying too. She wept as she dried their tears with the end of her sari.

"No, beti, you mustn't cry. We will soon be with Daddy." They made a sorry picture – the three of them sitting and sobbing their eyes out, missing Varun, wishing they were together again.

Apart from the bittersweet joys of motherhood, what kept Tara going in her months of loneliness was the postman. He became the next most important man in her life. Anticipation, satiated by news from her beloved, went on to create a deeper hunger inside her. Spinning in the spiral of hope, she lived from one aerogramme to the next. The tinkle of a cycle bell was enough to make her drop what she was doing and rush to the veranda, hoping to see the grey-haired postman, with his khaki mail sack strapped to his side. Sometimes, she would stay in the veranda all morning, leaning precariously over the trellised wall, waiting for him to come trundling round the corner on his bicycle.

The sight of the postman taking out a light blue aerogramme from his bag and pushing it in the rickety mustard yellow letterbox was all she needed to boost her flagging spirits. Luckily for her, Varun was a good correspondent, ensuring a steady stream of weekly letters. Letters that described the grey and cold English weather and the bland food he had to eat. Oh how he missed her rajma and chicken masala! Letters that spoke of love and loneliness and of a bright future together... soon. He missed her and the girls and understood this separation was tough on all of them. In just a couple of months she would be with him again, he promised. Her young heart was full of hope and love. No longer would she have to listen to cruel relatives who swore on all that they held holy that her husband would never come back... or worse still, if he did it would be with a 'memsahib in a tight miniskirt with a bob-cut'... an immediate connection to the 'vamps' in the Hindi films. They were liberal with their hurtful comments and unsolicited advice. Like starving carnivores, they hunted for gossip to feed on, for they were bored with their own uneventful lives.

"Didn't I warn you, Behena?" Billo tai reminded Mataji of her prediction. "I told you that Bengali doctor was no good. But who listens to me? Now he's gone and left her!" She was the meddlesome neighbour who made it her business to know about the affairs of the Bhatia family. Tara dreaded her visits because she left an insecure trail of fear in her wake. She probably spent a major part of her day with her ear pressed hard against the thin wall the houses shared, straining to hear conversation filter through bricks and mortar. Some 'Breaking News' that she could use in her daily gossip sessions. She had all the makings of a TV reporter.

"What will Tara, beti, do now? No husband and two daughters to boot!" Kunti masi pulled her sari pallav firmly on her head as she added her bit of masala, ready with her condolence speech on the death of a marriage.

"He must have found a 'gori mem' now he won't come back," predicted the local midwife who had helped deliver Jyoti, in that very house, two years earlier. "Didn't you hear? That's what Suresh, Pammi's son, did. He now has a desi wife and a white one! Chhee chhee!" she touched both her ears in a superstitious gesture, which actually looked like she was checking to see whether both her ears were still there or not. "Hai Ram! This is kalyug after all."

But Bebo, the vicious old crone with the warty nose, who lived downstairs, went one step ahead of everyone else. "If and when you go, just throw Divya into the sea! She cries all the time!" She offered this drastic solution to a tearful Tara, on how to put a permanent end to her younger daughter's constant wailing who was definitely not worth the trouble if she cried so much! "I will be the happiest when you are gone." She continued in this heartless fashion. "Then I will finally be able to sleep in peace, undisturbed by your daughter's ear-shattering banshee wails!"

Stoic as ever, Tara would swallow her tears, don her expressionless mask to hide her anger and resentment, and serve them tea and Marie biscuits. "Don't pay heed to what they say, beti." Mataji could read Tara's silences better than anyone else. "Take it in from one ear and out of the other." But their voices of doom constantly echoed in her head, keeping her awake during those long, lonely nights when she yearned for the secure comfort of her husband's arms. She had faith in him, for did he not marry her against his mother's wishes? Was that not proof enough that he truly loved her? But there was a germ of doubt, a little question mark in her mind that grew out of the seeds sowed by her relentless relatives and nosy neighbours. What if they were right? What if she had really lost him? What if he had forgotten her? What if...

Varun

Tara remembered the day when she had first met Varun. She was a shy eighteen-year-old girl sitting in his crowded clinic with Mataji, waiting for treatment. A persistent cough was troubling her no end. Waiting for her name to be called out, she stared at the black and white plastic nameplate hanging on the door. Dr Varun Guha. "*Guha?*" she read the unusual surname again. "*What kind of a name is that?*" She thought, *I wonder where he's from.*

Varun Guha was a self-made man, who had seen life from both sides.

Born in a small village, in what is now Bangladesh, Varun spent his early childhood in rustic simplicity. Living near a river, he learnt to swim around the same time he began to walk. Together with his brothers and friends he would row to school in his very own, tiny 'boat' made from a hollowed trunk of a tree. Many a time during their races back home, boats would overturn, and he would come home soaked to the skin, to face his father's wrath. His father was a strict disciplinarian, a no-nonsense man. He worked hard as an inspector in a steamer and navigation company to ensure that his family had a comfortable life. When Varun was about ten years old, his father was transferred and moved with his family to Bhagalpur, a small town in Bihar.

Even though Varun was a sickly child, tormented by gastric infections and amoebiasis, he was spirited. He would be the first one to sign up for any kind of competition, whether it was swimming, wrestling, kabaddi or rowing. He loved sports of every kind and invariably returned home with medals and cups. He was his father's favourite, amongst his five brothers and one sister. Often he would accompany his father on the company steamer and go fishing far out into the river. Varun was proud to be his dad's little helper and cherished these shared moments of togetherness.

Close on the heels of India gaining independence, relatives flooded their house. Victims of the partitioning of the country, they had fled from their homes in East Pakistan fearing for their lives. They had nowhere to live. Varun's father took them all in, with open arms. Aunts and uncles, with their children, filled the house, completely changing their lifestyle. For a while chaos reigned supreme. But no one in the family dared complain. Varun's father would not turn away these people who were in need and had come to him for help. Once the dust settled down, a quiet air of communal harmony spread like oil over troubled waters. Life in the household jumped back on track again.

Apart from his interest in sports, Varun was an excellent artist. Though he had not received any training whatsoever, with a few strokes of his paintbrush, he could make sceneries come to life. It was a God-given gift. Much to his father's dismay, he would spend hours lost among his canvases and paintbrushes. One day, in a fit of rage, Varun's father tore up all his paintings.

"Painters live in poverty and if they are any good, become famous only after they die! Stop wasting time like this, Varun. Enough is enough," he ranted. "I have told you before and will not repeat myself anymore. You have to study hard. Make something of your life. Become a doctor."

Varun silently looked on in despair as his works of art were shredded and destroyed. He was very upset but fear, respect and yes, love for his father made him obey his command. With a heavy heart he gave up painting and studied medicine… a basic course to gain a licence so that he could dispense medicine. When he passed this course his proud father set up a dispensary for him not far from home. Initially people from the neighbourhood trickled in, out of curiosity, but very quickly, as news of his expertise spread, Varun's practice grew.

Not allowing him to rest on his laurels, his father insisted that Varun now join a full-fledged medical college and pass his MBBS exam. "You have the makings of a good doctor. It is my dream to see you famous. I will be the proud father of a famous doctor." Obediently, once again Varun prepared himself for higher studies and got admission into a good medical college.

A couple of months later his father fell seriously ill. He had been complaining of severe stomach aches for a while and was rapidly losing weight.

"Don't worry, Baba. I will take you to Calcutta. They have the best doctors in the medical college there. You will be well in no time."

Varun took his father to Calcutta and got some investigations done. Expecting a gastric or intestinal infection, he was in for a shock when he got the report. His father was diagnosed with advanced stage cancer of the gall bladder.

"Your father's condition is serious." The doctor took Varun aside and informed him. "He does not have very long to live."

Dumbstruck and shocked, Varun could not believe what he was hearing. Within a nano second his life had changed. He wanted to weep and hold his father close and never let go. He felt like screaming in anger. He wished someone would come and say that "Don't worry, son, we will treat your father. He will be okay." But there was no one. Nothing. He had no one to turn to for help. Slowly he walked towards his father.

"It's nothing serious, Baba," he controlled the tremble in his voice. His eyes glistening with tears that threatened to spill over in an uncontrollable gush. "You'll be okay. I've got the medicines for you." He did not have the heart to tell his father this shattering news. He could not.

He kept this news a secret and told no one at home... not even his mother. He kept this horrific information to himself, praying for strength and courage. Hopelessly he watched as jaundice enveloped his father, taking away his strength and appetite, colouring him a deep shade of yellow. Instead of helping him, his medical knowledge hammered home the brutal truth. Impotent in the face of the lethal combination of cancer and jaundice, he waited desolately for death to take his father away.

A couple of nights later Varun woke up to his mother's screams.

"Wake up, all of you! Wake up! How can you sleep? Your father is dying." Her shouts filled the night, waking up his siblings and relatives.

Rushing, Varun was the first to reach him. Pushing the mosquito net aside, he held his frail father in his arms. "Baba, it's me. Varun." He wept. The tears he had held inside for so long flowed freely. The dam of courage was broken.

"Look after everyone, I..." Just like that, mid-sentence, his father whispered his last breath in his favourite son's arms.

"Baba... Baba! Don't leave me. Don't go."

Holding his father's limp, gaunt body, Varun wept the tears of a broken man. He was a doctor but he had not been able to save his father's life. His baba, who he respected so much, who he loved with every atom in his body, was gone forever. Desolate grief swept through him. His tears rained down on his silent, unresponsive father. He was now holding a body in his arms. A body that once was his father.

Ironically, his mother's wails and the sight of his weeping siblings filled him with a divine strength. He had to be tough for them. He had to rise above his anguish. The onus of looking after his widowed mother and six siblings had fallen on his young shoulders.

In shameless haste, all those relatives who had sought and received refuge in their home, left. At a time when they needed all the support and help they could get, Varun and his family were left high and dry, in the hands of fate. Alone. The very people who had sponged off them suddenly vanished. They were left to fend for themselves. Varun's mother had sold most of her jewellery to pay for his father's treatment. They were now living off their meagre savings. The cold fingers of poverty came knocking on their door.

Varun was desperate. He had no time to feel cynical or angry. Self-pity would get him nowhere. He needed to act fast. He had promised his father that he would look after everyone. Come what may, he would keep his word. Luckily he found a job close to the medical college where he studied. He was paid two rupees a month to write official letters in English for a businessman. Attending as many classes as he could, Varun would work for the rest of the day so that he could earn some money to send home. He had no money to buy the expensive medical books, so he borrowed books and lecture notes from his friends. He would then study all night for he had to return them the next morning.

He lived with a relative who made place for him to stay in his store room among his sacks of salt, offering him a jute bag to sleep on the floor at night. If it was not the mice, it was the mosquitoes that kept him awake. This relative's wife was kind enough to feed him a princely feast of two dry chapattis with a piece of jaggery a day. Of the two chapattis, he would fold one and hide it in his pocket for his younger brother who studied in a college nearby. He could not bear to think that he was eating while his brother stayed hungry. They met every day under the big banyan tree where Varun would watch his brother devour the rolled up treat.

Then one day he was caught.

"How dare you steal from us? You are biting the very hand that feeds you!" He was soundly thrashed for feeding his brother with their chapattis. "Haraamzada! You wretched ungrateful boy."

He stayed on despite the insults and the beatings. Whatever little help they dished out, he took with open arms. He could not afford the luxury of an ego. His poverty made him vulnerable and dependent on others. But it also made him strong... filling him with a determination that he would overcome this challenge life had mercilessly thrown his way. One day he would not need to turn to anybody for help. One day he would be in a position to help others... in a more humane way. He made a silent promise. A commitment to his father's memory.

"If someone helps you in your time of need you must never ever forget that. You must always be grateful even if someone gives you only a pin. Because that's what you needed at that time." Varun told his children, later in life. Advice that stemmed from his own experiences.

Life was harsh. People were cruel. Those were tough times but he was determined to become an excellent doctor and nothing would come in the way of his dream... his father's dream... even if he had to study all night to make it come true. He was an achiever. He learnt to be tough on himself for he could not afford to succumb to the inviting arms of self-pity and distress.

After passing his MBBS exam, Varun got selected for a registrar's post in a government hospital in Delhi. He still had a long way to go but he was on the first rung of the ladder of success.

Varun Meets Tara... and they Marry

Stethoscope strung around his neck, Dr Varun Guha sat at the table in his clinic and watched his ninth patient of the morning walk out. It was nearly 11:30. He was thirsting for a cup of tea and desperately needed a break. But the waiting room crowded with sick people indicated that he might even have to delay his lunch. He could hear people coughing and shuffling about outside. As he leaned back in his chair, his eyes fell on his prescription pad next to his blood pressure instrument. Dr Varun Guha, M.B.B.S. A deep sorrow shadowed his eyes as his father's face swam like a watermark on the clean sheet of paper. He missed his father. Time had not healed that wound. Sighing he pressed the bell and waited for the next patient to be sent in.

"Tara Bhatia," called the nurse from behind her cluttered table, looking at her list of entries. "Doctor is ready for you now."

"Come, beti" Mataji heaved her heavy body out of the uncomfortable plastic chair. Following her ample white figure, Tara stepped hesitantly into his chamber.

Awestruck, Varun watched as this figment of his bachelor dreams walked into his room. Her bright pink dupatta, accentuating her ivory skin, was draped delicately round her thin shoulders. Her long, thick black plait hung over her left shoulder firmly holding the dupatta in place. The tiny pearl earrings dotting her earlobes were her only adornment. Her innocent, ethereal beauty completely knocked him off his feet. Thank God he was sitting down.

"Please sit down." Varun suddenly remembered his manners as he realised that the two women were still standing and staring at him, waiting for him to speak. Mother and daughter, he presumed. Coughing violently as soon as she sat down, Tara covered her mouth with one end of her dupatta. Shyly she looked at him, apprehension reflecting in her big brown eyes. He was a skinny bespectacled man with a thin moustache outlining his upper lip. Why was he staring at her so intently with his dark black eyes? She felt as if he could look inside her mind and read her thoughts. Uncomfortably she looked away, letting Mataji give a detailed description of her ailment

What would the doctor say? Would she need an injection? She hated injections. She had to have so many when she had nearly died of typhoid a few years ago. Tuberculosis was rampant in those days and Tara was worried that something was seriously wrong with her again. She needn't have worried about that.

"Don't look so worried," Varun had to put her at ease. He had read the apprehension in her eyes. "It's nothing serious. Just a bad throat infection. You'll be ready to sing soon." He joked and was rewarded with a tremulous smile of relief. He wanted to say something witty and funny. He wanted to see her smile again. But Mataji's voice took over.

"Thank you, Doctor Sahib."

"Bring her again after she has had these capsules for a week." He reluctantly dragged his eyes away to look at the older woman.

Varun cured her throat infection. But who would treat his lovesick heart? Tara was too young and naïve to know that the minute he saw her, this man of medicine was hers. He became a man with an obsessive dream... a dream to marry this Punjabi beauty.

Luckily for him, Varun left such a deep and positive impression on Mataji that soon he took on the role of family physician. His congenial and convincing bedside manner encouraged confidence and bridged the patient-doctor gap. With his effortless charm and air of reliability, boosted by patience and perseverance, he managed to win over Tara's orthodox, die-hard Punjabi relatives. So, much against his own mother's wishes... this Bengali doctor became part of a Punjabi family!

Tara and Varun were wed on a hot and balmy June night. His dream was now a reality. She was his. So strong was his love for her, that he even agreed to a Punjabi-style wedding. He found himself going to his bride's house perched precariously astride a skeletal, moth-eaten mare, which could barely move once he sat on it! Bedecked with garlands he made a grand entrance accompanied by a few friends and the usual trumpeting and drum beating band belting out "Come September" and other standard wedding tunes

Putting his hard-earned savings to good use, he organised a small reception and invited his friends and relatives to meet his bride... the woman of his dreams. He even managed to scrape together enough money to buy Tara two saris... a baby-pink chiffon with a thin gold zari border and a turquoise blue silk with little white flowers all over. The short and romantic two-day honeymoon in Agra was the icing on the cake. It was all he could afford.

Letters from Varun

It was these saris that Tara clung to when she thought of those days and struggled with her pain of loneliness. It was these saris that soaked her tears when she hid her face in their soft folds, inhaling the fragrance of Varun's love. His sincere voice promising to send for her as soon as he had earned enough for the fare kept ringing in her ears. These delicate saris were her lifeline, each silken strand connecting her to him.

They had had long discussions regarding his decision to go to England to become a surgeon. She was the one who, ignoring her twinges of concern, persuaded him to pursue his dream. For she knew how much it meant to him. She managed to convince him that she would be fine staying with her parents till he sent for her. Deep down in her heart she had an unshakeable belief that soon they would be together again. So she turned a deaf ear to the ill will of gossip-hungry relatives, pulled out the weeds of doubt by the roots and threw them in their faces. Her two daughters were living proof of their passion and undying love for each other. She was confident and she was tough.

"Trrring – trring." The familiar bell of the postman's cycle cut into her reverie. It was a hot summer afternoon. The men folk were out at work. Jyoti and Divya were playing with their dolls on the cool cement floor in front of the pedestal fan. Divya was patting hers to sleep, while

Jyoti was trying to stuff a piece of chapatti in her doll's plastic mouth. Mataji was in the kitchen making herself a cup of tea, in spite of the heat. "Tea," she would say, "keeps the heat out of your system." Tara sat on a cane stool in her favourite place in the corner of the balcony. She was absently combing her long black hair, lost in a haze of thoughts.

The cycle bell jolted her out of her semi-somnambulistic state. Throwing the comb down in a Pavlovian response, she rushed down the stairs, tying her hair in a knot as she went. She nearly tripped over the pleats of her sari in her excitement. The postman waited patiently for her. By now he knew that the blue aerogrammes with English stamps on them controlled the young mother's heartbeats. He preferred to hand deliver them rather than simply put them in the letterbox. At least this way he got a chance to see pure, unadulterated joy in someone's eyes. It filled his heart with a warm glow in a strange vicarious way. "Another chitthi from bilayat for you, beti," he said, holding out the blue envelope, smiling at the eager glow in her eyes.

"Thank you, Hari Bhai," Tara said, eagerly snatching the letter from his extended hand and tearing it open as she climbed the stairs. As always, her eyes quickly scanned the page. A once-over before the proper word-for-word read. The smile faded from her face as the written words sank in. She could not believe what she was reading. The words seemed to lunge at her, sharp razors heartlessly cutting her dreams into little pieces. It could not be true! She collapsed in a heap on the top step, sobbing as if her heart would break. Her hopes had come crashing down like a house of cards.

"What's the matter? Tara?" Mataji came rushing out of the kitchen spilling the cup of tea over herself in her hurry to know the cause of the heart-wrenching sobs.

Mataji had a gentle, comforting air about her. She always covered her head with her sari pallav and she always wore white, even though she was not a widow. Earlier, whenever anyone died in the family, she would shed her coloured sari and don a white one. Unfortunately, at one point, so many people died in her immediate and extended family that she just locked up her coloured saris and continued to wear white. It probably seemed like less of a hassle at that time and then just became a way of life for her.

Ignoring the rapidly spreading sepia stain on her clothes, she tried to gauge the situation. She was shocked at the sight of her shattered daughter sitting on the landing, weeping her heart out.

"What's wrong, Tara? Has something happened to Doctor Sahib? Is he okay?"

Though he was her son-in-law, she couldn't bring herself to call Varun by his name. He had always been, and would always be 'Doctor Sahib' for her.

"Beti, say something."

Getting only sobs in response Mataji bent down and with trembling hands picked up the cause of this hysterical outburst from the floor, where it had fallen from Tara's listless fingers. Expecting the worst, she adjusted her spectacles and tried to focus on the neatly printed, tear-stained Hindi words. Varun's letter was terse, stating that all travel plans had changed. That she couldn't come to England. He would soon let her know his future plan of action. He did not substantiate his instruction with any reasons or explanations.

"Now, now, don't cry, beti," Mataji held her daughter's thin, heaving body close to her ample bosom. "I know what you are thinking but don't jump to conclusions. Have faith in God. Something must have come up for him to change his plans. You will go to him… if not now then a couple of months later. Don't lose heart."

She read the unspoken fear in her Tara's eyes. The fear that maybe he did not want her anymore. That maybe he had indeed found a 'mem', a white woman. But Mataji, bless her soul, was the epitome of optimism.

"Now stop crying and wipe your eyes," she continued firmly. "Hurry before Jyoti and Divya see you in this state! You know they'll start crying if they see your tears. I can't handle three wailing girls!"

She knew how the chain reaction of the girls' tears could go completely out of hand! Mataji's words – and then Jyoti's – penetrated Tara's clouds of sorrow.

"Mummy, potty! Potty! Mummmmmy!" Jyoti's desperate voice filled the air.

Hurriedly Tara wiped her eyes with her sari and rushed off to pick Jyoti up before she soiled her panties right there in the middle of the room! Mataji stared worriedly at her retreating back. Folding the letter again and again into a wad, wishing she could press it into nothingness, she tied it in the edge of her pallav. She could not risk anybody laying their hands on it. As it was, the neighbours were jumping to all kinds of conclusions at her non-Punjabi son-in-law's absence. Knowledge of this letter would just add salt to her troubled Tara's wounds. Angry with Varun's insensitive letter, she rushed to the prayer wall and sent up a quick prayer to all the Gods hanging there.

For the rest of the day Tara functioned on autopilot. She went through the motions of feeding her daughters but couldn't bear to touch a morsel herself. Every so often the words of that letter flashed in her mind, triggering an onset of sniffles. She, the epitome of patience, became irritable at their childish antics.

"Mummy, Divya's torn my painting!" Jyoti screamed after giving her sister a whack on the side of her head with her plastic pencil box. "I was painting a card for Daddy."

"Waaaa! Waaaaaaa!" Divya bawled loudly. "Mammaaaa!"

Impatiently Tara smacked both of them. "Behave yourselves, both of you. I have a headache. Now play quietly and leave me alone. I don't want to hear another sound from you."

Not getting their expected hugs, the girls were stunned into silence at her unprecedented reaction. What had happened to their loving mother who was always ready with a hug and a kiss? Mataji quickly came to everyone's rescue and whisked them away before they had a tantrum duet! She herded them into the warmth of the kitchen, where she reigned supreme.

"Your ma's not feeling well. Don't cry now. Come I'll tell you a story. Here have some batashas."

Thanks to childish fickleness and the sickly sweet bribe that they were busy stuffing into their mouths, they were soon distracted. Engrossed in Mataji's story about Akbar and Birbal, Jyoti and Divya soon forgot about their poor mother and left her to her troubled thoughts.

Next day, after a sleepless night, plagued by dreadful possibilities that she was too scared to put into words, Tara despondently finished her morning chores. She then complained of a headache and lay in bed all morning.

"Wake up! Mummy! There's a letter from Daddy! WAKE UP!" Jyoti shook her impatiently waving an aerogramme, like a matador, in her face. Blue had become Tara's favourite colour.

"Mummy!" Divya shouted too, trying to clamber on to the high bed, wanting to be a part of the action.

Lost in her depression, Tara had not heard Hari Bhai's cycle bell tinkling incessantly downstairs. Not getting the usual response to his bell, the postman had come upstairs. Breathless after the climb and from holding his breath past the smelly toilet he rested on the top stair, inhaling fresh air noisily. Seeing Jyoti playing outside the kitchen, he gave the letter to her. "Your papa's letter, beti," he wheezed, patting her gently on the head, "go and give it to your ma." Then taking another deep breath, he rushed downstairs, increasing his speed as he approached the stink zone.

Hearing the commotion, Mataji rushed down from the roof where she had been drying the clothes. Apprehensive at what the missive would disclose she watched Tara slit open the sides of the letter. It fluttered gently as her trembling fingers pushed the flaps apart.

"How's Daddy?" Jyoti chirped.

"How's Daddy?" Divya parroted.

"Shush," Mataji said holding them back, pressing their faces against her, nearly suffocating them in the soft cotton folds of her white sari. "Let your mother read in peace."

She stared intently at Tara's face trying to read the letter in the expression of her daughter's eyes. Relief ironed out the worried frown on her gentle countenance as she saw the lines on her daughter's forehead disappear and a smile light up her face.

"Thank you, God," Mataji whispered silently. She did not need to read what Doctor Sahib had written to know that all was well now. Releasing her iron-like grip on the children, she let them loose on Tara. Like bats out of hell they charged towards the bed.

"What does Daddy write? Tell us, na. Please read out the letter, Mummy." Jyoti was unstoppable.

"Daddy wants us to go to him. He's sending us the money!" said Tara hugging her girls joyfully. "We are going to England. We will be with Daddy again!"

"Yippee!" Jyoti jumped up and down clapping with glee. Not knowing what on earth was going on, but happy that everyone was happy, Divya clapped too! It was good to have her loving ma back again!

"What did Doctor Sahib write, beti?" Mataji asked quietly, once Jyoti and Divya were busy with their crayons and scrapbooks.

"He was confused and upset at what a friend of his advised him to do," said Tara in her forever forgiving, all-accepting manner. Varun had had an argument with an Indian colleague – Bimal – regarding Tara and the girls travel to England. Bimal had not arranged for his wife and three children to leave Calcutta and join him because he felt that a family would cramp his lifestyle. Looking after a family in a foreign land was not easy, warned this voice of experience (and doom!). And it was very expensive too. Bimal managed to convince Varun to cancel Tara's travel plans.

In a fit of Varun-like impulsiveness he wrote off a letter telling Tara to stay in Delhi. But for Varun, his family was his universe. He could not stay without them. After fretting and fuming for a day he realised that he had been a fool. He should have listened to his heart and not somebody else's advice. He cursed himself for he knew his impetuous letter must have caused Tara a lot of pain. Thus followed a second letter, close on the heels of the first one. With a short apologetic explanation for his previous announcement, he asked Tara to start her travel plans as he was soon sending money for the ship fares. Mataji gave Tara a relieved I-told-you-so hug and they wept tears of relief together. Life suddenly seemed bright and sunny again.

That evening Mataji took Tara and the girls to the Mandir to officially thank God! It was a very special day. Tara wore the pink chiffon sari, with the gold zari border, that Varun had given her and she dressed up the girls in identical red velvet frocks with red satin bows in their hair. Clinging to their mother's hands on either side, Jyoti and Divya followed Mataji's matronly figure down the narrow lanes of Old Delhi. Lanes where horses, cows, dogs, cycle rickshaws and people vied for right of way. Lanes where people stopped at the roadside stalls on their way back from work to eat hot jalebis or kachoris, washed down with a tall glass of steaming milk, expertly transferred in a long stream from container to glass, to ensure a good head of froth. During Dusshera, it was down these lanes that the ornate floats of the various local Ramlila processions would move to the loud beating of drums. People would lean over perilously from their balconies lining both sides of the lanes to catch a glimpse of the spectacle. They would shower flowers of respect and faith over the couple dressed as Ram and Sita sitting on decorated thrones with Hanuman, the monkey God, standing protectively behind them. Little boys and girls shouted joyfully and ran alongside the parade in excitement.

On the way Mataji stopped at the sweet shop to buy freshly made laddoos, which would be offered as prashad... a thanksgiving for her daughter's dream becoming a reality. In the mandir, they stood in a silent cluster in front of the beautifully ornate idols of Ram and Sita and stared in awe at the beauty of their faces. Following Mataji's instructions, the children joined their hands, bowed their heads, closed their eyes and thanked the Gods for bringing the smile back on their mother's face again.

Off to England

As soon as Varun had saved up enough money, he arranged for his family to join him in England. Tara was a brave and determined woman. On a cold February morning, with a smattering of English, and two young daughters to keep her on her toes, she followed her heart to England. Travelling by planes was a rarity in those days, and very expensive, so they went by sea, setting sail from Mumbai. It was a voyage that took fourteen days and seemed endless.

"God be with you," Mataji hugged and blessed each one of them, wiping tears of mixed emotions from her eyes. "Listen to your mother and behave yourselves," she warned, knowing what little terrors the girls could be. She would miss them terribly but she was glad that they were finally going. She feared for Tara who was so young and innocent and trusting. How would she manage the journey alone with two little children? They had prayed hard for this day. The Gods on the prayer wall had finally done their job. But now that it had finally dawned, she suddenly wanted to cling to them and take them back to the secure walls of her home.

Standing near the huge passenger liner, huddled up in a group of friends and relatives, Tara struggled with farewells and apprehension of the unknown. When it came to finally leaving, Divya and Jyoti followed the porter up the ship's ramp, skipping and jumping happily, blissfully unaware of the turmoil raging in their mother's heart. Holding on tightly to their tiny hands, Tara glanced backward with her heart in her mouth. One last long look to freeze the image of her family in her mind till they met again. As the ship set sail, they stood on the deck and waved furiously at the gradually diminishing figures of their loved ones.

The specks on the shoreline soon vanished and so did Tara's tears. She had to be emotionally tough. She was nervous and she needed her wits about her. The voyage was daunting, especially for someone who had rarely stepped out of the secure portals of her home, unchaperoned. But with the push of each wave against the ship's hull she moved closer to her husband. She had the determination to take on the world, for nothing could keep her from her 'raja'... the king of her heart.

Surrounded by water for so many days kept her religious fervour alive. The stormy days on the ocean were particularly scary but she took them in her stride. When giant waves effortlessly tossed the ship from side-to-side, Tara would not venture out of the cabin. Holding her daughters tightly, she would recite in a trembling voice verses from the "Hanuman Chalisa" that Mataji had given her. "Hanumanji will protect you and keep you safe," she had said, pressing the thin booklet in Tara's hands while she was packing.

"Jai Hanuman gyan gun sagar..." she chanted, praying for courage and their safety. But before she could reach the part where Hanuman leapt around, burning Lanka with his tail, Divya threw up in her lap. Not being able to cope with the vigorous rocking of the ship, she was violently seasick. Much to Tara's dismay, her youngest born was retching and throwing up for most of the journey through the Mediterranean Sea where the waters were the roughest. A couple of families who empathised with her situation soon took Tara under their wing and eased her into a comfortable level of security.

Finally, as the day of arrival dawned, she dressed up her daughters in new clothes especially bought for this occasion. As usual, they were identical dresses... navy blue satin, trimmed with white lace hand-stitched by their mother. They were beautiful, a labour of love. "Daddy will be so proud when he sees you," she said as she tied white ribbons in their hair. Their happy faces shone back at them in the reflection in their shiny black patent leather shoes. Divya was now ready to meet the enigmatic Daddy, whom she knew only through the eyes of her sister.

"We will be with Daddy soon," Tara said excitedly, herding them on to the deck. "Look! There's England!" she pointed at the distant horizon.

The girls stared hard at the water shimmering in the mid-morning sun, their eyes searching for what she could see. A few gulls skimmed the water. Divya pointed at them. Is that what Ma meant? She had no clue what her mother meant by "England". Jyoti kept jumping as high as she could to see the gradually growing speck in the distance that slowly but surely transformed into land.

"I can see England! I can see England!" she shrieked.

By now all the passengers were leaning against the ship's rails. The joy and excitement in the air was infectious. Divya clapped her small hands in wonder. As they drew closer, fuzzy, faceless forms turned into miniature people. The silent deck came alive with voices and waving arms as fellow travellers tried to spot relatives and friends.

"There's Payal!"

"Look, Rajesh Uncle is standing there and the fair lady with him must be Sally, his girlfriend!"

"Oh my God! That's Sheila! Sheila! Sheila!"

Shouts pierced the sky to draw the attention of identified loved ones standing on the pier. As soon as the ship docked, the Guha girls disembarked, following the crowd down the stairs.

"We are going to Daddy," sang Jyoti happily, hanging on to Tara's sari. Staring at the sea of faces from the safety of her mother's arms, Divya had no clue what this sudden animation was all about. Suddenly she felt tired and not so excited anymore.

"Stay close, Jyoti," Tara said, worried at the sudden surge of people. She secured Divya in the crook of her left arm and grabbed Jyoti's hand with the other. But Jyoti had spotted her father from between a sea of knees.

"Daddy! Daddy!" she shouted, waving madly to draw his attention, jumping as high as her tiny legs would allow.

Freeing her hand from Tara's unsuspecting grasp, she jumped the last two steps and with amazing precision, landed straight into Varun's arms and clung to him like a burr on a mohair sweater! Not recognising this vaguely familiar looking man, Divya threw her thin arms round her mother's neck, peering out from under her chin in fear at this stranger, wondering why Jyoti was hugging him so lovingly. Varun held Jyoti close in a bear hug and covered her face with kisses.

"My rani beti! My princess! How you've grown!" Heaven was his, now that he was reunited with the "girls" in his life. Thank God he hadn't followed Bimal's advice. He stared longingly at Tara's radiant face that was just as beautiful as ever.

"He's your daddy, beti," she said, trying unsuccessfully to untangle her neck from Divya's arms and push her into his.

As he swung her clinging leech of a sister onto the ground and reached out for her, Divya started to cry! No, she did not know who he was and definitely did not want to be taken away from her mother by this big stranger with the thick black hair and a moustache!

"Divya, beti, come to Daddy."

In vain Varun tried to release Divya's stranglehold round her mother's neck. Finally giving up with a resigned laugh and a pat on her head, he enveloped both of them in a joint embrace as Jyoti clung to his leg. Tara held herself stiffly, suddenly shy and embarrassed by his public display of affection. It had been so long since she had felt the power of those strong arms. She was with her beloved again. She inhaled deeply, taking in the scent of his nearness and woody cologne. It was the longest breath she had ever taken. Then she exhaled, slowly, releasing all those emotions that had bothered her these last few months. Her deceptively delicate and gentle appearance hid the steel inside. Her struggle was finally over. She was a survivor with a pool of strength and resilience that she dived into during the toughest times of her life. Luckily her children inherited a few precious drops from this pool.

A Son is Born

They were quick to adopt the Western way of life. Jyoti and Divya soon forgot their smattering of Hindi, their life in the narrow lanes of Delhi and, unfortunately, Mataji. They lived in a small county in Wales and were fortunate to get staff quarters in the hospital where Varun was working as a resident doctor.

Nearly a year after they stepped on to the shores of Britain, Tara buckled over in pain one morning. She was chopping onions in the kitchen. Luckily Varun was still at home, getting ready to leave for work. Jyoti and Divya were sitting at the small table in the kitchen finishing their breakfast of porridge. Or rather, Jyoti was finishing hers while Divya was using her spoon to make concentric circles of the gluey mixture in her bowl. She hated porridge and was trying to figure out how to throw the congealed mass into the bin without Ma noticing. This would be tough, because Tara was standing right behind her. Divya stared into the viscous depths; cross-eyed and hypnotised, as round and round her spoon went.

The knife clattered on to the floor, taking a few onion slices along with it. Divya looked around to see her ma bent, her face over the onions, as if she was eating them straight off the chopping board. With one hand on her huge belly, she clung to the edge of the yellow Formica kitchen counter with the other. As one, the girls hopped off their chairs and rushed to her side. Her ashen face was furrowed with lines of pain.

"Daddy! Daddy" Jyoti yelled, while Divya stood dumbstruck. Jyoti always had more presence of mind than her. "Something's wrong with Mum! Come quick!"

By the time Varun charged into the kitchen the pain had subsided. "It's okay, beti, don't worry," he reassured them looking at their stricken faces as he helped Tara to the living room sofa. Apprehensively Divya watched as her ma sank into its leathery lap. What was wrong with Ma? Was she going to die? Tears of fear crept into her eyes.

"I'm all right, Divya, Jyoti," Tara reassured them, smiling tremulously. "Everything's going to be okay."

The girls were hastily deposited in the safe custody of Mrs. Jones, their neighbour. Uncomprehending and fearful, they watched big-eyed from the window as their dad bundled Ma into the car and rushed off to hospital.

"Don't worry, my loveys," Mrs Jones was reassuring, "Mum will be back soon. She's going to have a baby. You will soon have a brother or sister to play with."

But Divya didn't want to stay with Mrs. Jones, she wanted Mummy. She didn't need a brother or sister, she had Jyoti, didn't she?! She was definitely angry and upset at how everything seemed to be spinning out of control. Her initial attempts at wailing died a quick death thanks to Jyoti.

"Stop being a cry baby, Divvy!" she said as sternly as a six-year-old can. No, Divya was not a baby. She was all of four years old! Her ego dried up her tears. She bit her trembling lower lip and swallowed her anger. "I guess as long as Jyoti's with me I'll be okay," she consoled herself, reaching out to cling to her sister's hand tightly.

Sure enough, their brother, Amar was born the following morning. Finally, Varun's dream of a boy child had crystallised into reality. God had heard his earnest prayers. Third time lucky! Sona Bai's prediction had come true. Yes, he now had an heir. The family name would not die. Tara's joy knew no bounds. Separation and heartache had become a thing of the past. Content that their family was now complete Tara and Varun settled down and concentrated on building their future in a foreign land. It was tough, but so were they! They were determined to face it together.

Childhood Dilemmas

Divya had strange memories of England, disconnected and dreamlike. Kept alive and stitched together with photographs and strands of stories she'd been told by others. Growing up sandwiched between her outspoken, gregarious sister and her parents'-dream-come-true brother was not easy. Being extremely reserved and a bit of a loner did not help either. She preferred to be part of the wallpaper design in social gatherings and family get-togethers. Petrified that someone would notice her, at times she wished she were invisible! Divya took on the role of a 'good' girl, always ready to help with the housework, choosing to help her ma in the kitchen, in her own small way, while her siblings took over the evening and entertained the guests. This arrangement suited everyone, and continued in this manner. Jyoti was relieved at her sister's willingness to do the "boring" housework and Divya was happy to potter around on her own among the pots and pans. Being irritatingly obedient was also part of Divya's 'good' image. Not wanting to irk her parents she would shy away from anything that smelt of trouble.

"Jyoti! Divya! Where are you? Supper's getting cold." Ma's voice rose to an impatient pitch.

"Let's just say we didn't hear her," Jyoti whispered conspiratorially.

They were playing tiddly-winks in the wooden shed at the bottom of the garden. The shed was their hideout where they spent many hours hanging out. They had stocked it with comics, favourite toys, small packets of Smarties and a tin of crisps.

"But *I* heard her," Divya said horrified at the thought of lying and facing Ma's anger.

She scampered off to do Ma's bidding, closely followed by her reluctant elder sister muttering "scaredy-cat" angrily under her breath. She was right. Divya was scared. Scared of being the cause of any unpleasantness. Scared of her dad's wrath.

Although she tried her best to please her father, a favourite family pastime, initiated by him was, what she now called, 'Let's make Divya cry'. He'd pick on her for no rhyme or reason and tease her heartlessly, till she burst into tears!

"Today Divya has to drive the car," he pronounced in his no-nonsense voice as they were getting ready to go for a picnic.

He plonked the five-year-old Divya on the driver's seat and stood back in stern anticipation while she sat there frozen with fear wondering how on earth she would fulfil his command.

"Come on then," he bellowed impatiently tapping his foot.

Realising that some action was expected from her, Divya stretched her arms as far as she could and clutched the steering wheel with her small hands, her short feet just about touching the end of the seat. After that she didn't know what to do. So she sat there statue-like, too scared to move.

"You'll sit there till you drive," he continued persistently. Sadistically.

"Let her be, Raja! Stop teasing her. She'll start crying now, you know that," Ma pleaded, trying to persuade him to stop.

He only relented once the desperate tears streamed down Divya's petrified, panic-stricken face. A seemingly harmless adult joke left a deep scar on her psyche, manifesting itself in different ways. For most of her childhood she would vomit every time she sat in the car.

"Do we have the plastic bag?" became a standard question before the family went anywhere in the car.

She tried her hand at driving much later than her siblings… only when she was in her twenties. And that too was a disaster. In fact she was twenty-one when Varun gave Divya her first… and last, driving lesson. Both Jyoti and Amar had learnt the skill effortlessly and zipped around the roads of Delhi in their little Morris Minor. Divya was the reluctant one but Varun decided that it was high time she also learnt how to drive. So after giving her a short theoretical introduction, Varun and a reluctant Divya set out.

"Drive very slowly and remember what I told you about the gears and the clutch."

She nodded, trying to swallow the lump that had settled in her throat. It was 5am. A time when Delhi roads are empty. Starting the ignition, she eased the car forward. Very slowly. Very nervously.

"Hmmm. Good." She saw him nodding from the corner of her eye. After one round of the block Divya picked up courage and unfortunately, speed.

Thwack! Varun hit her left arm sharply as his loud voice pierced her ears.

"Brake! Press the brake!" his eyes bulged out of his reddened face. Thwack thwack… her left thigh this time. Hard.

"Brake, Divya!" he bellowed desperately as the car hurtled towards a cow regurgitating in the middle of the road, blissfully unaware of her impending conversion to beef. "Can't you see that cow? STOP!"

Where the hell did that cow come from? Divya thought. It wasn't there on their first round. Her foot seemed to have got stuck on the accelerator. Childhood memories of being ordered to drive jammed her senses. Her reaction time fell way below zero. She froze. Grabbing the steering wheel from her inert hands, Varun swung it around to the left as Divya's foot discovered the brake and slammed on it. Missing a bovine tragedy by the breadth of its tail, the car climbed the pavement and stalled. The cow turned to give them a baleful look as the engine shuddered and died a spluttering death. Silence.

Completely shaken by the incident, Divya held her breath and waited, dreading what would follow. Varun slapped his forehead with his hand in despair.

"What were you thinking? Ha?!"

She stared ahead, not daring to turn, move or blink. Shallow breathing was allowed... but mustn't be audible.

"Why didn't you press the brake? I kept shouting Brake! Brake!" He continued his monologue. "Couldn't you hear me? You are stupid! Now let me drive," he said opening his door.

Silently she got out of the car on wobbly legs and relinquished the driver's seat to him.

"I don't want to learn how to drive," she whispered, crawling into the passenger's seat. "I will marry a man who has a driver."

Thankfully, he didn't attempt any more driving lessons. But more than that... thankfully Divya did marry a man who had a driver! And that's when she learnt how to drive... again!

Another hot favourite of her father's was making her sing.

"Now Divya will entertain us. Come on then, Divya. Sing for us," her dad ordered.

Obediently she attempted a song in a quavering broken voice, wishing the earth would open up and swallow her, or a bolt of lightning would strike him. He burst out laughing as the strange unmelodious sound filled the room!

"Why can't you sing like your sister? Jyoti, beti, you sing a song now."

Jyoti, who had been itching for her chance to prove her superiority, then took over with her nightingale-like voice, melodious and soothing.

"Ah! Good. Very good." Varun nodded his approval as Jyoti beamed.

"Okay, Amar, now you sing 'Twinkle twinkle little star…'"

Amar confidently belted out the nursery rhyme, complete with actions, as everyone, except Divya, fondly looked on. Her vision was blurred by tears of resentment.

She used to hate her father for making her feel so inadequate and stupid compared to her 'oh so talented' siblings. She was the odd one out, and was kept on the margins. How she hated and feared him then. This silent admission would inevitably be followed by guilt – after all he was her father, how could she think ill of him?

One extremely embarrassing family 'joke,' was often narrated as a conversation filler for visitors. It was about how Divya had won a drawing competition by fluke when she was seven years old.

"Divya, show uncle and aunty the cup you won in the art competition," Varun would say when there was an uncomfortably long lull in the conversation.

"She got the first prize by mistake!" he'd laugh as the guests donned their "we're interested" masks.

Knowing that Divya couldn't draw to save her life, Varun thought that by forcing her to participate in an art competition, she would somehow get over her inhibition and magically turn into a Picasso or a Monet! Dreading that once again she would disappoint him, she submitted her drawing and nervously waited for the judge's decision. She was so surprised when her name was announced as the winner of the 1st prize in her age group that it took a while to register.

"Divya Guha! Divya Guha! Could Divya Guha please come to the stage at once?"

The judge had to announce her name three times before it dawned on her that it was actually *her* and not someone else with her name who had won. Divya walked slowly to the stage as the announcement was made for the last and final time.

"Ah here she is! The first prize in the 6-8 year group goes to Divya Guha who has drawn this witch!"

Her drawing was held up for all to see as she looked on in horror. Witch? How could the judge call it a witch when she had drawn a fairy! Mortified, Divya went up and accepted her trophy. She had drawn a fairy that the judges mistook for a witch!! The only cup she had ever won was by accident! The cup became a showpiece. And the incident... a conversation piece.

Divya developed this strong need to prove her worth to her father... to make him feel proud of her as he did of his other children. A sort of over compensation. So what if she couldn't sing or draw or chat "intellectually" with people? She could work hard. She became a 'miss-goody-two-shoes'! It was taken for granted that Divya would help Ma in the house. She would always volunteer to clear up, help Ma hang out the washing and fold the dried clothes. If anyone lost anything, she was the one who would find it. "Divya, have you seen my snuff box beti?" Varun would ask her knowing that even if she hadn't seen it she would find it for him. She enjoyed the responsibility and importance that came with this role, hoping to get a few brownie points from her father. And it worked!

A Second Encounter with Death

After having survived the fire in her birthplace, it was in England that Divya faced death once again – a close encounter of the second kind! The family was being vaccinated against Yellow Fever, in preparation for a trip to Lagos, which finally never materialised. Varun sat there at the table with a medical tray fully equipped with cotton wool, spirit, syringes, ampoules of the vaccine and also an antidote (just in case any of them reacted adversely to the injection). To Divya's sensitive nose, the room smelt like her father when he came home after a day in the operation theatre.

Amar, being the youngest, was the first in line. Divya held her breath and watched in trepidation. He sat comfortably in Ma's lap, not knowing what he was in for – ignorance was definitely bliss! A quick jab, just a short wail and it was over. Tara heaved a sigh of relief as she made him sit on the bed and gave him his favourite toy car to distract him and keep him quiet.

"Jyoti!" shouted Dad, deciding to put her next in the queue. Divya exhaled silently. She still had some time before it was her turn.

"Come on, you're next! Where has she gone now?" A tinge of impatience laced his voice. "Jyoti!!"

After a quick search, Jyoti was dragged out from her hiding place under the bed, kicking and screaming! She was so petrified of injections that just the mention of the word was enough to make her vanish. Sometimes, even the smell of spirit did the trick.

"I don't want an injection! I don't want to go to Lagos!" she wailed.

"Be brave, Jyoti. Look at Amar. He sat so quietly while Daddy gave him his shot," Tara said in her soft stern voice. "Now sit still."

She held her tightly in her arms as Varun did the needful. Amar, who had quickly recovered from his short bout of crying, ignored his car, preferring to watch all this melodrama with keen interest. A still snivelling Jyoti got off Tara's lap with a scowl on her face, rubbing the red dot on her arm. Angry with everyone in general, she sat on the corner of the bed next to Amar. Clutching her newly injected arm with a pained look, she sulked.

Then it was Divya's turn.

"Come, Divya, beti. Come and sit in my lap," Ma coaxed. Acting braver than she felt, Divya clambered on to her ma's lap and stuck her arm out like a sacrificial offering. She had promised herself not to cry. Another one of her attempts at winning brownie points from her parents. This time for stoicism. Not only that, her siblings were watching, so she had to keep her upper lip stiff! Wincing as her father punctured her skin and pushed the needle into her muscle, she sat absolutely still mainly because she was petrified that any movement would cause the needle to break inside her arm. After pulling the needle out Varun wiped her skin with spirit and turned back to the table to prepare Tara's syringe.

"Good girl. You are the bravest of the lot. Not a sound."

But Varun's much longed for words of praise literally fell on deaf ears. Divya had silently collapsed in her ma's arms. Her eyes rolled back, showing only white and her head lay inert over Tara's elbow.

"Oh, Raja! Something's happened to Divya." Tara cried as she shook her inert daughter, slapping her face gently, trying to revive her. "She's fainted."

No, she hadn't fainted with fear; she had been given the wrong injection. Varun had given her the antidote by mistake. The result was severe vasoconstriction. Tara looked horrified as within seconds her daughter became as white as snow and listless like her favourite rag doll.

As a worried Varun massaged her, Divya started vomiting violently. Gradually she revived and got her colour back but she sure gave him a scare! He never recovered from the fear that he had nearly killed his middle child. Even now, when reminded of the incident, he shakes his head in disbelief.

"We almost lost you that day," he says.

"You nearly died in my arms. It was terrible!" adds Tara.

Having survived the 'fire test' was not enough for God, Divya decided. Like Spartan babies thrown off a cliff, she had to be absolutely fit to survive. So, she was put to the test again. For some strange reason God still wanted her to live! And she had to be tough.

A Bladder Problem

As a child, Divya was always too scared to stand up for herself, happy to let her elder sister fight their growing up battles. Luckily Jyoti did this with great élan and paved the way for both Amar and Divya. She had the gift of the gab and convincingly argued with their dad regarding many issues – from the inalienable right to read comics to being allowed to watch the Beatles on telly! Jyoti made life easy for them. Divya followed her happily, sheep-like in her complacency. There were times, however, when she had to fend for herself and unfortunately didn't do a very good job of it!

The morning bell rang for assembly. Children hurriedly dropped their bags in their classrooms and rushed to the school hall. The gathering of students for prayers before classes took on the semblance of columns and rows. Latecomers would have to stand up right in front next to Mrs. White, the principal. From her place in the second row Divya kept turning to look back at Jyoti, who was in the sixth row. Feeling an uncomfortable pressure in her bladder, she tried to attract her sister's attention. But Jyoti's eyes were shut. She was already lost in prayer. Desperately wanting to pee and not knowing what to do, Divya was unable to concentrate as the other children droned "Our Father who art in Heaven..." She was six years old and too scared to ask to be excused from assembly. After shuffling around for a while like Peter Sellers in 'The Party', she was horrified when she felt hot pee gush down her leg! She tried her best to press her thighs together and squeeze her muscles to control the flow... to make it just a trickle. But failed. How could such a small child have so much of water inside her?

She prayed that no one would notice, as she surreptitiously inched away, trying to act as if the yellow pool on the floor did not belong to her! But soon accusing fingers were pointing in her direction and the children around her started giggling and whispering loudly. She was so ashamed that she didn't dare look at Jyoti, certain she would disown her. A horrified Mrs. White naturally hauled her up... this is something British children would never do; they would ask to be excused! Divya stood in the corner of the principal's room as a very embarrassed father was called to take her home, where, needless to say, she literally got a dressing down!

"Why didn't you go to the toilet before you left for school?" Varun scolded. "And if you had to use the toilet in school you should have asked your teacher!"

Tears of anguish and embarrassment chased each other down her cheeks.

"Let her be." Tara came to her rescue. "She's still small and probably couldn't control herself."

"You are always protecting her, Tara! It was so embarrassing at her school!" he ranted. "I had to hear whatnot from the principal."

Once annoyed he was unstoppable. All the old skeletons were dug out to be rattled in front of her.

"She's like a bird when it comes to eating and takes forever to finish her meals."

He was nursing his anger because she had taken extra-long to finish breakfast that morning. She hated porridge and just couldn't make herself swallow that congealed mass! In fact, she felt like retching just at the thought of it.

"And she's as scared as a mouse in front of others! Can't open her mouth. When will she learn to be like Jyoti?" he continued relentlessly.

Yes, that was the problem. Why couldn't she be more like Jyoti?

Patriotism and Racism

A strict disciplinarian, Varun was also a very patriotic man. He loved and missed his motherland. Often, misty-eyed, he would talk with longing about his childhood in a sleepy village in Bengal. In his own way he tried his best to teach his children about India, its rich culture and their heritage.

"You should be proud to be an Indian. India is a great country," he'd say overcome by passionate fervour.

He spent sleepless nights worrying about his children becoming too "western" in their thinking.

"You keep track of Elvis Presley's farts and John Lennon's burps!" he'd exclaim in a sudden fit of displaced anger, picking on their favourite pop singers. "But do you know anything about Swami Vivekananda or Rabindranath Tagore?"

Then he would launch into a short history of the lives of these great people while they fidgeted impatiently waiting for him to finish. He was horrified when he realised that his children could sing "God save the Queen…" with great gusto but didn't know their own national anthem. So every other evening, after a tiring day at the hospital, he would herd everyone round the piano and as he went plinkety plink on the keys with two fingers, they tunelessly belted out "jana gana mana…" in different tones and pitches. A ferocious frown from him would silence their unsuccessfully suppressed giggles. It was a serious issue to him – and he would not tolerate anyone making light of it. The neighbours were initially surprised by the weird sounds coming from "those strange blackies" next door. They would peer from behind the lacy folds of their curtains, wondering whether they should walk across and investigate the origin of the noise. But they soon got used to their evening cacophonic jingoistic 'concerts'.

Being a 'blackie' in England was not easy in those days (the now common term 'Paki' had not been coined at that time). Though not very dark-skinned, (both Varun and Tara were the fairest in their families) the Guha family stood out everywhere they went and were made to feel unwelcome, sometimes subtly and at times with an in-your-face aggression. Too young to understand the needless anger and hatred behind such actions, Jyoti and Divya were horrified by their first experience. It happened with the fat lady who owned a corner shop near their school.

"If you promise to behave yourselves at school today, I will take both of you to buy some sweets," Tara promised Jyoti and Divya, as they got ready for their first day at school.

She was apprehensive about leaving the girls alone among strangers, especially foreign ones. She had come a long way from being a hesitant English speaker. With Varun's help she had quickly picked up the language and spoke it with confidence and pride. She had been priming them for days.

"Remember to say 'thank you' and 'please' and you must pay attention in class," she reminded them nervously.

"And, Divya, remember not to pick your nose! Use your hanky." Her thoughts were racing through all the 'Do's and Don'ts' list she had mentally prepared.

Divya nodded slowly as her ma's nervousness filtered into her consciousness.

"Jyoti, look after your baby sister," she continued as she combed Divya's hair and tied it back in a ponytail. She then divided the ponytail into two, yanking them apart with a sudden jerk to tighten the hold of the ribbon. A wavy clump that was so high and tight that she could feel her eyebrows rise with the pull, making her look permanently surprised.

"And don't worry," she ended, "I'll be there when the bell rings to bring you back home."

By now Divya's lower lip was trembling dangerously and her tear ducts flooding! The prospect of going to school did not seem appealing at all. Why couldn't she just stay at home with Amar and play with him? She looked at Jyoti to check how she was feeling. She gained some strength from her cheerful, stoic expression. Silently Jyoti reached out and held her sister's hand and pressed it with a "don't worry I'm here" squeeze of reassurance. Divya's drooping spirits lifted knowing she would be safe with her around.

Though those first few hours at school were a complete blank in Divya's mind, what she did remember was rushing out of class to the home time bell, searching amongst the crowds of milling children for Jyoti. She found her waiting for her near the main gate, next to Ma. Amar had been left in the care of Mrs. Jones, so that Tara could pick up her girls after their first day at school.

"How was it?" Ma asked eagerly as she hugged Divya tight.

"I want jelly babies and Smarties. One of each colour," she said in response to her mother's question.

Tara's promise to buy them sweets was still fresh in her mind.

"Okay, darling," she laughed at her child's one-tracked-mind answer. "Come on then. Let's go get some sweets."

With her progeny on either side, this beautiful lady walked to the corner shop, happy to have her daughters safely back among the folds of her sari. Although she had been busy with the cooking and looking after Amar that morning, the house had been deathly quiet without the constant chatter of her girls. Her colourful orange silk sari fluttered gaily in the breeze, turning heads in its wake. In those days an Indian woman in her traditional dress was still an uncommon sight. And Tara wore it with pride.

The bell hanging on the glass door tinkled and the metallic 'Open' sign clinked, announcing their arrival to the huge lady sitting behind the till. She looked like a snow woman with garish red lipstick and a red bow tucked in her blond halo of hair. Jyoti and Divya were arguing about the candies they would buy as they bustled in.

"I'm gonna get jelly babies and Smarties."

"I'll get sherbet drops and chocolate flakes."

Tara smiled at their infectious excitement and gently closed the door as the girls headed straight for the big jars of colourful sweets and chocolates.

"Oh! I am sorry," the fat lady said, exaggerating her pronunciation so that she could make herself clearly understood. "I have just closed for the day."

Her stiff upper British lip straightened into a red slash on her white face. She shooed them out, her fair face flushed with tolerant distaste and hurriedly hung the

'Closed' sign on her door just in case they had not understood the Queen's English! One never knew with these foreigners.

Before they knew it they were out on the street again. It had happened so fast that for a second they were stunned into silence and stood on the street disoriented. How could an 'Open' shop suddenly close like that in the middle of the day? Disappointed, Jyoti and Divya looked longingly at the sweet jars and turned to their mother, waiting for her explanation of the fat lady's unfriendly behaviour.

"Come, come," Tara commanded anxiously, suddenly unsure of herself. "Let's go home."

"But you promised..."

"I said let's go!"

The sudden firmness in her voice indicated that this was not open to discussion. Reluctantly the girls dragged their feet but allowed her to pull them away from the magnetic tug of the sweet shop.

"Don't feel sad, my darlings. I'll tell Daddy to take you this evening to buy some sweets," Tara forced some cheer into her voice to pacify them, angry that someone could ruin their plans so cruelly and thoughtlessly.

Turning back one last time Divya saw the fat old lady peering from the shop window, hoping they had believed her lie, waiting impatiently to hang up the 'Open' sign again.

When Varun heard the story he was livid at the unfairness of the whole incident. He promptly forbade them from going to that shop ever again. It irritated Divya because all her plans of 'after school treats' had gone down the drain. But it really bothered and worried Tara and Varun. How long could they shield their children from such open antagonism? They felt powerless and impotent in this foreign land.

Jyoti, Divya and Amar were largely sheltered from it but Varun had to bear the full brunt of man's cruelty to man just because of a difference in skin colour. One day he came back from hospital really agitated. He had boarded a bus that morning and was horrified when all the passengers stood up as one, and disembarked. They did not want to travel on the same bus as a coloured man.

Why, he wondered. Did they think he has some infectious disease? That his colour was contagious and would rub off on them? Was he an untouchable? The experience angered him and left him shaken. For the first time in his life he had been made to feel small. Humiliated in such a blatant manner.

But he did not let that incident keep him down for too long. As soon as he could, he bought his first car – a sky blue Austin Mini. It created quite a dent in his savings but at least he would not have to suffer such ostracism again.

However, it was the same story at work. His promotions were being stalled because he was not white. The racist epidemic was spreading its cruel tentacles, pulling them in to its folds.

Divya, on the other hand, loved England – the Beatles, Beano comics, and bacon for breakfast. Then there were toffee apples and the 'child-boggling' variety of chocolates. She saved up her precious pocket money to spend it on liquorice and Smarties. Every other weekend they'd pack their swimsuits and be taken to the beach to build sand castles and jump waves.

The Beatles had just become famous and much to the dismay of most parents, they had swept away the youth of England in a storm of pop music. Divya grew up watching hysterical girls on TV, screaming and fainting as the Beatles sang their way into young hearts. Getting a

'Beatle-cut' became the latest hairstyle for the boys. 'Beatle-mania' was there to stay. And she was happy to be a part of it. Life couldn't have been better.

But Varun thought otherwise. He didn't want to bring his children up in a culture that was so alien to his traditional ways. They knew no Rabindra Sangeet... he had no time to teach them, and Tara couldn't sing. Their knowledge of Hindi and Bengali was limited to a few words... no matter how hard he tried to enforce the "only Bengali to be spoken at home" rule, the children would struggle for a while and then slip into English. They had stopped eating with their hands, preferring a knife and fork instead. He was sure they would soon start using toilet paper instead of washing up with water. He felt dirty and disgusted just at the thought of such a possibility! And not only that... what would he do if the girls started dating at the age of twelve? Heaven forbid! But most important of all, his motherland needed him as a doctor and surgeon.

The die had been cast. They had to pack up, bid a tearful farewell to all their friends and with great resistance and resentment, head towards the country of their ancestors, towards an unknown future... one that Divya did not wish to belong to.

Back in India

Having grown up in England, ignorant of India's poverty, coming back to an India they did not know was, in a way, rather traumatic.

"Why are those people lying like that on the road, Ma?" Divya asked in horror as she looked at half naked people and lepers, maimed and starved, lying under trees on the roads of Delhi. Begging at traffic lights. A similar scene had caused Lord Buddha to give up his riches and go in search of the truth.

"They are poor and have no home," Tara explained patiently.

"But how come they don't have a home? How can they just live like that under a tree? What happens when they fall ill?" Divya's questioning mind needed reasons and details.

Her ma's patience soon ran dry as her answers failed to satisfy Divya's persistent queries regarding their situation.

"Enough now." Ma had no answers. "Ask Daddy this evening." Divya swallowed the next question as Ma's voice took on a stern tone.

She couldn't sleep for many nights after that. Wide awake, lying in her bed that she was now grateful for, she'd wonder where all those people would sleep at night, what they would eat, where they would bathe and go to the toilet! Did they not brush their teeth every morning? It was a rude and extremely disturbing jolt to her puerile senses.

Getting into the Indian groove was tougher than the shift to England. They were older now. Their roots, still tender, had been uprooted from the Welsh soil. Though they were now the same colour as everyone around them, they felt excluded most of the time. Everyone spoke Hindi, a language Divya did not understand. When she spoke English, people laughed and mimicked her Welsh accent. So she bravely attempted to speak Hindi, but that was worse. They went into hysterics! Oh how she hated it! Her form of refuge was silence. She stopped talking.

Initially, till Varun could find an apartment, they stayed in the one-roomed house in Sita Ram Bazaar, once again. The wheel had turned a full circle. Mataji was delighted to have them back after eight long years and tried her best to make them as comfortable as possible. But nothing could ease Divya's distress. She was 'homesick' for England. She hated the country of her father's dreams. The weather was awful, the food strange and the place where they lived was in a dirty and smelly part of town. People defecated and urinated on the roadside and there were cows, cockroaches, flies and mosquitoes everywhere.

There were more people living in that one-roomed flat now, including her uncles and their new wives! No one had any privacy whatsoever. A little store room downstairs had been converted into a bedroom. Her uncles and aunts took turns to use this space for procreation! Looking back, Divya now sometimes wondered... how did they decide whose turn it was? Did they pick straws? Did they work out some kind of rota? Something like... Mondays & Thursdays – Pappu Mama and Kanta Mami; Tuesdays & Fridays – Manoj Mama and Rita Mami. At night the rest of the family spread mattresses on the floor and slept in rows, dormitory-style. Divya developed the habit of covering herself from head to toe with a sheet, scared that either a cockroach would crawl up her leg or one of the fat lizards on the ceiling would fall on her while she slept. She often wondered how so many of them had lived like this several years ago.

Having to go to that tiny hole-in-the-wall toilet, on the staircase, was Divya's biggest nightmare. Apart from the fact that one of the door panels was nearly fully corroded, nothing had changed. Initially, Divya became severely constipated, preferring anal retention to using that Indian-style toilet. Finally, when it came to choosing between exploding due to an overstuffed alimentary canal or answering nature's desperate call, she picked up her courage and went. It did not get better with time. Each visit to that toilet was a terrifying experience for her. Concentrating on balancing her weight in the squatting position, she was scared that she would fall into the stinky, keyhole-shaped pot in the floor. This was not conducive to bowel movement! Toilet paper was unheard of and washing her bottom afterwards was out of the question. How on earth did people maintain their balance and wash their bum at the same time? One had to be an acrobat to accomplish this feat. Not willing to take any chances, she'd yell, "I'm done, Ma!" and Tara would come and wash her. Between her three children, Tara sometimes spent a greater part of the morning rushing down the stairs to wash some child's bottom! Divya longed for a commode that she could sit on comfortably and read a comic while she waited for gravity to work hand in hand with her peristaltic movements!

She also longed for fish'n'chips wrapped up in greasy newspapers. Just the thought of that oily, fishy smell made her mouth water. She wished she could bite into a 'flyer' − liquorice stick − and feel the sherbet powder filling dissolve on her tongue. She used to dream of "Tinker-bell," the ice-cream man who would drive his van down their lane and Pied Piper like, ring a bell to draw children out of their houses. She missed the little room in the attic she had shared with Jyoti, where Tojo, her stuffed teddy, and Milly, the rag doll, sat arm in arm, perched precariously on the windowsill. Her heart yearned for the familiarity of their backyard with the coal bin and the wooden shed at the end of their nettle-filled garden.

Divya was even ready to give up her most prized possession − her walkie-talkie doll − to go back to England and make funny-shaped snowmen with her friends. So what if they had left her locked up in a cupboard while playing hide-and-seek! Tired of playing the game, their fickle young minds had wandered on to 'hopscotch' while Divya sat in her well-chosen hiding place... in the dark among shoes and clothes, waiting to be 'found'. Ma's innocent question, "Where's Divya?" jolted Jyoti into action. Busy in the company of her friends she had completely forgotten about her baby sister.

"I don't know," she shrugged, suddenly reminded of Divya's existence. "We were playing hide-and-seek but that was about two hours ago. We couldn't find her and got bored of hunting for her so we decided to play hopscotch in the backyard."

"Well go find her now, you silly girl," shouted Ma. "How could you leave your little sister like that?"

A frenzied 'Divya-hunt' began and she was finally found and dragged out of the cupboard dazed but proud that her hiding place was so good that no one had been able to find. She wondered why Ma yelled at her instead of giving her a reward for winning the game.

Educating Divya

＊ / ＊

Finding a good school for Jyoti and Divya proved to be yet another ordeal in their rapidly growing list of 'trying to settle down'. Amar was still too young to go to school. To add salt to their nostalgic wounds they were rejected by the first school Varun applied to. They failed the entrance exam of this 'convent school' because they did not know Hindi, their mother tongue.

"Best of luck, my darlings!" Tara said, giving her girls a tight hug, as they went with Varun to give the very first exam of their lives.

"Just do your best," he advised as he left them with the lady in charge of admissions. An officious-looking lady with a brown register in her hands and a pen dangling from a blue cord round her neck.

"Follow me, girls," she said brusquely.

Holding hands Jyoti and Divya stumbled after her down the long corridor, their short legs trying to keep pace with her long strides.

"Good morning, Sister Prudence, I have two more," she said handing them over to a nun dressed in a pure white habit.

Never having seen a nun in my life, Divya was petrified at the sight of this white apparition, with no visible hair on her head but lots over her non-existent lips.

With a deep sense of foreboding, she tightened her grip on Jyoti's hand and prayed hard that this day would end quickly. It did not have a good feel to it.

"What's your name, child?" Sister Prudence whispered hoarsely, bending in Divya's direction.

She felt hot breath on her forehead. Her voice vanished.

"She's Divya and my name is Jyoti." Comprehending her sister's fear, Jyoti had come to the rescue.

"Okay, Divya, you have to go to this room," she announced in a no-nonsense voice, pointing to the classroom they were standing outside.

Prising Jyoti's hand out of Divya's tight death hold, the nun took her inside and made her sit at a desk in the front row. By now Divya's ears were buzzing with a fear so intense that she was paralysed. A 'bone-locking' fear that prevented her from running after Jyoti's fast retreating figure. She was given a short passage in Hindi to translate into English. Having never seen the Hindi script before, she stared at the sheet of paper for a long time, trying desperately to make sense of the strange patterns. What was she expected to do? Surrounded by strangers, she did what she was really good at... burst into tears like an automated sprinkler!

Divya looked around the room through her tears and saw some of the other aspiring students staring at her in amusement. But she couldn't care less. She wanted to go home. Jyoti went through a similar ordeal, but without the tears. She was made of stronger stuff. They did not pass the test. Needless to say the school was not impressed and the girls did not gain admission.

Luckily Varun's friend's daughter, Sheetal, solved their language problems. She took on the task of teaching them Hindi. Thanks to Sheetal's good teaching skills, they passed the next school's entrance exam and eventually ended up in a convent school with Irish nuns and strict discipline.

The nuns did not walk, they glided silently like swans on a placid lake, catching girls red-handed for breaking the rules, of which there were many.

"Pick up that sweet wrapper and throw it in the dustbin, child," Mother Stella's quietly stern voice would suddenly echo in an unsuspecting student's right ear. They never heard her creep up behind them. Nuns had sharp eyes and hypersensitive ears, all of them. And definitely wore rubber-soled, squeak-proof shoes.

In spite of the moral science classes and the eagle-eyed nuns, the boys of the adjacent school had followed their overactive hormones and managed to cut a hole in the dividing hedge for quick and easy access to the girls' Senior School classrooms! The huge church in the middle was a good meeting place to secretly pass love notes to each other, say a quick prayer and rush off to assembly.

But Divya hated school. She hated studying because she was never good at it. She hated the teachers because they were forever comparing her to her brilliant sister. She hated her elocution teacher, Miss Paul, who tried to teach her in her own innovative way how to open her mouth and speak. She made Divya stand at the back of the class with a wooden ruler, kept breadth-wise, protruding horizontally out of her widely prised open mouth. She was punishing her for continuing to speak through clenched teeth, in spite of several dire warnings.

"Now you will remember to open your mouth wider every time you talk!" she intoned as Divya stood there trying not to choke on the spit that had collected in her mouth. She could taste the wood pressing hard against her tongue and palate, as she clenched the wobbling ruler with her teeth. By the end of the period, the collar of her blouse was drenched by the rivulet of spit dribbling down the side of her mouth and neck. For many days she practised saying "How now brown cow" in front of the mirror, rolling the "r" and opening her mouth wide then pouting her lips for the "ow's" just like Miss Paul.

She developed an intense dislike for her Hindi teacher, Mrs. Singh, for the way she punished her for bringing an uncovered book to school. She made Divya take off her blouse in front of everyone and insisted that she cover the book with it! Luckily she was wearing a slip underneath.

"Why should you cover yourself if you can't cover your school books?" she screeched in explanation, as Divya stood there not making eye contact with anyone. She was scarred for life.

But what she feared most of all was end of term... the time for the results of the annual exams. She would dread the yelling she knew she'd get from her dad when he saw her poor marks... because let's face it – they were invariably below average! In fact, in an attempt to save herself from a showdown, Divya once took the liberty of signing her report card for him and told the teacher that he was out of town! She doesn't remember the consequences... traumatic, for sure, for they were deeply and irretrievably suppressed in her box labelled 'Painful Memories'.

Realising his younger daughter's academic Achilles' heel, Varun took it on himself to try and improve her poor grades. He decided that he would tutor her! That was very brave of him indeed, especially after his unsuccessful attempt at teaching her how to drive! Not a very good track record. After a tiring day at the hospital, he would invariably be in a foul mood to begin with. Undoubtedly, the last thing he wanted to do was teach. But he was bound by his duty as a father.

"So, what subject did you study today, Divya?" came his dreaded question.

"Geography," she answered meekly, her voice barely above a whisper.

"Speak up! At the mention of studies, you lose your voice."

"Geography," she repeated in a slightly louder quavering voice.

"Bring me your book," he ordered.

"Hurry up!" he bellowed as Divya dawdled, trying to delay the inevitable torment.

Reclining on the bed, his head resting on two pillows, he opened the book to the chapter she had claimed to have studied. Sitting stiffly on a chair in front of him with her wildly beating heart in her mouth, Divya's 'education' would begin. Jyoti and Amar would make themselves scarce at times like this; not wanting to witness what they knew would follow… their sister's annihilation.

"Come on then," he said sternly, scowling over the thick black rim of his spectacles, his foot tapping impatiently against the other, "let me see how much you remember… recite the chapter!"

Stuttering and stammering, she managed to say the first sentence and then forgot what little she had tried to memorise. Finally giving up, she sat there, tears streaming down her face.

"You told me you'd studied this chapter," he roared, "you lied!"

Chucking the book into her lap with a look of disgust on his face, he said, "Now go and learn the chapter. You will never achieve anything in life."

Threats of dire consequences invariably followed along the lines of –

"I'll remove you from this school and admit you in the government school across the road."

"You don't have to go to school anymore. I'll sack the maid and you can wash the dishes and do the sweeping and swabbing in the house."

He would fret and fume, sadly shaking his head at the thought of his daughter's doomed future.

As she sat there, a nervous mass of trembling twitches, he would go off in to an exhausted sleep. How could he slip into sleep so quickly? Maybe yelling at her had a sedative effect on his senses. Divya developed the art of switching off the minute he started shouting and replacing his rantings with Cliff Richards' soothing voice. "We're all going on a summer holiday..." would automatically begin to play in her mind, calming her frazzled nerves.

She'd sit there fuming inside... How the hell did he expect her to learn the entire chapter by rote anyway? What a nightmare! She hated studies, she hated him for taking the joy out of her learning and she hated herself for being so dull and for crying so easily. Why couldn't she be bright and talented like her siblings? He never ever tried to "teach" them like this. Why her? Divya promised herself then, never to pressurise or traumatise her child, when and if she ever had one.

But then again, Divya loved her dad. She loved him with all her heart and yearned for his stamp of approval and acknowledgement of her as a person not the object of his ridicule or an emotional punching bag. How she strived to please him! She felt so special when he called on her – not Jyoti or Amar – to pull out his grey hair with her tiny nimble fingers or press his tired legs and pull his toes till the knuckles cracked.

"Ooooooooooh! Hmmmmmmmmm! You have such gentle hands!" His response to her touch filled her with pride. Strangely, he found this very relaxing and would drift off to sleep under the magic of her fingers. Divya could still remember fanning him quietly with a hand fan, during a power cut on hot summer afternoons, so that he would not wake up from his deep sleep. As soon as the electricity went, she would hurry so that before the whirring of the ceiling fan could stop her hand fan would take over with a gentle swish.

But her competition was tough – she had to contend with her sister, his first-born-precious-child and her brother, his dream-come-true. They were clever and talented and they could do no wrong in his eyes. Why was she like she was... serious, stubborn, sullen, silent and unattractive? She was not to blame for her looks but whatever little joy she got out of dressing up and preening childishly in front of the mirror was rudely squashed with a "Your face is like an owl's," in Bengali. "Do you think you are Miss India? Why are you wasting your time? Go and study."

She had this deep-rooted feeling of animosity towards her father. There were days when she wished he would just stay at work in the hospital and not come home because she was so tense when he was around. She felt guilty reading a storybook or playing when he was at home. On hearing his car enter the drive way she would hurriedly stop whatever fun thing she was doing and sit with a text book open in front of her, pretending to study. Somehow she felt that in his presence the only acceptable activity for her was to study.

Having seen how cruel life could be, Varun was tough on his children. He had seen the darker side of life and wanted to equip them with skills that would help them take on the world, come what may. He had no patience for whiners and was intolerant with underachievers. No wonder he pushed them so hard, even at the risk of pushing her away from him!

Dad…
I watch you
as you lie asleep,
your stern face gentle in repose.
I read
the story of your life
in the lines on your face.
The struggle
and the heartache,
the deep yearning
that fuelled your ambitions,
the desires for your children –
it's all there in each wrinkle.
Your skin
etched by each emotion
comes alive before my eyes.
There, that line across your brow
talks of your childhood
and the struggle to carry on
after your father's untimely death.
Those lines
near your eyes speak of the woman
who stole your sleep…
and your heart.
That fine network there
has its own story to tell –

of your tireless striving
to achieve the high goals
you set for yourself.
I watch you
and as you lie there
unaware of my presence,
I wonder
what new dream is being born
in your mind?
And I say a silent prayer
that it comes true.

Adolescent Years

Once Varun had earned enough money to rent a flat they moved from their one-roomed dormitory life-style in Sita Ram Bazaar, to a slightly bigger place in a slightly "better" neighbourhood. The move couldn't have been better timed. Thanks to the procreative activities in the storeroom-turned-bedroom downstairs, the number of residents in the house had increased by a couple of babies.

The flat they shifted to comprised two rooms and a small hole-in-the-wall attic that was converted into 'Jyoti and Divya's bedroom'. It was tiny and if they stood on their toes and stretched up they could touch the ceiling. But it was their very own space and they loved it. Initially Jyoti and Divya would gingerly climb up the rungs of the metal ladder hooked onto the wall, hanging on to the sides for dear life. With practice, they were soon running up and down, without looking or holding onto anything, often even while reading a book!

Amar spent many hours of his childhood silently perched on the top rung of the ladder, peering into the room to see what his sisters were up to.

"Aaaaah!!" Jyoti yelled as Divya pulled a strip of waxed cloth off her thigh. Divya had the unenviable job of waxing her sister's legs. She turned to see Amar leaning into the room. His saucer-like eyes horrified as he took in the 'torture' scene. Jyoti was lying face down on

91

the bed with her dress pulled up to her bottom. Divya was bent over her bare legs, a butter knife in one hand and a strip of cloth, covered with sweet sticky wax and uprooted hair, in the other.

"Shoo! Go away, Amar!" she screamed waving the dripping knife at him like a sword.

"What are you doing to didi?" he asked inquisitively. "How can you do that? That's disgusting!"

"It's none of your business. Ma! Call Amar down. He's spying on us again!"

But he was also stacking these visions in a folder in his brain called "what girls get up to".

******

During Divya's adolescence, her Bengali uncles and male cousins were the bane of her life. There should be a law against such relatives, not allowing them within feeling distance of young girls, under section 999! The lecherous sods tried their hands (literally) on any part of her body they could touch.

One uncle would go into her room at the pretext of teaching her math. Taking advantage of the fact that she was alone, he'd shove his hand under her blouse and get cheap thrills feeling her young, teenage body.

"So what did you say the answer to the sum was?" he'd whisper in her ear, his hot breath sending shivers down her spine. No, he was not really interested in an answer. Divya sat like a statue, rigid with terror as his rough fingers rubbed her sensitive skin.

The first time he came to their house he beckoned to Divya saying "Come and give your *kaku* a *haampy*" in a thick Bengali-accented voice.

"Haampy??" What the hell was a 'haampy' she thought.

Seeing the lack of comprehension on her face, he laughed. "Come here, give your uncle a kiss," he explained, offering his cheek.

She was thirteen and very wary of the male species. Quickly pecking his bearded cheek, Divya ran off before he could hug her. He would always ensure that he sat next to her in the car and press his body against hers. Once he even pretended to count her ribs, his fingers moving slowly upwards. Instead of screaming for help at this intrusion into her privacy, rigor mortis would set in. Stiff with fear and hatred she would freeze into a block of wood. She learnt the art of floating into another level, blocking off her conscious mind completely.

The irony of it all is that when she was old and bold enough to work her way out of this trauma and talk to her parents about it, her dad refused to believe it. He became an ostrich, preferring to believe that his relatives were not capable of such gross misdeeds. He did not even bother to acknowledge the trauma on her adolescent psyche, let alone comprehend her fears.

Being too gentle a soul, Tara was not emotionally strong enough to voice any opinion that differed from her husband's. So, Divya was left to deal with it all by herself. The best thing she could do was to suppress it all and vow never to marry a Bengali – even though that resulted in a silent war with her dad. He stopped talking to her for two months. He was sure it must have been something she'd said or the way she'd behaved to provoke such a response from them. It's amazing how skilfully young girls are made to feel guilty for the actions of men.

College... and Boyfriends

Finally, and thankfully, Divya's school days came to an end. She surprised everyone, including herself by not only passing her Senior Cambridge exams, but getting a 1st Division as well. Her family couldn't believe it! It was just not possible.

I am sure they made a mistake while totalling the marks, she thought, swept by the flow of disbelief. But it was true. All her fervent prayers in the school church with the pre and post dabbing of holy water had helped. Her wishes had come true.

Making wishes had become an obsession with Jyoti and Divya. "Quick! Make a wish! There's a red van." Jyoti's excited voice filled the car. They were on their way to visit some relative or the other. Every time they spotted a red mail van on the road, they would close their eyes, make a wish, clench the wish in their tightly fisted hands and then, in order for it to come true, "throw" the wish on a passing black car! Rather complicated! But they did it each and every time without fail. Another way to make wishes come true was to make them under a railway bridge while a train passed over it. Whether it was a red van or a train, Divya's wishes were all the same – she always wished that she passed her exams with a decent grade.

Tara immediately went to the mandir and brought back laddoos as 'prashad' for everyone. Varun was relieved too. All those long tedious hours of teaching her had not gone in vain. He had probably thought she would never pass.

Thank God, Divya thought, *this horrible stage of my life is now over*. Much against her father's wishes, she opted to study psychology at university.

"Only 'mad' people study psychology. If you are not mad now, you will be after studying it!" he proclaimed. "Why can't you study English or economics instead? Something more normal."

But she was adamant. Jyoti supported Divya's decision and in her persuasive way convinced their father that she would definitely not become madder than she already was. He had zero expectations from her anyway, so it wasn't such a struggle this time. She was geared up for a life minus strict nuns and demoralising parent-teacher meetings. Divya really enjoyed her college days because for the first time in her life she was doing something *she* wanted.

Her love life at that point of time was negligible but that didn't bother her much. One major source of excitement for her was sorting out her sister's 'love life'. Jyoti was pretty, young and vivacious and boys flitted around her like proverbial moths.

"Come with me for a walk, Divi," she'd plead "I promised Sunil I'd meet him at the canteen."

Great! She was now supposed to be a chaperone.

"Ma, Divya and I are going for a walk to the library," Jyoti said smartly without batting an eyelid.

"Come back before Dad gets home and don't be too late," said Tara, gullible as ever.

Once they reached the canteen, however, Divya would have to make herself scarce and find ways of keeping herself entertained for the next hour so that Sunil and Jyoti could have their heart-to-heart! She always went prepared with a book to read, a habit that has stayed with her till today. But she did not begrudge this Queen Bee behaviour of her sister for she was basking in the golden sunshine of her newfound freedom. Finally free from the disciplinary shackles of school and childhood, she was determined to make the most of college life and the independence that went with it.

******

Not considering herself attractive, Divya was pleasantly surprised when Mike, a guy from Fiji, fell in love with her. He was skinny and really tall but his Afro hairdo made him look much taller. Somewhat like a 'jhool jharoo' – those long brooms you get to sweep away cobwebs from the highest, unreachable corners of the ceiling! He had come on an exchange programme and was studying in a neighbouring college. Sadly (for him) Divya was not attracted to him and anyway, she was too busy having a good time to get involved at that stage. But it did feel good to suddenly become the object of someone's attention. And what attention! He was so bowled over by her that he was even willing to be a "subject" for all the psychological projects and tests she had to complete to graduate.

"This way at least I get to spend some time with you," he said obligingly, attempting to delete all those guilty thoughts from Divya's mind that she was using him.

She had struck gold! Getting 'subjects' for the Practicals was tougher than administering the tests! A day before their Practicals Divya and her classmates would go scouting around for gullible guinea pigs. At the sight of this band of psychology students, friends and acquaintances were often seen doing a double take and crossing the street at breakneck speed, rushing off in the opposite direction that they had been ambling down a few moments ago! They dreaded the possibility that they would be dragged to the Psycho Lab and administered a variety of tests including IQ, Aptitude or Personality. Bunch of lily-livered chickens all of them!

But Mike was different. He would eagerly participate in any test Divya subjected him to, even if it meant bunking his own tutorials. Needless to say, the test results were not reliable. While she explained the test instructions, Mike would be too busy staring at her with the entire Milky Way in his eyes, probably distracted by all kinds of Freudian thoughts.

"Have you understood what you have to do, Mike?" Divya asked, waving the stopwatch she was holding, in his face.

"Huh?" he dragged his star struck eyes back to the multi-coloured blocks and the pattern card in front of him. "Oh yeah. I got it." He mumbled his lie.

"You want to come for a coffee or something after this? I sure could do with one." He was hopeful that one day she'd relent.

"Sorry, Mike, I have to write this up and submit it tomorrow."

"Oh okay. No problems. When's my next test?" Never say die! He was good for her ego, even though her test results went for a six!

Then there was Rajesh, Varun's college friend's son. He was a medical student who came to stay with the Guhas for a few days during his vacation. He was suffering from schizophrenia and depression and had attempted suicide a few times. The decision to send Rajesh to Delhi was a double-pronged one. Rajesh's father thought that the change would do him good and also hoped that Varun would be able to drill some sense into his head.

Being a student of psychology, Divya was rather excited, sadistically so, when she heard of Rajesh's problems of the psyche. She used him as a guinea pig and tried her hand at counselling him.

"So tell me, Rajesh, when was the first time you realised that your brain was like a bucket with a hole in it through which your thoughts were coming out?" She tried to add, what she hoped was, a professional tone to her voice.

She spent long hours listening to him empty out his mind and clutter up hers with irrational thoughts. She'd nod and hum and haw and look as empathetic as possible.

This is what he needs, she thought tiredly after an extremely long and boring session with him. *He needs a patient, non-judgemental hearing.*

This, as Divya learnt the hard way, backfired into 'transference' because one fine morning, about a week after his arrival, he boldly announced at the breakfast table that he loved her and wanted to marry her. Stupidly naïve that she was, it came as a shock to Divya. As for her apoplectic father, he nearly swallowed his spoon! Ignoring Amar's snorts and giggles, she hurriedly got her dad a glass of water as he choked and spluttered on his cornflakes. Varun looked at her accusingly. Once again she was to blame for some stupid wimp of a man's behaviour, but by now she was used to this and refused to let it penetrate her thickening skin.

"Finish your studies first, beta. Then earn and be independent and then think about marriage," Varun managed to say in an exaggeratedly tolerant, measured voice.

Varun was scared that if he scolded Rajesh, he would try jumping off the roof or some such melodramatic thing. If it had been anyone else, Varun would have slaughtered him on the spot for broaching such a topic, finishing him anyway in the process!

"But, Uncle," Rajesh pleaded, "Divya is the only person who understands me."

But Varun had already got up from the dining table and left the room... his way of ending a conversation he did not agree with.

The next day Rajesh disappeared leaving behind his suitcase full of clothes. Panic-stricken, Varun went crazy looking for him and in sheer desperation, informed the police.

Rajesh was finally found that night, at the railway station. The police found him sitting forlornly on a platform bench, staring blankly at the train tracks. He truly believed he loved Divya and was heartbroken at the rejection of his offer to marry her. In the blink of an eye he was promptly packed off home before he thought of doing something more drastic.

All she had done was to have given a patient hearing to his perceived problems, asked probing questions and made the right noises. Divya didn't for the life of her expect him to misread her interest. That's the danger of little knowledge and inexperience. In spite of her innocence in this entire drama, she felt guilty for some strange reason and stayed out of her dad's line of fire for a while, praying for his amnesia.

And Then There Was Love

Arjun was her first love.

Divya met him at Jyoti's wedding, at a time when she had given up all hope of ever finding the right guy and falling in love. Reluctantly she was coming to terms with the fact that she would die single and unloved. She would be agony aunt to all her friends for the rest of her life, lending her shoulder, ear and hanky now and then for their broken hearts. Arjun saved her from her complacent acceptance of vicarious living. He was the groom's friend. Though not the dark-handsome Mills & Boon type, he had a deep, sexy voice and dark bottomless eyes you could lose yourself in. And he was very tall and gaunt, in a Clint Eastwood kind of craggy way. He was in the navy and sailed for eight months at a stretch. Divya met him when he was home on his four-month annual leave.

After perfunctory introductions by common friends, she felt his eyes follow her everywhere as she rushed around greeting guests and collecting presents. But there was no time for her to wallow in his attention. She was in demand, as she had never been before!

"Divya! Jyoti needs a hair pin... her veil is slipping off her head."

"Divya! Could you get Jaanvi aunty her shawl from the car?"

"Divya, beti, please get me a cup of tea, I have a headache."

Weddings can be so exhausting, she thought as she finally collapsed on a chair behind a pillar, away from the blaring shehnai-spouting loudspeaker, hoping no one would find her.

"Can I get you a cup of coffee or something? You look like you need a drink."

A deep voice emerged from the bushes next to the pillar.

"*Oh no! There goes my hiding place,*" Divya sighed resignedly. Nearly falling off her chair, she turned and looked up. All the way up, into Arjun's eyes. She was surprised at the concern she saw there.

"Oh I'd love a cup…" Not giving her time to finish her sentence he disappeared and materialised again instantly like a magician, holding two cups of steaming coffee.

"Voila!"

"Gosh! That was quick!" she exclaimed.

"I'd kept two cups of coffee on the table behind you, hoping you'd take me up on my offer," he confessed sheepishly.

She laughed. "Thanks I really needed this. Greeting so many people has dried up my throat. It feels like sandpaper. My vocal cords have never been exercised so much as they have today."

She was a bit nervous by his attention. "Stop blabbering," she told herself sternly.

"I've been watching you all evening. You must have walked a couple of miles by now. How you do that in a sari with such high heels is really commendable," he continued. "Maybe I should walk beyond you just in case you trip... then I can catch you!" Hope filled his eyes at the thought.

"Hahaha! Actually the truth is that my feet are really killing me," Divya replied. "I wish I had worn flats instead of these pencil heels... but I am so short. Vanity!" she blurted, feeling unsure of what to say as his eyes stared unblinkingly at her.

"Come to think of it, you are a bit on the small side, aren't you?" he teased. And then on a serious note, "But you are one bundle of energy!"

They sat and chatted over coffee. She must have drunk at least three cups of the bitter brew within the space of an hour. By the time the wedding was over, Divya was on a caffeine high. They exchanged phone numbers and promised to meet again. He had all the time in the world and she needed someone to help her fill the depressing void now that her sister had married and left home.

Arjun would pick her up from college every other day and take her for long mo-bike rides. Initially she felt awkward sitting astride his bike. Like a true blue prude, she kept her bag between them like the Great Divide and held his shoulder gingerly with her fingertips. But he soon sorted that out.

"Hold on tight!" he shouted. "There's a pothole coming up."

And he'd break and then accelerate ensuring that she had no option but to hold him real tight... or else risk falling off!

He soon took care of her bag too.

"Here, let me hold your bag," he said as she was trying to cling to her bag and clamber onto the bike at the same time.

Instead of returning it once she was on, he just slung it around his neck so that it rested against his chest. With gay abandonment, they sped around the streets of Delhi. It was so exhilarating! Divya loved clinging to him and resting her head against his lean back, inhaling deeply. Givenchy Gentleman filled her senses. Sometimes he would drive with one hand, the other one snaking backwards round her waist to draw her closer and hold her captive. Ah the impetuosity of youth! She loved the feel of the wind playing with her hair, even though she looked typhoon-hit by the end of the ride. Driving at 70 mph he once gave her a yellow rose, drawing it skilfully and magically out of his shirt pocket.

"I love you!" he shouted as the bike wobbled at his distraction.

She laughed in sheer ecstasy as those precious words danced in the breeze around her. Divya preserved that rose bud in the pages of her diary for posterity! Its yellow fragrance eternally trapped in the pages of time.

Arjun taught her how to kiss. But their first kiss was quite a disaster.

It was one o'clock in the morning. The roads were dark and empty as most of Delhi was lost in slumberland. Arjun had taken Divya out for dinner to "Tandoori Nights", famous for its variety of tikka platters. To avoid yet another fabricated explanation to her parents, Divya was spending the night at her friend Sujata's place.

"Don't worry about being late," Sujata pressed the house keys in her hand. "Go on then... Just have a blast!"

Dinner and drive over, Arjun parked outside Sujata's, building under the dark shadows of a neem tree. Switching off the ignition he turned to Divya with a strange look in his eyes. The moonlight found its way through the leaves to rest gently on her yellow silk shirt. Silver on gold.

Here comes my goodnight hug, she thought sleepily. Not used to alcohol, the vodka in the 'Peach Passion' cocktail she had drunk was befuddling her cognitive abilities.

He took her in his arms and she wrapped hers around him, enjoying the warm feel of his embrace. And then...

"Open your lips, D," he urged. A hot whisper against her mouth. Holding her chin gently, he tried to prise open her tightly clenched mouth with his. Sitting in the constricting confines of his car, their bodies were straining, awkward and twisted. She felt a muscle in her lower back complain at this odd angle, as the gear stick pressed uncomfortably against her thigh.

How do they do it in the movies? she thought. This is so bloody uncomfortable.

"Hey, loosen up, it's only a kiss," he softly reassured her as she sat contorted in his arms. Stiff... a product of adolescent abuse.

"Don't be scared, honey," and, in spite of the gearstick embedded in her thigh, she gradually relaxed. Her limbs melted into a vodka-induced, limp mass of bonelessness and her lips trembled uncontrollably like a goldfish out of water. Involuntarily she opened her mouth, and he slipped in his tongue! Taken unawares, she was unprepared for this strange sensation. She had experienced the feel of a wooden ruler in her mouth... but not this – this wet, spongy mobile intruder! Horrified, she clamped her mouth shut nearly biting his tongue off in the process.

"Ouch!" he screamed in pain, looking disbelievingly at her. His passion flew out of the half open window.

"Why did you do that?" Divya asked moving away from him, her eyes reflecting her distress. Leaning against the window, she wiped her lips with the back of her trembling hand. Sensing the panic in her voice, his anger vanished.

"It's okay, honey. I am sorry I came on too strong. It's my fault. Must be the whisky." He apologised holding her close, patting her head tenderly, trying to calm her down.

"I didn't mean to scare you, sweetheart," he whispered. "It's okay. Calm down."

They sat like that, her head to his chest, till she stopped trembling. Then he escorted her to the gate of Sujata's house. That's the last I'll see of him, Divya thought sadly embarrassed as he drove off. Nobody expects to risk losing his tongue during a kiss!

There was no news from him for two whole days. Divya was too mortified to call Arjun. She wilted in silent despair. Two days later as she walked out of college, her heart did a tiny summersault when she saw him leaning against his car, his sunglasses perched jauntily on top of his head. Shy and awkward, she slowly walked towards him wondering what to say.

"Thank God you're finally here!" he said coming forward to meet her halfway. "I've been waiting for nearly an hour, hoping against hope that you wouldn't bunk classes today."

He hugged her quickly in a very proper, acceptable-in-public way.

"Hi, D," he smiled.

"Hi."

Silence... an uncomfortably long pause that echoed in the space between them.

"How's your tongue?" she ventured hesitantly (better than... cat's got your tongue?), broaching the subject of her mental despair and his pain.

"More than my tongue, it's my bruised male ego. No one has ever reacted to my kiss like that before."

The laughter in his voice was enough to set Divya off. She was in splits... and so was he. She leaned against the car for support. The entire episode suddenly seemed hysterically funny. Throwing caution to the winds she hugged him hard and tight, happy to have him back. The college durwan looked suspiciously at them, wondering whether he should reprimand them for 'misbehaving' in public. The principal had instructed him to be strict with young students displaying such "ultra-modern behaviour".

"Let's go for a coffee," he said disentangling himself, pushing her gently into the car just as the durwan was about to take a step in their direction.

Their next kiss was slow and gentle and not at all traumatic. In fact, this time round Arjun was a bit wary, not knowing what to expect.

"Be gentle," he warned jokingly, his lips smiling against Divya's!

Miss Paul, her elocution teacher, should have taken a few tips from him... such a more pleasant and exciting way to teach her the skill of opening her mouth (without the help of a ruler!).

He made her feel beautiful and womanly and special. Divya suddenly grew up and overnight became more confident. She felt worthy of love. It's amazing what a little tender loving care can do. There was the proverbial spring in her step. A lifting of her spirits. Her spirits were at an all-time high and she would let no one ruin her moments of glory. Her father would have had a major heart attack if he came to know about Arjun. She couldn't let that happen so Divya became an adept fabricator. She lied with a straight face not scared of going to hell (but saying a few silent "Hail Mary's" just to be on the safe side – an offshoot of her convent education).

"I've got extra classes, so I'll have to stay back late today."

"After class I might go to the documentation centre to do some research work for my thesis."

Surprisingly, and thankfully, her parents never questioned her sudden spurt of academic activities. In fact, they welcomed this studious change in their middle child.

Arjun took over her thoughts completely. She was a puppet in his hands. They would hold hands and go for long walks on the wooded ridge, near Delhi University, or sit in the coffee shop chatting for hours or just happy to stare silently into each other's eyes. They sat through many films but did not get to see much of them having bought tickets for the last row. Their young love found its naïve expression in those dark halls where lips found each other fleetingly and tightly clasped hands conveyed the longing of their hearts. If Divya did not meet Arjun, her days seemed incomplete and interminably long, the lonely hours not wanting to end. She was swept off her feet by the tidal wave of first love and she was happy to drown in its turbulent waters.

"You really do justice to a sari," Arjun said one day when Divya had made an extra effort and worn a sari, praying that the pleats wouldn't fall out. She felt like never ever taking that sari off again! In fact, she still had that sari, safely wrapped up in moth balls and muslin. A memento of her first love.

Ahhh... first love. The most intoxicating emotion ever. Cherished and preserved in the sanctity of your mind, to be relived through answers to innocent questions of children and grandchildren. Tell us about the first time you fell in love... An evergreen favourite.

Divya's first love, unfortunately, did not survive the test of time and distance.

As with all good things, Arjun's leave came to an end. He had to join his ship. Divya took to writing long letters filled with love and loneliness. She posted these thick missives every other day. Unfortunately for her, and their relationship, he was not much of a correspondent. When he did write, the letter would have to wait till the ship docked at a port so that it could be posted. In those pre-mobile, pre-email days, the silences were long and stressful.

"He doesn't love me anymore."

"He has found someone else."

In a strange way, history seemed to be repeating itself. When her dad left for England, Ma had the security of marriage on her side. But apart from a heart full of loving moments, Divya had nothing. Plagued by inexperience and doubts, she became insecure, at not knowing anything about what was going on in his life. No contact caused a slow silent death of their short-lived relationship. Maybe, if they could have stayed in touch things would have been different and she would have been sailing the seven seas with him. The captain's wife. But then, perhaps, she was just another girl in another port for him. Just another holiday romance.

Divya desperately needed an agony aunt for her broken heart... Jyoti was miles away, married and living in London. How she missed her, especially at times like this when she needed someone to console her. But she had to clamber out of her well of lovesick self-pity. It was a long and arduous trek and she slipped and fell a few times. She skinned her heart and bruised her ego... but she made it.

The Hunt for a Husband

Once Divya had graduated, the 'husband-hunting' began in full earnest. She felt like a sack of potatoes that her father had been carrying for too long. She was a heavy burden and needed to be offloaded at the earliest. She put her foot down when she was made to parade in front of a Bengali family, who had come in search of a bride. She felt like an exhibition piece on display.

"Ensure that you are home early today, Divya. We are having visitors," Varun said in a voice that did not entertain any questions on the matter.

Somehow Divya had a gut feeling that something fishy was going on. She followed Tara to the kitchen, turning to her for answers.

"Come on, Ma, tell me the truth. Who's coming this evening?"

A bit of probing and arm-twisting revealed that it was going to be a matchmaking evening.

"We've heard that the family is very 'good'. They are keen to meet you," Tara said apologetically, knowing Divya's aversion to such issues. "You never know... some good may come out of this." As positive and hopeful as ever, Tara tried to make her see reason.

Some more pressure and Divya got the entire story out of her mother. It seems the 'boy' lived in the U.S. and was so busy earning money that he had entrusted his parents to find a 'suitable bride' for him! He had complete faith in their choice. Divya's hackles rose immediately.

What a wimp of a guy, she thought angrily, *he can't even take some time off to come and see the woman who would be his bride, the one he would have to live with for the rest of his life*. She promised herself that she would make it difficult for them to 'choose' her for their docile, namby-pamby son.

Divya purposely lingered in college and reached home barely five minutes before the "good family" was supposed to arrive. Much to her parents' dismay she refused to change from her jeans into a sari.

"There's no way I'm going to dress up and act coy and demure in front of 'bride-hunters'," she informed her ma adamantly as she tried to persuade her to wear a sari.

"Stop arguing with your mother and go up and change right now," Dad intervened in his 'do-it-or-else' voice.

Divya's 'Capricorn' spirit bristled and her chin shot out in stubborn protest. "I hate wearing saris," she lied, remembering how happily she had worn one for Arjun.

Just as their argument was taking an emotionally nasty turn, she was saved by the doorbell. It was too late… they had arrived. Ignoring her dad's dirty looks and his hurriedly whispered command, "Do pranam. Touch their feet," she sadistically decided to enjoy the evening at everyone's expense. She knew there would be hell to pay for later but was beyond caring.

"Come come, Mr. Mukherjee. Mrs. Mukherjee. Welcome." Varun and Tara rushed forward to greet their daughter's potential parents-in-law.

"Namashkar," Divya said from a distance, standing safely behind Amar.

Four members of the absent prospective groom's family had come bride-hunting for him – his parents and two married sisters. The three women, decked up in their Banarasi silk sarees and gold jewellery, looked like Christmas trees. A thick line of sindoor filled their centre parting dividing their heads into two well-oiled hemispheres. An in-your-face, bright red proclamation of their married status. After a decent interval of social niceties, the third degree began over cups of tea, samosas and rasagollas. Divya reluctantly carried the tray of snacks and served them, as Amar sniggered in the background.

"So, did you make these?" asked the father, staring at her through his bushy eyebrows as he bit into a hot samosa.

Shaking her head, Divya heard Amar cough, as he nearly choked on his samosa. She shot him a "save me" look. Me and cook???

"Well you can cook, can't you?" Was there a thread of worry in the old man's voice? Not waiting for her answer, he continued, curious to know about her culinary skills. "What all can you cook?"

Ah... now he's finally come to the point, she thought. *Why doesn't he just hire a cook for his son?*

"No, no, I haven't made these," Divya said hurriedly. "These are bought from the local shop down the road. I hate cooking. But if push comes to shove, I can boil an egg and make a toast." She smiled sweetly. "It's called survival cooking."

He shook his head sadly, putting a red cross on item number one of his mental checklist.

"And can you sing?" he persisted. A 'good' Bengali girl should be able to burst into Rabindra sangeet on request!

"Sometimes, but only in the bathroom. And that too I sing only rock-and-roll. Or maybe head-banging acid rock sometimes," Divya said cheerfully using the term she had heard Amar speak so often. "It helps to clear my mind." She refused to make eye contact with her parents, thinking of all her horrific childhood singing sessions.

"Grrumphngngt." That was Amar again stifling his laughter, rather unsuccessfully.

"Acid rock and you? You should have seen their faces!" he said later amidst hysterical howls of laughter.

Divya knew she was pushing her luck and could sense her dad's mute fury at her totally juvenile behaviour. But he couldn't say anything in front of guests. She was protected by the presence of these strangers. Meanwhile, the boy's mother sat silently with a strange look of anticipation in her eyes. Her thinning, jet black hair was tightly twisted in a small knot at the nape of her neck. It looked like a small brinjal hanging on to her head for dear life. *Waiting to be plucked,* Divya thought mesmerised by the image. Ignoring Divya completely, Mrs. Mukherjee kept looking at the drawing room door. It was as if she was waiting for something to happen... someone to come. It was only later, just before they left that the reason for her expectant expression became clear.

Before Divya could be asked the next question, she was sternly ordered by her dad to take the heavily bejewelled sisters upstairs.

"Go upstairs. Take them to your room," he said with a gentleness that she knew was put on for the guests. Only she could hear the underlying steely threat of "just you wait till they leave..."

Angry at being made to feel like a two-year-old punished for bad behaviour, she obliged. Actually she was glad to get away. Mr. Mukherjee was beginning to bug her. Their jewellery tinkled and shone as the sisters

112

clattered up the stairs. They lifted their saris high so as not to trip over, exposing very hairy legs.

Maybe I could introduce them to the art of hair removal, Divya thought wickedly. While the two pairs of parents discussed her future possibilities on the bridal market, the two sisters soon took over from where their dad had left off and continued with the interview upstairs!

After a cursory inspection of her room, the Metallica sisters sat on the edge of Divya's bed. There was not much place on the bed anyway for there was a pile of clothes strewn across it in colourful disarray. She had tried them on hastily that morning before deciding what to wear to college. By the time she decided on a pair of skin-fit jeans and a sleeveless cowl-necked top, she realised she was running late for her 10 o'clock class. There had been no time to tidy up and put the clothes away. Divya blessed herself silently for this unusual mess, hoping that they would think she was an untidy person. Ignoring the bed, she pushed aside a pile of Mills & Boons and clambered on to her desk and waited. Silence. The ominous quiet before the storm.

"Would you like to listen to some music?" Divya asked trying to fill the uncomfortable gap with her inane words.

"Elton John? Neil Diamond?" she rambled.

After all, they were still her guests. She had to be polite. But it was as if she had not spoken. They stared at each other and then on mutual consent the barrage of questions began. A session of synchronised interrogation.

"Do you ever wear saris?"

"No," she lied, swinging denim-clad legs, "I live in my jeans. And at home I wear shorts, they are so comfortable to hang out in."

"Can you stitch?

"Naaah."

"Knit?"

"Nope."

"Maybe paint?" they asked in desperation, hoping she had some talent hidden somewhere.

Divya shook her head, feeling a bit sorry for them. But she wasn't in any mood to help them.

"Oh I have better things to do in my free time," she said airily, "like reading Mills & Boons," she picked up a book to show them the cover of a TDH (tall, dark and handsome) man passionately kissing a PYT (pretty young thing), "or chatting with my many boyfriends," she ended.

Yuck! She sounded like a brazen brat to herself! Many boyfriends? She was still recovering from her Arjun experience and licking her wounds. But she quite liked the image she was portraying. She wished she had long pointy nails painted a deep scarlet. It would have been perfect. She wished she had a camera to capture their changing expressions.

Horrified and visibly disappointed they lapsed back into an uncomfortable silence and this time Divya did nothing at all to put them at ease. No, she was definitely not suitable for their beloved brother. She read it in their eyes. They heaved a collective sigh of relief when they were summoned downstairs. It was time for them to leave. And time for Divya to face her parents' ire.

Just before departing, the boy's mother came out of her reverie and spoke up for the first time that evening. She turned to Varun.

"Doctor Babu, let us see your daughter at least once," she squeaked. Her voice sounded unused, like somebody testing a mike.

Her husband probably never gives her a chance to speak, Divya thought nastily.

You could have heard a cockroach burp! The stunned silence that followed seemed to last forever.

Who the hell did she think I was, Divya thought. The maid? Maybe I looked like one to her since I was not dressed to the nines for the 'occasion'. She realised why she had been given the royal ignore throughout. For once her father was at a loss for words.

"Pardon me?" he said politely, clearing his throat, wondering if he had heard her correctly.

"If your daughter is not here then maybe you could give us her photograph so that we can at least see what she looks like and inform our son," she persisted, as her tinsel offspring looked at each other, horrified at their mother's obvious gaffe. "He is going to call up tonight."

"*She* is my daughter," said Varun, pointing a finger accusingly at Divya. She tried to look blasé but wished she were invisible.

Ping! The coin dropped. A look of utter shock washed over the lady's face as she quickly slipped on her spectacles and inspected Divya afresh. A disappointed "Oh" was all she could bring herself to utter... or rather squeak. To give them credit, the rest of her family was really embarrassed by this lack of observation and dense behaviour. All of a sudden, they were in a hurry to leave. After uncomfortably abrupt farewells, they left.

"Completely crazy family!" Amar couldn't stop laughing! Thanks to Mrs. Mukherjee, Divya did not get the dreaded scolding she had expected from her parents. They were also bemused and amused by her strange behaviour.

"What a waste of an evening," Divya said taking advantage of the general mood. "Till I complete my post-graduation, 'marriage' is a forbidden word in this house," she announced loudly in true Capricorn stubbornness.

"Furthermore," she added with continuing bravado, "I will NEVER marry a Bengali, NEVER!" she'd had enough of male Bengali relatives pawing her body and couldn't bear the thought of spending the rest of her life with one!

The irony of her life was that though she married a non-Bengali, she ended up living in Bong land – Kolkata! And much later... hold your breath... falling in love with a Bengali! She agreed with that wise person who said, "Never say 'Never'." The 'Bong Connection' just wouldn't let her go.

Her aggression caught her dad unawares because she was left to continue with her studies in peace. But as her final semester drew to a close, Divya's future hung over her head like the sword of Damocles.

Wedding Shehnais

That's when Ravi came into Divya's life. He lived in Kolkata and was spending a few days with his Delhi relatives, who also happened to be Varun's patients. He was gentle, polite... and available. He showed a reasonable amount of interest in her without seeming too pushy. She was stressed with the marital pressures coming from the home front. She weighed her options...

– he was not a Bengali (major plus point!)

– he was good-looking (bonus)

– he had a good sense of humour (very important)

– he was well read (great! at least they could have an intelligent conversation) ...

So what if he was seven years older than her, a bit old-fashioned and still wore very flared bell-bottoms. That's it! She decided he was the best choice going. She would have preferred to go to Vienna for higher studies – her application had been accepted. Perhaps, if she had been one of her other aggressive siblings she would have gone. But marriage was written on her cards and before she completed her post-graduation, Divya was unofficially engaged.

Ravi and Divya went out a few times and tried to get to know each other, asking questions that seemed important at the time. Feelers of the games people play.

"What kind of music do you like? I hope you like the Beatles! And Simon & Garfunkel?"

"No thrillers aren't for me. I enjoy reading Bertrand Russell and Herman Hesse."

"Oh yes! I love going to the movies. The mushier the better."

They rose and fell a couple of notches in each other's eyes depending on the answers.

"Would you like a cigarette?" he asked, politely offering her an open pack of Marlboro's. He felt like a smoke and his offer was just out of sheer courtesy.

Divya had tried smoking a few times but only behind the closed doors of her bathroom, never in public. And after each trial she would spray the bathroom liberally with perfume, rinse her mouth with Listerine and then chew some gum just to be on the safe side. She couldn't risk her dad finding out about his docile daughter's tobacco experiments. But what the heck, she thought impulsively, let's test him.

"Thanks." She deftly took a cigarette and held it expertly between her lips, waiting for him to light it.

Immediately, she plummeted in his esteem. Taken aback that she smoked, he took a while to recover before he put a flame to the cigarette. Inexpertly, Divya inhaled trying not to choke on the sudden inrush of smoke. She had marred his mental picture of a "good, homely girl". Well, served him right! Why did he offer cigarettes if he didn't want to see her smoking?

At the end of the sizing up they decided that, despite the smoking, tying the knot was not such a bad decision after all. They sealed the deal...and their fate. He proposed to her over a cup of coffee in the Oberoi Maiden's Hotel and she accepted.

"I found my maiden at Maiden's," he told everyone.

He was witty, too.

So Ravi and Divya got married. It was a 'mixed' wedding with a bit of both Bengali and Punjabi rituals to keep all the relatives happy. But in spite of that, wedding politics and gossip were at their peak! Relatives had a gala time pointing fingers at each other, trying to find out surreptitiously what each one was giving, ready with their criticism and comments. As she sat there in their midst, dressed to the hilt, she felt like a mannequin. Her aunts were busy fingering her necklaces, inspecting her sari, and lifting her henna-stained hands to see how heavy her gold bangles were.

Ravi refused to come to the wedding astride the traditional "ghori" (mare) – not after his friend, Anuj told him what he went through when he got married.

"There I was in my entire bridegroom's splendour, sitting astride this white horse," Anuj recounted, "when suddenly it neighed loudly, reared up on its hind legs and took off!"

A bee had stung the horse's backside. Anuj charged past his bride's house like Ivanhoe going for a jousting tournament. Clinging to the horse's neck with one hand and his turban with the other, he barely managed to stay on the garlanded saddle. The mare-with-groom-hanging-on-for-dear-life were finally stopped by worried relatives who thought Anuj had galloped off because he had developed cold feet! He must have developed a sore bottom... that much was certain!

Ravi decided to take a safer option and came sedately in a car decked with flowers instead. As he sat in the car, waiting for the driver to come, his cousin's wife gave him her month old baby to carry.

"Please, Ravi, I hope you don't mind holding Akash and taking him along with you in the car," Priya gushed breathily as she shoved her little bundle into his arms. "He'll sleep all the way, so don't worry."

Before Ravi had a chance to react she closed the car door with a bang on his surprised face and rushed off in a blur of silver and pink silk, leaving a trail of Chanel 5 behind. She loved dancing, especially at weddings. She rushed to join the other women swing their hips and twirl around to the beat of a popular Hindi film song that the band was playing. As a result, when Ravi stepped out of the car in front of Divya's house, he had a babe in arms. A shock wave washed over her relatives and neighbours. People were nudging each other, whispering and pointing at the groom gingerly holding a baby.

"Poor Divya… she is marrying a man who already has a baby! He must be a divorcee or maybe a widower."

"I wonder why Dr Guha is marrying his daughter off to a married man. |She'll have to bring up someone else's child."

Blissfully unaware of the rumours doing the rounds, Divya sat in all her finery trying to look coy. Waiting to be called to the 'mandap', she wondered what the hell she was letting herself in for. Suddenly she felt panicky as the enormity of her decision hit her. She desperately wanted to run to the safety of her bedroom and lock the door. She wasn't ready to go away and leave the secure shelter of her youth. She did not want to take on a new family, new responsibilities… she did not want to get married!

"I've changed my mind!" she wanted to shout. "Go home, everyone, I'm not getting married."

She froze and broke out in cold sweat at the same time. Her stomach churned and bitter bile filled her mouth. Crazy thoughts shrieked like banshees, whizzing around in her mind, like the ghosts in the Casper comics she had read as a child.

But it was too late to step back. She could hear the band playing "Come September" – a big hit in most Punjabi weddings at that time. It was a funny sight to see suited-booted men and heavily decked up women suddenly begin to twist or do a 'bhangra-cum-shake' fusion when they heard this tune.

There was a sudden rush of activity and Divya's friends and cousins swarmed around her, giggling and cracking silly jokes about the groom. The 'baraat' had arrived. Relatives wanted to help her get up and escort her to the 'mandap' where Ravi was waiting for her minus the baby. Thankfully a breathless Priya had relieved him of her still sleeping baby.

Divya had always wondered why a bride is helped by her friends to walk towards her future husband... as if suddenly she has no strength in her legs. Cynically, she used to think it was because they wanted to be in all the photographs. But now she realised the need. She was thankful for their support because, petrified by the unknown future, she was overcome by a debilitating weakness. Her knees trembled and her legs threatened to give way as one foot followed the next in a robotic walk.

No one should ever marry for the wrong reasons. But then what is the "right" reason to get married? Love? There was no way she would have been given the time to fall in love with someone and then marry him. And ironically, a 'love marriage' was completely out of the question in her family of ostriches (even though her own parents had married for love). So she took a deep breath, swallowed the bile and agreed to marry. It was a silent compromise she made with herself.

The heat of the fire pushed into her face, pressed on by a sudden autumn breeze. Divya closed her watering eyes – tasting smoke and a strange kind of sorrow. A feeling that brought out the butterflies in her stomach, drying her mouth. Making it difficult to swallow.

"Om shanti shanti shanti…" the pandit chanted and on cue, Ravi and Divya threw handfuls of aromatic 'samagri' into the flames of the 'havan' and repeated their marriage vows after him. Soon she would be leaving the cosseted security of her youth… her family and friends. She would be starting a new life with a man and his family. Soon she would be a wife... his wife. A man with whom she had shared a couple of thoughts and a cigarette, over coffee a few times. A man she barely knew. Glancing sideways at Ravi through the double curtain of her lowered lashes, thick with mascara, and the maroon net of the veil covering her head, she wondered whether similar apprehensions were going through his mind. Thoughts of sharing his home and hearth with another, of a new family, of a changed lifestyle...! Sitting on the low throne-like chair, dressed in his cream silk sherwani, he was the epitome of the perfect groom. But his handsome face showed no emotion as he stared into the flames. And why should it? He wouldn't be leaving his family to become part of another. His life wouldn't be as completely turned on its head, as hers would be.

Why was she doing this to herself? Instead of thinking of exciting romantic thoughts of their impending first night together, like most other brides would do, Divya was needlessly winding herself up into a state of frenzy. She thought of Asha, her dear friend, who got married four days earlier. She had always been accommodating and in control. When they had last spoken, she had seemed happy and ready to make the compromises that marriage demanded. Compromising. Adjusting. Adapting. Just the thought turned Divya's premarital feet to clichéd cold. Maybe there was something seriously wrong with her.

She needed more oxygen as her chest constricted in panic. Another spasm of nausea engulfed her as her churning stomach threatened to reject her morning cup of tea. She had fasted and not eaten all day as part of the rituals required of a bride-to-be. Her empty stomach nervously gurgled and rumbled in protest, the embarrassing sound luckily hidden by the pundit's chants. What would happen if she extinguished the fire by throwing up in it? Definitely a first in the history of Indian weddings. Swallowing a mouthful of bile, she closed her eyes and concentrated on her breathing to calm this assault on her senses, praying for this gastric upheaval to subside. Her jewellery began to feel like an anchor weighing heavy on her neck. Like a drowning woman, her henna-ed hands clutched the deep silky folds of her gold and maroon Tanchoi sari as she blinked hard, not wanting her mascara to run. Even in this dramatically emotional moment, vanity reigned supreme! No wonder brides keep their eyes lowered, she thought. It's not coyness. It's just so that the world won't see the panic and fear in their eyes as the reality of the situation hits them!

Blocking out irrational thoughts Divya tried to concentrate on the words of wisdom that the pundit was preaching, as he tied one end of Ravi's white shawl to the brocaded maroon end of her sari pallav. A tight symbolic knot of togetherness. Her father, sitting opposite the pandit, took her hand and placed it in Ravi's. A transfer of ownership. It was as simple as that. She was being given away. Given from one man to another.

There were still many more rituals to follow. Many more holy mantras to be recited before they could be pronounced husband and wife. Divya needed to pay attention to what the pandit was saying because every now and then he asked her to repeat a 'shloka' after him. But her mind was restless, thoughts strained at their reins, clamouring to be set free. Here was a fire sanctifying the beginning of her married life! What was it about fire that affected her so deeply? It was as if these flames ignited smouldering embers of her memories, bringing them back to life.

Her birth had been tempered by fire.

The sounds of conch shells and her Bengali relatives ululating brought Divya out of her trance, with a jolt. The rituals were over. Still in a daze, she stood up on trembling legs. She touched the sindoor on her head and wiped the red flecks that dusted her nose. Impassively she stared at the powdery red sindoor stains on her finger tips... proof that she was a married woman now! Ravi and Divya touched their parents' feet for their blessings and a sudden shower of petals rained on their heads. Friends and relatives rushed forward to congratulate them. A new chapter in her life had begun.

The Kolkata chapter…

'Twas not so very long ago
I came here as a bride
my heart radiating love's glow
my head held up in pride.
As I took on the role of wife
that flame began to die
is this where I would live my life?
I could not help but cry.
Horror-struck I looked around
crowds of people everywhere
garbage rotting on the ground
traffic polluting the air.
The humid weather drained me out
there were power cuts galore

corruption rampant all about
I could take it no more.
But as the years passed in a blur
my attitude changed its stance,
as I realised I'd sentenced 'Her'
without giving 'Her' a chance.
Kolkata had slowly grown on me
quieter than the night
now when I look around I see
things in a different light.
I feel 'Her' magic in the air
'Her' warmth, it fills my heart
I cannot help but despair
I hadn't loved 'Her' from the start.

A New Wife and a New Life

No longer just a woman but now a wife, Divya left Delhi, the place of her youth, and went to live in Kolkata. It was only then she realised and appreciated the kind of trauma a woman undergoes when she has to switch, not only cities, homes, families, lives, but also roles and identities overnight. She also realised how sheltered her upbringing had been... and that was definitely a disadvantage.

Marriage for her, the supposedly ultimate goal for most women at the time, was like opening a veranda door on the twenty-first floor to step out... only to find nothing there. Feet, expecting hard ground, feel for solid but cycle wildly through thin air instead. Stomach heaving, you freefall into emptiness. It was like an illusion. Why hadn't anyone warned her about this? But it wouldn't have made a difference. However well prepared one might be, when it actually happens the gut-wrenching, heart-stopping reality of it all really hits you hard and knocks you off your feet. It happened to many women yet not much importance was given to "post-marital depression". You were expected to accept the change and take on the role of wife, daughter-in-law, and sister-in-law with the same familiarity as slipping on an old nightgown! Divya began to look at newly married young women with admiration and respect.

"We are your family now," she was told by the members of her 'new family', "forget your parents!" Their light-hearted attempt at inclusion. Many a truth is said in jest! Hard hitting truth. Callous jest.

Not very high on the sense of humour scale, Divya was disturbed. *How dare they*! she thought, angered by the presumption that she should discard her own family and accept a strange one with the snap of two fingers and a blink of an eye.

In a household of three men (Ravi, his younger brother and father), Ma ji, Divya's mother-in-law, reigned supreme. She was not used to having another woman in the household dynamics. Simple and gentle in her ways, she tried to make Divya's transition an easy one in the way she knew best. A week or so after she had joined the family Ma ji came to her with a bunch of keys of different sizes, all bound together in a heavy ring of silver with tiny bells dangling from a shell hooked on to it.

"Here, beti," she said putting them in Divya's hand and closing her fingers firmly over them. They jangled noisily – heralding the end of her freedom. The wedlock keys! "These are yours now. You take charge."

The handing over of keys: An age-old tradition. A symbolic relinquishing of power (sometimes done reluctantly and sometimes not at all). A figurative acceptance of the bride into her new home. Ma ji was willing to step down from her 'powerful' role of matriarch of the house. The cold keys of the house sat heavy in Divya's hand, burning a hole in her palm.

"No, no, Ma ji. You keep them," she said, hurriedly giving them back to her, not wanting to hold them for even a second longer than necessary.

"But all new brides look forward to running a house." Puzzled eyebrows rose delicately at her new daughter-in-law's nearly violent reaction.

"Not this one," Divya replied with gentle firmness. "Thanks, Ma ji, but you keep them."

Was it her imagination or did Ma ji look relieved as her power was returned to her, intact and unblemished? Divya was relieved too. She was definitely not ready to take on the responsibility of running a house.

She tried to dissolve herself in the uncharted waters of her new role. But it was tougher than she thought. The feeling of complete aloneness had never been so strong. She was utterly homesick! It was paradoxical. How could she be homesick? *This* was now her home!

It became part of her daily, masochistic routine to sit by her bedroom window overlooking the mango tree and re-read her mother's letters, weeping copiously as she did. Tara's letters spoke of love, loneliness and maternal sorrow. She missed Divya intensely, especially during the evenings, she wrote. No one could fill the void at that time of the evening when they used to sit and discuss their day and talk about mundane issues over a hot cup of tea.

"You know, Ma, in Dr Pal's class, the first two rows are always empty because when he speaks, his spit sprays the people sitting close by. So we sit at the back just to stay out of his spit range!"

And Tara'd laugh as Divya launched into a detailed description of her lecturers. She loved making her mother laugh and used to look forward to these shared moments.

"I wish I could have gone to college like you and Jyoti," a pale shadow rippled over Tara's fair face fleetingly. "I would have loved it; just like you do. Well at least I was lucky to go to school," she sighed.

When Divya left Delhi, Amar was in his first year at college. Lanky and leggy, with a rapidly roughening voice, he was too busy rebelling against Varun's dictums, intent on enjoying his newfound independence with a vengeance. And anyway, teenage boys have their own agenda – and that does not include inane chatter with a despondent mum.

Tears blurred Divya's eyes and washed the blue ink of the words. The letter soon looked like a Rorschach ink blot. A work of modern art – 'Ma's life in Blue'. She longed to wrap her arms around Ma like an umbilical cord and keep her close forever. The first couple of times Ravi tried his best to console his young bride, calming her down in his mature, quiet way. But Divya could not get out of this tragic spiral of depression. It was too much of an effort.

"You shouldn't have got married if you can't stay away from your family," Ravi finally said, irritated by her juvenile behaviour. "And anyway, this is your family from now on. Grow up, Divya!"

This was not what he had bargained for when he decided to marry. Fed up with a constantly snivelling, depressed wife, yearning for her mother, Ravi decided that he had had enough. He called up Tara and asked her to stop writing to Divya. So she did. It was a blow to her maternal instincts but much against her wishes, she obliged. He was her son-in-law after all... a powerful person who called the shots in a Hindu family. It was as if her lifeline had been severed.

"Ma, why don't you write to me anymore? I've written three letters and you haven't replied to even one of them!"

"Oh I've been so busy, beti. I am so sorry. We've had guests every evening. I just get so tired by the end of the day." Tara made up some lame excuse each time. It was only much later that Divya came to know the real reason for her mother's sudden silence. But by then she had got a toe hold on the slippery slope of change.

A rather desperate and drastic measure on Ravi's part to stabilise a new relationship, but to be honest, it probably did help Divya in a way... a sort of forced cutting of apron strings. Why hadn't her parents sent her to a hostel when she was young? She thought angrily. At least then she would have got used to living away from them.

Time heals... but she was not given the luxury of time for her severed umbilicus to heal. She was expected to integrate into her family-by-law from the very first day. Instantly. Thrown into the deep end of the marital pool, she had to learn to frantically swim towards happiness and not sink in her self-created quicksand of depression. She became a good actress, adept at hiding her feelings and switching her moods... bordering on schizophrenia.

Ravi seemed happy that his plan had worked. Satisfied at this change, he did not want to delve deeper into his wife's psyche. Letting him think that he had succeeded, Divya waited eagerly for times when she was alone at home so that she could sneak a quick phone call to her mother and hear her comforting voice. She had no friends in this foreign town and did not venture out on her own. She had nowhere to go and nothing much to do but wait for Ravi to get back home from work every day.

"Give it time... it'll grow on you," Ravi placated when she cribbed about Kolkata. "Give yourself time."

She waited for something to happen. She was impatient. She was stupidly naïve. She was young.

The Devil's Workshop

The initial, novel rush of romance soon fizzled out like a Diwali cracker and Divya settled down to becoming just another housewife, flipping through recipe books and rustling up exotic meals to impress her husband and his friends. "Cooking Without Tears", "Exotic Eats from the East", "Desserts to Delight Your Man" lined her bookshelf, pushing her collection of Mills & Boons to the back.

Great. Just what I had wanted out of life, she thought ironically. She resigned herself to becoming a typical upper middleclass Indian housewife. Dressing up and going to kitty parties. Getting a pedicure and a facial at a fancy upmarket beauty parlour. What she saw in her marital crystal ball sent involuntary shivers up her spine. Her life revolved around her 'Lord and Master' — Ravi. Obviously he was delighted and lapped up all the attention. His wife had finally been moulded to suit his needs. What more could a man ask for?

But Divya continued to silently miss her family, friends and the cold Delhi winters. She missed her room filled with adolescent dreams and rosy romantic fantasies. She hadn't wanted to grow up so fast. Marriage was considered a shortcut to maturity. She had wanted to take the long road. She began to feel trapped and restless... as if her education was being wasted.

She tried to entertain herself by finding different ways to fill her empty days. Her idle mind became a research centre for stimulating strategies to shake her out of the limbo she had settled into. One fine morning she woke up energetic and excited as a plan grew in her brain. She would give Ravi a surprise, she decided... she would re-arrange their bedroom and give it a new look.

After their daily morning ritual of "Bye darling" a peck on the cheek and a walk with Ravi to the gate, Divya began putting her thoughts into action. It was a lot of physically intensive work but she knew it would be worth it. The room was full of heavy antique teak furniture that must have previously adorned a noble zamindar's house. At the risk of getting a slip disc or a hernia, she shoved and heaved, pulled and dragged them around all by myself. She did not want anybody interfering in her plans. She worked nonstop and, by early evening, was nearly done... as well as done in!

"Ahhhhh!" She groaned as she pushed the last bit of furniture, the heavy armchair, with its maroon and gold brocade upholstery, into its new position by the desk.

Tired after the back-breaking day, she lay down on the newly positioned bed and surveyed the room with pleasure. The four-poster bed had been pushed against the window to catch the early morning rays of the sun; the ornate bookcase now had pride of place next to the door and the roll-top desk fitted perfectly between the bed and the pillar. Excited at what she had accomplished, Divya waited eagerly for Ravi to get back from work. The room looked different. More spacious. Definitely an improvement to what it had been a couple of hours ago. She was satisfied. Maybe she could find a job as an interior decorator, she thought. The slam of the main door followed by firm footsteps burst her occupational bubble.

Lying there, she felt her heartbeat accelerate. She hadn't felt such childish exuberance in a long time.

"Hi!" she said cheerfully, as Ravi entered the room. From her horizontal position on the bed she searched for pleasant surprise and approval in his face, waiting for him to say something like "Wow! This looks amazing!"

"Hi, Divs," he said smiling down at her before the change registered. "Are you okay? Why are you lying down?" Concern. Then silence. Stunned silence. She watched his smile disappear in slow motion.

"What have you done?" he said, looking around in disbelief. By now his lips had disappeared into a thin line. More than surprise there was shock... more than approval, condemnation. "You moved the bed! ... And my desk... And the brass lamp!"

In dismay and horror he named each item of furniture that had been shifted, as if ticking off a checklist in his mind. Her heart sank with every tick.

"Don't you like it?" she asked, suddenly feeling foolish. The dark cloud on his face was the answer.

Ravi did not like it. She learned that the hard way. In fact, he did not like change of any kind in his life.

"Why did you have to rearrange things? I like the room the way it was. It's been like that ever since I can remember," he grumbled, and settled on the cane chair in the veranda with his evening cup of tea.

A furious and upset Divya spent another back-breaking couple of hours shifting all the heavy furniture back to their original places. On her own. So much for attempting to bring some excitement into her life!

A Lesson Not Learnt

A few years later, Divya tried another attempt at giving the flat a new look. This time it was the living room that was the focus of her attention. As she was shifting two book cabinets from the study, Ravi awoke from his Sunday afternoon siesta and came out to investigate the cause of the commotion.

"What do you think you're doing?"

"What does it look like?" she retorted.

No time for niceties after six years of married life. And anyway, with cabinets positioned in different stages of transition and so many books strewn on the carpet, one didn't have to be a member of Mensa to figure out what she was up to.

"Books??!" he exclaimed, staring in horror at his Jean Paul Sartres and Bertrand Russells lying arm in arm with her Barbara Cartlands and Robert Ludlums.

"In the drawing room? In MY house?" He couldn't get over her presumption. "Books look awful in a living room."

"No they don't!" Divya had been raised surrounded by books. "You are so wrong! Books lend character to a room… any room! Even the kitchen."

She was tired, hot and bothered and didn't really need this kind of interruption. Once she started something she just wanted to see it through and get it over and done with. His mouth took on his stubborn 'I-won't-budge' look.

"Well," his voice was laced with steely determination "In MY house there won't be any books in the living room."

That silenced her. You could have heard the soft drip of a leaking tap! Her words of argument froze on her lips. This was a battle she couldn't fight. Without another murmur she shifted everything back to their original place, remembering her earlier futile attempts at rearranging furniture. She could have kicked herself for being such a slow learner. But what really hurt most was the "MY house…" bit. It was like a royal seal of possession warning her not to touch things that weren't hers, not to step over the ever-deepening boundary line.

It is true, she told herself sadly, it wasn't hers. This was his house. The house in Delhi was her father's house. Who was she trying to fool? Wake up and smell the coffee, woman! At the end of the day there was no place she could call her own. The sooner she learnt and accepted that, the happier she'd be. She swallowed bitter tears of reality and self-pity as she put the books back on their shelves.

Of Words and Wit

Despite his rather rigid notions of the place of books in his house, Ravi enjoyed books. He was erudite. A bottomless well of information. His knowledge was eclectic, wide and varied. He believed in 'serious' reading, in every sense of the word. Thrillers and mush (Divya's literary diet) were not for him. When reading Bertrand Russell or Conrad or Sartre, he was always armed with a dictionary and notebook close at hand to jot down interesting quotes and new words and their meanings. As a result, though his vocabulary was astonishing, he took forever to finish a book.

"It's amazing how you read so fast," he said admiring her speed. Divya could read up to three books a week. "How do you do it?"

"I skip the boring parts."

He was horrified when she sheepishly confessed that not only did she skip words but also short paragraphs! Sometimes descriptions could be so longwinded and tedious.

"How can you do something like that? That's sacrilegious."

"Oh, but I get the gist of the story. If I read as slowly as you I'd definitely forget the beginning!" she retorted. "And anyway it's too much of a bother looking up a dictionary. Breaks my flow..." was her offhand reply, shrugging off the niggling feeling of 'maybe I should read properly'. "It's quicker just to ask you the meaning than to look up the dictionary!"

He was shocked into disapproving silence.

Every morning, over cups of tea and Thin Arrowroot biscuits (a hot favourite in Bengal) they'd sit in the verandah and share the newspaper. Ravi would get the Business and Sports pages while Divya grabbed the front few pages. After reading the headlines she would struggle through the quick, easy crossword while he would crack the cryptic one.

"Hey, Ravi, what's a 9-letter word for 'Antique phonographs' beginning with 'V'?" she asked frustrated at not getting a clue.

"Victrolas," he said, without even looking up from what he was reading!

He just had to look at an anagram for a few seconds to know what it stood for. Once Divya was done with her bit of the newspaper, she would pass them on to him. Meticulous as ever, he would put all the pages together in the right order and then read it from the first headline to the last word, remembering the minutest of details. Having a sieve-like mind, Divya marvelled at his incredible memory and was deeply envious. But sometimes his fantastic memory worked against her, especially when they argued. Like an elephant, he remembered all the 'unacceptable' things she'd said and done and forgotten many moons ago, and mentally filed them carefully for future reference. At the opportune moment he would pull each one out from the deep recesses of his mind, air them and file them back again... probably alphabetically or chronologically!

Ravi had an amazing sense of humour and wit too. His innovative puns and spontaneous one-liners were famous amongst their friends.

"So come on, Ravi, tell us your latest joke…" they'd implore at a party that was beginning to limp like a stale lettuce leaf. Then there was no stopping him.

"Have you heard of the karate champion who joined the army and killed himself when he saluted the General?" he asked straight-faced as everyone burst out laughing at the visual imagery. Soon he would have everyone in splits.

"You can't get through life without a good sense of humour," he would say while reading *Laughter is The Best Medicine*. He had all the volumes. Admirably, he didn't lose his sense of humour in spite of all the pain and suffering life dealt him. He clung to it ferociously right till the excruciating end.

Ankylosing Spondylitis Takes Over

Soon after their first wedding anniversary, Ravi fell seriously ill. He developed such a severe pain in his back that it left him stiff and immobile. Any kind of movement was painful but if he didn't move the stiffness increased. It was a vicious cycle that couldn't be broken. Painkillers and anti-inflammatory medicines soon became an essential part of his daily diet.

Before their marriage he had complained of stiffness in his lower back. In fact, on the day of their wedding, he had been unable to sit on the floor for the traditional havan ceremony. So they sat on overstuffed red and gold armchairs that looked like low thrones. Varun and Tara were told that a suitcase had fallen on Ravi's back when he was travelling somewhere and that the old injury was still bothering him. But the truth was that he had Ankylosing Spondylitis, just like his father.

Ankylosing Spondylitis?? When they were kids, Varun had told his children about many unusual ailments that he had come across in his professional life but he hadn't mentioned this one. Divya had never heard of the disease before, but within the first year of her married life, she came to know enough of it to last her a lifetime. She borrowed medical journals from libraries to read about it.

She learnt about calcification, autoimmune diseases and 'bamboo spines'. She tried to understand the implications, the management, the prognosis… everything.

"No there is no cure for it but give it time, it should burn itself out," they were reassured by doctors. "It is a self-limiting disease that mainly attacks young men."

Although equipped with theoretical knowledge about this wretched affliction, and fully aware of the enormity of his problem, the young couple were not prepared for what ensued.

Within a year Ravi's disease had spread like wild fire, calcifying his entire spine into a single unit… a 'bamboo-spine', stiff and rigid. When he turned, there was no segmental rotation. He had to move his entire body, like a stiff plank of wood. Calcium was being deposited on his inflamed hip joints too. Layer upon layer. Limiting his movement. It was a nightmare that shook them completely.

Divya hesitated to tell her parents the intensity of the problem… there was no point! They would just get upset and there was not much they could do anyway. She took it on as one of God's inexplicable tests and attempted to at least pass, if not get a distinction! Little did she know that the test was going to be unbearably long and agonising. And that she would fail miserably...

Progressively Ravi needed the support of a stick to walk. He began to stoop − five feet eleven soon became five-six. His strides became smaller. His spirit lower. He would watch Divya as she did her yoga every morning.

"You are so lucky to be blessed with such a flexible body," he'd say as she kicked her legs up in the air in one swift fluid motion, balancing herself on her head. She could do a headstand and stay ramrod straight in that inverted position for a while.

"It's all thanks to dad," she explained. "As kids, he'd force us to get up early in the morning and exercise for an hour. I used to grumble so much then but now, I guess it's serving me well."

"How I wish I could do some of those exercises," he'd say sadly, fascinated by the way she'd twist her torso, arms and legs in different yogic 'asanas'.

Her exercise regimen, however, was for working days only. On weekends and holidays she'd laze around in bed ignoring Ravi's prodding.

"Come on, Divya. Get up and exercise," he'd coax. "Don't take your health for granted.

"Ooph! It's Sunday, Ravi," she'd mumble drowsily into her pillow. "Have a heart. Let me sleep."

"That's the irony of life… people don't realise what they have till they lose it." Ravi would continue till he realised he was talking to himself when he heard a gentle snore from her side of the bed.

He felt powerless as the disease ravaged his body, slowly but ruthlessly. He could not sit on the low chairs in the house, so the furniture had to be modified. His writing table was raised by a foot and the chair padded up to increase its height. Since he was unable to bend, he was dependent for all the 'below-the-waist' activities Divya took for granted – cutting toenails, wearing socks and shoes, soaping legs and scrubbing feet. He needed her help to get in and out of bed.

More than the pain, what really bothered him was this change in his life. He was losing his freedom to do all those things he could earlier achieve on his own. He hated this dependence on Divya and often she became irritable too. If it was not easy for her, it was hundred times worse for him. When he dropped something by mistake, he would have to call someone to pick it up from the floor for him because he could not bend.

"It would be so nice to live on the moon. Things would float around instead of falling down," he said with dry humour, as he helplessly watched his pen roll down to the floor. Cursing gravity, he tried to make light of his frustration.

In Search of a Cure

Divya held Ravi's hand as he underwent acupuncture. He lay prone and helpless on the examination table. Needles punctured his skin protruding vertically from both sides of his spine.

The 'shopping' for advice and treatment had begun. The search for relief. The hope for a cure. Divya took him to doctors, homeopaths, acupressurists, colour therapists, aroma therapists, magnet therapists, sadhus, miracle men… the works.

She learnt how to help him exercise, just by watching the physiotherapist in action. She'd come back from work and help him with his exercises, believing and hoping that the disease process would slow down if he exercised more often, after all, it was supposed to burn out at some point. Then of course, there was never any shortage of sympathetic people to give unsolicited suggestions and advice.

The 'astrologers' − "Wear a ruby ring on your middle finger. The rays of the sun through the ruby will be beneficial."

The 'feng shui experts' − "Shift your bed so that it faces west. And remember it shouldn't be under a beam." "Oh no! You have your bathroom in the wrong place. Not good at all!"

The 'ayurveda specialists' – "Boil this mushroom in water and drink it every morning before you rinse your mouth." "Mix this powder in hot castor oil and rub it on your joints every night before you sleep."

They tried them all. Each and every one of them... except shifting the bathroom, which was practically not possible.

"You must take him to this 80-year-old sadhu who sits under a peepul tree in a village 50 miles away. He cured my brother-in-law of cancer," said another well-meaning friend.

They rushed to the village to find that they were not the only ones in search of a cure. Hundreds of people of different ages, with different ailments, but unified in hope, waited patiently for the 'darshan'. Unable to stand for too long, Ravi sat in the car while Divya stood in line along with the others. Through the milling heads she managed to get a glimpse of the sadhu sitting on a stone under the tree.

After waiting for hours in the heat in the serpentine queue, their turn finally came. Divya rushed to help Ravi out of the car. Facing the cross-legged, half-naked skinny sage they waited for a miracle to happen. His brownish-grey hair was matted and hung in long dreadlocks down his bare back. His wild beard ended just above his belly button. Through half-shut eyes he watched them approach. After a brief glance in their direction, he called them closer.

"Aao – Come to me," he commanded, gesturing with a quick inward flick of his hand. Divya helped Ravi move forward. His legs were stiff after sitting for so long. Closing his eyes, the sadhu placed his left hand on Ravi's right hip and held his right hand against his forehead in blessing. Divya closed her eyes praying for a miracle... for his prayer to work. After about two minutes of silence the sadhu slowly opened his eyes.

"Have faith in God and you will be cured," he intoned. "Tie this around his left wrist," he dangled a red plaited cord in front of Ravi, "and this around your waist," he told Divya, handing her a longer black one.

"In your last life you were a prince. You had a big harem. Because of your excesses then, you are suffering now. But don't worry. Come and see me after three months. You will be cured. You will run to me. Now go." His extremely mobile wrist flicked outwards. Divya bent down and left some money at his feet before she was gently pushed aside by the impatient person waiting for his turn behind her.

She helped Ravi back into the car. Once he sat sideways she lifted both his feet together in slow motion and held them up while he shifted and twisted in his seat. Ravi, a prince with a harem in his last life? Excesses? Of what use was that bit of information now?! An uneasy feeling of anti-climax filled her mind as they went home. This is not what they had expected. Strings of different colours?! How could that help him? Obediently, if sceptically, she tied red around Ravi's wrist and black around her waist.

One can never tell how these things work, she thought. Not superstitious by nature, she was unhappy to be dragged into all this mumbo-jumbo. But she was willing to give it a shot. After one month of no improvement she hesitantly broached the topic.

"Would you mind very much if I removed this cord from my waist? It is rather uncomfortable. And it hasn't really helped you, has it?"

She need not have worried. Ravi shared her feelings of doubt. After untying their cords, Divya wrapped them up in a muslin cloth and threw the bundle into the Ganga, with a silent prayer for forgiveness.

Friends meant well but they couldn't change the course of destiny. Ravi and Divya were ready to go anywhere, meet anyone and try anything for they were desperate, yet hopeful. Each suggestion, followed through with an anxious persistence, died a quick and sad death as there was no improvement in his condition. Despite their shattered hopes, they would boost each other's sagging spirits and plod on.

"Medical science has advanced so much I am sure they will soon come up with a cure for this wretched disease," Divya would console Ravi. Fighting to keep the flicker of hope alive, they picked themselves up after each blow, persevering… not ready or willing to give up. But the disappointments gradually began taking their toll. They were weary with despair.

A major chunk of Divya's day was spent either in clinics waiting interminably for doctors who did not respect other people's time or in helping Ravi with his physiotherapy and taking care of him. She was young and strong and determined to make a go at winning this round.

It's not easy
living life like this
watching loved ones suffer
helpless
in the ruthless hands of fate.
Emotions oscillating,
swinging uncontrollably
walking the tightrope of life
swaying over stormy waters
nothing to hold on to

no one to turn to
trying to find some meaning
in this madness

Insecurities of Man

Brought up by an alcoholic father and a meek, submissive mother, Ravi's childhood was traumatic. His mother transferred all her love and attention to her younger son and used Ravi as her shield. He grew up feeling the need to protect his mother. He grew up into an intense, man, rigid in his habits and thoughts. He felt insecure and unloved... till he married Divya. He had her to love and be loved. But he still needed constant reassurance and reaffirmation of Divya's love for him. She had to beg and plead with him to allow her to visit her parents – he just didn't want to let her go.

"You just met them in December," he said to her after they got married. It was July. Seven months since she had seen Amar and her parents. He was apprehensive that if she left Kolkata, she would not come back. It was a fear, intense and irrational. After a lot of sulking and cajoling he relented and reluctantly bought Divya's train tickets, permitting her to go for two weeks.

While Divya was away he missed her deeply and phoned every day to tell her so. "I miss your snores at night." "I miss doing the crossword together." "I miss the sound of you pottering around in the room." But she was too busy to feel the separation as strongly as he did. She was having a good time with her parents and going out for lunches and dinners with old friends. For her the two weeks ended too soon but for him each day seemed endless.

When she returned Ravi was impatiently waiting at the platform. As the train came to a halt, he frantically searched for her in the milling crowds at Howrah station – a place where it's difficult to find anyone at the best of times. Avoiding coolies balancing the suitcases piled on their heads, beggars of all ages and passengers in a hurry to get out, he slowly walked the entire length of the train. He looked with anticipation at the passengers getting off each coach door, expecting to see Divya. But she wasn't there. He panicked. His prediction had come true – Divya had decided to stay back in Delhi! She was not going to come back.

Turning back for a second round of the platform, he spotted her standing there guarding her two suitcases. It was hot and humid. Sweat had glued his kurta to his body. He was hot and irritable.

"What took you so long to come out?" he exclaimed agitated at the thoughts that were still swirling around in his mind. His angry voice was tinged with relief. His face was flushed with the heat and the anxiety of his thoughts.

"You couldn't possibly have expected me to leap out as soon as the train entered the station?" she said, visibly upset.

This was not the kind of welcome she had expected after a fortnight's separation and all those "missing you" phone calls. Actually, since she disliked crowds, and detested being pushed and shoved around by coolies and passengers, she'd waited inside the train, disembarking once the crowd had eased. That's why it had taken her so long.

He relented and gave her a sweaty hug. "I am so happy to see you. Thought you weren't coming back."

This extreme insecurity was also reflected in his decision to not have a child. For three years, as Divya's maternal instincts bubbled and boiled inside her, he was adamant about this decision. Every drop of blood of each menstrual cycle was a reminder of her biological clock ticking away furiously, ready to explode like an atom bomb. But he would not budge: no sex without a condom, and that was that. He was apprehensive that her love for him would diminish if they had a child. He did not want to share her love.

"You will have no time for me once a baby comes between us. You'll love me less. And anyway, I strongly believe that this world is not such a great place to bring a new life into. There are too many people weighing the world down already," he rationalised.

Meanwhile, Beeji, his grandmother, a true Punjabi matriarch, began questioning this delay in Divya's conceiving, as a visual sign of her poor fecundity. Her fertility was called into question. Subtle hints were not Beeji's style. She believed in full frontal attacks and that too just below the belt. She was convinced that there must be something definitely wrong with her grand-daughter-in-law's reproductive abilities. Maybe she had defective ovaries. Maybe her tubes were blocked. Her unfortunate, eldest grandson had married a barren woman! All these comments were cleverly made in Ravi's absence. Not once was he subjected to such comments or any kind of third degree as Divya was!

Displacing her anger at this unfair torment, Divya would take it out on Ravi. But her words were like water off a duck's back.

"She means well. Don't take it to heart," he would try to placate her.

Divya was desperate, so she took matters in her own hands and took her plea to a higher realm. She turned to Ma Kali, the mother goddess. She went to the Kali temple, famous for making wishes come true and prayed fervently for a child, instead of praying only for Ravi's health like she used to.

Pregnancy and Thereafter

A month later Divya conceived. No, it wasn't planned…
the condom had burst! Ravi's face fell as did his post-
coital elation.

"Your nail must have torn it!" was his instant reaction.

But her nails were short. The contraceptive was
defective. She didn't feel like arguing. She didn't want to.
She simply kept her excited reactions to herself and
silently blessed the prophylactic manufacturers. She knew
in her heart that this was an act of Divine intervention, for
believe it or not, at the very moment that it happened, the
image of Ma Kali – black face, protruding tongue and all
– flashed in her mind. She hoped that one of the eggs
floating around inside her was at the right place to be
fertilised by one of the sperm that had managed to leak
out of the torn rubber. She sent a quick prayer of thanks to
the goddess for helping with the first step of conception.
The very next morning she started experiencing morning
sickness. How could the symptoms of pregnancy start so
soon? The power of the mind is amazing! Divya was
thrilled but sadly, Ravi did not share her elation.

"Call Dr Bose and ask her about those morning after
pills that they keep advertising on TV," he said.

He wanted her to take some pills to induce an
abortion.

"No! I am not going to. And you can't force me to!"

For the first time in her life Divya stuck to her guns and refused. What she had yearned and prayed for had happened and there was no power on earth that would make her change that. Ravi raved and ranted, tried logic and emotional blackmail, but she refused to give in. Her mind was made up. Thankfully, once he realised this, he gradually stepped off his high, emotionally insecure horse and got involved in the joys of her pregnant state. Placing his hand on her blossoming abdomen, he'd wait patiently to feel the baby kick.

"I just felt it right here! Below my hand!"

"Must've just been gas." Feeling bloated and flatulent seemed to have become her permanent state of being.

Ravi accompanied Divya for her ultrasound tests and watched in fascination as the doctor pointed to the pulsating shadow on the screen, and said, "Can you see that? That's your baby's heart beating away."

Soon Ravi took on his new role of 'father-to-be' very seriously and began pampering Divya indulgently. He would ring up from work many times during the day to see how she was feeling.

"Did you do your breathing exercises after breakfast?"

"I hope you are not feeling nauseous anymore."

"Did you have your vitamins?"

He even went along with her for her evening walks. He was the epitome of love and concern.

Apart from Divya, the happiest person in the household was Beeji. She was so excited about the fact that soon she would be a great grandmother. Divya's pregnant state was proudly announced to all and sundry, as if it added glory to the family name. Thank God her fears of her so-called "barrenness" were unfounded. Divya was now considered worthy of Beeji's attention once again. She made a jar full of a sickly sweet mixture of semolina, dry fruit, lotus seeds, sugar and ghee for her, as a reward for the good news.

"Eat two tablespoons of this every morning on an empty stomach and mark my words you will have an easy delivery. The baby will just slip out," she said.

"Drink milk and eat lots of coconut," she advised, "then the baby will be fair... not dark like you."

Divya was too happy to be irritated by what Ravi called Beeji's 'well-meaning' comments.

With each passing month, much to Dr Bose's dismay, Divya gained weight rapidly.

"All this 'eating for two' is nonsense! If you carry on like this, you'll find it very difficult to lose all this weight after your delivery," she admonished. "You better start going for walks every evening."

Not wanting to look like a sumo wrestler for the rest of her life, Divya started her evening walks on the roof.

But her hunger had an identity of its own... something she had no control over. Much to Ravi's amusement, she developed strange cravings to eat unusual combinations of food. In the middle of the night she would struggle out of bed and quietly shuffle into the dining room to eat chopped tomatoes and choco-chip cookies! During the hot summer months she gorged on mangoes for breakfast, mangoes for lunch and yet again, mangoes for dinner. She simply could not get her fill of them. Sadly, the mango season soon came to an end and with it her gastronomical desires took a turn for mint and cheese sandwiches. She consumed vast quantities of mint chutney till even her dreams had a green tint to them. Her burps became nice and minty. She loved it! Nine months seemed too long a time to indulge in such crazy diets. When she stood up she was a baby elephant and when she lay down, a beached whale.

Getting out of bed was a Herculean task and took forever. A crane would have been hugely helpful during that time. Soon Divya's belly ballooned so she couldn't even see her toes! She felt ungainly and awkward and just moving was a tremendous effort. But nothing could cloud her joy. This baby was God's gift to her and she cherished it with every part of her expanding being.

Her clothes seemed to have shrunk considerably. She gave up after unsuccessful attempts at trying to button up her dress by sucking in her breath, pulling and stretching the cloth at the same time. She would walk around with buttons undone. Longingly, she looked at her jeans and salwar-kameezes and then pushed them to the back of the cupboard, not knowing whether she'd ever be able to fit into them again. It was obviously time to get a new wardrobe... an XXXL one!

"I am now living in kaftans," Divya told her friend Gita one day. "At least they come in a free size."

"Hey, don't worry, Divya, I'll take you shopping," Gita said when she heard her plight. She had three children and was well versed with the travails of pregnancy.

"I know just the right shop for you... and they have pretty reasonable stuff too!"

Promptly at ten the next morning, her car honked at Divya's door.

"Coming!" she yelled from the verandah window as she slipped on her flat shoes. She had temporarily given up wearing her pencil heels because of her fluctuating centre of gravity. Now she was short and round. Breathless from her laboured journey down the stairs,

Divya held her huge abdomen and struggled into Gita's low car.

"I need a mini truck to cart me around," she said and Gita laughed with an understanding nod.

"Yup! You are huge. Are you sure you don't have twins in there?" She looked pointedly at Divya's stomach propped against the dashboard. "Or triplets maybe?"

Divya opened and closed her mouth a couple of times like a goldfish.

"Please, Gita! Have a heart!" she cried, as visions of trying to hold three babies in her arms flashed through her mind.

"Okay, okay, Divs! I was only joking. Come on relax. Take a deep breath. Please don't have your baby in my car!"

They were cracking jokes and laughing hysterically by the time they reached the shop. Divya was exhausted when she got back home. She had struggled in and out of at least ten different outfits before settling for three dresses that were huge and tent-like but at least she could breathe in them!

******

Once the morning sickness phase was over, Divya began enjoying the role of an expectant mother. She busied herself knitting, crocheting and stitching an entire wardrobe for her baby. Dresses, nappies, sweaters and booties soon filled the shelves, displacing sarees, blouses and petticoats. Preparing for her unborn child became her passionate obsession. Her baby was going to be the best-dressed baby in the city of Kolkata. She wanted to finish so much before her delivery. It was as if she was racing against time.

"Have you seen those new vests of mine?" Ravi asked one morning, getting ready for work. "The ones your mum gave me."

Uh oh! Divya looked at him guiltily.

"I had a fantastic brainwave this morning, Ravi," she said sounding really defensive. "Since your vests are new and so soft I cut them up and made little inners for baby. See!" She held up the cutest, tiniest vests with lacy crocheted edges. Luckily he laughed at her eccentricities and she heaved a heavy sigh of relief.

"I'm sorry, I should have asked you first but when I got the idea you were at work and I was too impatient to wait for you to get back," she apologised.

"That's okay," he said forgiving her impulsiveness. "But they look too small... are you sure they'll fit?"

"Of course," Divya said confidently.

But she was wrong. They were a couple of sizes too small and were finally used as clothes for a doll!

The only dark cloud in Divya's sunny skies was something very disturbing that Dr Bose had told them.

"As you know, Ankylosing Spondylitis is more common in males. And it is usually congenital," she informed the parents-to-be. "Just as Ravi got it from his father, chances are that if you have a son, he might have the same disease too."

Then began her inner turmoil. Till that moment Divya had never given much importance to the gender of her child. She had just wanted a normal, healthy baby. But now things had changed. She spent all her waking hours praying for a daughter.

The Birth of Tanya

With clockwork precision, Divya's labour pains started on the very day Dr Bose had predicted. It was as if the baby was aware of her obsession for punctuality.

"This is it," she gasped, as the belt of pain tightened around her abdomen. "Call Dr Bose."

"Bring her to the hospital once her pains are ten minutes apart," Dr Bose calmly told a very worried Ravi.

So in his meticulous way, Ravi sat next to Divya's bed for the next four hours, holding his watch and timing her contractions.

"Now," she said her face distorted in pain.

"Okay your last one was twelve minutes ago. We'll wait awhile," Ravi said as fastidious as ever. "She said ten minutes."

"No!" she screamed panic-stricken at the possibility of delivering the baby at home. "I don't care what she said. Take me now!"

They woke up Tara, who had come to Kolkata for her daughter's delivery, and rushed to the hospital in the middle of the night. While Ravi attended to the admission formalities, Divya was taken on a wheelchair to the Labour Room. Struggling out of her clothes, she wore the white hospital gown that the nurse thrust into her hands before rushing off to attend to another expectant mother. It was a busy night in the maternity ward.

Alone in the sterile pre-delivery room Divya lay on a gurney, dreading her next painful contraction. The intensity and frequency of the contractions were increasing slowly but surely. Stiffening in preparation for the onslaught, she bit her lower lip between clenched teeth and gripped the sides of the gurney, as razors of pain ripped through her insides. The nurse in charge would enter now and then to check her baby's heartbeat and the extent of her dilation. She had a strange funnel-shaped instrument that she held against her ear and pressed hard against Divya's abdomen.

Such an out-dated method of hearing the heartbeat, she thought, in all her pain and worry. *I hope she knows what she's doing.*

Suddenly there was a flurry of activity as she rushed from Divya's side to the phone on her desk. She spoke loudly and urgently into the telephone, "Dr Bose, please come immediately, I can't hear the baby's heartbeat! I think it's a case of foetal distress."

The umbilical cord had wrapped itself around the baby's neck, threatening to strangle it.

"Don't let them operate on you," Beeji's parting words rang in Divya's head. "Nowadays doctors are knife happy and just need an excuse to cut you up. They don't want to wait for a normal delivery."

She wept. *Please don't let anything happen to my baby,* she prayed fervently. Tara and Ravi were sitting in the waiting room, oblivious of her state. She refused the nurse's offer to call them for she did not want them to see her in such a condition. Divya always had this inexplicable need to be on her own when very upset. Dr Bose rushed in ten long minutes later, reassured her that everything would be okay, and prepared her for surgery.

"Don't worry, everything is under control. Now calm down. You'll soon have a bonny baby in your arms." In the early hours of the morn, her daughter was born by caesarean section. Ravi, who was waiting outside the OT door, heard her first shrill cries of protest as the doctor spanked her little bottom.

Once again God had answered Divya's prayers. She had given birth to a scrawny, wrinkled, bald, baby girl. She was beautiful. She was hers. She was Tanya.

Holding her for the first time was a humbling experience. Apart from a blue eyelid, due to the pressure of the umbilical cord, she was healthy. This little creature was her very own miracle. She had done it… with a little help from God, the condom manufacturers and of course, Ravi! She felt so protective and overwhelmed by a maternal emotion that is indescribable and indefinable, yet universal, so they say… a love that is stronger and more powerful than life itself. She knew at that very moment that Ravi was right. She would love her child more than him… she would love Tanya more than her own life! Luckily, Ravi's attitude changed too.

"I never ever imagined that I could love another person as much as I love my little princess," he confessed a few months later, surprised at this new and unfamiliar emotion he was experiencing.

******

They say that breast feeding is supposed to be one of the most sensual experiences in a woman's life. They also say it's a pity men can never know the deep satisfaction and feeling of completeness that accompanies this maternal act. Well, 'they' are wrong! Breast feeding was the bane of Divya's newly maternal life. Unfortunately for her, not only did she have cracked, painful nipples but had developed an extension of her breast glands ("wings") under her arms. All the milk accumulated there in painful sacks. So initially, breast feeding Tanya was something she did not look forward to. The nurse, who must have earlier worked in a concentration camp, would stride into the room every morning with a steel bowl of boiling hot water, small previously-white-now-grey towels and a steely look of determination. She would then, with enviable single-mindedness, proceed to clamp boiling hot towels in Divya's armpits and on her tender breasts and twist them hard.

"Just to facilitate proper flow of milk," she would mumble while Divya screamed in agony! Nurse Hitler even used a suction machine to pump milk from her breasts. She felt like a bloody cow! This, together with her post-surgery pains ensured a quick fading away of her maternal instincts.

One morning, when the nurse coldly said, "You are crying now but just you wait and see, after nine months you'll be back here pregnant again, saying you want a son!" Divya felt like shoving the suction pump up an unmentionable part of her anatomy. *She was definitely in the wrong profession. She should have been an executioner,* Divya thought savagely.

"Baby's hungry," she sang as she entered her room with a glint in her eyes and a little bundle in her arms.

"But I've just fed her, how can she have digested that so soon?" Divya moaned as Tanya was thrust unceremoniously into her arms. She didn't want to go through that entire milking process again. But the minute she held her baby close to her heart, the world transformed into a gentler, more beautiful place. Suddenly the 'executioner' had a halo on her head instead of the white cap and her sadistic smile seemed angelic.

Tanya would open her eyes staring at her mother quizzically, probably wondering what the drama was all about. Divya would gently stroke her blue eyelid lovingly, thanking God for saving her. Then Tanya would smile lopsidedly (or was it gas?) and Divya was her slave for life! How she loved holding her perfect little hands and kissing the soft soles of her tiny feet, deeply breathing in her baby scent. Maternal bliss. All that pain and discomfort was forgotten as Divya held her world... her universe was in her arms.

Someday
when you grow up
I will tell you of the joy of love...
Of the ripples of longing
that seep through your being
washing away your senses
Of speaking volumes without words
in the comfort of silence
wishing time would crystallise
forever.
Someday
when you grow up
I will tell you of the pain of love...
Of the tremendous loneliness
when you are apart
Of the heartrending pain
as you walk away
knowing that a part of you
is left behind
knowing that you will never

be the same
again.
Someday
When you grow up…

******

Divya dreaded Dr Bose's visits too. She would bustle in with her band of medical interns following her at a respectful distance just like in 'ER' the medical TV serial she loved watching. After the usual "How are we this morning, Divya?" followed by a brusque "Let's take a look," she'd whip her sheet aside to proudly display her caesarean scar to the oohing and aahing students!

"Isn't it a beauty? So neat and smooth, you can barely see it. A bikini cut," she boasted, proud of her skill with the knife.

As the students pushed each other to get a better look at the caesarean scar on Divya's abdomen, Dr Bose would go into the details of her case. Embarrassed and blushing at the fact that so many people were seeing her in this state of undress, Divya would either close her eyes to shut them out or develop an intense interest in the designs on the ceiling, wishing the fan would fall and create a diversion, a distraction. By the end of her stay in the hospital, she had become quite shameless. She could bare her bosom and abdomen on request without batting an eyelid. And she had Dr Bose to thank for that!

Fathers were given special visiting time in the mornings. On the dot of eight, Ravi would step into the room a big smile on his excited handsome face.

"I just saw Tanya from the nursery window. Her face looks so pink and wrinkled. She actually looked at me when I tapped on the glass and smiled!"

"Obviously she'll smile. She's got a full stomach. I've just spent the last painful hour feeding her," Divya would say wearily. He gave her a hug and launched off into a detailed description of the cot he had got for Tanya and by the time he left she was smiling once again.

"Remember to bring the dress you wore as a baby," she told him, sentimental as ever, "I want Tanya to wear that when we go back home tomorrow."

So Tanya left the hospital wearing her father's thirty-year-old, threadbare baby smock, smelling of mothballs.

Bringing up Baby

Tara stayed on in Kolkata for about a month to nurse Divya back to health. She helped, as only a mother can. She first lovingly bathed Tanya in her little tub after massaging her with mustard oil. Then it was Divya's turn. She poured water on her carefully, ensuring that her caesarean site remained dry. She even slept with Divya, so that she could get up in the middle of the night when Tanya cried hungrily for a feed. She seemed to recognise Tanya's every grunt and gurgle and put meaning to each sound.

"Tanya's hungry," she'd say gently lowering a wailing Tanya into Divya's arms, or, "she wants to pee," as Tanya scrunched up her face and made a funny mewling sound.

Tara was the one who took on the challenge of toilet training Tanya at such an early age. The minute she noticed a change in her body language or facial expression, she'd quickly take Tanya, to the toilet and hold her small body over the sink. There she'd stand patiently making a sound like a pressure cooker's whistle, "sh, sh, sh," and return only once her mission was accomplished.

Divya dreaded the day her ma would leave and go back to Delhi. How on earth would she manage on her own? But that day soon dawned. Once she left, Divya had to shift to another room because Ravi complained that his sleep was disturbed when Tanya cried at night. What about her sleep? And her need to be with him? Sometimes she would wash soiled nappies, weeping at night, feeling so alone and depressed – delayed postpartum blues at its peak! She missed her stoic and silent mother.

Ma…
I think of you most
on days like these
when I'm feeling really low…
Of your silent strength
and gentle smile
…the way you helped me grow.
To you I turn
with my troubled mind
when my days are dark and grey,
your caring touch
and loving words
just sooth the pain away.
When I had to leave you one day,
you just stood back
and let me go,
silent tears
streaming down your face,
it was hard for you, I know.
From you I learnt
of love and life
of giving and forgiving
and this sees me through

my darkest hours
when life seems not worth living.
At times like these
I long to run
to the shelter of your heart
For I know
you'll be there for me –
miles cannot keep us apart.

"Enjoy each and every moment of her growing up – the tantrums and all," Dr Bose advised when Divya cribbed about something inconsequential regarding Tanya. "Before you know it she will be out of diapers and into discos! Then you'll long for these diaper days again."

What she said put Divya on track again. It made so much sense. She began to enjoy each precious stage of Tanya's infancy. Looking at life through her eyes made the world seem such an exciting place all over again. Her eyes would grow big with wonder at the sight and sound of a dog barking or a monkey chattering and swinging from a tree. She loved birds and could stare out of the window for hours, clapping her tiny hands at sparrows and crows, chortling with delight as they flew away. Divya began to do the very same 'juvenile' things that she had tolerated disdainfully in other new mothers.

"Bowbow, bowbow!" she shouted excitedly, rushing into the room where Tanya was playing on the floor with an ugly stuffed monkey eating a plastic banana. It was her favourite toy. Picking her up, monkey and all, Divya took her to the window so that she could see a dog barking at a cow. She was in a constant state of alertness, watching out for unusual sights and sounds – anything that would thrill Tanya and make her laugh, for her laughter headed

Divya's 'Top of the Pops' chart. It was so musical and tinkly.

And as Tanya grew older Divya's obsession increased.

"Tanya can sing 'Twinkle Twinkle little star' with all the actions," she'd excitedly tell her friends.

"Come on, Tanya, sing for us," and Divya would push Tanya gently into the centre of the drawing room. Obediently and a bit shyly she'd give a childish rendition of the rhyme, gesturing with her small hands, while her mother sat back silently mouthing the words, bursting with pride. To give them credit, Divya's friends tried to look equally animated and even clapped obligingly after her 'performance'. It was exhilarating.

Getting a Job

When Tanya was just six months old Divya found a job. That was one of the many turning points in her life. It happened one morning when she was playing with Tanya in the veranda while Ravi read the newspaper. She heard him clearing his throat noisily.

He's about to say something serious, she thought, knowing his habits by now, and sure enough...

"There's an opening for a job that is just up your street, Divya. They need a counsellor," he said reading out the advertisement from the 'Vacancies' column. She didn't show much interest – she was far more interested in playing 'this little piggy...' with Tanya and watching her chortle.

"I really think you should apply and see what happens," he persisted.

She applied and got an interview call.

"Go for the interview just for the heck of it," he advised. "If you get the job then you can decide whether you want to take it or not."

So nervously, Divya went for the first ever job interview of her life.

"I knew you'd get it!" he exclaimed happily when she proudly waved the offer letter in his face a week later.

Excited at the prospect of her first job, she confirmed her acceptance immediately. The extra income would be welcome. The drain on their finances due to Ravi's treatment was enormous. Thankfully, Ravi was careful with his money and had invested well. She was not much of a spender either. Her needs were few and limited. She stopped buying books, but being an avid reader kept her hobby alive by becoming a member of the local library. She rarely wore the jewellery with which she had been festooned when she got married, preferring to keep it all safely locked up in the bank. Buying clothes was something she seldom indulged in and they hardly ever ate out. She needed money mainly to take care of her basic day-to-day needs but disliked asking Ravi, or for that matter anyone, for money. Though he never refused if she ever asked him, she was reluctant to do so... her ego always got in the way. With this job, she would not only have her own money to spend as and when she wished, she would also be able to contribute in her own small way, to the household expenses.

Surprisingly, though Ravi was the one who had persuaded Divya to work, he was apprehensive at the same time. First it was Tanya who had taken up most of her attention and now, with the job, she would hardly have any time for him. And then, the prospect of her earning and becoming financially independent was daunting. His Indian male pride of being the breadwinner of the family was being threatened.

"Don't let the money go to your head," he warned her, "it's only a pittance anyway!"

Yes, he was right, it was only a pittance. But so what if it was a mere Rs.800/-? It was her very own hard-earned money. She loved this newfound freedom, this feeling of being a working woman. She got to meet more and more people, made many friends and thoroughly enjoyed her work as a counsellor. Listening to everyone else's problems, made Divya put hers on 'hold'.

Her confidence and self-esteem grew in direct proportion with her promotions. Her savings grew too and soon she didn't have to ask Ravi whether she could go to visit her parents in Delhi, she just booked her tickets and informed him. She realised that it was true − earning her own money gave her autonomy, a feeling of being in control of her life... and, in a way, did go to her head!

******

Divya's job kept her on her toes all day. It was demanding and hectic but it was her lifeline. She loved it with a passion. She had just finished writing the report of the last counselling session. The clinic was empty. Everyone left at the dot of five. Divya sat back enjoying the silence after the buzz of activity during the day. Tanya smiled at her from her soft board, a bright toothy smile. Ready to call it a day and hurry home to her, Divya stretched her tired shoulders and pushed her chair back when the phone rang. Irritated at the thought of being held back she picked up the receiver.

"*I just called to say I love you...*" Stevie Wonder sang in her ear! A crank call she thought banging the phone down. As she began arranging the files according to the next day's appointments the phone rang again. Once again Stevie Wonder's dreamy voice crooned through the earpiece. The person was a real pain... whoever he was, she thought.

"Hey! Don't hang up... it's me," she heard Ravi take over from Stevie as she was about to break the connection.

"Ravi?!"

"Yup. I'm sorry for what I said this morning... I didn't mean it."

This morning's argument was over the guest list for Tanya's birthday party. Her first birthday was still a month away but with the eagerness of new parents, they were planning a huge bash (if Ravi had his way) or a small get together (if Divya had hers).

"She won't even understand what's going on and will just be cranky and clingy with so many people around," Divya had argued.

"Fine," he shouted. "Let's just cancel the plan." And he threw his list of fifty names into the bin. She had stormed out of the house, frothing at the mouth.

"Let's go out for dinner, shall we? Chinese," he continued, not sure whether he had been forgiven or not.

"Okay, sweetheart. I'm on my way home."

She couldn't stay angry with him for too long. Definitely not when he behaved like this... caring, loving, and wanting to make up. Hurriedly Divya grabbed her bag and rushed out of the building, thinking of a revised guest list. Walking as fast as her short legs could carry her, she played her daily game of making it to the bus stop in time. Dodging dogs and cows, avoiding potholes and people, it was like a video game. It was always a race against time. But she always made it just as the chartered bus trundled down Park Street.

Sounding like a steam train, she clambered on to the bus and sank into her seat next to the window, gasping for breath. The roads were chock-a-block with people, cars, scooters, buses... office rush at its peak. Her mouth watered in anticipation of the promised Chinese meal, as her thoughts shifted to dinner. Yes, she was hungry. Divya loved this forty-five-minute journey back home. A journey filled with the anticipation and eagerness of being with Tanya again. The two hours they spent together before her bedtime was something both of them looked forward to.

Joys of Motherhood

Getting Tanya to sleep was a Herculean task. Her energy levels seemed to increase as the sun went down. Tired, after a day's work Divya would lie by her side, patting her head gently hoping her humming would lull Tanya to sleep. Ready to drop off herself, she would peer at her baby's face only to see her twinkling eyes staring at her, shining in the dark! She was wide-awake. Often it was Divya who fell asleep while Tanya lay beside her content to play with the satin belt of her emerald green dressing gown, while she gently snored.

"Mummy! Lulla I want lulla," she'd lisp, demanding a lullaby, waking Divya up mid-snore with a jolt. She became an expert at singing "Golden slumbers kiss your eyes" in her sleep.

Tanya resisted sleep for as long as she could, straining desperately to keep her eyes open. It was as if she felt she would be missing out on something exciting if she succumbed to the arms of slumber. When asleep, she looked angelic and innocent, so delicate and fragile that Divya could just stare at her for hours, suppressing a strong urge to pick her up, waken her and hold her close again!

Weaning Tanya was another major battle. A battle of the bottle!

"BOTTLE! I want my bottle!" she'd wail as Divya held her tight and tried desperately to hold a glass of milk against her mouth.

"See that crow?" she'd ask, pointing at the window, "it's taken your bottle away. Crow! Crow! Come back! Bring back Tanya's bottle!" she'd shout shrilly in maternal desperation.

Trying to distract her, Divya managed to pour in a small mouthful of milk as she calmed down for a moment and looked out of the window for a crow with her bottle in its beak.

"My bottle!" Not finding any crow, Tanya screamed flailing her legs and arms, knocking the milk all over her mother.

"Now see what you've done! Naughty girl!"

It was also a battle of egos, neither side ready to give in. She'd cajole and plead, rave and rant but to no avail. Strangely, Tanya would drink water from a glass but for milk she needed her bottle.

Finally, Divya calmed down and gave in when her doctor asked her, "Why are you getting so upset? She'll soon grow out of it. Have you ever seen a teenager drinking milk from a bottle?" She smiled at the doctor's words and at her unnecessary pig-headedness. Her common sense worked wonders and Divya settled down with renewed determination to enjoy the joys of motherhood. Much to Tanya's relief (and unspoken surprise), the crow returned her milk bottle!

Tanya Goes To School

When Tanya was just two years old Divya decided she needed to go to a playschool.

"She should be with kids her age doing mischievous things, running around and playing, not watching soppy Hindi soaps on TV with Ma ji," Divya argued as she put her case forward to Ravi. "Surrounded by adults all day, she's losing out on her childhood and is growing up too soon. And anyway it's just for two hours."

Luckily Ravi gave in, mainly to keep the peace of the house! Tanya was thrilled with her new schoolbag and tiffin box. She paraded up and down in her brand new uniform.

"I am going to thoool," she proudly told everyone as she waved them goodbye, not knowing what was in store for her. Ravi and Ma ji stood at the door to see her off as Divya held her tiny hand and led her away. Turning back, Divya saw Ma ji dabbing her eyes with the edge of her pallav.

Such needless drama, she thought insensitively. *She's only going to school*. Little did she realise that she would soon be taking on the role of 'Melodrama Queen' playing her part to perfection. Unfortunately, Tanya's first day at school was distressing for her as well as for her mother!

Hand in hand they walked through the heavy iron gates of the school, down the shaded path to the playground. Newly admitted children stood with their parents in small clusters waiting expectantly for the teacher to tell them where to go.

"Tanya?" Divya saw the lady she had met two days ago when she came to pay the fees, walking in their direction. She recognised Tanya from the photo on the admission form she held in her hand. Tanya looked at her shyly and nodded with a smile.

"Come," she said, holding Tanya's free hand and the three of them walked towards the school building. "I'll take you to your class," she continued, addressing Tanya, ignoring Divya's presence. "You're going to have a lot of fun."

She left them at the entrance of the classroom, rushing back to escort other children. Mickey Mouse and Daffy Duck shared the walls of the room with Wendy the witch and Casper the ghost. Tanya looked around in wonder as they stood at the door but did not let go of her mother's hand.

"Please, ma'am, just leave her here and walk away. Do not look back," the nursery teacher told her sternly as they were about to step into the classroom. "And don't worry, she'll be okay."

Her kind appearance seemed to be in contradiction with her tone and her expectations. How could she ever imagine that Divya, a mother, could do something like that? The teacher grabbed Tanya's free hand in an attempt to draw her in. Tanya suddenly tightened her grip on Divya's hand sensing something unpleasant was about to happen. Having been brought up to blindly and unquestioningly obey teachers, Divya wrenched her hand away from Tanya's tiny clinging hand.

"I will come back soon, darling," she whispered in her ear, quickly hugging her. Then she walked away before Tanya could react. It took all she had, to resist the urge to turn around and run back.

"Mummy! Mummy, don't go! I want my mummy!" Tanya's cries rang in her ears.

A few steps away Divya hid behind a tree and peered back. The sight of her precious one standing there looking for her, big drops of tears pouring from her eyes was unbearable. She wept. Her little ray of sunshine was unhappy and she was the cause of her misery. She was the one who had insisted that she join this school. Ravi was right, it was a bad decision. She was a bad mother. Heartless and horrible. She was certain that Tanya was wondering why her mother had just left her like that among strangers and walked away. She must be thinking that she'd never see her mother again. With every thought, Divya cried some more not caring that she was in a public place and that she must have looked weird hiding behind a tree like that.

To hell with it! I won't send Tanya to school, I'll teach her myself, she thought irrationally, deciding to rush back and grab Tanya in her arms and take her home. As soon as she stepped out from her hiding place, the teacher shut the classroom door. She must have read her mind. On that first day of Tanya's school Divya stood there weeping behind the tree for two hours, waiting for the bell to ring so that she could hold her princess in her arms again. Yes, she could definitely have become the uncontested winner of the 'Ms. Melodrama Contest'!

******

If getting Tanya to sleep when she was a toddler was tough, waking her up when she started going to school was another 'bed' game altogether! And particularly more excruciating on cold winter mornings. "Trring, trring!" the shrill persistent alarm cut cruelly through each layer of sleep, pulling Divya heartlessly out of her dream. It was 5:30 am.

"How could that be possible?" she thought. She had just fallen asleep. Covering her head with a pillow, she snuggled deeper into her duvet. It was very cold and dark outside her quilted world. She had no desire to leave the snug warmth of her night space.

Let Tanya miss school today. One day won't matter, she thought sleepily sliding back into the first layer of sleep. But where the alarm clock failed, Ravi took over.

"Wake up, Divya, Tanya'll miss her bus if you don't get out of bed." His hand emerged briefly from under the folds of his quilt to shake her out of her comfortable stupor. As she straightened out of her foetal position, her feet pushed the hot-water-bottle-now-turned-cold, and it fell to the floor with a thump. Bleary-eyed, she struggled out of bed, shivering as her feet landed on the cold marble floor. Muttering under her breath, she stumbled to the bathroom to wash the sleep out of her eyes. Cold water did the trick instantly. Wide-awake, she was now on 'autopilot'.

"Tanya, wake up, babe," Divya shouted, struggling into her socks and woollen housecoat. She stared longingly at her bed, temptation battling with duty, as Ravi turned over with a grunt and went back to sleep.

"Tanya! Tanya!" her voice preceded her as she entered Tanya's room. Two little fingers, forming a V, shot out from somewhere under the quilt heap on the bed. Tanya rotated in her sleep, usually ending up at the other

179

end of the bed in the morning! Once she had even fallen off the bed as a result of her nocturnal travels. The two fingers silently held up meant, "two minutes more please". Invariably obeying her wordless plea, Divya would succumb to the temptation of her warm bed. Sliding under her quilt she would hold her small body close to hers, generating a loud string of protests as her cold hands found warm skin. She loved these moments of complete togetherness, even though they were only for two minutes.

"Okay, two minutes are up, babes," Divya would mumble much against her wishes, as Tanya stretched and yawned.

"Please, Mum, just hold me for one more minute. I promise I'll get up then," she'd plead sleepily. "I still have some sleep left in my eyes!" she'd explain.

Or sometimes… "I'm trying to open my eyes, Mum, but I can't. They're stuck!"

And they'd cuddle some more, both of them wishing that the clock would stop ticking.

"Okay, hon, you better get up now or you'll miss your bus," Divya said untangling their reluctant limbs, forcing herself to get out of yet another warm bed.

Then began the preparation for 'Her Royal Highness Princess Tanya' to get out of bed. Still snug under her quilt, she'd stick one tiny foot out for a sock to be put on. After much cajoling, the other foot would come out. Once the socks were on it was time for her cardigan. One arm at a time. She kept her eyes tightly shut through all this, clinging to the last dregs of sleep. She did everything in slow motion on those mornings when it was always a race against time. It was a wonder she never missed her bus!

"Time's up, darling," and with one sweep of her hand Divya would pull the quilt off her, as she shrieked in annoyance! This was their school day 'getting-out-of-bed' ritual... and they loved it.

"Come on, darling, hurry up," Divya'd say rushing kitchen-wards. "Stop dilly-dallying. Your bus will be here any minute." Now that she had managed to wake Tanya up, she had to make her breakfast and prepare a snack for her tiffin to take to school.

"Do you want toast or cornflakes for breakfast?"

"Toast," she'd mumble sleepily.

"*Toast*?! Then why did you make me buy cornflakes yesterday?"

And sometimes her question would vary a bit...

"Do you want cornflakes or porridge for breakfast?" Silence. Then..."Cornflakes" came Tanya's wary reply.

"But I've made porridge for you. Now you better eat it!"

Tanya soon realised that the questions were trick questions. They were actually meaningless, for no matter what she opted for, the choice was finally her mother's! Surprisingly, she always fell for it. This was just another one of their inane early morning banters.

******

On weekends and school holidays, however, it was a different story altogether. More like a 'getting-into-bed' ritual. Without fail, Tanya would wake up early all by herself and clamber into her parents' bed. Settled comfortably between her father and mother she'd whisper noisily first in Divya's ear, "Morning, Mummy," then in Ravi's, "Morning, Papa," jolting them out of deep sleep.

"Come and sleep, darling. Sleep with Mummy, Tanya, honey," Divya would mumble. Refusing to open her eyes she'd hold her close hoping she'd let her sleep for a while.

"Mummy! Papa! Wake up! No school! Let's plan what we'll do today," Tanya's cheerful voice chirped, excited that she didn't have to go to school, covering their faces with slobbery kisses till they were forced to open their eyes. *Why couldn't she be like this on school days?* Divya wondered, perplexed at her early morning energy levels.

"Papa's got a wonderful plan for today, babes," she said throwing the ball of parenthood into Ravi's quilt. "Don't you, Ravi?"

"What's it, Papa?" Tanya turned her excited attention to a heavy-lidded Ravi.

Let Ravi handle the holiday mornings, Divya thought as she sank back into the precious embrace of sleep.

The downside of working was that she hardly got to spend time with Tanya… she was missing out on a major chunk of her childhood. So, when Tanya was five years old Divya chucked up her job for one that gave her more time to be a mother.

Tanya Learns

Soon Tanya made lots of friends and began to look forward to going to school. Proudly Divya would hug and kiss her as she learnt new words and poems and discovered more about the world around her. Full of stories – some made up, some real – she would wait impatiently for her mother to come back from work so that she could regale her with her tales. As she tripped over her words in her enthusiasm, Divya would stare lovingly at her animated face, listening in wonder as she let her imagination take over. She could put Enid Blyton to shame with the stories she wove. Her teachers loved her too. She would come back from nursery school with bright red lipstick kisses on her cheeks and smiley stickers on the pages of her diary.

Then she learnt how to write and Divya's joy knew no bounds. Hungrily she read her daughter's scripts and encouraged her to write more. Invariably, she'd come back from work to find a little note for her stuck with Sellotape on the main door. She still had each and every note Tanya scribbled to her.

"mummy I am going bicos you shoutd at me" (Divya had scolded her that morning because she was still toying with her breakfast while the school bus honked downstairs.)

"dear mummy I love you. my name is Tanya" (just in case she thought someone else had written the note!)

"My dear mummy I have been good today please take me for ice-cream love Tanya"

"Good news − I got all correct in maths. Bad news − In Hindi ma'am wrote does not pay attention in class" (She was refreshingly honest.)

"I am very sorry mummy. Please I beg you not to get angry. I promise I did not even know how my pencil box broke…"

She loved to write and rapidly discovered the joys of writing. She learnt to express her emotions through the written word and filled up the pages of her diaries with daily anecdotes, feelings and dreams. Her very first 'essay' in school brought tears to Divya's eyes. It reflected the compassionate, sensitive side of her. She drew a picture of a man with a stick and wrote, "I feel sad because my papa has a leg problem and he walks with a stick."

Ravi's illness hurt Tanya to the core. She had converted a corner of her room into a mini temple. Pictures of gods and goddesses of different religions found their way there. Jesus Christ, Shiv ji, Lord Krishna, Buddha, Sai Baba stood shoulder to shoulder with each other, innocently and silently conveying the 'God is one' message. She would spend long hours in the prayer corner of her room, praying to all of them to cure her papa. Her little heart could not bear the thought that of all the people in the world, her precious papa had to suffer so much.

"Why can't Papa play 'catch-catch' like Rima's papa?"

"Why doesn't Papa take me to see the circus? Deepak's father is taking him."

"Why is Papa always in so much pain? Will he get better?"

"Why does he walk in such a strange way? My friends make fun of him. Why can't he walk properly?"

So many questions to which Divya had no answers, but she tried her best to answer her truthfully.

Her friends' reactions to Ravi's disability upset her enormously. Young children can be thoughtless, and so cruel in word and deed.

"Oh dear," said a visibly upset classmate of Tanya's, who had come visiting, "I sat on the same chair as your father. I hope I don't get his disease!"

Another so-called friend mimicked Ravi's awkward gait, as the rest of the group looked on and laughed. Needless to say, Tanya never wanted to speak to them again. At this rate she'd have no friends!

"They don't know any better," Divya tried to console her teary-eyed daughter. "Just forgive and forget. Don't take it to heart, darling."

But Tanya could not understand why people were so mean. How could her own friends make fun of her papa? How could they not understand his sorrow and misfortune? There was a lot in store for her to learn. She was exposed to so much suffering, sadness, and the unkindness of fellow human beings from such an early age and as her mother, Divya could do nothing about it. Frustrated and angry at her helplessness, she held her close, wiping Tanya's tears... and her own. She had failed in her vow to shelter her from life. She could not protect her daughter from this harsh reality.

Divya prayed for the wisdom and strength she needed to fill the lacuna in Tanya's life created by Ravi's disability.

"So what if Papa can't take you swimming? I will," She reassured her unhappy daughter. She did not want her to miss out on any opportunity in life, whether it meant going for dance practice, mountaineering or participating in a nature camp. Divya attended all the functions and ceremonies to mark Tanya's achievements – Prize Days, Sports Days, her dance performances, the Investiture Ceremony when she was made School Prefect – she was there. She juggled her time and attention between the demands of her work, Tanya's extracurricular activities and of course Ravi's treatment. Come what may, she went, but she went alone. Sadly, Ravi's restricted movements, due to his disability, prevented him from attending such events. But try as she might, Divya could not completely fill the void of his absence.

"I wish Papa could have come," Tanya would sadly say with longing in her voice, her eyes welling up. It hurt him too and he felt frustrated by his limitations. The only option was coming back and describing the details of the event and showing him the photographs. But that was never enough… it was nowhere near the real thing.

******

Unknowingly and unconsciously, Divya passed some of her childhood fears on to Tanya. The minute she heard "Come sit on my lap, sweetie," spoken (maybe innocently) by a male friend or relative, she'd cringe and go all cold inside. She'd quickly send Tanya off on some errand or the other before she could comply.

"Go to the kitchen, Tanya, and get some biscuits," or "Go and finish your homework, Tanya, remember you have to study for tomorrow's test."

She would not allow her innocent daughter to experience the kind of abuse that she had gone through as a child. She had to protect her daughter from that. The 'no-nonsense, no-argument' tone in Divya's voice must have registered, for invariably Tanya obeyed her in spite of a visible glint of a question in her eyes. "I've just finished studying so why does Mum want me to study some more?!" But she knew she was not allowed to argue when her mother had that particularly stern look on her face.

Divya also stuck to the silent promise she had made to herself many years go − she never pressurised Tanya about her school work.

"Did you do your best, darling?" she asked her when Tanya did poorly in her Geometry test.

"No," she whispered meekly, expecting a yelling.

"Well okay then, no point crying over spilt milk. Next time give it your best shot."

And she could see the look of relief in her child's eyes. She should never be scared of me, Divya vowed. She was a part of her and even if she did something wrong, she needed to know that her mother's love was unconditional.

The Birthday Present

"Mum, please can I have a sister for my birthday?"

This was Tanya's usual request that would be voiced a few weeks before her birthday. Being an only child, she longed for a sibling. As the intensity of her loneliness increased, her request was voiced more frequently throughout the year, and not just restricted to birthdays. Often the request became a demand and then a tantrum!

Divya had always wanted to have at least two children but she now had to be content with only one. Ravi – his disease and his attitude towards the whole issue of children; the fear of having a boy with ankylosing spondylitis in his genes; her own feelings of inadequacy at handling her present situation; the home environment... so many conditions prevented her from being able to fulfil this particular wish of her daughter. But how could she explain all this to her young daughter? How could she expect her innocent mind to understand the complexity of her plight? Divya tried her best to compensate by filling this void and packing Tanya's days with an assortment of activities and visits to friends. But she would have none of it.

"You were so lucky, Mummy, you had Jyoti mashi and Amar mamu when you were small. Why can't I have someone?" she'd try to reason with her mother.

She wanted a sibling, a playmate. Someone who would be with her all the time – who would sleep with her, they would play and fight together, gang up against their parents, giggle about their mischievous pranks, share their secrets. Divya thought of Jyoti and Amar and what they'd shared as kids. She did not blame Tanya for there is nothing as strong and precious as the bond between brothers and sisters. It saddened her tremendously to know that Tanya would be missing out on such a unique relationship. But there was not much that she could do to resolve this issue.

"Okay, if you can't give me a sister or brother, get me a dog," she reluctantly offered a compromise. However, that was not possible either. Both Ravi and Ma ji were not fond of dogs and refused the idea of keeping one in the house.

"It'll stink."

"It will chew up all the legs of my antique furniture."

"It will have ticks."

They came up with a host of reasons in favour of their decision.

Seeing her so desolate, Divya decided to surprise her with a pet that would be acceptable to all – a parrot. She didn't have a clue how to go about buying a bird, so she approached her friend, Madhu, for help. Her house was like a mini aviary. She would be the right person to guide her. Madhu rang up two days before Tanya's birthday.

"Hi, Divya! I've bought your parrot and a cage too. Come over this evening and collect it."

Cage? She hadn't thought of that! How would she have brought the parrot home? Bless her, Divya thought thankfully.

Excited at the prospect of finally getting Tanya a pet, she went to Madhu's house straight from work.

"It's in the balcony."

They walked through the landing lined with cages full of birds of different breeds, colours and sizes. It was quite fascinating.

"Here you are," she pointed to a cage on the table. "That one's yours. Or should I say Tanya's?"

The parrot was perched on a metal swing fixed in the cage. As Divya entered, it cocked its head to one side, acknowledging her presence. "Seems like an intelligent bird," she told Madhu. "Maybe Tanya could teach it a few words."

Then, balefully looking her straight in the eye, it let out a strange squawk and fell backwards! Horrified, Divya peered at it as it lay there, inert on the floor of the cage, its legs stiff, up in the air. It was like a scene straight out of a Walt Disney cartoon.

"Maybe it doesn't like red," she muttered, removing her bright red stole.

"Oh my God! It's dead," stated Madhu in a shocked voice, prodding it with her finger.

"That's not possible! You've just bought it."

Divya couldn't believe it was dead. *How does one give mouth-to-mouth resuscitation to a bird?* she thought staring at its half open beak. What did it die of? A cardiac arrest brought on by her presence? She stood there stunned, heartbroken, selfishly thinking about what she would give Tanya now. So much for pets, she thought sadly. Well at least she had tried. Divya stopped on her way home and bought Tanya a Barbie doll instead.

The Accident

"Mum," wailed Tanya staring at her reflection in the mirror "my plaits are all wonky! I can't go to school looking like this!"

In dismay Divya turned her around to look and sure enough the left plait was higher, standing up like an antenna and the right one wilting, drooping down.

"It's okay," she lied. "There's no time now. You'll definitely miss your bus."

Tanya stamped her foot and pursed her lips. Recognising the beginnings of a tantrum, Divya redid her left plait at super speed. Not giving her time to check in the mirror, she grabbed Tanya's schoolbag and water bottle and rushed with her to the bus stop.

"I've made your favourite 'bhelpuri' for tiffin today," she tried to appease her distress, as they ran across the street to the bus stop. It had the desired effect for immediately Tanya's face lightened up. Divya gave her hand a tight squeeze. She was such an easy child to please.

Thankfully they saw Anupam waiting at the corner with Ritu, his daughter. Though late, they had not missed the bus. It arrived within seconds of their reaching the corner.

"Hi, Anupam," Divya greeted him, wondering how he always looked so energetic and fresh every morning compared to her dishevelled appearance.

"Bye, darling," she hugged Tanya, helping her onto the first step of the bus. Waving a distracted bye to Anupam, Divya headed home, her mind shifting to 'work' mode. She had enrolled for a one-year course in Special Education at an Institute not too far from home.

I must remember to finish my child's case study, she thought. *And I also have to submit two assignments today.*

Her mind was buzzing with things she had to do. Studying after such a long gap was a challenge to her rusty grey cells. She was one of the few "senior" students amongst a batch of just-out-of-college kids. But she loved the back-to-school feeling again. For the first time in her life she was actually enjoying studying. The phone rang just as she was tucking in the pleats of her sari.

God! I hope it's not Trishna, she thought, *she can't stop talking and I'm already running late for work.* Ma ji came out of her room to answer the phone but Divya made it there before her. "It's okay, I got it."

"Hello," she said in a slightly breathless, business-like voice that she hoped conveyed 'it's-not-a-good-time-to-call' to the listener.

"Divya, it's me, Anupam."

"Oh hi..." before she could complete her sentence he continued, sounding serious.

"There's been an accident with the bus. I am coming to pick you up. We'll go to the hospital together."

She felt as if she had fallen in freezing water. She could not move, breathe, speak. She just stood there staring at the phone, as if it was about to explode in her hand.

"What's wrong?" asked Ravi, sensing bad news. "Tell me, who was it? What has happened?" he held her shoulders, worried at her silence.

Divya felt an involuntary tremor course through her body, growing in intensity. The phone fell from her hand.

"Accident. Tanya's bus has had an accident," she somehow mumbled. Ma ji sat down in stunned silence.

"She's going to be okay," Ravi said firmly. His voice seemed distant, as if it was coming through a tunnel. "Think positive. Everything is going to be okay."

"I'll come with you, beta," said Ma ji, too worried to stay at home.

Ma ji and Divya rushed downstairs to Anupam's waiting car and jumped in. Divya looked back and saw Ravi standing at the window, watching helplessly. He must have cursed his disability... his inability to rush to the hospital with them. The car was thick with silence and heavy with unspoken fears. She tried to speak but the words stuck in her throat. She stared at the hospital looming ominously ahead of them, not knowing what to expect there.

The emergency room of the hospital was chaotic as all emergency rooms generally are. But that day it was filled with school children of different ages, most of them covered with blood and crying. Parents milled around in the hall, some relieved that their children were safe, others hugging their injured children, visibly upset. Bad news travels fast. The bus had collided with an oil tanker – luckily an empty one. Anupam found Ritu in a state of shock but physically unharmed. Divya worriedly scanned the faces, searching for Tanya. She couldn't see her anywhere.

"Can you see her?" she asked Ma ji in a choked voice.

"No," she whispered back, barely able to speak.

They searched everywhere, asked the nurses and doctors, "Have you seen a little girl with two plaits? My daughter. Her name's Tanya. She's only six years old. She was in this bus. I can't find her."

Heads shook from side-to-side as she babbled. No. She was not there. She wept, not knowing where her baby was or what condition she was in. Where could she be? What should she do?

"Go to her school," said a parent seeing Divya's state. "Maybe she's been taken there by someone."

She spotted Tanya's teacher who had rushed from school on hearing the news.

"Have you seen Tanya, Mrs Gupta?" she asked her hopefully. At least she would be able to recognise her.

"No I'm sorry, ma'am," she said helplessly. "But don't worry, check at home or then go to school," she advised.

She was on the verge of hysteria. Tanya was lost, injured, and untraceable.

"Let's go home first. Ravi must be worried," said Ma ji, thankfully making a decision and taking charge of the situation. Anupam had already left with Ritu, so they took a taxi and went home. Divya prayed and wept all the way. It was one of the longest journeys of her life.

She ran up the stairs, leaving Ma ji to pay the cab driver. Ravi opened the door on the first ring of the bell.

"Tanya's inside," he said before she could say anything. "She was brought home by a lady. She's okay."

When the accident occurred, passers-by rushed to help. They took all the children off the bus to the safety of a bus stop nearby. A woman in a car just behind the bus spotted Tanya in the midst of the melee standing all by herself, schoolbag in one hand and her broken water bottle in the other. She looked desolate and was crying. She picked Tanya up and carried her to the car. Fortunately, Tanya was able to guide her home. Divya thanked all the gods above that she had forced her to learn their address by heart.

Ravi's relief knew no bounds when he opened the door and saw a strange lady with a kind face standing there with Tanya in her arms. He could have hugged and kissed the lady for being Tanya's guardian angel but restrained himself and thanked her profusely instead. Holding Tanya close, he heaved a tremulous sigh of relief. He was shocked by her state. Her face was flushed and cuts and scratches crisscrossed her cheeks. Her white uniform was torn and red with streaks of blood, her plaits had come undone and her dishevelled hair was matted with grease from the floor of the bus and blood. The blood was not hers, it was the bus driver's. When the accident occurred, Tanya had been sitting in her usual place on the front seat of the bus, next to the driver. With the impact of the collision of the tanker and the bus, she fell forwards onto the gearbox. The driver who was seriously injured fell on top of her and the entire windscreen shattered and fell on both of them. She had glass in her hair and a few bits came out of her mouth.

Taking Tanya to his room Ravi cleaned her wounds as best as he could. Unable to bend, he helped her stand up on the bed and then wiped her face with Dettol-soaked swabs of cotton. He was in for another shock for when he removed her uniform he found that she was badly bruised down the entire length of the right side of her body.

Rushing into her room, Divya found her lying on the bed, dazed.

"My baby's okay. My princess. I love you so very much."

She was blabbering deliriously as she clung to her, tears of relief rolling down her cheeks. Tanya lay in her arms, listless like a rag doll, staring back at her silently with her big brown eyes. They visited the doctor that evening.

"Apart from the trauma and the bad bruise," the doctor said, "physically she is okay. Don't send her to school for a few days," was his advice.

The question of sending Tanya to school didn't arise for she was in a state of such severe shock that she did not talk for two whole days. Divya took leave from her course for a few days to be with her and help her get out of her traumatised state. Fear made Tanya insecure and she clung to her mother, unwilling to let her out of her sight. In Divya's desperate attempt to get her chatterbox back she did all the craziest things possible. She sang funny songs and clowned around. Anything to get her to smile. She made her favourite food and pampered her, grateful that she was safe and nothing serious had happened.

"My bottle broke," Tanya wept, more upset about her favourite water bottle breaking than her bruised little body.

"Don't worry, sweetheart," Divya smiled tearfully, gently hugging her. "We'll buy you a new one," she promised. "A better one."

She must have aged a few decades that day.

The First of April

April Fool's Day was a day when Tanya and Ravi would invariably gang up against Divya and be at their juvenile best.

"No," she'd think on the last day of March, "this year I am definitely not going to fall for their pranks."

But each time she was caught unawares. This particular year was no different. Her reaction to a telephone call from her parents and siblings was a major source of entertainment to Ravi and Tanya. The ringing telephone followed by the announcement, "It's a call from Delhi!" would culminate in her dropping whatever she was doing, pushing Tanya off her lap (if she unfortunately happened to be there at that moment) and rushing to the phone, stumbling over furniture and anything that came in her way as she went. Such was her eagerness to talk to them!

On this particular first of April, Divya was cooking in the kitchen when she heard the phone ring.

"Hello, Daddy! How are you?" she heard Ravi shouting.

In those days, a trunk call generally provoked people to scream at the top of their voices. "Yes, she's here. I'll just call her," he continued. "Divya! Divya! Where are you? It's Dad calling from Delhi!"

In the middle of kneading dough, she rushed to the living room to answer the phone, her hands still sticky with bits of dough hanging from her fingers.

"Hi, Dad," she said picking up the receiver.

"Hello, beti. How are you?" squawked Tanya's voice from the phone extension in the bedroom.

Divya stared at the receiver. During that nano gap between wondering what had happened to dad's voice and realisation, she was foxed. Tanya rushed into the room with Ravi close behind and they burst out laughing hysterically as they saw the incredulous look on her face. She could not help but laugh with them, acknowledging the ingenuity of their idea.

"Ha, ha, ha! April Fool! We fooled you again!" they chortled with glee at their success.

Divya stomped back to the kitchen plotting her very own devious plan. After a decent interval, when the excitement of their prank had died down, it was her turn... the revenge of the mummy!! She picked up the tomato ketchup bottle and liberally poured it on her hand, letting it drip down to her wrist. Clutching her left forefinger, she rushed into the bedroom where Tanya and Ravi were re-living their joke and cackling at the success of their prank. "It was a brilliant idea, Papa... Mummy fell for it!

"It was funny wasn't it!"

"Could you get me some cotton wool and Dettol please?" Divya said in a voice that reflected no panic but understated urgency and pain. Holding her "bloodied" finger in a visible but not so obvious way, she rushed to the bathroom. *I could have won an Oscar for my performance*, she thought as their horrified looks and a volley of questions followed her retreating back.

"What have you done?

"How did you cut yourself?

"Should we call a doctor?

"So much blood, you'll definitely need stitches."

That's it! She couldn't take it anymore and collapsed in a paroxysm of laughter on the edge of the bathtub. Tears of mirth and victory rolled down her cheeks. But they still hadn't realised that she was fooling them. The tears brought on concern.

"Does it hurt? I'll just call Dr Sen. Tanya, get some ice. Quick!" Ravi took charge. "You'll also need an anti-tetanus injection."

Tanya rushed back in record time with a bowl full of ice cubes. "Here, Mum, press this against the cut," she said in a worried voice.

Laughing uncontrollably, Divya rolled off the edge, sliding into the bathtub. That's when the penny dropped. Tanya and Ravi stared at each other and then at her sprawled in the bathtub.

"It's only sauce! April Fool!" she said licking her fingers, weak with hysteria.

"You scared us! That's not fair!" they said in unison.

"All's fair on April the first," she said, glad to have had the last laugh.

Burmese Pakodas

"Hey, Mum!" Tanya wandered into Divya's bedroom one Friday evening.

Ravi was fixing her a drink – a tall glass of Vodka and Sprite with a sliced green chilli for flavour. She had settled down in her rocking chair lost in the pages of a romantic book, her feet up on a wooden stool. They were in a relaxed TGIF ('thank-God-it's-Friday') mood.

"Yes, darling?" Divya said reluctantly closing her book in the middle of a steamy paragraph. Tanya had always been and would always be more important than any book... no matter how exciting. She pulled Tanya on to her lap and gave her a tight hug and a slobbery kiss.

"What's it, sweetness? Tell me I'm all ears now," she fibbed absently, her mind still going over the detailed description of the passionate embrace. The embrace she had to give up, mid-kiss.

"Don't, Ma! First listen, na!" Tanya shrugged her arms off, objecting to this mother-handling.

Uh oh... she means business. This is going to take a while, Divya thought. So giving the book one last longing look and she gave her daughter her undivided attention.

"What's the matter, honey? What's bothering my babushka?" she said, her 'I'm-all-here' body language sign switched on.

"Ma," she started. "Why don't you ever cook something interesting for me?"

Oh no... please not this!

"My friends bring such delicious tiffin to school – chow mein, samosas, pakodas, dhoklas – and guess who makes it for them? Their *mothers*."

Divya should have seen this coming ever since Tanya started describing her friends' snacks in obsessive-compulsive detail.

"Today Sheena's mum gave her biryani for tiffin and there was this amazing coconut chutney with it. And you know what Shalini got? Delicious aloo tikkis and cheese balls. And me?? No one wanted to share my tiffin because you gave me boring jam sandwiches!"

"Well it's better than the banana sandwiches we were given as kids," Divya retorted. Cold comfort! It's true. When she was in school, Ma would often use mashed bananas as sandwich spread. By break time, the insides of the sandwiches had turned a peculiar shade of black. But she ate them.

"Anyway, darling," she continued placating, "I'm sure Sheena's or Shalini's mums don't make all that early in the morning. They either order the cook or just go and buy the stuff from the market."

She tried her best to burst the perfect mother-cook image that Tanya clung to so dearly, but sadly, she refused to be side-tracked. Cleverly, she changed her tactic and tried pulling the emotional strings bit.

"I want to offer my friends something different and tasty and say that *my mother* has made it," she said plaintively.

"Okay, dear... but you'll have to wait for winter to boast about your mother's cooking skills," Divya explained. "Right now it's too hot for me to cook."

Divya had developed an aversion of unknown origin to cooking, happy to leave it all to Lakshmi, their cook and Ma ji. As a result, she was not fussy about food – she could eat anything as long as she didn't have to cook it.

"This just proves that you just don't care what I feel."

Oh dear… she was soon going to hear violin strings!

"You always feel hot!" she said accusingly.

"Want to play scrabble?" said Ravi cheerfully, coming to Divya's rescue, amused at her dilemma, successfully distracting Tanya by dangling the carrot of her favourite game. Divya took a long swig of her much-needed drink.

What would she do? She fretted. Sweating over recipe books and rustling up exotic dishes was now history. A dish that could take her three hours to prepare would disappear in front of her eyes in ten minutes! So much blood, sweat, and tears for a burp and a smile of gastric satiation. She would rather crochet a lacy doily that would last a lifetime. She had now reached that stage in her life when she entered the kitchen only on birthdays or if someone put a gun to her head. And Tanya was using the most dangerous gun in human history – emotional blackmail. In fact she was getting a bit too trigger happy for Divya's liking! She had to set her image right. Her daughter's 'reputation' was at stake.

"Do you have a recipe for something that tastes great but is easy to make?" she asked her friend, Ananya, the next day. She was the epitome of a super woman… she was a perfect wife, a fantastic mother to her two children and to top it all, a successful business entrepreneur. *If she hadn't been my friend, I would hate her*, Divya thought as Ananya beamed in sadistic delight.

"Seems like Tanya's taste buds are stirring! Or is it Ravi, whose stomach is complaining about Lakshmi's cooking?"

As she told her friend the story, Divya could see her mind flicking through the pages of her turmeric stained, much-used recipe book.

"Burmese Pakodas!" she exclaimed as the Eureka bolt struck her on the head. "It's the easiest snack to make. I assure you Tanya'll be licking her fingers, asking for more."

Divya definitely did not want that kind of a situation to arise. Trouble is, the minute you cook well, everyone's expectations sky-rocket and the requests to keep dishing out yummy food become more and more frequent.

******

She was happy with her 'she's-a-pathetic-cook' reputation that she had acquired after her disastrous attempt at chilli-chicken. Her hand had slipped while pouring soya sauce over the marinated pieces of chicken and then while they were frying she had to rush off to answer the phone. She came back from her chat to find smoky, shrivelled up black pieces of charred fowl stuck to the bottom of the pan. Her heart sank as she scraped them into the serving dish. As thoughts of ordering in some food filled her head, she spied the ketchup bottle sitting innocently on the shelf. Yes! God had shown her a way out of this sticky situation. She liberally poured dollops of tomato sauce. Red soon disguised the black. At least it looks colourful, she thought.

"It tastes a bit like charcoal," said Ravi as Tanya wrinkled up her nose, pushing her plate away. Silently, Divya chewed a rubbery red and black piece and swallowed it with great difficulty.

"Okay," she decided, enough is enough, "who wants dosas instead?"

She could feel the dining room tension slip away replaced by instant relief as Ravi stopped pretending to eat and Tanya leapt to the phone to place the order.

Her "dessert attempt" was not too successful either.

"Divya's made a strawberry soufflé," Ravi proudly announced to their newly made friends, Sita and Sujoy, who had come for dinner. Since Lakshmi, their cook, had prepared the entire meal, Divya decided that her contribution to the evening would be dessert.

"Wow," they said in polite unison.

"Oh God!" she jumped up in dismay at his words. "I forgot to take it out of the freezer!" Instead of the soft, creamy, mouth-watering soufflé that the recipe promised, out came this rock hard, pink block!

"That's great," Ravi joked as she tried to cut it with the sharpest knife in the kitchen, "now we can officially break the ice!"

"You need a hammer, or maybe a chisel," Sujoy said helpfully, laughing as she turned different shades of red.

"It actually looks like a giant Digene tablet," Tanya chipped in, thinking of the antacids Ravi used to eat with his painkillers.

"Good," Ravi took off from where she had left. "It'll help to digest the acidic comments!"

They were in splits. Well at least they were having fun, even though it was at her expense. That frozen soufflé was the death knell, or should one say the executioner's block, for Divya's culinary attempts. She heaved a sigh of relief. Now nobody would pester her to cook again.

But, unfortunately, 'one-up-mothership' had raised its ugly head again. *I can't let Tanya down*, Divya thought as she pulled out her long-lost apron from the deepest, darkest corner of her kitchen cupboard. It had a musty, unused smell to it. Once again she tied the apron strings round her waist and marched into the kitchen with resigned determination. Burmese Pakodas coming up...

Burmese Pakodas. The name had an exotic ring to it. Divya closed her eyes and could just visualise Tanya offering them proudly to her friends with a "My mum made them" tag. The evening was hot and muggy but she did not let that deter her. She was a woman with a mission. With her recipe book held open by her spectacle case and perched rather dangerously on the shelf above the gas stove, she set to work. She chopped the vegetables, ground the ginger and garlic, and prepared the batter for the pakodas. Soon, she was perspiring, as if a tap had been turned on her head.

"Think cool," she told herself, trying the visual-imagery strategy. "Think that you are sitting in Darjeeling." She began humming "rain drops are falling on my head..." loudly, trying not to think of the rivulets of sweat trickling down her back. She lit the gas burner and waited impatiently for the oil to heat. Staring at the flaming wok, she could feel the molten lava of irritation frothing inside her, ready to explode.

How the hell did I get roped into this? she thought, longing to take a shower and sit under the fan with a cool drink.

Someone should invent pills that burst into different flavours in your mouth and then expand in your stomach, filling it up at the same time. Chilli chicken pills, cheese toast pills, lemon tart pills... her mind wandered to the myriad advantages of such a revolutionary invention, the main one being – No More Cooking! All working women would bless her. Maybe she should patent her thoughts! The spluttering oil and the prickling sensation in her eyes dragged her out of her reverie, bringing her back to reality with an unfeeling nudge. Using her hands she scooped up little handfuls of the mixture and dropped them into the smoking oil. They sizzled and turned a deep brown within seconds.

"I can't take this anymore," she decided as she carefully took out the first batch of pakodas. Frying small handfuls at a time would take forever. She needed to get this over with. She wanted out!

It's like my life, she thought, as the heat evaporated all powers of rational thinking from her mind. *I start something with great gusto, get impatient and then want it to end real soon.* She snapped out of her philosophical haze, drops of sweat stinging her eyes, as the oil beckoned invitingly.

"I'm sure there must be a faster way to do this." Throwing caution to the wind, she picked up the bowl and poured its entire content of batter into the oil. She could always cut it into smaller pieces once it was done.

"Hey, Mum. What's cooking?" Tanya sauntered into the kitchen at that very moment. "What's this?!" she stared into the pan pointing at the huge bubbling mass.

"Burmese pakodas," Divya said weakly, wiping her sweat-flushed face with the back of her hand, leaving a yellow streak of batter across her hair and forehead.

"Pakoda?? It looks more like a Burmese Pagoda!" Impressed by her own wit, she cackled hysterically and rushed out of the kitchen to report the latest 'mother's culinary disaster' to her father. Et tu Tanya.

The huge blob wobbled dangerously as Divya used a flat steel spatula to shovel it out of the wok on to a plate covered with brown paper to soak the oil. It looked well done, crisp and brown all over but its appearance was deceptive. Her ingenious plan of cutting it into small pieces backfired for when she cut one edge of it she found that it was uncooked – yellow and raw inside.

Yup, just like me, she continued on the 'life's-a-Burmese-pakoda' track. *Tough and hardened on the outside but soft and mushy inside.* She was so pleased with her analogy that it diluted the dismay she felt when Ravi and Tanya rejected the pakodas on sight, condemning it without even a trial!

"It looks like a Thanksgiving turkey that we need to carve! Pakodas mean more than one monolith right?" asked Ravi mischievously.

"At least try it," Divya urged bravely, putting a small piece in her mouth.

"Actually don't," she added hurriedly.

They laughed as she hurriedly spat it out. Even *her* pride and ego could not persuade her to swallow that particular culinary disaster! It lay, for days, under the gul mohar tree of their lane... even the dogs refused to eat it! As for Tanya, she readily agreed to take Haldiram's samosas for her friends. Divya wasn't asked to cook for a long time after that. Bless those Burmese Pakodas – they played a major role in ensuring her absence from the kitchen!

The Need for Breathing Space

Internecine family quarrels and financial misunderstandings soon led to the collapse of the family business. Before long, Ravi was 'jobless', sitting at home trying to make some money by dabbling in the stock market. Three of their four cars had to be sold and the drivers discharged. There was a drastic change in their standard of living. The proverbial coat had to be cut to fit the cloth of circumstances. Stepping down in life is tough but they had no choice but to accept and adapt to this new lifestyle. God kept them on their toes to test their tolerance and ability to withstand all kinds of anguish at the same time. But the drop that made their cup of torment overflow was Ravi's illness.

With each passing year, his condition deteriorated. Now that the disease had spread painfully to all the major joints in his body, disabling him... he was more or less housebound. Nothing seemed to help. The only option was surgery, which he refused outright.

"I'll definitely need a blood transfusion for such a major surgery. What if I get AIDS from the blood?" he argued. He read up extensively about Total Hip Replacements on the Internet. "The implant has a life of only twenty years. What will I do after that? Go in for another surgery?"

"But for twenty years you will lead a normal life. And who knows, the way medical science is progressing, they may come up with a breakthrough by then." Divya's persuasive voice fell on deaf years. He was adamant, and closed to reason.

So life limped on. Sadly, Divya's family became more and more dysfunctional and bringing up Tanya became more or less her responsibility. She was at her wit's end and was having difficulty coping with her hydra-headed problems. Her alcoholic father-in-law would terrorise them in his state of inebriated bravado. Ma ji, being too mild and gentle, could not put a stop to his home-wrecking behaviour. Ravi's way of handling the situation was to herd Tanya and Divya into the bedroom and lock the door. There they would sit for hours behind closed doors, listening to his drunken shouting. Tensely they'd wait for the intoxicated storm to blow over and for him to subside into a stupor.

Life became claustrophobic and Divya hated having to live out of one bedroom when they had such a big house. She would think twice before inviting people over because her father-in-law would immediately take over the bar… and the party! Her brother-in-law, also suffering from the same Bacchus-ridden affliction, was not coping too well with his marital problems. Every other day there would be a drunken drama in the house… the stuff of Indian "soaps".

She dreaded the midnight knock on her bedroom door that became more and more frequent with each passing day. Along with many other ailments, her father-in-law suffered from cardiac asthma. The attacks generally occurred in the early hours of the morning, between 1 am and 2 am. An attack meant respiratory problems and he would have to be rushed to the emergency ward of the nearest hospital and admitted to the ICU.

"Divya! Ravi!" Ma ji's panic-stricken voice penetrated the dense layers of sleep, pulling a reluctant Divya out of REM. "Wake up! Hurry!"

Knowing exactly what she was expected to do she shook Ravi and staggered out of bed. Automatically jumping into her jeans, she grabbed her handbag while Ravi called an ambulance.

Being the only "driver" in the family, Divya was handy to have around. She drove behind the ambulance with Ravi, wide awake by then.

Often she'd have to rush in to the doctor's room and wake up the only doctor-on-duty. Grumpy at being woken up, he'd yawn sleepily and shuffle out clutching his lungi, while her father-in-law sat on a wheelchair, wheezing and gasping for breath. After a cursory, half-hearted examination, the somnambulistic doctor would inject him with some life-saving drug, put him on oxygen and then admit him to the ICU. Ravi and Divya would sit in the waiting room, cooling their heels, this routine event too familiar and frequent to perturb them.

By the time the formalities were over, the night sky was lightening to the dusky rose-grey of dawn. By the time they got home it was too late to go back to sleep. Divya lay with her eyes shut, wide awake. Groggy at work, she OD'd on coffee to keep herself alert. After a couple of days in the hospital, she brought her father-in-law back home so that he could he could get back to his chain-smoking and booze-guzzling again. He suffered because he couldn't give up his addictions. They had to endure along with him, for no fault of their own. Initially, she used to get really upset at these incidents but as the frequency of each episode increased, Divya soon became stony cold and blasé about them, furious that they had to suffer because of someone else's death wish.

She worried about the effects of these melodramatic antics on her daughter's psyche. Tanya would stand frozen in a corner, her eyes wide with fear as her young mind tried to comprehend the drunken drama unfolding in front of her. Ravi's inability to take a stand and deal more firmly with the situation angered Divya. Why was he turning a blind eye to this serious issue? Couldn't he see what was happening? Didn't he realise how his wife and child were being traumatised? This was not a healthy atmosphere for a child to grow up in. She definitely did not want to continue living in such an environment.

She had to take Tanya and get away. She needed breathing space…

I need to take a trip somewhere
and go off on my own.
It doesn't mean that I don't care
my heart's not made of stone.
Just being by myself will help
to ease the pain away
I'll do exactly as I please
cherishing every day.
When I have sorted out my mind
and had enough of me
I'll return again to be with you
but till then set me free.
I'll rest against the old oak tree
lost within a book
or simply watch the world go by
contented just to look.

Divya's escape came in the form of her inflamed appendix. She needed an operation so, along with Ravi and Tanya, she went to Delhi for the surgery. It was a relief to get away from the walls of her bedroom that were slowly closing in on her. Taking advantage of the fact that they were in Delhi, Varun tried in his own way to persuade Ravi to agree to undergo surgery of his hips.

"Think about it, Ravi. Not only will the quality of your life improve tremendously but your entire family's too," he implored.

He arranged appointments with orthopaedic surgeons and personally took him for all the visits. No luck. His suggestions and persuasions were stonewalled. That's when Divya announced that she didn't want to go back to Kolkata. She had had enough and did not want to be a part of an alcoholic household anymore. Desperate, she was even willing to leave Ravi and stay alone with Tanya. Her decision to remain in Delhi, where she would definitely be able to get a job, was supported by no one but Amar. Solid as a rock, he empathised with what his sister was going through. But he was too young and could ultimately do little. Jyoti, still in England, was unaware of her sister's problems. Divya thought it best not to trouble her with them, for there was very little she could have done from so far away.

Ravi refused point-blank to leave his family and shift. He could not understand why she was behaving so irrationally. As far as he was concerned, her life was comfortable in Kolkata and she had no cause to complain. Her parents were too traditional and orthodox. They made it clear that now she was married and her life was with her husband and in-laws.

"You have to live with them and face life bravely," was Varun's unhelpful advice. "You can't give up so easily. Don't be soft."

Ravi and Ma ji promised that things would change for the better and that Ravi would have the operation within a few months: False promises, just to make her change her mind. Though she was desperate, Divya had to give in and with a heavy heart she found herself back in Kolkata. She had nowhere to go… no one to turn to. She had no place to call "my home". She swallowed her pride and her sorrows and accepted their victory and her defeat. She now understood why women in such situations commit suicide… it's that 'pushed-in-the-corner' feeling of no one to turn to, no refuge. She learned an important lesson, then: she needed to be financially independent in order to take such a major step of starting out on her own. She could rely on nobody but herself. How important it is for women to earn money! And to think she had regretted at some point the overpowering sense of autonomy felt by a working woman.

Angry at his wife's "unacceptable" behaviour in Delhi, Ravi did not talk to her, unless required, for a whole year. It was a cold war and she froze into a block of ice – mentally and physically. All those promises made in Delhi had been hollow and were conveniently forgotten the minute they landed in Kolkata. It was just a ploy to get her back. She was so hurt and angry at this Judas-like behaviour that she made a silent, somewhat childish, vow to never get emotionally involved in Ravi's medical /health issues. If he didn't want an operation, so be it. It was against her nature to be unpleasant and rude so she took him whenever required, for whatever kind of treatment, wherever he wished… but refrained from interfering and kept her thoughts to herself.

Reluctantly she accepted her role as nursemaid. With a determined thrust of her chin, she suppressed all her dreams and desires and soon it became a way of life for her − to exist... not live. She became an avid reader and escaped into the world of words. She overcompensated and channelled all her energies to her work and to bringing up Tanya. Her relationship with Ravi became strained and stilted and soon they didn't have much to talk about. They hid behind the silent impenetrable walls of their egos. In spite of their personal problems, it still hurt to see him suffer so much. Husband and wife ended up as patient and caregiver.

A Nurturing Job

For the first time in her academic history, Divya topped the course that she had been studying. She read the mark sheet so many times that it formed a permanent image in her mind... but she still could not believe it. Under no pressure to perform or prove her worth to anyone but herself, she had excelled. It felt strange. In a daze she accepted all the praise and congratulations.

The Institute offered her a job as a special educator. Without a second thought, she accepted. She found refuge in her new job, teaching children with disabilities. The work was God's way of giving her strength and direction at a time when she needed it most. She learnt so much from those special children and their families. Their persistence and courage made her realise how ungrateful she had been for all that she had... how she had taken so much for granted. People tended to look at her with awe and respect when she said that she was working with people with disabilities.

"It is tremendous work that you are doing."

"Such a noble profession."

"It must be so rewarding."

"You are truly amazing."

They listened with a look of disbelief on their faces when Divya brushed aside their praises saying that she was the one benefiting from this experience.

"I am actually doing it for myself," she admitted honestly. "These children teach me something new about life every day. In fact, I have learnt more from them than they have from me."

These children could do so much with so little. Like any other child they wanted affection and attention, giving their own pure, unconditional love in return. From them she learnt to count her blessings and adopt an attitude of gratitude. It was there, within the walls of that incredible haven, that she found her mentor, Mrs. Raina. This remarkably strong yet gentle lady, who was at the helm of the institution, became her role model. Unknowingly, she became the guiding force in Divya's life, giving her the strength and courage to follow the path she had chosen. She had implicit faith in Divya's abilities, and ensured that she was given all the opportunities to grow academically and professionally.

It was as if God had sent Mrs. Raina to look out for her. Divya's experiences at work held her in good stead at the personal front. Her attitude changed and she stopped crying herself to sleep. After many moons she slept right through the night on a dry pillow. She cursed herself for having wasted so many precious hours of her life in the self-destructive arms of self-pity. She developed a deeper understanding and sensitivity to the debilitating effects of Ravi's disability. She felt as if her vision had cleared after a long period of blindness. And though sometimes the bright light hurt, she became larger than her problems... determined, hardened and tough.

It was at this point that she was offered the opportunity to go abroad for higher studies. One March morning, Mrs. Raina called Divya to her office and informed her that she had selected her out of all the staff to upgrade her skills. She would be awarded a scholarship for a fully funded post-graduate course in Special Education but she would have to go to Britain. She would be away for a year. Divya was so excited she couldn't believe her ears. It was a well-timed opportunity that she desperately needed. She reached home, the wonderful news bubbling in her like a shaken soda bottle, impatiently waiting to be let out.

"One whole year?! How could you even think of leaving me and going away for so long?" Ravi said, aghast when she told him.

"What's one year in a lifetime?" she said, visibly upset at his reaction. "It's such a fantastic break for me. You should be proud that out of all the employees in the organisation, I have been selected."

"Yes, yes. I am proud of you," he said impatiently. "It is a good achievement. But tell them you can't go. One year is just too long."

He shook his head firmly. He had made up his mind. Divya's delicate bubble of joy burst. Ravi's insecurities were like the tentacles of an octopus. They wrapped themselves tightly round her, choking her freedom, cutting off her oxygen supply. She felt claustrophobic. The pillow of self-pity was drenched that night. Dejected, she went back to work the next day with swollen eyes and turned down Mrs. Raina's offer.

"I am sorry, Mrs. Raina, but I can't accept your offer." She blinked rapidly to hold back the tears that glistened in her eyes. "Ravi is not comfortable with me going away for a year. He says he can't stay without me for so long." Quickly she turned, wanting to leave the room before she broke down.

"Wait, Divya!" Mrs. Raina was shocked. "No. You have to go. You deserve it." She got up from her chair and

217

held Divya's shoulders firmly, preventing her from rushing out. "I am going to try whatever I possibly can to ensure that you avail of this offer. Do you want me to talk to Ravi?" She was even willing to fight Divya's battles for her.

"No thank you, Mrs. Raina. You don't know Ravi," she replied. "Once his mind is made up, no one can change it."

"Let me see what I can do about this." She refused to give in. "We'll work out something."

Two days later, Divya was busy checking children's' files at work when Mrs. Raina walked into her room, a triumphant look lighting up her beautiful face.

"You're going to England. I've had a chat with the University Board and explained your case to them. You don't have to go for one year at a stretch. Now you will need to go twice, for only three months at a time. But you will finish the course in two years instead of one."

She had persuaded the university authorities to allow Divya to complete the course in two years as long as she continued working on her dissertation while she was in India.

"So now you won't be away for a whole year at a stretch. Ravi just can't refuse this offer," she enveloped Divya in a genuine embrace of victory. "I told you we'd come up with a solution."

Divya went home apprehensive but with a heart full of hope. Over a cup of tea, she put forward this new, modified plan to Ravi.

"Even three months is much too long…" he began to argue.

But this time Ma ji intervened on her daughter-in-law's behalf.

"No, Ravi," she said firmly, "Divya must go. It's a great opportunity for her." Divya could have kissed her feet. "You go, beti. I am here to look after Ravi."

She gave Ma ji a tight hug, thanking her profusely, blessing her silently for her support. Joyfully she rang up Mrs. Raina and gave her the good news.

"I can't thank you enough for all that you've done for me." Divya would be eternally grateful for all the trouble she had taken to ensure that she joined the course.

England

With a newfound eagerness Divya started planning her trip to England. Ravi's silent disapproval bothered her but did not dampen her uplifted spirit. Tanya was initially excited as her mother's contagious energy infected her. She handed her a long list of all the things Divya could buy for her.

"You will be buying stuff for me so they might as well be things that I want and like," she said wisely.

Tanya did not have much faith in her mother's choice! Once the excitement of anticipated presents faded, the reality of her three months' absence set in.

"You'll be gone for so long, Mummy!" her eyes welled up. "I'll miss you very much," Tanya wailed, clinging to her at the thought.

Adding fuel to fire Divya started crying with her as well! Ravi couldn't fathom his wife's behaviour. Why was she crying when this is what she had fought for? Women were beyond his ken! Knowing that she was really looking forward to the trip, Tanya covered up her feelings in an unusually mature manner.

"We'll be okay, Mummy. You just have a wonderful time."

In spite of her brave words Divya knew the loneliness she anticipated. Tanya had already begun to miss her. For the first time ever she was leaving her little bundle of joy alone for such a long period of time. It was heart wrenching for both of them.

The day of departure soon dawned. Packed and finally ready to leave, Divya hugged everyone and said goodbye. Tanya and she wept as they held each other tight.

"I'll bring you lots of lovely presents. I've kept your list very carefully in my diary."

"No I don't want anything," Tanya sobbed. Presents suddenly seemed so unimportant.

"Promise me you'll enjoy yourself!"

"I promise, darling."

Divya tore myself away from her precious daughter's arms and forced herself into the waiting taxi.

"Bye!" she waved to everyone, as the cab let out a fume of polluting smoke and jerked forward. "I love you!" They blew kisses at each other. She was on her way.

By the time she reached the airport she was composed and ready for new experiences. She felt apprehensive about travelling alone and going to a foreign place. She needed to have her wits about her. As she flew towards England on silver wings, an amazing light-heartedness set in. For the first time in her entire life she was on her own. She was neither wife nor daughter; sister nor mother. She was there in her own capacity, as a woman. Suddenly it felt great to be on her own.

She loved everything about England − even the weather that everyone seemed to complain about. So many sights awakened childhood memories, taking her down the cobbled paths of reminiscence. The red telephone booths, the double-decker buses, the fish 'n' chips corner shops and the handsome bobbies in their smart uniforms, brought on warm feelings of yesteryears.

One Friday evening, after a late tutorial with her supervisor, she got on to a bus that would take her to her PG accommodation from the university. Sitting down next to a middle-aged English lady she propped her heavy bag full of books on her lap. As she settled back in her seat she smiled at her co-passenger. A friendly, tired, end-of-the-week kind of smile. In response, the lady got up to leave and hissed, "Go back to where you belong! Paki!"

Immediately unpleasant memories of the fat lady at the candy shop flooded her mind. Yes, in spite of the fact that the streets of the British Isles had many more 'coloured people'; racism still appeared to be a thorn in the English rose. But Divya did not let that untoward incident dampen her spirits. She felt youthful again even though she was the only "senior student" among all the younger students. She vowed to enjoy each and every nano second of her freedom. Close on the heels of that pledge followed a silent prayer, blessing Mrs. Raina for making it happen.

She was back in the country of her childhood... the country that she had left so reluctantly thirty years ago. She stayed with an English couple and their cat, preferring to stay as a paying guest rather than in a hostel. Her research work took care of a major chunk of her weekdays. She enjoyed sitting in the university library, which was so big that one could easily lose oneself in its maze of corridors. Surrounded by volumes of knowledge, her first couple of minutes would be spent gazing in childlike wonder at the tome-laden shelves, deeply inhaling the musty smell of books. She would then be prepared to start her day.

There were days when she was so engrossed in her work that she would forget to eat lunch. She met some interesting people there, who like her, had come to study from different parts of the world. She made some good friends too. They did all the touristy things together, sight-seeing, posing next to the tall guards at Buckingham Palace trying to make them smile, drinking cider and Pimms and of course shopping. She loved buying gifts for her family and friends back home. She had managed to buy small mementoes for everyone, even for Lakshmi, her cook. Though she had bought everything on Tanya's list, there were so many things she just couldn't resist.

"Tanya will love this Charlie Brown pencil box," she told Scholastica, her Nigerian friend, as they meandered down the aisles of Tesco. "And it's full of chocolate gold coins too!"

"Wow!" she said, adding a bright pink electronic organiser to her heavily laden trolley. "She'll have so much fun with this Personal Diary."

Cherishing her stay in England, Divya was determined to stretch every moment to the maximum. She was like a caged person suddenly let loose. Breaking away from the gravity of her stress filled home, she felt weightless and free. Like a dandelion floating aimlessly in a sudden breeze.

The trips abroad came at such an opportune moment in her life. They were like sparks that recharged her dying batteries, energising her flagging spirits to take on the demands of her life with renewed vigour. Just when the colours of her life had begun to fade like an old Polaroid photograph, Destiny stepped in with her paintbrush and palette. Divya's cup of joy overflowed with the vibrant hues of renewed hope again.

Reality

Soon Divya was back in Kolkata and England seemed like a distant, if fascinating dream. Life hit her on the head with a 'the-respite-is-over' reality cudgel. Having tasted freedom, she wanted to run away again. It was a struggle to get back into the shrivelled up skin of her previous existence. If three months were enough to make her feel this way, thank God she had not gone for a year! She would have hated coming back to this lifeless life.

Nothing had changed in her absence. The same problems related to health and hearth besieged her home. What kept her sane through the entire ordeal was Tanya. She was the light of her life and often Divya wished that time would move slowly so that she could savour for longer her innocent years. She wanted to silence the ominous ticking of the clock and hang on to time. She wanted to cling to Tanya and never let go so that she could keep her sheltered from life's jagged edges. Unhealthy though it may seem, she became Divya's reason for living. Probably this intense feeling was too big a responsibility to thrust on such tender shoulders. But Tanya filled her life with love, laughter and joy. She was sensitive to her mother's moods and knew how to make her laugh when she was feeling low. Divya was kept busy with Tanya's adolescent crushes and heartbreaks, her ambitions and dreams. Realisation of the reality that soon she would not need her flapping, squawking mother-hen's attention, saddened her. She grew up too fast. All too soon her little baby was neither little nor a baby anymore!

Since the time
you came out of
my womb,
tiny and quivering –
almost birdlike,
you have been
slowly
flying away from me.
I long to hold you
close to me...
forever
in my arms.
But
with each flutter
of your growing
limbs
the gap widens.

Divya was complacently trying to settle down to a fatalistic "this is the way my life is now... I should be happy with what I have" attitude. But she was not happy... she wanted more. 'This' was definitely not the way she wanted her life to be. She did not want to die a hard, bitter cynic. She clung to her conviction that 'Life is beautiful', not wanting her circumstances to change this belief. She wanted to live life to the fullest.

She spent long hours introspecting, trying to quell the turbulence in her mind. Taking one step back she reviewed her situation. She was still young and had many friends. She needed a social life. Why should she become a recluse? She was doing everything she possibly could for Ravi. As long as she didn't neglect her duties towards him why couldn't she be happy? Why couldn't she enjoy life? She had to get out of this dangerous state of inertia and nobody could help her but herself. She had to kick her own butt, no matter how physically impossible that might sound!

So Divya started accepting invitations and began going out on her own. But she had not considered the vicious wagging tongues of the middle-classes in Kolkata. She soon realised that it wasn't easy being married yet going out for social events on your own. The first party she went to was the toughest. It was an acid test of her brave attempt at breaking out of the 'couple' mould. People looked behind her shoulder as they spoke to her, their eyes searching for Ravi. Subjected to a third degree, she had to answer a constant volley of personal, prying questions.

"Doesn't Ravi mind you going around on your own like this?"

"Has he given you permission to come by yourself?"

"What about your in-laws? Don't they say anything? Don't they object?"

She was made to feel guilty for her single presence, as if she had committed a crime. And perhaps she had. Perhaps she should be there nursing Ravi and not out partying, trying to enjoy a few moments on her own. Going against the norm is considered a crime. And the norm was that married women did not go out on their own.

"No, he hasn't come because he wasn't feeling well." She got tired of repeating the same story and hearing the same polite, pseudo-sympathetic noises. Nobody was really interested – she was just one of their topics of gossip… a filler in their later conversations.

"How can she party when her husband's unwell at home?"

"I am sure they don't get along."

Some of them were even divorcing them! Divya nearly threw in the towel, thinking that maybe, it was just simpler to take the coward's way out and stay at home. Thankfully, her rebellious nature reared its stubborn head. How could she allow a bunch of gossiping women, (yes, sadly they were all women) take charge of her life? After all, they didn't know her situation. They didn't know what she went through at home. They were living by their own set rules of 'what should be' and she was definitely doing 'what shouldn't be' in bold red! Perhaps they were envious. Who knows? They resisted her breaking free and tried to bind her down with the thick twines of social norms. But Divya fought back with a vengeance for she was fighting for her sanity. Knowing that she would get as many jibes as she was willing to take, she realised that it was up to her to put her foot down. So she put both her feet down. She would take it no more. She learnt the art of selective hearing, skilfully fending off their questions with a few of her own. She learnt to play their games but the rules were hers. She pressed the mute button to cut off their taunts and danced to her own music. She became thick-skinned.

That steep rocky road
to the future is mine.
I'll have to walk up it
one day at a time.
Sometimes I may stumble,
sometimes I may fall
But my destined path
I can't change at all.
I may be alone
with no one to lean on.
If that is my lot
God, please make me strong.

She didn't want anyone's sympathy. "Poor Divya... such a tough life she leads." She had no patience or time for that. Life simply had to carry on. "How's Ravi? I really admire you..." was often just a way of getting information to be discussed in hushed tones at the next party. But she didn't want to end up being a conversation piece. More often than not there was no genuine concern. Everybody had their own battles to fight, their own crosses to bear. Nobody was really interested in hearing someone else's tales of woe more than once. Twice was pushing it and three times brought on the onset of selective hearing! Divya learnt this the hard way when she began to actually see people switching off at the very start of her description of Ravi's condition.

"Last night his knee was all swollen up..." she would begin and mid-sentence she would 'see' little blurbs of their thoughts light up above their heads: "Oh there she goes again with all her problems. All I asked her was – How's life? – Oh anyway, what colour sari should I wear to tonight's party?" At one level it was comical, at another... so superficial.

So a neutral "Everything's okay, thanks," became her usual response. Then she'd hear the silent sigh of relief when she changed the topic to something more 'interesting', like the latest Bollywood blockbuster.

In the eyes of the world, her status was rather confusing and difficult to understand. Though married, Divya was in a sense single; and though single, not free. If women bitched about her, it gave men the licence (or so they thought) to be licentious! Men friends, whom she had known for many years, revealed themselves as chameleons, suddenly changing colour and taking on a different persona in her company. She was the subject (or victim?) of many flirtations – some light-hearted, others a bit more serious.

She was alone in an ocean of sharks – circling her in ripples of lust disguised as sympathy and concern. They circled closer and closer, closing in, waiting for the suitable moment to grab a bit of her. Was she becoming paranoid? At first she shrugged it off as her overactive imagination but it happened far too often to ignore. At a party, a hand would linger on her back or sari-clad waist (in those days she actually had a slender waist!) while escorting her to the dinner table. Did she really look so helpless that she needed to be escorted like that? The hugs took on a slightly more intimate touch, becoming too tight and too close for comfort. 'Hello' and 'goodbye' handshakes lasted longer than necessary and felt different – an intermittent pressure, a gentle pumping of her hand, conveying some cryptic, Morse-coded message with intimate undertones.

Divya was struggling with her own baggage, desperately trying to keep her head above water. Her mental state was fragile. It would have been so easy for her to succumb to her emotional and physical yearnings for support. How she longed for a strong shoulder to rest on for a while, a reassuring embrace, a gentle kind of loving. But she was not free and anyway, she was overflowing with puritanical values imbibed from the Irish nuns at school! Initially embarrassed and awkward, she soon became an expert at handling unwanted attention and fortified the shield she had built around herself. But then, she was a warm-blooded woman with the normal level of active hormones. So, of course, there were times when it was an effort to hold back and she stood on the precipice of temptation, nearly yielding. Maybe if the situation was reversed Ravi would have gone ahead and had an affair, she tried to rationalise. Okay, if not an affair, he would have had a few one-night stands? But she held back.

"You are too serious about life…" what Arjun had told her, many years ago echoed in her head. He was right. She held her reins tightly, not willing to release her hold, too scared to cut them loose… to free her from herself.

The Baggage We Carry

As Ravi's condition grew from bad to worse, so did his relationship with Tanya. They developed a 'hate-hate' relationship. Divya hoped it was a passing phase but, unfortunately, it lasted for a very long time. Tanya was growing into an attractive and intelligent young girl. She had her share of heartaches and infatuations. She went through the usual teenage belligerence and 'parents know nothing' attitude. And then, as with other teenagers, there was the phone of contention.

"As soon as she comes back from school, she spends all her time chatting on the phone with boys. Last month's phone bill was too high. And anyway, when is she going to study?" was Ravi's usual complaint.

Rigid in his ways, he did not even try to understand the fact that Tanya was going through the ambivalent stresses of adolescence and that of growing up in an environment as depressing and stressful as the one they had provided her. To sort out this issue, Tanya was allotted 'phone time' on a daily basis and that proved to be successful in keeping blood pressure levels under control. But there were other issues too.

It had been a real tough day at work. Divya's head was still reeling with end of the month reports and deadlines. She opened the main door to an unusually quiet house.

"Hey, guys, I'm home!!" she shouted, forcing some cheer into her tired voice.

"Hi, Tanya," she said opening the door to her silent room.

Great! They've been at it again, she thought as she saw a prone Tanya on the bed, her head hidden in her crossed arms. Suddenly Divya realised how much she looked forward to Tanya's "Mum's home!" cheerful announcement to the world when she got back from work every evening. She ached to hear that. Putting her bag down, Divya sat next to her and gave her a tight hug.

"What's wrong, darling?" she asked, knowing full well that she and Ravi must have had yet another spat.

"Nothing," Tanya whispered, turning to snuggle into her mother's thigh. Her expression contradicted her statement. Her lower lip trembled and her eyes welled up with the unshed tears she'd been holding inside all afternoon.

"I know something's the matter, hon. You can't hide anything from your old Mum, remember?"

"You'll tell Papa if I tell you," she confirmed Divya's doubts but continued anyway. "He said that he's never going to talk to me," she hiccupped, sobbing silently. "He got angry and is going to send me to an orphanage."

"What did you do to make him so angry?" Divya stroked her hair, feeling a little red spot of fury behind her eyes expanding, rapidly threatening to flood her senses. "No one can send you anywhere, my love," she reassured her, holding her trembling body tight, shielding her from the terror of her imagined future.

No adult had the right to make a child so insecure. Divya was livid. How dare Ravi plant this seed of fear in her? She seethed inside. Her father's voice echoed in her head, threatening to take her out of school to work as a housemaid as punishment for not studying. It's all a power game, she thought angrily stomping off to have it out with Ravi. This was all she needed after a long crazy day at work and a crowded bus ride back home. She longed to have a shower and wash off the pollution and other people's body odours from her sweaty body. Oh for a cup of tea... No point! She had to get this sorted out before she could indulge herself.

Ravi was sitting in the verandah, his walking stick resting between his legs, pretending to read the newspaper.

"Hi," he said.

"What happened today?" she said in response to his terse greeting.

"You've already spoken to Tanya so you must have heard her version of it. She's definitely filled your ears with her complaints against me, so why are you asking me?" he grumbled. "You won't believe me anyway."

Divya's huge red bubble expanded and burst with a deafeningly silent explosion, colouring her vision.

"I'm sick and tired of coming home to this strained atmosphere every evening," she said exasperated. "Why are you so rigid? Why can't you accept the fact that she's just a child... our child? What could she have done that's so bad that warrants the threat of sending her to an orphanage?" She could hear her voice rising to a high pitch. She had to keep telling herself to calm down... breathe slowly.

"*You* don't have to face it every day," he countered.

"Every day," he repeated, "she'll come home from school, chuck her bag on her bed and ask what's made for lunch. When she's told what's cooked, she has a major tantrum – 'Oh joy! Daal and beans!' – you should hear the sarcasm dripping in her voice. She complains about lunch no matter what's cooked. She has no respect for Ma ji, no respect for me and takes all her comforts for granted." He exploded.

If Divya's pitch was high, his was on the verge of hysteria! She was beginning to feel sorry she'd asked him.

"So I told her the only way she'd appreciate what she has is when I send her to an orphanage. Then she'll understand!" he went on and on in this fashion.

Ma ji came out of the room as his screaming voice went out of control.

"Orphanage??!!" Divya shouted, not willing to take this anymore. "Couldn't you think of a better, less traumatic way to handle this? Why on earth do you have to terrify her like this? Can't you just scold her or explain things properly to her? Or better still see that lunch is something more appetising than beans! She's only a child for heaven's sake!"

"From tomorrow you people decide what is to be cooked," Ma ji said, adding a few drops of her own comments to their fire before retreating to her room.

"Great!" Divya said to the ceiling fan, throwing her hands up in a fit of frustration. "*I'll* get up early, make Tanya's tiffin and breakfast, take her to the bus stop, send her to school, rush back and get ready for work so that I don't miss MY bus and in all this find time to tell Lakshmi what to cook! Why don't I just give up my job instead?"

She heard a door creak in the stunned silence and realised that Tanya was standing behind her bedroom door, listening to their tirade. She had to put her anxious mind at ease.

"And by the way, if you want to send Tanya to an orphanage, she won't be going alone. I'll be going with her," she said still speaking to the fan, wondering which orphanage would take in a mother and daughter. She hoped Tanya had heard this and felt less insecure about the threats. All this was so unnecessary and unpleasant.

"All Ma ji's got to do is TELL Lakshmi what to make, not cook it herself," she continued, not willing to let go. "I'm sure you can think of something more exciting than beans and daal. As a child did you like beans? If I remember well, Ma ji said you were the fussiest child this side of the equator! But you've forgotten your own childhood."

"What's the point of my saying anything," Ravi fumed. "You'll always take her side. She's got you round her little finger. But mark my words, you are spoiling her."

Dire threats of Tanya's bleak future for which Divya was entirely to blame was his usual conclusion to their frequent battles over issues related to Tanya. A war of harsh words that reflected their own personal baggage of insecurities.

The Empty Nest

Impulsively, Divya decided that the only solution was to send Tanya away to Delhi for her university education. She needed to get her away from this madness that was tossing them around like autumn leaves in a Kolkata Nor'wester. She was emotionally bruised and battered, too weary to fight. She had to rustle up all her strength and courage to send her sunshine away.

I have no right to cling to her just because she is my source of energy. I have to let go, she thought fatalistically.

She felt that she could manage on her own and face whatever problems she had to as long as she knew Tanya was happy. Was she doing the right thing? Should she let her learn to deal with the situation herself and stay on? This was Tanya's family too and Ravi was her father. It was a tough decision... an emotionally loaded one. After Tanya passed out of school, padlocking her heart Divya bundled her off to Delhi. Thanks to her excellent school results, she had got admission in a good college. Though heartbroken, Divya felt that it was something she had to do.

Your tiny hand I held in mine
– I have to let it go
You've grown so very fast my love
Why does it have to be so?
Once your lips smiled just for me
I was your world – your galaxy
Now you've gone so far away
I close my eyes, your face to see.
I'd kiss your childhood pains away
And wipe away those tears.
I pray God gives you the strength
To face life's unknown fears.
I long to hold you in my arms
And never leave your side
But till then, these lonely tears
Behind a smile I'll hide.

Even though Tanya would stay with her grandparents Tara and Varun, Jyoti promised to look after her. She had come back from England a few years earlier and had settled down in Delhi with her family. Raghav, her son, was four years younger than Tanya.

"Don't worry, Divi, we'll have a blast! I'll be her local guardian. She can stay with me."

Hearing that was like music to her frazzled nerves. Tanya and her sister got along like Siamese twins! In fact, they were like clones. They shared the same views on life, had similar habits, tastes and mannerisms. They were blind believers of 'retail therapy'. Shopping, for them, was a great de-stressor. In fact, they didn't need any excuse whatsoever to shop. They were chronic shopaholics. A 'Sale' sign was like a magnet for them, leading them into temptation.

"Do you really need another shirt? You have so many clothes at home," Divya admonished. They'd gone shopping for shoes when she suddenly felt herself being dragged inside a boutique. Tanya had seen something she liked!

"But, Mum, I've always wanted a lime green one. It's my favourite colour. When I close my eyes I can just see myself in it!" pleaded Tanya, looking longingly at the light green shirt on the mannequin.

No doubt it did look good but one can't end up buying everything that looks good. There had to be a limit somewhere.

"I'll buy it for your birthday," Diva said postponing the eventuality with a half-hearted promise. Seeing the salesgirl approach in their direction she frogmarched Tanya firmly out of the shop.

"Birthday?! That's three months away!" Tanya screeched. "Going shopping with you is so boring. I love shopping with Jyoti mashi," she said petulantly.

Off they'd go, aunt and niece, arm in arm. They'd window-shop, enter shops randomly and spend hours trying on clothes, shoes and junk jewellery and end up buying a few things too. Divya, on the other hand, was content to stay at home and babysit little Raghav.

Jyoti had many friends and loved to party.

"Let's have a party tomorrow night," she'd suddenly announce. "The zing is fading in our lives."

"But you had one last Saturday, just six days ago! My zing is still very much alive and vibrating!" was Divya's response.

"What a wonderful idea, mashi!" was Tanya's.

Effortlessly she'd organise a party with good food and great music. She loved to be surrounded by people and so did Tanya. Another drop in their sea of similarities.

Great, Divya thought, *Tanya will have a wonderful college life*. Jyoti would ensure that her college days were full of fun. But, sadly, that was not meant to be, for her sister left the country a couple of months after Tanya joined college. O the plans of mice and men!

******

Once Tanya left Kolkata and home, Divya knew it would (and could) never be the same again. They would now have to look forward to holiday visits to be together once more. Soon she would get a job and then live on her own. This was the beginning of a brand new life for her daughter.

Divya prayed hard for her happiness. "It's hard letting go" is the biggest understatement only appreciated by parents who have experienced it. She felt as if some major organ was being torn away from her un-anaesthetised body, leaving her hollow and bleeding inside. The pain was tremendous, the gap too big to fill. She regressed to her earlier days of night-crying and pillow-wetting. She missed Tanya so much, but since she was the one to have sent her away, she had to be brave and hide her sorrow during the day.

4 o'clock in the morning
I'm still lying wide awake.
Thoughts of you
race through my
sleepless mind.

Your cheerful voice
and carefree laughter
fill my senses.
Overwhelmed
by a heart-wrenching longing
to see you...
hold you close to my heart
breathe your very essence
into my being
I blink away
the rush of tears.
Time
is supposed to
ease away the pain
but it doesn't seem
to get any better.

The empty-nest syndrome set in with a vengeance. Instead of drawing closer, like some people predict, Ravi and Divya drifted further apart. Their relationship went rapidly downhill. As a counsellor, Divya was helping so many people sort out their problems but failed miserably with her own. Just another one of the little ironies of life. She spent more and more time at the club library after work. On holidays she preferred to sit in the veranda immersed in a book or writing letters to Tanya. In a repeat performance, she would read her letters over and over again, just as she used to read her mother's letters soon after she got married. Rolling each word and sentence in her mind, feeling each emotion, reading between the lines, tears of loneliness blurred her vision. Tanya wrote amazingly well. Her pages described her days at college and were full of wit and humour.

"You are never to buy a birthday card for me," Divya had once told her after Tanya had presented her with the most exquisitely handcrafted one, with a poem composed by her inside. Her favourite card was in the form of a booklet:

Even when her gaze that once spoke
Of diaphanous dreams,
Became a tapestry –
Came apart at the seams,
And was dimmed by the darkness of a birthless void,
Where hope could haemorrhage and sanity be destroyed,
She fought off the phantoms from her morgue of space,
And brought me up with serenity and grace.
As karmic perimeters closed in,
She curled up in a foetal position,
Trapped with nowhere to go...
In quiet submission.
She smiled at me with only pure love to show.
I knew nothing but her iridescence,
her glow.
She locked the doors to her dungeon inside
Made peace with the demons who once ran alongside,
Clawing for her hide.
She sheltered me from the vapid vacuum inside.
She held her breath to blow life into my sails,
Never letting me partake of her travails –

As serrated edges of memories
Marched in cold-blooded concatenation
And aspirations leapt like lemmings,
To their liquidation.
Mozart became a weird vibration,
Replaced by the cacophonous tune
Of the Pied Piper of Guilt
And sadness overflowed its banks
Of barren silt.
The same breeze that scattered her sighs
Over stagnant hills and vales,
Echoed in my depths
And conjured up a gale
To shake off dismay from our world
Fight for joy in life's unfurl.
Should your gilt-edged aura
Ever be darkened
By mirthless spells,
It will be driven away, mother,
By the rage of angels.
For rarely has the earth carried a soul
Who makes the scarred and broken
Once again whole
By smoothening jagged edges
With her bare hands
It is a sacrifice few will understand.
She rises like a phoenix from the gallows
Creates pools of love, never shallow.
She taught me to

Experience, exult, exhale and endure,
Solemnise, sensitise, synergise and soar
Discard the disease and seek the cure.
Ma,
You splashed colours
Into my world of black and white
Arched hallways of dreams
When yours had no respite.
Taught me to grow
And in simplicity and delight
Taught me without wings
The art of flight.
You are the torchbearer of the night...

For someone as young as her, Tanya had a deep and unique power of understanding and empathising... and an eloquent way of expressing it.

Ravi's Operations

All the doctors Ravi went to, with Divya in tow – and they went to many – advised surgery. He was desperately searching for a doctor who would say that he didn't need an operation. A doctor who would give him the answer he was looking for. At this stage he was crippled by his deformity. With a 'bamboo spine', hips fixed at odd angles and swollen knees, he could barely walk. The pain was getting worse too. Finally, a renowned doctor bluntly told him that he would soon be bedridden if he didn't get operated in the near future.

"In fact you should have had you're your hips replaced many years ago. How have you managed like this for so many years?" said one doctor, surprised at the advanced stage of the disease. "You have delayed it for too long. Your knees have also got affected."

When he finally decided to go in for a total hip replacement in Kolkata, Divya suggested Delhi because she knew she would not be able to manage on her own. Organising the rarest of rare O negative blood, to-ing and fro-ing from the hospital, there would be hundreds of things to do. She just did not possess the stamina anymore to go through it alone. At least in Delhi they had medical and family support. And Tanya was there too. When Ravi agreed to go to Delhi, Varun took over and organised it all. Divya did not have to lift a finger.

So Delhi it was. Ravi and Ma ji left for Delhi. Divya stayed back by herself in Kolkata for a while. Her long leave from work would start only after a week and that's when she would join them. She had organised wheelchair assistance for Ravi so that he did not have to walk too much at the airport.

"Bye, Ma ji!" Divya hugged her and then bent down to tightly embrace Ravi who was sitting awkwardly in the low wheelchair.

"Bye, darling. Have a safe flight and give Tanya all my love."

She dropped them off at the airport and drove back home feeling strangely numb. She had been functioning on reserve for far too long. The dark, empty house welcomed her with a deathly silence. It seemed strange to be on her own after so many years; happy to just potter around in the house she enjoyed her space and the solitude. A sudden peace descended on her. She prayed that this would be the turning point in her life and that things would change for the better. That the operation would be successful and Ravi would lead a 'normal' life like the doctor had predicted. "You'll be able to go for long walks, swim, climb stairs… everything." Not in the mood to eat, she lay down on her bed and drifted into deep sleep.

Thank God tomorrow's Sunday, was her last conscious thought.

Early next morning, poised on the edge of alertness, she lingered in bed listening to the silence before dawn. Curled up under her blanket, snugly sheltered from the cold breeze wafting in from the window, she could hear the early morning sounds of the neighbourhood stirring awake. Sleepily, reaching out to Ravi's side of the bed her hands touched his cold pillow. She was alone.

"Aaaargh!!" Her eardrums rattled as a loud sound blasted the remnants of her sleep from her mind. She nearly shot out of bed to dial 100 to inform the cops that a neighbour was being murdered! As the sleepy fog rapidly cleared in her head, realisation dawned – it was the new neighbour clearing his throat of phlegm, as only Indians can. "Aaaaaargh pthoooooooo!" That awful sound took over the role of an alarm clock for, unerringly at 6 am every day, he'd shake the dreams out of her eyes with this strangulated noise.

Then Divya waited with bated breath for what she knew would follow... the claps. Loud, rhythmic thunderous claps reverberated in the quiet morning air. No it was not someone heralding the onset of dawn with applause, thankful that he had survived the night to see another day. It was just the neighbour. Mr. Bhagat, in the house on the right, doing his yoga. Clapping hard is supposed to stimulate various pressure points on the hands and is good for one's health. Well... at least that's what that man believed.

With the loud claps as a backdrop, the banging started. Divya's house was surrounded by such noisy people! The maid had come to the Sharma's house at the back and was banging on the door loudly. She was too short to reach the doorbell. She continued till Mrs. Sharma screeched, "Kaun hai?! Who's there?" from the 2nd floor window. Who on earth did she expect every day at 6:15am? Divya thought sourly.

Then came the next predictable sound – the van reversing out of the narrow lane, a Hindi song blaring as it backed. Ah!! Some music at last, albeit loud and jarring for that time of the morning. Pressing her 'snuggle pillow' over her head she tried to blot out the sounds. Finally giving up the pretence of sleeping and she got out of bed to make herself a much-needed cup of tea.

Making tea is a comforting ritual. In her languorous early morning state of mind, she stood there in the kitchen, waiting for the water to boil. Watching the little bubbles of water rise to the top and turn to gold with the tea leaves, had a strange kind of hypnotic effect on her. In a semi-drowsy state, she took her cup of tea to the veranda and sat in placid harmony with the world. She decided she would do nothing all day. Any activity seemed like too much of an effort. Making tea had drained her of energy. She had just tipped the last warm sip of tea in her mouth when the phone rang.

"Good morning! I am okay," she said cheerfully, knowing that either it was Ravi, Tanya or her parents wondering if she had survived her first night of solitude.

******

In a well-known hospital of Delhi, Ravi underwent five operations within three days of each other – both his hips were replaced with implants, his knees were repaired and the toe of one foot needed to be immobilised and fixed. It's amazing how all that trauma and agony can fit into one sentence.

Giving him anaesthesia was a major problem. Since he could not bend his neck the tube could not go in via his throat easily and since he had calcium deposits in his spine and joints, giving him spinal injections was not possible. An expert anaesthetist was needed and fortunately the doctor had a proficient one in his team.

He needed eleven bottles of blood – the O negative type. Thankfully, Varun organised this with ease. Ravi now had more steel than bone inside him. "You are an iron man now," Varun said jokingly. He had to learn how to walk again and his progress was slow and painful. The physiotherapist came home every day, to help him exercise his weakened muscles and guide him through each step. From walker to elbow crutches, Ravi bravely persevered… and progressed.

After two months they were back in Kolkata. Soon Ravi graduated from his crutches to a walking stick. Not bent in an awkward angle anymore, he seemed so much taller. He and Divya went for short walks around the block and even went swimming as the doctor had predicted. They started entertaining friends and accepting invitations for dinners. Their lives began to gain some semblance of normalcy again.

But this was just a short-lived respite. It was the ominous lull before the storm. God had other plans for them… another test was coming up, looming large like a gigantic tidal wave.

Another Blow

They were caught completely unawares by the next hurdle that had been erected in their chequered lives. After exactly one year of all those operations, Ravi started complaining of pain in his left leg and hip.

"You must have pulled a muscle while getting in and out of the car," Divya said, massaging the area with a balm. "It'll ease out soon."

They didn't lose much sleep over it. But the pain did not go for it was caused by something that changed Ravi's life forever. His left hip had collapsed and with every step he took, his implant was pushing deeper into his pelvis. Over the years, the disease had destroyed the quality of his bones. He had developed osteoporosis. His bones had become soft and could not take the weight of the heavy implant. Divya rang up the doctor in Delhi and read out the X-ray report over the phone.

"Another operation is imperative," he said. "Come to Delhi."

A hip reconstruction surgery. All that pain and suffering had to be endured again. They were devastated but there was no other alternative.

"Why? Why? Haven't I suffered enough?" She had no answers to Ravi's painful questions.

"It will be okay," she tried to be positive. "You'll soon be back on your feet again," she said not looking at him for she couldn't bear to see the deep unbearable despair in his eyes. Furrows of pain had completely altered his handsome face.

The doctor told Ravi not to bear any weight on his left leg till he had the operation. He now walked only if he had to, bravely hopping around with the help of the walker that had been put away in the storeroom a year ago. They prayed that the other hip would not collapse because of the uneven weight bearing. Once again they made plans to lock up the house and go to Delhi.

All this stress and anxiety was taking its toll on Divya. She was becoming a nervous wreck. Friends just had to show a bit of concern and she would break down and cry. Her tear ducts were working overtime. It was as if her whole world was collapsing around her. She longed to curl up in a little foetal ball and let the world pass her by. But that was a luxury she could not afford. She had to get a hold on herself. She could not let depression get the better of her. She needed to be strong for her family – for Tanya and Ravi. But she was tired... emotionally, physically and mentally weary to the core of her very being.

This time around it was a different ball game altogether in Delhi. Varun did not handle this disappointing news very well. As a father he realised his daughter's agony but he was bitter and angry about the entire situation. He felt that the entire treatment had been unnecessarily postponed for too long. In his opinion, precious years had been wasted. A younger body would have been able to withstand the trauma of such major surgeries better than a fifty-two- year-old one.

He needed someone on whom he could vent his frustrations and anger at this needless delay in Ravi's treatment. Unfortunately, since Tanya was staying with him, she became the scapegoat and the target of his displaced wrath. Overcome by his own distress, he unreasonably blamed her for Ravi's condition. He did not realise or even try to acknowledge what she herself was going through and the fact that she needed emotional support herself. She was living her own private nightmare, seeing her beloved father suffer so much. Divya felt trapped – squashed in a club sandwich of her husband, daughter and parents. She spread herself thinly like oil on troubled waters... hoping and praying the gale would blow over soon. "This too shall pass..." became her silent and desperate mantra.

The Blood Ordeal

Ravi clung to Divya's hand as the two hospital attendants wheeled him out of the room. "Don't worry, darling," she whispered in his ear. "We're all praying hard for you. It's going to be okay." She only had words to give him… just words.

She increased her speed, trying to keep pace as they pushed the gurney.

"Okay, madam, you cannot come with us now," the attendant said gently as they approached the OT.

Ravi smiled tremulously at her as she hugged his thin body tightly. And then she was alone, standing in the corridor facing the swinging OT doors. She was still standing there half an hour later, when the attendants came out with the empty gurney.

"Madam, you can't wait here. Please go to the waiting room." This time a hint of impatience laced the attendant's voice. He had no time for sympathy.

With feet of lead she walked out slowly. Tanya rushed towards her followed closely by the rest of her family. She hastily pasted her smile back in place.

"How was Papa?"

"Was Ravi okay?"

"Did they say how long it'll take?"

Questions, laced with concern, flew around her and all she could do was nod and smile sadly. She had no answers. Once again they waited in the lounge of the same hospital, waiting for the operation to get over. Each one silent, lost in prayer and undisclosed, anxious thoughts. Suddenly the door swung open.

"The patient has lost a lot of blood. We urgently need two more bottles of blood," said the bare-footed attendant, his green mask still in place over his mouth.

Varun was unwell and therefore unable to help. Panic-stricken, Tanya and Divya rushed to different blood banks, each in different directions, miles away from the hospital. Divya had visions of Ravi dying on the operation table due to blood loss, his body alabaster white. Think positive, she kept repeating inanely to herself. She was ready to donate her blood, as that was the procedure, in exchange for a bottle of O negative blood. At the blood bank, however, she was in for a shock.

"Sorry, madam, this is a rare blood group and there are other people waiting for blood before you," the doctor informed her in a matter-of-fact voice. He was about to turn away when, there, right in front of all those people standing in the queue, Divya broke down. She wept tears of helpless despair. What would she do now? Where would she go? She became hysterical as each drop chased the other down her cheeks.

"My husband is on the operating table and needs blood urgently," she sobbed. "He will die if there is a delay. Take all my blood if you want!" she sobbed dramatically. "You have to help me! You have to give me blood!"

Realising that there was only one way to get rid of this hysterical woman, the doctor calmed her down with a brusque, "Okay, okay I will try and organise it for you. Let me see what I can do."

In spite of being so overworked, she held Divya's hand and led her into her office, away from the jostling people who were literally baying for blood. Divya's head was pounding and her eyes seemed like balls of fire. But this was not the time to think about herself.

"Here, drink some water," the doctor said, offering her water in a plastic cup.

She was professional and gentle at the same time. Divya took a long sip as if her life depended on it. All that crying had drained her.

"Lie down on the examination table for a while. I need to check your BP before you can donate blood."

The bed sheet looked as if it hadn't been washed since it was woven. But Divya didn't have the strength or the choice to resist. Obediently she clambered on to the examination table. As soon as she lay down her bones turned to jelly and the room began to spin gently. She felt mildly intoxicated. No, she couldn't let this happen. She needed her senses about her. She had been using all her strength and will power to cling firmly to the reins of her body and mind. Lying down at this time was not such a good idea. It loosened her hold. She struggled to get up.

"Lie still." The doctor held her down. "Take a deep breath and calm down," she continued as she strapped the belt around Divya's arm and set up the blood pressure apparatus.

Her voice reverberated against the walls of Divya's mind, echoing loudly. She shook her head violently, to get rid of this woozy feeling. Her pressure was checked three times. It was sky-high.

"You cannot donate blood in this condition, madam. In fact you should take complete rest. Is there someone with you?"

"No, I have come alone."

"Alone?! You are in no condition to be going anywhere by yourself." Worry and concern filled the doctor's voice.

"I'll be okay, doctor. I am okay. My husband is in a critical condition. I have to rush back to him with blood. He will die if I don't go back soon."

One part of her wished she could do just that – lie there forever on that grimy table. But she shot up, holding her head in an effort to control the spinning universe. She needed blood.

"So what'll happen now?" Divya asked in a panic-stricken voice, realising the implications of what the doctor had just said. If she couldn't donate blood, she couldn't get it. The doctor was one of the angels God sent down at an opportune moment to lighten Divya's load, for she agreed to forgo the exchange of blood for her. Thanking her profusely, she took the precious bottle of blood in the ice-packed case and rushed out as fast as her wobbly legs could take her, hoping she would make it back to the hospital in time.

Surprisingly, at the other blood bank, Tanya was undergoing a similar experience. She could get blood only if she donated her own blood, she was told. Unfortunately, this was not possible since she was found to be anaemic. Thinking about her father lying in the operation theatre, she broke down, just like her mother. Luckily, a lady sitting there observing the entire incident, took pity and offered to donate her blood! What a bloody nightmare it was (pun intended!) for both of them. Completely shell-shocked but proudly armed with blood, Tanya rushed back to the hospital. Mother and daughter reached the hospital around the same time only to hear that the operation was over! The blood was not needed after all! It took them quite a while to recover from the emotional trauma of their experience. But the operation went off well, and that's all that mattered in the end.

Back home, Divya was giving a brief description of their 'blood ordeal' to a well-meaning uncle's innocent question, "How is Ravi?" when Varun intervened.

"They are too soft," he said, scoffing at their ordeal. "Such emergencies happen during surgeries. These things have to be taken in your stride. You can't break down so easily." He spoke from experience, from a doctor's point of view.

Divya was still walking on an emotional tightrope. Her taut nerves sizzled and when she heard his seemingly heartless words, a fuse blew in her ravaged, fragile mind. As it is she was teetering on the edge of a mental precipice − she lost control and fell in to the abyss of hysteria! She raved and ranted and wept uncontrollably.

"*Soft*? *Soft*?! How can you call me 'soft'? Do you have any idea what I have been through in the last twenty years? If I was 'soft' I would have been in a mental asylum by now!"

There was just no stopping her. That word "soft" hit her hard where it hurt most. It was like the last straw. She screamed and shouted at her father like she had never done before. All the years of bottled up resentment, anger and stress boiled and bubbled and came frothing out in a lava-like flow of incoherent words. Refusing to be placated by her shocked mother, Divya brushed aside Tara's desperate attempts to calm her down. They were both horrified by her Jekyll & Hyde behaviour. What had suddenly happened to their docile, quiet-as-a-mouse daughter?

Her uncle, probably feeling guilty for having asked what he thought was a polite question left in a hurry, embarrassed to witness their family drama. Tara somewhat understood the cause of her daughter's outburst but Varun could not tolerate such unacceptable conduct from his progeny, and that too in front of a third person. He did what he usually resorted to when upset and angry – he stopped talking to her. But caught up in her own mesh of dilemmas, Divya was beyond caring.

Mystic Powers of Buddhism

Within a week Ravi was discharged from the hospital. Once again he had to go through the physiotherapy route of learning to walk again. He persevered relentlessly, taking it literally in his stride. By now 'Pain' had become his middle name. It was during this time that a family friend introduced him to the practice of Buddhism. He began chanting 'Nam-myoho-renge-kyo' with hope. Hope that some light would filter in to the long, dark tunnel of his life. He found so much strength and solace that he initiated Tanya into the practice. She adopted it with such deep-rooted belief, as if her whole life depended on it. Voraciously she followed the dictum of the Lotus Sutra – to practice, study and have faith. Her conviction was unshakeable and amazing.

"Mum, you should chant. Just see incredible things happen to people. Our life condition will change."

She was very convincing because she believed in the mystic powers of the Lotus Sutra.

"It's not as if problems vanish, but you acquire a life condition so strong that you don't feel as if you have any problems! And the best part I like about it is that you can change your karma! You don't have to accept whatever life doles out to you because "Nam Myoho Renge Kyo" means, 'I dedicate my life to the Mystic Law of cause and effect.' As you sow so shall you reap. You enter with borrowed faith but then gradually grow your fledgling wings and fly independently as your life changes direction in front of you, because you accumulate a lot of good fortune practising for yourself and for others. In the process of helping others overcome their obstacles, struggles and the pain of shattered dreams, you help yourself heal."

Tanya was passionate about her belief and her explanations were really convincing. That's when Divya began chanting too. She would hear bells tinkling when she chanted and experienced an indescribable feeling of peace. It was indeed mystic, beyond the powers of human comprehension. In a dramatic reversal of roles, Tanya became her teacher, her guru. There was a diametric change in Tanya's attitude. She became so positive in her approach to life. It was this practice that gave her tremendous courage to cope and inspired her mother too.

A couple of weeks later Divya returned to Kolkata. Alone. Ravi and Ma ji would have to stay on for another month, maybe two, till the doctor was satisfied with his condition. But she had a job to get back to. In a way, she was relieved to get away. The solitude would heal her. She needed to be on her own. To be an ostrich for a while and hide her head deep in the sands of seclusion.

Little did she know that God had a surprise in store for her. A bittersweet surprise that threw her off gear for a long time and turned her life on its head, whirling it around in a centrifugal frenzy. It was a gift of love that came to her in her darkest hour. And though it came with its baggage of guilt, it brought sensation back into her numb heart. It was Sanjay's love.

Sometimes
I feel like a
winter tree
all feelings shed
cold and
bare to the world
My dreams...
like branches
frozen in space
mid-step
an incomplete
dance.
Sometimes
I feel like a
summer cloud
in the clear morning sky
touched by love's sun
colours changing
with your smile
drifting
light and free.
And sometimes
I just don't feel at all
Numb.
Anesthetized
Oblivious.

Tanya's Revelation

Sanjay entered Divya's life soon after Tanya was born. They were introduced to each other at a Christmas dinner party hosted by Parvati, a common friend.

"Divya, Ravi, you've got to meet Dr Sanjay Ghosh... the best child specialist around town!" Parvati gushed breezily and rushed off to greet someone else.

"Hello, Dr Ghosh." Divya held on to her red silk sari to stop it from sliding off her shoulder and tried to shake his hand at the same time. She should have pinned it up to her blouse with a safety pin, she thought hiding her irritation with a smile.

"Please – only Sanjay." Dark eyes, that twinkled as he smiled his acknowledgement, stared at her. His hand firmly grabbed hers and shook it gently.

"Oh okay... Hi, Sanjay!" Divya looked down at the hand that still held hers. Long artistic fingers clasped her stubby ones. Nice hands, was her passing thought as he slowly released the pressure of his fingers and finally let go.

"Hey, Divs! Long time!!!" Ritu, an old friend distracted her attention. Inhaling quickly and deeply, for she knew what was going to come, Divya disappeared in Ritu's arms, her face pressed against her heavy bosom. Today's fragrance was Lily of the Valley!

It was the first time Divya had gone out, leaving Tanya with Ma ji. She was fat and matronly and still struggling to lose all the excess weight she had put on during her pregnancy. Her maternity clothes, baggy and shapeless, were still a part of her wardrobe. When she walked in her red and white sari she was sure she resembled Santa Claus in drag. It was beyond her imagination that someone would find her remotely attractive. But Sanjay did. He fell in love with her, way back then. And she was clueless.

Reluctantly Sanjay turned his attention to Ravi and shook hands. Together, they headed to the bar to fix themselves a drink. They got along so well that evening that another meeting in a not so crowded environment was fixed. From then on there was no looking back. Their meetings – both planned and on the spur of the moment – were frequent and informal. Sanjay would drop in unannounced after his clinic, for a drink and a chat or Ravi and Divya would go across to his place for a game of Bridge. Attending parties at each other's house became an accepted part of their lives.

For so many years, Sanjay kept his feelings for her close to his heart, shielded from the radars of the world. Either he hid his feelings well or Divya was just preoccupied and unobservant. Or both. Patiently he waited for her, never knowing whether it would always be this one-way, silent and distant loving or whether it would materialise into something more 'up, close and personal'. Slowly but surely he paved the road for her – the road that led to his heart. He was so confident of his love for her that he did not wait for reciprocation of any kind. He did not need it. He was content just loving her from afar.

It was only many years later that someone was perceptive enough to sense what was going on inside his heart. Ironically, that someone was Tanya. Young as she was, just about twelve years old, she was the one whose antennae honed in on his feelings for her mother.

Sanjay came visiting one evening. As usual, Divya and Tanya walked down to the gate to see him off, a courtesy they displayed towards all their guests. They stood there shaking hands in the car park, exchanging the usual social niceties that go on for a while before departure.

"Take Care."

"Thanks for a lovely evening."

"Bye. Come again."

An impatient Tanya watched keenly as they continued in this inane fashion. Her mental radar beeped frantically, registering the presence of an unidentified emotion on her mother's horizon.

"Sanjay uncle has the 'hots' for you," she declared matter-of-factly, with true teenage candour, as they finally waved goodbye to the moving car.

"Hots??! What rubbish!" Divya scoffed going red in the face, wondering at the same time, where on earth her daughter could have picked up such a word.

"I'm telling you, Mum," she insisted. "He held your hand for so long and didn't want to let go! And didn't you notice the way he kept looking at you? He couldn't take his eyes off you!"

Divya laughed, perplexed at her innocent observation, not realising that she had unwittingly hit the nail on the head!

"Must have been because of this electric blue design on my shirt. It sort of jams your signals and makes you go all cross-eyed," she said, dismissing it lightly.

She didn't take her seriously, for Tanya had a habit of saying crazy things and pulling her mother's leg. She had a fertile mind and an overactive imagination. Ravi took this teasing lightly too. Listening with a look of benign amusement, he often added a few of his own comments and observations. Divya was often the butt of father and daughter's harmless banter.

"Pankaj uncle refused to budge from your side all evening," Tanya said after they came back from a New Year's Eve party. "Mum, you better be careful… I'm sure he has a crush on you! He turned his head all the way round like an owl just so that he could keep track of you. At one point I thought he'd fall flat on his paunch."

They all burst out laughing at the thought of fat and flabby Pankaj spinning like a top perched on the bar stool.

"Oof, Tanya! Your descriptions are ridiculous!" Divya snorted.

"Have you noticed how Manish uncle smiles when you enter his shop? Normally he looks so disagreeable, as if he's got a perpetual bad smell under his nose! But when he sees you his face lights up like a bulb."

Tanya thought her mother was beautiful, and that all men – married and single, old and young – were bowled over by her presence. Bless her!

But, strangely, that remark about Sanjay "having the hots" for her stuck like chewing gum somewhere on the edge of her mind.

Chinese Food... Or Games People Play

Divya and Ravi attended Sanjay's marriage and were there to shower blessings on his new born baby boy. He even took them to his new apartment before he shifted in, proud and excited at the prospect of owning his own space at such a young age.

"You just have to see the view from the roof... it's breathtaking!" he said as they followed him up the stairs.

"Wow!" Divya said taking in the Kolkata skyline of palm trees and ponds, "You are so lucky to be living in such a scenic place. Miles away from pollution and crowded streets."

The cool monsoon breeze played with her hair, pulling it out of the wooden clasp and tossing it around.

"You should leave your hair open more often," he said, smiling as she tried to bunch it up into the clasp again. "It looks good."

"Good?? You need to get your eyes tested." She laughed.

"She looks like Medusa at the moment," Ravi joined in good-humouredly.

It was the comfortable banter of good friends.

Hind-thought is fifty-fifty. Looking back, it seemed as if Sanjay wanted to include Divya in all his happy moments – to share them with her. Yet she had no idea of this flame that was burning in Sanjay's heart. This ember with her name glowing on it that burnt brighter and brighter each day, fuelled by every meeting. And meetings there were many…

One night Sanjay came just as Ravi and Divya were getting ready for dinner. Tanya was spending the night with a friend – a pyjama party. And it was the cook, Lakshmi's evening off, so the menu was boring, a simple 'rice and daal' with some leftovers from lunch. An uninteresting meal to serve a guest, Divya thought, even though that guest happened to be a good friend. Impulsively she decided to pay a visit to the restaurants close by. She knew that if Sanjay heard her plan he'd object vehemently. So while he and Ravi chatted and watched the cricket match between India and Pakistan, she mumbled something about going downstairs. She needn't have bothered for they were too engrossed in the match to pay much heed.

They probably won't even notice my absence, she thought as she gently closed the main door.

She nipped out to the nearest Chinese take-away to get some food: Vegetable hakka chow, garlic chicken, and crispy baby corn. Definitely a more appetising menu than what she had to offer! Not wanting to disturb cricket-lovers, she didn't ring the doorbell when she returned. Instead, she struggled with the key and the food packets she was carrying, juggling around the boxes till she finally managed to open the main door.

As soon as she entered, the strong aroma of oriental food preceded her into the apartment. It wafted into the living room, heralding her presence. Ravi had just gone to the kitchen to fix their second round of drinks. Sanjay stood transfixed near the TV watching the last crucial over of the match, when he heard her shuffling in.

"Where had you vanished?" he asked, turning.

His face registered enlightenment as he saw the source of the Chinese aroma and the answer to his question in her arms. Seeing her laden with packets of take-away, he strode across the room. The tower of boxes wobbled precariously in her arms, threatening to collapse.

Thank God! Divya thought, *he's coming to help me. Just in time.*

But instead, he held her by the shoulders and shook her, eyes sparking! A rapid wave of emotions manifested itself in his changing facial expression and body language.

"You said you were just going downstairs. You lied!"

"Ah... so you did hear me," she said. "I thought you guys were too busy watching the match." But uh oh... why was he so upset?

"Hey! Don't get so hassled," she continued, "it's only some noodles and stuff. If you keep shaking me like this we'll have to eat dinner off the floor!" she said, shrugging off his hands that seemed to have got stuck to her shoulders. She couldn't for the life of her understand his over-reaction.

"It would help if you took some of these boxes off me before they fall down." Her exasperated tone splashed over him like cold water. *Whatever had happened to chivalry*? she thought, looking pointedly at his hands still on her shoulders.

"Sorry," he said sheepishly, catching a box just as it was about to fall. Suddenly aware of what he had been doing, he was relieved to find some other occupation for his hands.

"But you shouldn't have taken the trouble, Divya. Going off alone at night like this. You lied!" he reiterated, upset that she could have done something as juvenile as fibbing.

"Hey, Sanjay, cool it. I didn't lie. I just didn't say where I was going."

"Well, I could have gone with you," he conceded lamely.

Okaay, it's just one of those games people play, she thought stepping away. Something smelt fishy here and it was definitely not the Chinese food.

"Hmmm something smells really appetising," Ravi inhaled deeply, as he walked into the room oblivious of any undercurrents. His walking stick in one hand, he held a tray with two whiskey filled glasses balanced on it in the other.

"Ah Fung Ling! So that's where you went! Wonderful. You've just earned yourself a drink!" He was pleasantly surprised at the cause of Divya's disappearance.

"You should drop in like this more often, Sanjay. That way, at least I'll get some good food to eat!" Ravi joked. He loved eating good food but unfortunately was saddled with a wife who preferred to do anything but cook!

A True Friend

Sanjay was a friend, in every sense of the word, to both Ravi and Divya. He enjoyed spending time chatting with Ravi over a drink, sharing their love of music and cricket and discussing the stock market. An afternoon spent sipping cold beer and watching India thrashing Pakistan at cricket was something they both looked forward to. And the post-match analysis was equally enjoyable.

He was very fond of Ravi and that's why his intense feelings for Divya weighed on his mind. Heavy with guilt. He watched in despair as Ravi's condition deteriorated rapidly over the years.

Much later, when he revealed his feelings for her, he spoke of his anguish and angst... of long sleepless nights when troubled thoughts kept him awake. Of the double-edged sword of love and guilt that he carried in his heart. And the agonising ecstasy of it all.

As for Divya, blissfully unaware of his private torment, she continued to use Sanjay as her sounding board. It was so easy for her to just pick up the phone with a problem, confident that he would have a solution for it. Sometimes it was not even a problem, just a concern that she wanted to air or a thought she needed to share. It was such a comfortable relationship because he seemed to understand her every mood even before she aired it. He just had to hear her voice and he'd be able to gauge her temperamental temperature and predict quite an accurate emotional forecast.

"I am feeling emotionally exhausted," she confided in him, after a hectic day at work followed by a long wait at a doctor's clinic with Ravi. "I don't think I can take this strain anymore."

"You are an amazing woman and like a teabag, your true inner strength shows when you are in hot water," Sanjay responded, trying to boost her flagging spirits.

"But this particular teabag has been in hot water for so long that there's no strength, colour or flavour left in her," she complained.

"You have no idea how strong you are, Divya. I really admire the way you handle your problems with such élan," he continued, his positive strokes pulling her out of her puddle of despair.

They could talk for hours over the phone. He became her shoulder to cry on and her source of encouragement – a reaffirmation of her abilities to live in spite of it all. He watched her (in awe, as he often said), as she held on to life by the horns and carried on regardless. Actually, she was just so petrified to let go, lest she got trampled on! It had become a way of life for her. She had suppressed all her desires and dreams and become a stiff-upper-lipped stoic martyr. She'd managed to achieve a zero expectation level from life. She had arrived at this sorry state of existence after wasting many precious hours, submerged in the self-destructive pool of self-pity and sorrow, successfully locking herself up in a windowless world and throwing away the key she thought no one would find.

But Sanjay had picked it up along the way. He had kept it safe to be used at an opportune moment to let her out... free her from her self-made prison of dying dreams and feigned bravado. Did she realise how tired she was of holding herself stiff and proud against the relentless storm, just waiting for cracks to develop and be humbly shattered? Divya didn't, but Sanjay did.

******

Over the years she had got used to just going ahead and doing things on her own. No 'handholding' to help her along the way! And anyway, there was no hand to hold for support. If it had to be done… she had to do it. There were no options on that front. No point complaining. In a way it made her stronger, confident in her ability to do odd jobs that 'normally' the man of the house takes on. So what if Ravi couldn't do it himself, he would take her through the steps and make the task as easy as he could by drawing out a checklist for her. Being a perfectionist, he was thorough in prepping her. In doing so he equipped her with skills that saw her through many a situation.

"Ensure that the mechanic checks all these things," he said, handing her a long checklist as she set off to get the new car serviced for the first time.

"If you don't supervise them, mechanics tend to do a slipshod job and then charge you for things they haven't done. And remember to talk confidently or else he'll know how little you know about cars."

As he continued, Divya could feel her hackles beginning to rise. Though irritated, she reluctantly had to accept the fact that he was right. If she was to drive a car, she needed to be capable of ensuring that it was in good running condition. Waving an impatient goodbye, she left before he had a chance to go over the checklist with her again, for the third time!

Divya was apprehensive, never having been to a service station before. She didn't know what to expect,

271

but what the hell... this was the only way to learn. Wanting to avoid the office rush, she reached the service centre bright and early in the morning and sure enough, she was one of the first to drive in. Silently blessing Ravi, she confidently went through his checklist with the mechanic.

"... And please ensure that you replace the oil filter and check the level of the coolant," she concluded, hoping that her expression didn't reveal her ignorance.

Sending up a quick prayer that he would do a good job and not cheat her, Divya went to the waiting room and settled herself on an uncomfortable plastic chair. Armed with a book and a bottle of water, she was resigned to the long wait while her car was serviced. Before she finished reading the first paragraph she heard the door creak loudly as it was pushed open. Looking up she was pleasantly surprised to see Sanjay walk in. A couple of days ago she had mentioned the scheduled free servicing appointment but had not expected him to be here.

"Hi, Divya," he said cheerfully.

"Hey, Sanjay, how nice to see you! What a lovely surprise." Carefully inserting the Tom & Jerry bookmark Tanya had made for her, Divya closed her book.

"How come you're here? Do you have a problem with your car?"

"No, no, I just wanted to ensure that you weren't being taken for a ride! A garage is no place for a woman. I'll just be back," he said and sauntered off to talk to the mechanic regarding her car.

He returned soon.

"It's going to take at least two more hours," he reported.

"No problem," she said nonchalantly. "I've come well prepared." She waved the book at him. "As long as I have a book I'm okay."

"What are you reading?" he enquired. "Oh no! Mush again!" he laughed, when he saw the book she held up. The couple in a passionate clinch on the cover explained it all.

They sat and chatted in that musty waiting room and the hours just slipped by.

"Don't you have to go to work today?" Divya asked suddenly aware of the time and that he was probably getting late for his clinic.

"It's okay. I've told them to reschedule some of my patients and that I'll be a bit late coming in."

No bells rang in her dense head. She was still oblivious to 'non-platonic feelings'!

"It's so sweet of Sanjay to go out of his way for me," she said, as she gave Ravi details of her morning. "He checked the car himself before I left the service station."

"Such a decent guy," he agreed.

Later when she turned the yellowed pages of her memory, so many incidents stood out in her mind. Bright red sign-postings of his love for her to which she was blind... Like the night of his birthday bash when he followed them home in his car.

Driving in a Storm

Ravi and Divya were the last to leave Sanjay's house that night. A son et lumiere was going on in the heavens above. Dense clouds, singed by serrated streaks of lightening, hung heavily in the night sky. Dark grey against black. Deep rumbles with intermittent cracks like the sound of a whip rippled through the air. Divya looked dubiously at the sky as they stepped out on to the pavement. The drizzle, though light, was a steady one.

"Bye!" Ravi and Divya said in unison, a synchronised wave complementing the farewell as they turned back once and then hurried towards their car. Holding Ravi's walking stick with one hand, she pulled open the passenger door with the other. As he lowered himself on to the seat, she bent down to lift his legs and give him the assistance and support he needed to get into the car. Handing him his stick, she stood up. As soon as she closed the door the heaven's ripped open, letting loose a sky-full of monsoon rain. Someone had turned the shower knob to full blast! But she did not get wet. Sanjay suddenly appeared behind her and whipped open a huge umbrella over her head.

"Thanks so much!" She shouted over the downpour. "Go inside or you'll get drenched."

"Don't worry about me," he said, following her to the driver's side.

Keeping her sheltered with the umbrella, he opened the door for her to get in. She quickly slid in as the sky cracked apart with another jagged bolt of lightning.

"Drive very slowly and carefully. The roads being the way they are will get flooded in no time and you won't know where the potholes are," Sanjay cautioned before shutting the door with a firm bang.

The area was a low-lying one. The residents used to jokingly say that the roads got waterlogged even if a dog urinated on the road! The light evening drizzle had metamorphosed into a deluge.

Turning the key in the ignition Divya tried to lip-read Sanjay's last minute instructions. But she couldn't hear a word for the drums of thunder and cymbals of raindrops on the car roof were belting out a symphony, drowning his voice. Nodding vaguely, she waved a hand at his umbrella-hidden figure. Releasing the clutch, she shot forward splashing the sidewalk with a spray of muddy water.

"Ooops! I hope he didn't get wet," she mumbled to herself.

"Gosh! It's like a river! The drainage system is the pits!" Ravi complained. "All the water is accumulating on the sides so try and stay in the middle of the road. There'll be less water there. And don't take your foot off the clutch."

She heard his voice of experience as she focused her attention on staying in the middle of the empty road. Before his disease had disabled him, Ravi had loved to drive. Often, he spoke longingly and nostalgically of his drive from Kolkata to Shillong with a college friend. "Now you have a pretty chauffeur to drive you around," she'd joke when his voice threatened to take the downhill path of depression.

Within minutes the road was completely flooded. Divya could feel waves of water hit the underbelly and sides of the car, rocking it gently. This was her first experience of driving through a waterlogged road. She was tense with apprehension, worried about how would she get Ravi home if the car stalled. She couldn't leave him alone in the car. Wading with him through the rapidly rising water was unthinkable and dangerous. Worse comes to worse, they'd probably just have to sit in the car till the storm dissipated and the water level went down, she thought as she silently navigated the car. Peering through the windscreen, she got fleeting glimpses of the road as the wipers struggled to push aside the sheets of water. Now you barely see the road, now you don't. Opaque, translucent. Opaque, translucent. The wipers swished valiantly in their continuous battle against the rain.

All of a sudden she saw a pair of headlights shining in her rear-view mirror. She breathed out a sigh of relief. They were not alone. God forbid, if anything should happen, at least there would be someone to help.

"There's someone else out on the road on a crazy night like this."

Ravi exhaled loudly, releasing the voiceless tension he had been holding inside. He must have been anxious too, Divya thought. As the headlights approached, they began to flicker and then flash. On Off On Off. A Morse code of lights.

"I think the driver behind us is trying to tell us something," she told Ravi. "He's flashing his headlights."

"Maybe the back door is not closed properly," Ravi said.

"Can't be..." she began. "Oh my God! I think it's Sanjay! Looks like his car."

Recognition, surprise and relief all compressed into one sound wave filled her voice as his car came closer.

"Only he would do something as crazy as this!" she mumbled to herself. But she felt more confident driving in the secure glow of his headlights. Now if the car stalled, he was there to help. The intensity of the rain seemed to lessen – or was it just her imagination? Her fears definitely vanished. Feeling herself relax, she concentrated on the road ahead.

Divya had a compulsive habit of following rules unquestioningly, especially while driving. It was the obedience drilled in by those ladies in white – the nuns – from her school days. So when she rolled down her car window and stuck her hand out to indicate that she would be turning right, it was not only sheer habit but also just her being a law-abiding citizen. It was such an unnecessary act because they were in the midst of a heavy downpour, it was past midnight, and apart from their cars, there was not a single car or soul on the road!

Driving closely behind them, Sanjay was amused by her neurotic behaviour. Although it was a reflex on her part, it provided him with enough material for humorous conversation at the next few parties.

"It was raining so heavily, I could barely make out the turning. Suddenly I see the right indicator light in Divya's car blinking. Then believe it or not, she rolls down her window and sticks out her hand in the rain to let me know that she's turning right!"

His eyes twinkled at her as laughter followed his narration. What *Divya* always remembered, however, was his concern for their safety and the way he followed them home at that late hour, in such treacherous weather – to be there just in case the car stalled on the waterlogged road. And still no warning chimes of possible deeper emotions.

Silent Admirer...

Divya's 40th birthday dawned. *So what's so special about this day?* she thought cynically, as she brushed her teeth, peering at the sleep-filled eyes staring back at her from the mirror on the wall next to the bathroom cabinet. A network of worry lines on her forehead and around her eyes and fine wrinkles on her upper lip greeted her. "Ugh!" she quickly looked away, not liking what she saw, not daring to look further down the length of the mirror.

"Hurry up, Mum!" Tanya banged on the door, interrupting her self-appraisal. "We're all waiting in the dining room for you."

Tanya loved the excitement of birthdays. She would decorate the table with flowers, cards and brightly wrapped presents. Bunches of balloons hung from the lamp holders, with tails of colourful streamers fluttering gaily in the breeze. She did her best to add a festive touch to all their birthdays, making them special with her attention.

"Mum! Have you gone off to sleep in the loo?!" she continued, as impatient as ever.

Dingdong, dingdong. The doorbell silenced her thumps.

"I'll get it!" she shouted, scampering off excitedly to open the door.

Oh! To be young again, Divya thought marvelling at her energy as she came out of her room.

It was the flower man. Divya had received a huge bouquet of yellow roses.

"Who's it from, Mum?"

"I don't know, darling," she said, foxed by the message in the card. "*From a silent admirer*" it stated. No name or address. Studying the card closely Divya tried to recognise the handwriting, but failed. Someone had made her birthday different by adding this mysterious air to it. She couldn't for the life of her come up with a name. It did feel good, though, to know that somewhere, someone admired her silently.

"Ha ha ha! Mum's got an admirer!" Tanya shrieked loudly, as elatedly she showed the bouquet to everyone.

"A silent admirer," she chanted as she waved the card at her mother. Then began the guessing game. Everyone had a go at it.

"Must be Ankur," said Ravi. "He seems to have a soft spot for you."

"No, no," Tanya said. "Manish uncle is definitely the one. He's forever making eyes at mummy when we go to the shop! And he always gives her a special discount."

"No, beta," said Ma ji, getting carried away with the rest of them. "I think it must be Prakash. His daughter has learned so much under your guidance that this is his way of showing his thanks."

They put forth their reasons for choosing contenders for the post of Divya's "silent admirer!" She joked about it with them, rejecting each name as "definitely not the one!" She did not know who it was, but she was sure in her heart that they were all wrong. She did not know anyone who would spend so much money on such a big bouquet of roses for her. All day she waited for someone to call, enquiring whether she had received the flowers. But there was no enquiry.

Five years later she finally learnt the true identity of that silent admirer. Sanjay. Unobtrusively, in his own quiet way, Sanjay had made her feel good about herself that 40th birthday. He needed no acknowledgment for his gesture. Thinking back, she often wondered how anyone could be so selfless. If she had done something like that, she would be the first person to ring up and ask if the flowers had arrived.

…and local guardian too

It was when Divya stayed back alone in Kolkata for the first time that Sanjay officially took on the role of her local guardian. Ravi and Ma ji were in Delhi and she would be joining them after a week, in time for Ravi's hip replacement operations.

"Is everything okay?" Sanjay would phone just when Divya was feeling like an ant that someone had stepped on. As if he knew she needed the comfort of a shoulder. A positive stroke. How did he know her moods? He was psychic. He could tune into her wavelength. He became her soul mate, a barometer of her emotions… her guardian angel.

When the phone rang at 8:30 every night, Divya would just pick up the receiver and say, "Hi, Sanjay" because she was so sure it was him! And it was.

"Hi, Divya! Hope I'm not disturbing you." He was his usual polite self. "I just wanted to make sure that you're okay. Do you need anything? Money? Groceries? A chat?"

Her days seemed incomplete without a call from him. For Divya it was still just a sign of concern from a very special friend. A friend she could rely on. A friend she could be herself with.

"Are you eating well? I worry about you staying all by yourself."

Not content with her reassuring answers to his third degree, he dropped in unannounced after work one day. Seeing is believing.

"Hi, Sanjay," Divya opened the door, her face reflecting the surprise in her voice at his unexpected arrival.

"Hi, Divya. Sorry to drop in just like that but I wanted to see for myself that you are okay."

"I'm absolutely okay. See?" She twirled a mini pirouette to prove her point. But he didn't wait for her to finish her slow spin.

Walking right past her, he strode through the dining room to the kitchen, with Divya following close on his heels. Going straight to the fridge, he was shocked when he opened it.

"I knew I was right! You haven't been eating anything!" he concluded, peering into its empty depths. She laughed, amused at his expression.

"An empty fridge does not a starved person make! And anyway, since I'm leaving in a few days I decided not to buy food."

"You are a crazy woman. What are you having for dinner?" his investigations continued.

"Actually I had a heavy snack at tea-time," she said sheepishly, hoping he wouldn't ask her what the snack was. Four digestive biscuits was a snack but definitely not a heavy one.

Throwing his hands up in Gallic frustration at her confession, he ignored her protests and took her out for dinner.

"I had a feeling you were skipping meals." He took his self-appointed responsibilities as her guardian rather seriously!

A year later when Ravi's left hip collapsed, Divya watched incredulously as their lives collapsed around them. Ravi's pain was excruciating but more than that was the fear of what would happen. It was insidious, hanging heavy above them like a loaded gun, weighing them down with its dreaded anchor. This was the beginning of his final suffering. She tried to comfort Ravi but her words rang hollow and bounced off the wall he had erected. He was the one who was at the centre of this maelstrom that was destroying their lives. He withdrew into silent depression as she cried into her pillow all night, questioning the unfairness of it all.

In this crucial time of need, Divya crumbled and failed miserably in her role as the pillar supporting her family. The tide was too strong for her to swim against. She succumbed and let herself be swept along its powerful current towards depression and despair.

Unaware of the latest storm that was wreaking so much havoc in their battered lives, Sanjay rang up for a chat. Divya's dam exploded and waves of anger and pain gushed out.

"Why does it have to happen to Ravi?" She wept on the phone. "He will have to go through all that agonising pain again. Hasn't he had more than his share of suffering?!" She continued blubbering uncontrollably. "There's no way he can survive another operation."

Sanjay let her vent her feelings and managed to calm her down with his gentle words.

At six o'clock the next morning, the doorbell rang. Wondering who it could be so early in the morning, Divya opened the door to find Sanjay standing there. She looked like something that the neighbour's cat had mauled and dragged in! Her eyes were red and swollen, like boiled gooseberries, from crying and lack of sleep; her hair was a knotted mess and her once-white-now-grey nighty was tattered and worn out, with holes in all the wrong places. She was not expecting anyone so early in the morning! Frankly, she was too upset to really care. She peered at him, registering the shock in his eyes when he saw her ravaged, tear-stained face.

"Divya! What have you done to yourself?"

And that was all she needed! She fell apart and couldn't stop crying! He sat her down, his fingers burning holes in her shoulders, and gave her a pep talk to boost her morale.

"You have to be strong at a time like this. Strong for Ravi and Tanya. You can handle it... you've done it before. You've weathered many such storms."

He realised the enormity of the consequences of their situation. She could not possibly collapse at a time like this.

"Faith. You mustn't lose faith. It will be okay."

His voice was soothing and like a tranquilliser gradually numbed her anguish. Soon, Divya had a hold on herself. But even then she did not realise that she had a hold on him! Thank God she was blissfully unaware of his emotions – she was too busy clinging desperately to the last threads of sanity.

Confession and Confusion

The night Divya came back alone to Kolkata after Ravi's hip reconstruction operation, she was emotionally and physically done in. She had still not recovered from the traumatic experience they had undergone in Delhi. At 8:30 pm the phone rang, its shrill bell boomeranged off the walls of the empty house and reverberated in her throbbing head.

Let it ring, she thought, trying to ignore it. *I can't bear to talk to anyone just yet. In fact, I don't want to talk to or meet anyone for the rest of my life!*

She wanted to just curl up in a cocoon of self-pity. She was not strong enough or ready to face the world. But the ringing was incessant. In her heart she knew it was Sanjay. The phone stopped ringing but within seconds started again. She should have known he wouldn't give up. She had to give in.

"Hello," she managed. Her deadpan voice discouraged conversation. She could think of nothing to say.

"Hi, Divya, Sanjay here. How are you? You must be tired after your journey so I won't talk for long. Please let me know if you need anything. Do you have enough cash?" then… not waiting for an answer, "I will send you some money tomorrow."

Worried about her being on her own again he needed reassurance that she was okay – mentally and, yes, financially.

"No thanks, Sanjay, I am okay. I promise I will ask you if I need anything," she said wanting to end the conversation quickly.

But, knowing that she would never ask anyone for anything, he said he would send her a blank cheque first thing in the morning.

"I leave it to you to fill in the amount you need."

So much faith in her… so much concern.

"I could have taken you to the cleaners. Filled in your cheque, emptied your account and become a rich woman," she told him much later.

But at that moment he was touching her freshly exposed nerves. She couldn't take it anymore. Anger, exhaustion, despair, self-pity… the gamut of emotions boiling and bubbling inside her, finally gushed out. She broke down.

"Why aren't you listening to me?!" She wept angrily, "I'm telling you I don't need anything!"

She banged the phone down before he could say anything. She was all by herself, with her worries and fears. Standing there she let the tears flow unabated… unseen. She stared at the phone in delayed regret for what she had done. It was unpardonable to displace her feelings in this way.

Is this how you repay true friendship? He was only trying to help, she silently reprimanded herself. She needed to apologise for her unacceptable behaviour. He would understand and forgive her. As she reached for the phone, her mobile phone beeped.

A message from Sanjay. "I am sorry. It's just that I love you and can't bear to see you hurting this way."

Wham!! She felt as if she had been torpedoed! Too weak to move, Divya sat on the floor and stared at the screen of the phone for a long time as if it were a time bomb, ready to explode! She read the message again and again. Why? How? When?

"What's wrong with him? This can't be happening to me!"

A million questions flashed through her mind, chasing each other in a frenzied whirlwind. No answers. She had no one to turn to. She couldn't talk about her unusual situation to anyone but him!! She needed to talk to him and get this straightened out.

"It's true," he stated seriously, when she called him up. "I do love you."

For once Divya had nothing to say to him. She was at a loss for words. Her superego took over.

"It is not right. We need to meet and work this out," she said shakily, playing for time to sort out her thoughts.

Always eager to meet her, he readily agreed. "Let's meet at the Club at eleven."

Divya reached the Club the next day, on the dot of eleven. Sitting under a tree in the manicured lawn, she nervously waited for him. *What should I say? What would he say? How should I behave?* Her stomach churned in apprehension as she saw his familiar tall figure striding across the greens.

"Hi, Divya! Sorry I'm late. I got stuck in a jam." He spoke naturally as if nothing had happened.

Maybe she was overreacting. Maybe he was just pulling her leg. She felt foolish and embarrassed. For the first time in his company she felt awkward and was at a loss for words.

"Lemonade?"

She nodded silently as he called the waiter and ordered two drinks. Staring at him, trying to gauge his mood, she was in a quandary.

"Hey, are you okay? What's wrong?" worry filtered into his voice as her silence registered.

The floodgates of her tightly reined emotions burst open.

"How can you behave as if there's nothing wrong? How can you just sit there and act normal and order lemonade after what you said last night?"

Yes, after a sleepless night, she sure was upset.

"I am sorry, dear. I know Ravi's operations have taken their toll on you. The last thing I want to do is add to that and be the cause of your distress. I know it must have come as a surprise to you but it is something I have no control over." He admitted in a voice as gentle as always, trying to calm her down.

"Okay," she said reaching for the lemonade, her mouth suddenly dry. "I'm all ears."

And then Sanjay opened his heart to her. The warm winter sun filtered through the leaves as she listened to him in stunned silence. With each word he uttered she could feel their chemistry changing.

"It must be so tough for him to expose his deepest emotions, risking ridicule and rejection," was her first thought as he stared into her eyes and bared his soul.

"No, I cannot accept this. This is crazy and has no future. You are crazy... There are too many people involved who would get hurt." She desperately tried to make him see reason.

Pat came his reply... "The question of your acceptance doesn't arise. I have loved you for years... silently, from afar and I will continue loving you regardless... You cannot stop me from feeling this way about you."

It was overwhelming, superseding anything she had ever experienced in her life. If there is anything such as true unconditional love, this is it. She tried her best to dissuade him...

"I could take your love, use you and then drop you. Just like that!" she said trying to put the fear of rejection in him.

But he laughed at this femme fatale image of her that she had tried to rustle up.

"I could hurt you and ruin you," she continued seriously, ignoring his amused look of disbelief.

"But why? Why now? Why have you kept silent all these years and decided to tell me now?!"

"I just couldn't stand it anymore. I couldn't bear to see your suffering and pain. I wanted you to know that I am there for you. I wish I could protect you from your life."

She tried her best but failed to convince him about the futility of it all. She didn't want to lose a friend. She didn't want him to get hurt, he was too special. Suddenly she felt unsure of herself. Like a teenager out on her first date being wooed! Nervously she twirled the straw in her fingers as he held her gaze and in his honest, straightforward way, continued to speak of his love for her.

How he hurt inside every time life dealt her a raw deal (and there were many of these). How he wished he could take away her pain. How he was sure his love would help her through the darkest phase of her life... and give her strength and sustenance. How the guilt of his feelings for her kept him awake at nights because he cherished his friendship with Ravi. How he had never loved anyone like this before. How he wished things could have been different. How he would love her till he died…

Divya went home in a daze, not knowing what had hit her. She vented her feelings in her diary…

Is it so easy to get swayed? Is this another one of God's tests? I am so confused at the way things are happening – at the way my life is spinning out of control. Do I always have to be strong and rational? Why the hell can't I let go and bask in the glory of it all? I'm a coward! I'm so scared of doing something that could hurt so many people. It is so heart-wrenching to hear confessions of undying love – such a heady feeling – that the temptation's too strong. Resisting such emotions is going to be really tough. I'm human after all, with all my longings and desires, hurt and pain. Feelings of physical and emotional needs are immediately suppressed every time they rear their ugly heads. Ugly?? Well, no. Actually I feel they're ugly because I'm not able to handle them the way the world thinks I should. Am I not entitled to some happiness in this life? If I pass this test what will happen? Saint Divya?? Do I want to pass? Maybe I'll scrape through. But, God, I want you to remember one thing when you are evaluating my life on this earth – I did try, so go easy on me... Please!

******

Beset with a kaleidoscope of emotions and thoughts, she had no answers to the questions that inundated her mind. Sanjay's simple and candid confession was like a streak of lightening cutting through the dark clouds that were covering and hiding her blue skies. Providing light, yet fracturing her protective shield at the same time. It

290

seemed strange to think of such a silent, one-sided love. What kept that love alive inside him for so many years? Wasn't unrequited love supposed to simply fizzle out and die a quiet unheralded death? Despite her staple diet of mushy romantic novels, filled with declarations of undying love, Sanjay's kind of love was something new to her. Bewildered and shaken, angry and anxious, she reacted violently to his confession. She did not want to step out of the numbing comfort zone she had so diligently created around her. She did not know how to handle ripples in her secure well... and this was more like a tidal wave!

Who gave you the right anyway??
To rekindle the dying embers
in my heart
and fan them
with your pure love?
To make me laugh again
and fill my darkness
with your light?
To make me cry silently
at your honesty
and the sheer futility
of it all?
To put me on this emotional roller coaster
with no one
to hold on to?
To create so much havoc
in my life
and then sit back

and watch me
spiral out of control?
Who gave you that right?

She began having intense conversations, or rather arguments, with herself, with schizophrenic undertones! Pendulum-like, she swung from acceptance to rejection and denial and then back again. Her life was going through its roughest patch, there seemed to be no light at the end of the tunnel. She was blinkered by her circumstances – perhaps for her own good and sanity. Her life with its array of problems demanded her complete, undivided attention. She was juggling the fragile crystal balls of her existence. Maybe she should have dropped a few along the way and lightened her load a little. But, instead, she gathered more! She became an expert juggler and in the process developed tunnel vision. Missing everything going on around her, she was just concentrating on preventing each one from falling down and shattering into a million pieces.

She could not handle any complications at this point. Yes, he was a complication, she decided. Yes, she liked him… very much… but did she love him?? "What is love anyway?" said the cynic in her. No, she did not want to be the cause of hurt to so many people. His family, her family. And what about the guilt factor? Her deeply ingrained catholic values were up in arms ready to battle with her irrational need for love. She was confused. Scenes from the film 'Ryan's Daughter' swept through her mind when the heroine's head is tonsured (as a punishment doled out by the villagers for her adultery). She would be an adulteress… a sinner… a home-breaker. This couldn't be happening to her… a wife (for whatever it was worth) and a mother. At forty-five, she was supposed to be satisfied getting her emotional fulfilment from books (the mush that she lapped up greedily). And what about her physical needs? Celibacy was a state she had learnt to accept. She had no choice, so she did not question it.

Introspection

Life carried on around her as if nothing had happened. Night turned into day and day into night, ignoring her earth-shattering dilemma. Her life was on autopilot. She continued breathing in and exhaling, eating and drinking, sleeping and waking up to face another day. She prayed for guidance. For strength.

Ravi and Tanya called every day.

"Are you okay?" An innocent question that released so much guilt. But why did she feel guilty? Sanjay was the one who was in love with her!

"Remember to take your blood pressure medicine every morning."

"Don't forget to lock all the doors at night. It's not safe these days."

They worried about her living all alone. What if someone broke in, burgled the flat and knocked her unconscious? Or worse still stabbed her to death? But that should have been the least of their fears. Someone had actually broken into the hardened shell of her heart, knocking her senseless. She had her own set of worries. The emotional storm in her mind was tossing her around heartlessly while she struggled without a life belt to keep her head above water.

She did something that she had not done in years… she stood in front of the mirror and looked closely at her reflection. What did Sanjay see that was so different from what the mirror had to say?

"You are so beautiful," his words rang in her ears.

Although he appreciated Divya's looks, her body image of herself was very low. She did not think that she was remotely attractive. "Don't think you are Miss India" Varun's words rang in her ears.

Maybe it's my profile that attracts him, she thought, turning this way and that, going cross-eyed trying to get a side view of herself.

Maybe my figure turns him on, she thought, eyeing herself sceptically.

All she saw was a wrinkled, greying woman with sagging breasts (that had failed the 'pencil test' miserably – a pencil box would probably fall but a pencil would definitely stay secure under them!) and a healthy middle-age spread. What could he possibly see in her?

She analysed and introspected, fretted and fumed. She went through various emotional stages before, mentally exhausted, she finally reached a reluctant acceptance.

Denial. No it's wrong. They were both married. She had her responsibilities towards Ravi and Tanya. She simply could not encourage this.

Anger. How could he stir up a hornet's nest of emotions that she had so successfully repressed and hidden in the deepest dungeon of her mind? Why didn't he just leave her alone?

Fear. Would she be able to handle the momentous opening of her Pandora's box of passion? Would she be able to take it in her stride or would she get swept away?

Relief. Yes, she was still attractive as a woman to someone and worthy of love.

Through all her turmoil, while she was tying herself up in Gordian knots, Sanjay remained calm, like a pillar. He was amused by the havoc he had created in her life! In a way he had partly achieved what he had planned... diverted her mind from the burden of problems that were suffocating her. He had energised her — made her want to 'live' again. He just stated his feelings and sat back with his arms folded, watching her spin dizzily out of control.

Don't do this to me
I cry in despair
Do it! Do it!
Life's oh so unfair!
Don't break down this wall
I've built in my pain
Tear it down and help me
Learn to love again.
Many lives will get hurt
If I give in to you
But I'll lose out on love
That's so pure and so true
Let me be on my own
Like I've been for so long
Let me rest on your shoulders
I'm tired of being strong.

The Kiss

Tossing her dilemma aside, fate decided to take the matter out of her hands. As luck would have it, Divya needed help urgently with some important paperwork. Ravi usually handled their income tax work. A novice in such financial matters, she had no clue what to do. So she called up Sanjay for advice. He would definitely know what she should do. He could only come late at night, he said, after his last patient left.

"I hope that's not a problem, Divya," he said, "I know you go to bed early."

"Of course it won't be a problem," she reassured him. "Come whenever you can. My beauty sleep can wait. I need to get this issue sorted out as soon as possible."

Though there was a palpable change in their relationship since his declaration of love, Divya tried to act as normal as possible when he came that evening. After all, he was still her dear friend and she liked him very much. They sat and talked about how to sort out the financial issue and he gave her the name of an accountant who would be able to help her in future. Once her problem was out of the way they relaxed, listened to some music and had a couple of drinks. She was pondering on whether to ask him to stay for dinner when he glanced at his watch.

"Goodness! I hadn't realised how late it is! I am so sorry." He apologised, standing up and knocking back his drink in a quick gulp. "I'd better be going now."

She agreed. It was late indeed.

"Thanks so much for your help, Sanjay," she said moving forward to open the door. "I don't know what I would have done without you."

With amazing precision, he caught hold of her hand and swung her around, straight into his arms. A perfect pirouette! Not giving her time to recover from her centrifugal spin, he kissed her, long and deep, setting her senses off in a counter spin!

"Sanjay!" she gasped, when he released her for air, "I think you better go home now."

Not giving him any time to react, she turned him around and pushed him out of the door with all her strength. Hurriedly shutting the door, she leaned against the wall unable to stand. Weak with emotions she had forgotten existed. She was scared. But, to her surprise, the fear was heavy with relief! Yes, she could still feel a strange sensation deep down inside. A pleasurable, tingling sensation. Yes, there still was a woman alive in her. And then piggy-backing on this awareness, came *guilt*! With trembling fingers she picked up her cell phone and began typing out a message. Her fingers were too slow for her rush of thoughts… how he should never have done what he did. How he was ruining their friendship. But he beat her to it. Before she could complete the message, he called.

"I am really sorry. I hope you are okay."

"You should be sorry, Sanjay, but you don't sound sorry in the least," she said in her sternest, 'convent school' voice.

He laughed! Here she was seriously contemplating the situation and he laughed! How *could* he?

"I love you very much, Divya. And you're right, I'm not sorry. I could kiss you again… and again," he said in a deep, serious voice that made a weak-kneed Divya hurriedly lean against the wall before she collapsed in a heap again!

As direct and disarming as always! How could she resist? She was fighting a losing battle!

I remember
the look on your face
as you spoke of your love –
old and concealed…
now vulnerable and revealed.
I hear
the subtle nuances
of your words
as they break free…
overpowering my questioning mind
with your honesty.
I feel
the gentle touch
of your hands
wiping my eyes…
tears brought on by a
maelstrom of emotions
released
by your love.
I see

the unspoken passion
in your eyes
as silent whispers
from my heart
mingle with
the stark reality
of your thoughts.
Remembering...
hearing...
feeling...
seeing...
I live
in a perpetual state
of
expectation, longing and
love.

He had patiently been chipping away the walls of the fortress she had erected around her. But that kiss was her undoing! It was the stick of dynamite that blew a huge hole in her bastion walls! He gave her no choice – and actually, to be honest, she had stopped looking hard enough for excuses. With each of his text messages, phone calls and visits, the intensity of her resistance decreased.

Another Birthday

Divya's birthday came and with it a free-floating anxiety. Tanya and Ravi called from Delhi to wish her. It was bright and early in the morning.

"Happy Birthday, Mummy! What are you doing? Did you sleep well? Did I wake you up? I miss you." A bubbly stream of words gushed through the telegraph lines.

"Happy Birthday, Divya!" Ravi's subdued greeting.

They were on speakerphone and their voices sang in a duet of emotions.

Tanya's cheerful tone lifted her sprits. Ravi's voice was laced with pain, reflecting his despair and her heart went out to him.

"Thank you, thank you! I was just hanging about in bed, snug under my quilt, waiting for your call." Divya injected a shot of enthusiasm in her response. "Have you started climbing up stairs yet?" She was eager to hear about some improvement in his condition.

"Only when the physiotherapist comes," he said. "Each step is unbearably painful and I get so exhausted by the end of it. I miss you and I miss home. I'm tired of living like this." He was getting frustrated and homesick.

"Just think, soon you'll be able to climb stairs on your own," she said encouragingly. "I know you're missing home but please don't rush back till you can walk on your own and climb stairs with ease. You still need regular physiotherapy."

Divya put the phone down unable to pinpoint the cause for her restless feeling. This was her reality. This was what she should be focusing on. Not Sanjay. Definitely not matters of the heart. She was all alone and dejected. She did not feel like celebrating. She'd managed to dissuade her friends from dropping in. Lying listlessly on her bed, she put in six CDs on a loop so that she could read and listen to non-stop music without having to get up. Consoling herself that it was just a day like any other day, she closed her eyes and lost herself to the hypnotic melody of the London Philharmonic Orchestra. She slept the deep sleep of the exhausted mind. When her eyes opened to the shrill ring of the doorbell, it was dark. Switching on the lamp she couldn't believe her eyes! The clock showed 7 pm. She had slept for four whole hours! The music was still playing. Norah Jones.

Must be Gita. I forgot to tell her not to come, she thought, getting out of bed, angry with herself at this supposed oversight.

Gita was not only a dear friend but also a pillar Divya often leaned on. Thinking of how she had helped her buy maternity clothes eighteen years ago, she allowed herself a small smile. But even though she was special, Divya wasn't ready for company. She was in a brooding and insular mood.

"Coming! Coming!" she yelled over the dreamy voice of Norah Jones, as the bell rang again.

Switching on the light in the entrance, she peered through the 'magic eye' in the door and saw Sanjay standing there, laden with gifts!

"Oh my God! I should have known he would come," she chided myself. "I hope I am looking presentable enough."

She was wearing a faded pair of jeans with a soft grey sweater that Tanya had sent for her birthday. Conscious of her clothes and dishevelled appearance, Divya opened the door just as his finger was moving towards the bell for the third time.

"Ah! I was beginning to wonder whether you were at home or not. Sorry to drop in unannounced but I was passing this way and thought I'd take a chance," he said as she ushered him in. "Happy Birthday, my dear!"

"Why were you sitting in the dark?" he asked putting the colourfully wrapped gifts on the centre table.

"I fell off to sleep listening to music."

The soft glow of the entrance light vanished as she switched on the lights in the living room.

"Come. Sit." She blinked at the sudden assault of brightness on her eyes.

"Thanks." He settled down on the low sofa, adjusting the cushion to make more space for his large frame.

For an unbearably long moment an awkward silence hung between them like a thick curtain. And then they spoke together, as if on cue.

"So what did you do today?" he said, clearing his throat.

"How nice of you to come," was her inane comment.

Staring at each other at the absurdity of their stilted conversation, they burst out laughing. They were behaving stupidly. They were friends after all! The curtain lifted.

"Sorry but I don't have anything to offer you." Divya apologised, suddenly remembering her Mother Hubbard status. Her larder was bare!

"I don't even have any birthday cake."

"I thought as much," Sanjay said. "That's why I picked up a small cake on the way."

He whipped out a chocolate cake from a cardboard box, like a magician.

"WOW! Kookie Jar! I love their confectioneries."

"I hope you don't mind my taking such liberties like this."

"Oh, Sanjay! How could I possibly mind? This is such a sweet and thoughtful gesture! Thanks ever so much." Suddenly her wilted spirits were blossoming again.

As they chatted, Neil Diamond took over from Norah and started singing "Juliet" in his to-die-for deep voice. Divya jumped up impulsively, grabbed his hand and pulled him out of his chair, catching him unawares.

What the heck, she thought, *It's my birthday!*

"This is one of my favourite songs. Let's dance," she said, holding his shoulders lightly with her fingertips. It had been ages since she'd danced with anyone.

She was short. Bare-footed on the carpet, standing on tiptoes, she barely reached his shoulders. She felt his hand move gently but firmly up her back as he drew her closer. Stiff and conscious of this sudden proximity, she cursed her impetuousness. But it was too late! The moment took over. Taking the path of least resistance she gave in. Melting in his arms, she rested her head against the firm cushion of his chest. Yes, this is what she had longed for. It felt so good. His warm breath of love filled the lacuna in her heart. They close danced slowly to every song after that, regardless of the beat. Rock & roll or slow love songs – they dance cheek to cheek! Actually, they didn't even need the music for they didn't notice when it stopped. They didn't talk. Words were redundant. They danced the evening away. And that was one of the best birthdays she had have ever had!

Thoughts entwined
Restless fingers
Send messages
Of love
Steps forgotten
We stand
Swayed by passion
The music takes over
And then
The silence.
Come...
let me be your wings
Let me take you
to greater heights
Unknown
Unreached...
Let me set you free
Free to chase the stars
hug a cloud.

Love-struck

Divya closed her favourite book, 'Bridges of Madison County', with tears in her eyes. So moving, yet such a simple love story. Such refreshing, 'straight from the heart' honesty. *Everyone should read this book*, she thought with conviction. *She* was reading it for the third time. Many of her friends had scoffed at the 'silly sentimentality' of it, but she was unmoved and firm in her admiration of the story. She had even bought the film with her favourite actors – Clint Eastwood and Meryl Streep in it, and seen it a couple of times. Being a die-hard romantic, she had read many love stories, but this one was different... so pure and satisfying. It struck a chord in her heart that vibrated for a long time... in rhythm with the music of her heart. She could relate to it so well.

Profound thoughts filled her mind. Why do people belittle stories of love these days? Why has love become something to hide away? Why are we ashamed of acknowledging the gentle tenderness that love brings our way? It set her thinking about Sanjay and herself. No, this was not an ordinary relationship, she concluded. It went beyond the boundaries of earthly bonds. It was ethereal... surreal... yet real. He was so very special to her. He made *her* feel special.

Affecting her power of reasoning, love had dissolved her brain to mush. As if she had never loved before. As if no one knew what love was but she. Their relationship was unique... like no other had been or ever would be. Did everybody in love think this way? Surely not. Undoubtedly hers was the pure 24 carats. The Real McCoy... but the truth is what you feel, at any given moment in time. And she sincerely believed that Sanjay and she actually grew into "us" (just like Francesca and Robert from the book). He became so much an integral part of her life, present in her mind just like a Figure-ground Perception Test – ever present in the background but popping to the foreground at the slightest pretext!

Divya began to write poetry, as people in love generally do. The muse of love poems had turned its spotlight on her! How had she survived for so long in such a state of limbo? The floodgates of her barricaded repressions opened to the sound of trumpets. She was inundated with the cool, refreshing waters of new love. Life was beautiful once again.

Though the intensity of her problems did not change, she took on life with renewed zest and zeal... as if she had swallowed a whole bottle of pep pills!! She didn't know when the transition in her feelings exactly happened. All she knew was that suddenly she was feeling young and womanly and attractive... and loved. Her love for Sanjay was born in the darkest moment of her life, unconsciously fuelled by her desire to live, her need for solace and affection. It was nurtured by his deep love for her. He had liberated her from herself and helped her to shed her mantle of denial. He had cut her self-restraining shackles and set her free. Free... to be herself without fear; to be happy without guilt; to live without doubt; to celebrate the wonder of life. She was just one step away from becoming obsessive... about him.

At work, her concentration waxed and waned. At the slightest pretext, her thoughts flitted to him on gentle wings of fancy. She, this middle-aged professional, holding such a responsible post, started indulging in juvenile behaviour. During serious meetings she was at her delinquent best! All her doodles ended up looking like his name in modern art form. Freud would have had a field day analysing her works of art! Without any conscious effort on her part, she would write different adjectives beginning with 'S'… strong, silent, sensuous… her pen was uncontrollable. It had a life of its own. Her colleagues started commenting on the dreamy faraway look that had taken over her usual harried 'I-have-the-whole-world-on-my-shoulders' look.

******

One evening, Divya went to Sanjay's clinic on some half-baked pretext and felt a deep pleasure seeing him at his workplace… observing the professional side of him. Sanjay the paediatrician. The waiting room was full of babies and infants ensconced in the arms of accompanying adults. They were in pain, some distressed, some subdued, with different ailments. She could hear his calm, reassuring voice as he spoke to his 'little' patients, coming down to their level, making them smile.

I wouldn't mind falling ill if he was my doctor, she thought.

She sent in a short note with the nurse just before the last patient went in, to inform him of her presence. Immediately his head popped out of his room for a second.

"What a wonderful surprise! I'll meet you downstairs in five minutes."

Later, standing at the corner of the road, waiting for him to come down, Divya was suddenly overcome by apprehension and guilt – unsure of her actions and herself.

What's wrong with me? What the hell am I doing? A married woman, a mother, waiting for her date??! My daughter should be doing this, not me!

She was all set to hail the first taxi that came her way and rush back home.

I'll SMS my explanation for my hurried disappearance and surely he'd understand, she thought as she stepped off the pavement, waving to stop a cab trundling in her direction.

Then she saw him striding confidently towards her. He waved as soon as he saw her, assuming that she was waving at him.

Uh oh! Too late! she thought, feeling tense and relieved at the same time. *I guess it's meant to be.*

The cloak of depression and doubt that fell heavily on her quickly dissipated as they greeted each other with a smile.

"Sorry to keep you waiting, Divya. Gosh! It's been a long day. I need a drink."

Holding her elbow, he steered her to the nearest bar. After her first few sips of Bloody Mary she could feel the tension slip away. Their chats were interspersed with silence. A comfortable silence. A silence neither felt any need to fill. It was just so reassuring to be with him. The evening was over too soon.

******

With the proclamation of his love, everything changed between them. Naturally. The guilt and apprehension made it an erratic journey… one step forwards, two steps back. "Sealed with a kiss" took on its literal meaning… their kisses sealed the change in their relationship forever. There was an unspoken rule regarding this change. A rule that they adopted naturally, unquestioningly. No longer could she call him up at home, just to have a long chat. He hesitated to call her up too.

It was their guilt that was the catalyst. And that's what Divya had feared. It was sad, for in a way she had lost a dear friend. But she had gained true love. You win some, you lose some…

She eagerly started looking forward to Saturdays when he would take her out for a drink or a quick lunch. Sitting in a cafe, reading a book she would wait for his call, checking her mobile phone every now and then.

"Reaching in five minutes" his SMS would flash on her screen, or "Sorry, caught in an emergency will meet in 30 minutes" and she'd order another coffee, thankful she had her book to keep her company.

A strange nervous tension would flow through her as she waited for him. A trepidation that eased the minute they were together. They did strange, juvenile things like crossing the same road a couple of times, just so that they could hold hands while crossing! The firm pressure of his long artistic fingers, wrapped around her slender ones, would increase whenever he looked at her. A silent message of love spoken by his eyes, expressed through his hands. The gentle massage of the ball of his thumb on the back of her hand left a tingling trail on her hypersensitive skin. Hands can convey such secret heartfelt desires!

They perfected the art of driving with one hand… one hand on the steering wheel, the other in a hand lock! Whether it was Sanjay's or hers – the car became their space… their oasis in the chaotic world. She could block out her reality with a slam of the door. How she wished that their long drives would never end... that they could live out the cliché and keep on driving into the sunset.

Thankfully Divya had come a long way from her childhood fear of driving! She actually enjoyed driving now and loved it increasingly more because she could always feel Sanjay's presence in the car, the pressure of his hand over hers as she changed gears. She could imagine him leaning against the window just staring at her with his deep dark eyes.

Another highlight of their drives was the traffic light. Red lights meant positioning the car strategically between two vehicles so that occupants of neighbouring cars could not indulge in the entertaining, voyeuristic activity of peering in!! That's when they would share whatever little tokens of love they had picked up for each other!

"See, I've got the latest Robbie Williams CD for you."

"I got this book for you – promise you'll read it?!"

But there was also a risk of driving with Sanjay... the distraction of proximity.

"Oh no," Divya disentangled her hand from his as she watched a policeman signal her to stop. "I didn't realise there was a traffic light there," she said in dismay, steering the car to the side.

"Yes, madam," the cop bent over his huge paunch to peer inside the window. "Where were you looking? You drove through the red light."

"I am really sorry, bhai, my brother," she pleaded, hoping the "brother" bit would work. "I promise it won't happen again."

"You should see that your wife drives properly," the cop rebuked Sanjay, who in turn promised to do so, with a smirk on his face.

"I'm letting you off this time," he relented after Sanjay's assurance that she would follow all traffic rules.

"Thank you, bhai!" The relief in her voice shone on her face.

"It's all your fault," she blamed a giggling Sanjay as she drove off. "You were distracting me with your stares. You are forbidden to look at me when I drive!"

She was a challenge to his self-control and will power. But he handled it well and never pushed her to do something she was not emotionally ready for. Both of them knew that they were stuck in a situation from which it was impossible to extricate themselves. Restrained by the seatbelts of conscience, they carried on in this frustrating-yet-in-a-way-fulfilling fashion… wanting more and more, yet happy with the precious time they got to spend with one another.

Ravi Returns

Ravi came back from Delhi, accompanied by Ma ji. He was still weak after his second surgery and not completely healed. But he needed to get back to the secure familiarity of his home. At the airport, Divya waited for him to come out. It broke her heart when she saw him. He was in a wheelchair pushed by an airport attendant. Ma ji followed close behind walking as fast as she could, trying to keep pace with them. Though he looked healthy, Divya could see from his face that Ravi was still in a lot of pain.

"Welcome home," she said rushing forward to hug him and then Ma ji.

She first opened the car door for Ma ji so that she could sit in the back seat of the car and then turned her attention to Ravi. Trying her best not to hurt his bandaged leg, she managed to get him off the wheelchair. Taking all his weight on her shoulders she struggled to help him get into the car.

Meanwhile a small crowd had gathered. A crowd of bored people waiting for their friends or relatives to arrive from different parts of the world. A crowd of people that stood and watched dispassionately as a woman struggled to help a disabled man into a car. A silent crowd of impotent spectators. It took a while and a lot of backbreaking effort to manoeuvre Ravi onto the car seat. As she shut the door, the crowd slowly dispersed, not interested anymore. Divya felt like shouting, "The show's over." One shouldn't expect any help from anyone, she thought sadly as she got in next to Ravi.

"It's so good to be back home," he said as she fixed his seat belt and then hers before turning the ignition. The engine purred gently into life.

"It's great to have you back," she responded, lightly touching his shoulder and then shifting the gear from neutral to first.

"Never thought I'd miss Kolkata so much."

They talked about Tanya for the rest of the journey. She would miss her papa and grandmother extremely. Ravi was already missing her so much. She was like a vibrant breath of fresh air in his static life. Had her college exams not been round the corner, she would definitely have accompanied him to Kolkata. Finally they reached home but they had to get him to the first floor.

With the help of the building 'durwans' Ravi was seated on a chair and carried upstairs. He sat at an angle, on the edge of the seat – for his body was like a plank of wood – unbending and stiff. His face was lined with pain and exhaustion. Apprehensively he held on to the arms of the chair. He hated this complete dependence on others. What if they dropped him? He would not be able to save himself. Divya's heart went out to him. But there was very little she could do.

"Please be careful you hold the chair tight. Don't hurt his bandaged leg," Divya instructed, anxious about the turns in the staircase. "Don't worry, Ravi, I'm here behind you."

He was pleased and touched to see the living room. She had decorated it with colourful bouquets of fragrant flowers to welcome him home. He looked around. Relief momentarily flooded his flushed face. He was home. His

314

home. It was good to be back to the place of his birth. He had been away for three long, agonising months.

"Come lie down you must be exhausted after your long journey."

She helped him on to the bed and went to the kitchen to make tea for everyone. Forcing herself to push Sanjay out of her mind, she gave Ravi her whole attention. He needed her.

******

Three days later a wound on his hip that had not healed properly started oozing . That's when all hell broke loose and the clouds of depression that had been kept at bay blocked their sunshine again. Frantic calls were made to the doctor in Delhi. History was repeating itself.

"Keep it covered," was the doctor's stopgap advice. "Change the bandage regularly and keep the wound clean."

But long-distance treatment was useless. He needed help. Immediate help from a physically present doctor, not one at the other end of a telephone line. Divya managed to contact an experienced local doctor who, though very busy, agreed to come.

"I can come but my driver's on leave," said Dr Mitra. "So would it be possible for you to arrange transport for me?"

"Yes, yes, doctor," she said in a relief-filled voice.

"Okay. Great. I can come only at 10 pm."

"No problem, Dr Mitra. I will come and pick you up."

She was willing to promise him the moon. They desperately needed his intervention and advice. She went and picked him up from his clinic late at night. After a

315

thorough examination, antibiotics and ointments were prescribed.

"His wound needs to be cleaned and the dressing done every day. We can't afford to let this infection spread," he told Divya in the car as she dropped him back home.

When the discharge showed no signs of abating, Dr Mitra decided to operate yet again.

"I want to remove a wire in Ravi's hip implant that I feel is causing this problem. I know that giving him anaesthesia is an issue. But don't worry I will call a very experienced anaesthetist to assist me."

The hospital, that he was attached to, was miles away from their house. It was in Howrah, across the River Hooghly. But there was no alternative. It had to be done... and Divya was the one who had to do it.

"The doc says that it's just a minor operation," she tried to reassure Ravi as he dejectedly got prepared for yet another surgery. She organised an ambulance to take him to the hospital while she and Ma ji followed in her car. He was to be operated the next morning.

They reached the hospital an hour before the operation was scheduled to start.

"This is it!" Divya hugged him as he was being wheeled out of the room. "Just think that this is going to be the last operation you have to undergo. Once Dr Mitra takes out that wire everything'll be okay." Ravi nodded silently, his eyes trying to believe her.

They waited outside the operation theatre for three hours. They sat in silence, lost in their thoughts. The OT doors swung open and Dr Mitra strode out still in his operating gown. The green mask dangled around his neck.

"Ravi's absolutely okay," he answered the question in their eyes, as they stood up to meet him.

"Thank God," Ma ji said, exhaling the breath she had been holding on to for so long.

"Here," he said giving Divya a thick, twisted shiny wire. "We took this out of Ravi's hip. Keep it as a souvenir. Hopefully he will be better now."

******

Every evening, after work Divya drove down to the hospital to see Ravi and meet Dr Mitra. Her mood would swing from hope to despair, waxing and waning, depending on Ravi's state of mind and physical status and the doctor's feedback. Together with that, the long drive during rush hour was fatiguing. There were days when she was so mentally and physically drained that she felt like throwing in the proverbial towel. She turned to Sanjay for the positive strokes that he so enthusiastically gave.

"Hey, that's not fair… you can't think of throwing in the towel… though I would love to see you without it!" messaged Sanjay, making her smile.

She was so caught up in her crazy schedule that they hadn't met in what seemed like an eternity.

"I love you so much and I'm so proud of your courage to get back to reality… you epitomise goodness. But I know how many tears you have within you. I love you too much to see you suffer. I admire your inner strength."

He was always there ready with his messages and phone calls, boosting her flagging morale, giving her the strength to carry on.

A week after the operation, Ravi's stitches were removed. Divya took leave from work, arranged an ambulance and brought him back home again.

"Don't worry I will send someone to do his dressing on every alternate day. His wound should dry up soon and the oozing will stop," Dr Mitra reassured them.

Though glad to be out of hospital, the numerous operations had taken their toll on Ravi. "When will all this end? I am fed up of my condition!"

He was weakening – physically as well as mentally. Anyone would. It was too much trauma for a person to withstand.

"You can't give up, Ravi. You have to keep fighting. Miracles do happen."

Divya tried her best to keep his flame of hope burning but it was affecting her too. She was burning out. Removing that wire did not help. The wound did not dry and the oozing continued. Along with the pus, it was as if his strength and spirit was oozing out too.

A Love Divine

Sanjay helplessly watched her struggle. Often he had to pull her out from the abysmal depths of dejection that she allowed herself to sink into. He made her laugh and let her cry. He was her guardian angel. Without him she would have given up and vanished from the face of this earth!

So what if they couldn't meet as often as they wanted to? They vented their feelings, shared their guilt and doubts, bared their souls and kept their love alive through emails…

My S

I know you don't really like it when I get all sentimental, but you've got to allow me just this once! Let it all be here in black and white for you to read again and again… and remember how much you've helped me. I mean each and every word I'm about to write, even though it may sound rather dramatic.

I want to thank you for not giving up on me. For persevering in your endeavour to break down the wall I had built around me. Relentlessly, you took down brick by brick, brushing aside my resistance and all my attempts to stall you. … You made me feel like a woman again – desirable and beautiful! I know initially I resisted but it was because I did not want to create any ripples in my dull and complacent existence.

Yes, it was a mere existence because what the world saw of me and the 'true me' were poles apart. I'd stopped expecting anything from my life and had become this accepting, unquestioning, boring person. Then you happened to me!! You stormed into my world and set me free... from myself. You gave me hope that in spite of what life was dishing out to me, I would still find happiness. You pulled me out from the bottomless pit of despair I was sinking in and gave me the strength, in your own quiet and gentle way, to face life. You gave me the courage to carry on. At times when I felt I couldn't take it anymore, you had faith in my ability to cope. You have helped me through so much and have always been there to pick up the pieces every time I fell apart. You made me whole again with your amazing, sincere love. This is just the tip of the iceberg of how much you've done for my bruised and battered soul. I could write volumes about this and would probably run out of paper and ink!

But do you realise the implications of what you've done??? I'm sure you do and that you are scared and worried about what's happening. Well so am I! But there's no going back now, is there? I often wonder what the next chapter of our story will be. Whatever it may be, you must always remember that you have a very special place in my heart – and you always will. This love I have for you was born out of your pure love for me and it grows stronger with the passing of each day. I selfishly take all that you have to offer, but I'm greedy and I keep wanting more! How much I have given you in return, however, is one big question mark! But you never complain, do you? You just keep giving of yourself, expecting nothing in return.

I'm learning not to fight the flow of life and am selfish about things that bring me joy... and you happen to be one of my main sources of happiness!! I am fortunate and blessed that you came into my life and filled it with your love. Thank you.

Goodbye for now, my love.

Take Care. D

Dearest D,

You are right when you say that I was part of a process... perhaps all through this relationship I was always hoping you will find some inner strength (like you did in the past), to cope up with all the setbacks in your life. I was also beginning to get involved in this process, as it was more than fascinating to get to know someone with such a beautiful mind (not to mention looks!). To confess, at times I felt so miserably sorry, for your state of being (I know how you hate the word) that I would yearn to give you few moments of wonder happiness... so that you could get back to playing the role you are destined to play in life. Perhaps I am responsible for it all, and my sudden stoic bursts of silence did not last long enough. I knew that I was getting you in a tailspin and you were slowly "spiralling out of control" and yet, I did nothing to control myself.

You know, I am not a rationalist or a conformist... and I shall continue my journey as a seeker and as a dreamer, I assure you of that. And, D, you have been a source of limitless love, direction, light and energy...

I thank you for taking me through this process... perhaps I was destined to go through these moments, however traumatic they may be...

I love you...

S

Dearest S

My day has been a bit hectic till now (and its only 1 pm!!). But then it's Saturday... this baby's day out!!! I went to collect my plane ticket – am going to Delhi first on 1st. Oct and back on 9th. (conference) and then on 21st. and back on 5th Nov (holiday). Haven't told R about conf. yet. Shall tell him on Monday! Then I went for a haircut. Was looking like Engelbert Humperdinck before – am now looking like Dev Anand!!! After this I'm having lunch with a friend and rushing back by 4 pm to meet another friend who's coming for tea.

So you see my Saturday is going to be just the way I like it – action packed!!

Love you, darling

D

Dearest D,

I know I need to respond to you more often... I'm sure you will excuse me again for being too involved with my life ... but that's just the way it is for the moment.

... you know, D, you are a very special person and yet I do not give you the hug you deserve... perhaps in the wisdom of my foolishness I shall realise that every sunset has its own special expression, even if you miss a few with the hope that there shall be many more to follow... I cannot possess you and yet I can... that's the wonder of this relationship... it supersedes physical, emotional and mental desires... it's sublime and infinite...

I will keep loving you till I die... perhaps at times silently ... and perhaps at times overtly... in the glass capsule of our journey...

I love you and your poems...

S

Divya yearned to hear from Sanjay and hungrily read each message and email he sent, memorising each word, each emotion. His love was her oxygen. She couldn't get enough of it. She was beyond reason and logic. She knew there was no future in the relationship but then... what is 'Future'? What is 'Now'? There is no 'Now' because as soon as it's registered in your consciousness it joins the 'Past'. And future soon becomes 'Now'. Crazy philosophical thoughts rationalised the guilt, creating a skewed balance of emotions. She needed to get away from the magnetic power of his presence, yet she couldn't prise herself away. She was being sucked into the eddy of his love. Destiny stepped in and plucked a reluctant Divya out of her quandary. She was invited to present a paper at a conference in Delhi. The timing was perfect for her confused mind. She immersed herself in preparing her presentation. She loved going to Delhi because it gave her a chance to spend some time with Tanya. The thought of meeting her daughter and her parents lifted up her flagging spirits. Ravi reacted as expected, when he heard her travel plans.

"Why can't someone else present the paper? Why do you have to go to Delhi?" His insecurity reared its head up once again. But Divya was tired of being his crutch. She organised a nurse to look after him. Knowing that he was well looked after, she went.

My S

Sorry but this is a depressing mail!!

It was like a damn bursting. The minute I settled down in the car with my mother and Tanya on either side, I just broke down. All I needed to set me off was mum's hug and a kiss from Tanya and all those pent-up emotions that I had hoarded inside me for so long came gushing out! I wept copiously. No longer did I have to be this stoic, 'can-take-it-all' woman who is always in control.

Yes, it was cathartic for both Tanya and I and it had to happen at some point otherwise I would have gone mad! Tanya, bless her, was just amazing! I think we needed this release and though I felt lighter I had a migraine for the next couple of days!! We discussed life and death – knowing deep down inside that we have to be strong for the inevitable. I hate to think about it but I can see that Ravi's given up. I know that no one's immortal and it's difficult to talk about the impending death of a loved one... but then nobody should suffer like this. It is just so unfair. But then who am I to judge the fairness of life?? I'm certain there's a deeper meaning behind all this. Everybody's got their own cross to bear and no matter how much you love someone, you cannot take away the pain and despair, especially when you know that there is no hope.

Coming to terms with a situation like this is, needless to say, very tough... but then I am sure that there are many people who have had to face tougher situations than mine. Often I feel I'm not handling it well at all and that I can't cope anymore. But my guardian angel is always there for me – sending positive strokes and rekindling my faith in my coping abilities and strength!! I know I always end up thanking you in all my mails but then I can't help it! And anyway, words seem so insufficient and meaningless – I can't ever seem to find the right words to express the depth and intensity of my feelings for you. I can just hope and pray that you are fortunate enough to get a guardian angel like mine... to be there for you always.

I am sorry to have written such a depressing letter, especially when you are not feeling too well but I had to get it out of my system. And this is just one of the occupational hazards of being such a conscientious guardian angel (the other, more exciting hazards I shall come to later!). I sincerely hope you are feeling better now. I don't want to nag but I do wish you'd take some time off during your day to exercise, meditate and just look after yourself. That's one thing nobody else can do for you. So please put your health on the top of your priority list.

You are and will always be in my prayers. Take care for you are precious to me.

I promise my next mail will not be so morbid! I love you.

D

Dear D,

I wish I had your courage to confess my inner feelings... perhaps I am too scared of the consequences....... sadly... that's the way it is. Dearest, you are an incredible person and I love you and am not really ashamed... it's just my stupid guilt pangs which destroy these blissful moments, you know when I drop my defences and face the truth. I realise the enormity of the expression 'true love'!

I will embrace you
In silent cadence
Till I die.
And I too will slow dance...
Even in steps unmatched
And in broken harmony,
Till I die.
I will stare at you

Like a blind man
Searching within...
And
I will selfishly accept
your single moments
of abandon
Till I die.
I will
Wet in tryst
Stare at the crystal gaze
Of life's glass hour
In fullness!
And I will never die.
I love you.

S

My dearest S,

You are really and truly amazing!! I often wonder whether you are in the right profession or not 'cos you write so well. I am actually at a loss for words after reading your poem and will hold it close to my heart... always.

D

The short trip to Delhi was good for Divya, and for Tanya. It was her respite. It did not, however, affect her feelings for Sanjay... or his for her. If anything, it proved that absence does make the heart grow fonder.

Dearest D,
And I too will
let the cool summer breeze
flirt with
my still curtain (of day dreams)
and unwrap million folds of
joy
when memories of
a warm Sunday afternoon
Splurged in a
spiralling climax
In a moment of pulse
and then in the
quiet stillness
I rest my head softly
upon a bosom full of
kindness
in serene
quietness of release
I remain... asleep.
S.

All too soon Divya was back in Kolkata and it seemed as if she had never left. Miles away, in Delhi, Tanya fretted. The distance made it that much more difficult for her. Her father's suffering was too much for her to take. Unable to concentrate on her studies she would call up at night, and open up her heart to her mother. Her mind was a boiling pot of thoughts ridden with despair, worry and sorrow. Her inability to be physically near her father when he needed her depressed her no end.

"Mum, there are times when I feel that I'm not doing my duty as a daughter. I should be there with Papa. He needs me. You need me." Guilt, like an infectious virus, was attacking her too.

"Beti, you must never give up hope. Cling to it fiercely as long as you live. There is nothing without hope."

Pop phil. (popular philosophy) or rather "Mom Phil" as Tanya coined Divya's words of wisdom, was all she had to give her. Divya understood Tanya's feelings for they were a reflection of her own.

"You have to think of your future and your career, darling. Papa doesn't want you to give up everything and sit by his side."

She longed to give Tanya a reassuring hug and console her. But the miles stood between them. Tanya took to what she did best...Writing. She wrote long letters to her papa. Letters full of encouragement and hope. Witty and humorous letters that brought a smile on his pain-stricken face. Letters that wiped away the separating miles, making him feel her nearness though she was so far away.

"There's a letter for you from Tanya."

These words were enough to light up Ravi's eyes and pep up his despairing spirits. He'd put on his spectacles, which he kept near his pillow, and hold the pages in his weak, trembling hand. Scanning the pages, he read quickly, devouring each word like a starving man. After some time he'd read her letter again. Slowly. Savouring its flavour, its wit. Then he'd keep it under his pillow, within easy reach, to read again and again.

Both Divya and Ravi missed Tanya tremendously but they couldn't cling to her and keep her with them for their own selfish reasons. That would be as good as clipping her wings. They had to set her free, as they reluctantly did. And she flew. But unfortunately their circumstances did not let her soar carefree among the sun-streaked clouds, as she should have. The leaden anchor of paternal despair weighed her down.

Divya too was chained down to the gestalt of her life. Her reality kept pulling her down, holding her back every time she tried to spread her wings and fly. The distant, beckoning horizon taunted her as she clamped the lid tightly shut on her emotions. At times, she would masochistically let herself be flooded by the vanity of remorse. The only times she treated herself a few precious moments of freedom was when she was with Sanjay.

S Dearest,

I better warn you that I'm in a very introspective mood and all sorts of strange thoughts are going through my mind!!

You know me like a book you've read a thousand times... you can even read between my lines – and I'm not talking only about the lines on my palm!! You've seen me through so much of my chequered life, lifted my spirits when I was low and made me feel good about myself again. But sometimes I feel that I've been selfish and have been thinking only about myself – my needs, my doubts, my everything. I know you've got your share of problems to deal with (relating to work, health, family etc.) and what can I do for you? Have I ever been able to do anything for you... soothe you when you're troubled? Share your worries? But you know, if you ever need me in whatever way, I'll be there for you. Promise me you'll remember that? Promise?! Sorry for this strange mail... but I did warn you!

Knowing what you do to me...

you still hold back
as your superego takes
over
bound by life's mundane demands
stuck in a groove...
unable to break away
yet wanting to...?
And you let
simple pleasures slip by... untouched...
for you are trapped
in the nothingness
of your glass bowl
your free spirit
restrained...
subdued.
I long to pluck you out
free you
in the ocean of love.
But the eddy of your conscience
drags you away
pulling you to the safety
of your oystered bed.
But what of me??
I gather my dreams –
leaf by leaf –
green turning to brown...
brown crumbling to dust.

With all my love... D

Dearest D,

Even as I cling
to myself in outward calm
I seldom realise
that
I am but a coward
hiding behind a glass
fragile
and colourless
waiting to be broken
into a million fragments
of
meaningless pieces
so much like the
brown crumbling
dust...
Love me tonight while I dream of your beautiful self.
S

Dearest D,

...yes in life's journey these moments are to be remembered... moments of togetherness and distance... you may be right when you say that distance gives a much better perspective to life... especially when one has a very passionate and reaching mind. You dearest, epitomise the true intensity of love and passion... I love every moment I spend with you

Your
S

A Great Despair

Ravi underwent two more surgeries within the space of three months. But his problem still continued. He developed two more sores on his left leg. The discharge from these wounds flowed relentlessly. Their biggest nightmare was now confirmed. His body had rejected the implant. Osteomyelitis had set in. The infection was eating away his bones. It was as if the very essence of his life was flowing out of his wounds in a slow and steady stream. Dr Mitra too was despairing of the situation.

One evening soon after his last operation, Divya was getting ready to leave the hospital. Visiting time was over.

"Bye, Ravi. I'll come again tomorrow after work." She leaned across the bed and hugged him. "Sleep well."

She was dizzy with sheer exhaustion. She stumbled down the corridor bustling with relatives, who like her, were on their way out. As she stepped out of the main doors of the hospital, the nurse called her. She had a message from Dr Mitra. He needed to see her before she left. Resigning herself to the fact that she would now get stuck in heavy office rush, Divya turned back. Shaking her head to stop the escalating buzz, she ran her fingers through her hair and hurried to his room.

Must be wanting to discharge Ravi soon, she thought as she knocked on his door.

"Come in, Divya. I've been waiting for you." His voice was serious. "Please sit down."

Instantly she knew that she did not want to hear what he was going to say. She perched herself on the edge of the chair and apprehensively looked into his kind eyes. Clearing his throat, he broke their eye contact and looked away. Taking off his glasses, he rubbed his eyes, wearily.

"I don't know how to say this but I am sorry we can't help you here anymore. It is better that you take Ravi back to Delhi again."

Divya did not know what to say, how to react. She stared at him, his words still floating around in her tired mind.

"But, doctor..." she tried, frantically searching for words. But her static filled brain was receiving no signals. It was jammed.

"What'll I..." she made another attempt in a quavering voice.

"How can..."

But he held up his hand and silently stopped her. He wanted to finish what he had to say.

"We've tried our best but there is nothing more that we can do here." He repeated. "His body has rejected the implant that was put in when he was operated in Delhi. The infection is now spreading in his body. The doctor who did his operations in Delhi will know what line of action to take. Maybe he will remove the implant."

The drumming of his fingers on the table reverberated loudly in her head. What was he trying to tell her? That he was turning them away? That there was no hope? That Ravi would never be able to walk again? That... that...

"*Stop it!*" she wanted to scream as she stared at him aghast, uncomprehending for a while. She felt like reaching out and holding his hands to stop the machine gun sound of his fingers. How could he just sit there and hand her this verdict so calmly? He was a doctor he was meant to heal, not send her away. As the enormity of his words sank in, the room started spinning. She couldn't breathe. Her body refused to stop trembling. She made a complete fool of herself and collapsed in a hysterical heap. The stress had finally taken its toll. She felt as if the weight of the whole world was on her shoulders and the earth had given way below her feet.

"Why, Dr Mitra? Why?" But he had no answers... just an ever expanding silence.

"There's no way I can take him to Delhi again," she cried, wiping her eyes with the cuff of her sleeve. "Whatever the course of treatment, it has to continue in Kolkata and you have to help me, Dr Mitra," she sobbed.

He was silent.

"P-p-please, D-d-doctor," she hiccupped.

"Okay, okay, don't be upset. We'll see what we can do." He was quick to console her recognising the onset of hysteria. "I will have a meeting with the doctors here and get back to you."

She rubbed her eyes and dabbed her nose with the hanky he had hurriedly pressed into her hand.

Funnily, at that moment Divya had an out-of-body experience for a second. She viewed the scene dispassionately from above. It had the makings of a TV soap opera.

Silly woman, if you have to weep in public at least remember to carry a hanky in your bag! she silently chastised herself.

Dr Mitra was sympathetic but she knew he was helpless. If he did not know what to do how could she, a lay person? She looked around his sparsely decorated room. The serene face of Lord Krishna stared at her from a calendar hanging crookedly on a hook. Suddenly she thought of the "prayer wall" in Mataji's house in Sita Ram Bazaar. Where was God now that she needed Him? She tried to think of a prayer that she could send to the heavens. Something to give her guidance. To help her. But her mind was blank. It was futile − her attempt to request for Divine intervention. Using up all her reserves of strength, she put on her social mask, thanked the kind doctor and stumbled out of his room, still clutching on to his hanky as if it were her crutch.

She was overcome by an irrational anger at Ravi and his mother. Why did they have to rush back to Kolkata? Why couldn't they have waited till he had healed completely? Maybe all that pushing and twisting on the plane, during the journey, had caused some damage to his implant. What should she do now? What could she do?

Fatigued, she sat in her car in the hospital car park, wishing she could just sit there forever. She clasped her hands tightly as if to strangle the gut-wrenching pain. She let her tears flow not caring about the inquisitive looks she got from passers-by. Resting her head against the steering wheel she sobbed uncontrollably... angrily... helplessly. The sun sank. The skies darkened. Time passed her by slowly. Just a handful of cars were left in the previously packed parking lot. She must have sat there for hours, rooted by her despair. She just couldn't get a hold on herself. That's when her mobile phone rang. It was Sanjay... psychic as ever!

"Hi," his calm voice passed through the foggy pea soup in her mind and registered.

She couldn't talk.

"Hello, Divya. Can you hear me?"

She tried to say something but choked on her words, breathing heavily.

"What's wrong, dear? Are you okay?" he said anxiously into the voiceless space. "Talk to me."

But she had no words to give him. Nothing to say. Only an ominous silence.

"Say something, Divya." Concern laced his voice. "What happened?"

She couldn't... the words got stuck in her throat, emerging as out of sync hiccups. That's when he got worried.

"Is there someone with you?" he asked.

"No," she managed a broken whisper.

"Where are you? I am coming."

That's when her deeply ingrained social behaviour reared its head. No, she was miles away. She couldn't let him come all the way. What could he do anyway? What could anyone do? She had to handle this herself. She took three deep breaths and managed to tell him rather sketchily what she had just gone through.

"I am coming, Divya," he repeated. "You just wait there for me," he said horrified at what she had to go through alone, upset at the state that she was in.

Another three breaths and she was calmer.

"No, no! Don't come I am better now," she said in a voice stronger than she felt.

"Are you sure, dear? If I leave my clinic now I will be there in an hour."

"I am okay, Sanjay. Please don't worry. I'm leaving the hospital now so please don't come."

"Please drive carefully and call me when you reach home," he said, frustrated at not being with her when she needed him.

Driving is an excellent activity to indulge in when you are upset and hassled! Especially driving in an Indian city. You have to focus on the road, be careful you don't run over pigs, cows, dogs, cyclists, and people rushing across the road to test your reaction time (or how good your brakes are!). Other male drivers want to overtake you just because you are a woman, potholes and speed breakers suddenly appear to check whether you are alert or not. You have to give it your 100%. You have to be all there. So she drove. She drove with a vengeance. She drove for hours. It was therapeutic. She went around the city, in some of the most crowded lanes. Speeding, slowing, stopping, honking. She drove till the relentless tears stopped and her eyes were parched... empty, like her soul. She turned to God again. She prayed for strength.

"God, if you are giving me all this shit, at least give me a spade to dig my way through and the strength to shovel it aside."

What would she tell Ravi? Tanya? Ma ji? They would be devastated. She prayed for the right words...for courage and wisdom.

Take these crazy thoughts
from my mind
Wrap them up
seal them
airtight and secure
Lock them in
a feel-proof box
and lose the key.
For they torment my mind
wildly stir
my restless soul

pull me down
knock me out
leaving me breathless
curled up
on the floor.

Life carried on, as it must. It never stops does it? Once again Divya brought Ravi home in an ambulance. Inquisitive neighbours peered from behind their curtains. A crowd gathered as he was taken upstairs. This time on a stretcher. He started losing hope in his future.

"You can't give up," she admonished. "Do something to keep occupied. Watch TV, read, write. You write so well, why don't you write about your experience so that other people with ankylosing spondylitis will know what to expect. It would really help so many people."

But he shut her out. Her words did not register in his mind. He just lay there staring at the ceiling.

"Don't lose hope, Ravi. There are people who have come out of worse conditions. You have to have faith."

She tried in vain to boost his morale but her words fell on deaf ears. She was talking to an impenetrable wall. Not ready to give up, she would force him to do things – get up, walk a few steps, eat. She cajoled and pleaded, raved and ranted.

"Please eat just one spoon. You need to eat to be strong enough to fight the disease."

But to no avail. She could not reach him. He took refuge in his silence. Mentally and physically he was becoming weaker and weaker. He had lost the will to fight… to live. The disease had won. Divya had lost him.

In all this Sanjay was her constant solace. He strived to reduce her mental agony in his own way as he scaffolded her crumbling world with his love.

Dearest D,

I know this will sound crazy at the end of the day... but you are a miracle and I am lucky to have known you over the years. I cherish every moment I have been with you, as they are all special seconds of completeness. S

My dearest S,

Is this what I wanted from life − is this the way I want my life to be? Is your life the way you want it to be? I know nobody's happy with their lives; they always have something to complain about. But don't get me wrong... I'm not complaining! I do acknowledge the fact that I am blessed with much more than most people and when I look around me I see that each and every person is fighting a tougher battle than mine! It's just that I always feel there's this vacuum inside me... a kind of emptiness... this feeling that I should be doing so much more than what I'm doing. I don't know if you understand what I'm saying but I don't blame you 'cos sometimes even I can't understand this incompleteness inside me. So when you say I'm a 'complete woman' I disagree with you. There's so much I want to do but somehow I'm not getting the time. I think I'm trying to rush things and should ease off a bit. But then I feel that time is just zipping by and soon I'll be too old to live all my dreams... then I look at Dad (who is such an amazing man!) I think people should learn to live like he does! I just think about his day and I feel tired! He packs each second of his day with so much that it makes you re-look at your way of living life! So what if he's nearly eighty? − he still finds time and has the energy to go to the nursing home, write poems/stories, paint, teach underprivileged kids and has started a new community project where he counsels all the senior citizens who go for walks to the park and gives free medical advice!

Love you from the bottom of my heart

D

Panic Attacks

"Divya, beta. Could you come home please? Now."

Although Ma ji's voice was as polite as always, Divya detected anxiety and panic. She never called her at work unless it was an emergency.

"Now? What's the matter, Ma ji? Is Ravi okay?"

She was in the middle of a meeting and was running late in her schedules for the day.

"Ravi says he can't breathe. I'm worried, beti." Her voice quavered.

"I'm coming, Ma ji. Don't worry." She dropped everything.

Trying not to think about the accumulating backlog, she postponed all her appointments and rushed home. She had to remind herself to drive carefully as she concentrated on changing gears and avoiding potholes. Her sweaty hands slipped on the steering wheel. She narrowly missed hitting a cow but made it home in record time. God! I hope he's okay, she prayed as she parked the car and rushed upstairs. She fumbled in her bag for the house key... lipstick, pens, fresheners, bills... where the hell was her key?! Her hands trembled.

"Stop!" she told herself. "You need to calm down before you enter the house. Take three deep breaths."

On her third inhalation, Ma ji opened the door. Impatiently waiting for her arrival, she had heard Divya's car.

"Thank God you're here. We need to get a doctor urgently. He says he can't breathe." She was in a flap herself.

"What's wrong, Ravi?" Divya said rushing to his side, forgetting his rule of taking off shoes before entering his room. He lay on his bed gasping, his eyes wide with panic. Bending over him she stroked his head, trying to calm him down.

"I can't breathe," he managed to whisper.

"Okay. Calm down. I'm going to get a doctor. Hang in there."

Picking up her handbag and the car keys, she charged off again.

"Try the polyclinics," Ma ji said to her retreating back as she clattered down the stairs. "Some doctor will agree to come home."

That was the problem... getting a doctor to "agree to come home", she soon realised, as she did the rounds of all the clinics in the neighbourhood. All the doctors she met refused point-blank.

"Sorry, madam, but I don't make house visits anymore. Bring him here and I'll see what I can do," said the first doctor.

"But I can't do that. He's bedridden and will not be able to come. Please, doctor, he can't breathe." Frantically she pleaded, in vain.

Back in the car, Divya burnt rubber to the next clinic... and the next. But it was the same story each and every time. As precious time flew by, she wondered how Ravi was. What she would do if all the bloody doctors refused. "They shouldn't be in this profession," she fumed. She thought of all the times her father had rushed off on emergency calls at all times of the day and night… never refusing anyone who turned to him for help. She wished he were with her in her moment of crisis.

She was fast becoming an ideal candidate for a nervous breakdown, she thought as she entered a clinic in the next colony. Seeing the hysterical look in her eyes and hearing the desperation in her trembling voice the doctor thankfully deigned to come, on the condition that she'd take him in her car and then drop him back afterward.

"I promise I'll do anything. Just come. Please hurry."

She was so grateful that she even carried his briefcase for him as they hurried to the car. And he let her. Rushing home, they found Ravi calmer. His breathing had eased out.

"It was a panic attack," the doctor announced. "It happens sometimes with chronically ill patients."

After checking Ravi's pulse and blood pressure, he left, thousand rupees richer than he had been five minutes ago.

"I'm so sorry," Ravi apologised. "I don't know what happened. I just couldn't breathe."

******

That was the first of many such attacks. Attacks that came with no warning… that lurked around the corners of each day, ready to pounce on them. Attacks that scared him with their intensity. Attacks that whittled away into Divya's psyche, leaving her trembling and ready to collapse.

They needed a dedicated doctor who would be ready to come in such emergencies. Most of the doctors in the colony had by now, at some point or the other, come to their house. All these doctors now refused to come after a visit or two. Unfortunately, the main reason for this was Ravi. Each of those doctors had been meted out the same treatment by him. Ravi would 'prepare' for a doctor's impending visit with a long list of questions…

"Should I try and sit up? For how long? What can I eat? Can I take all the medicines together? If not, what gap should there be between each tablet?"

The questions went into great detail, covering at least two pages, if not more. With each question, Divya could see the look of impatience creep into the doctor's eyes and hear an abruptness appear in the tone of his voice. The initial pleasant bedside manner was soon replaced with brusqueness and an apparent eagerness to leave. By the middle of page 2, the doctor would check his watch a few times, stop listening to the questions, prescribe a few medicines, and leave. Upset, Ravi would then complain bitterly about the doctor, curse the entire medical profession and finally refuse to take the recommended medicines.

"He didn't even examine me properly so how can he prescribe these tablets? On what basis? He's a useless doctor," he would conclude. "God knows where you picked him up from!"

The complaints were constant, as was the long list of questions. Doctors came and went but Ravi rejected each one of them for he was not getting the answer he was looking for… the answer that his wound would heal, that he would recover completely and walk again.

Understanding what he was going through, Divya tried to reason with him, failing which she started losing her cool. She was stuck in a catch-twenty-two situation. She couldn't ignore his complaints about his health, even though she knew most of the time they were psychological and stress based. It was getting extremely difficult for her to handle. She began to question her ability to cope with the situation.

Staying Afloat

Feeling inadequate and alone, she clung to Sanjay's words like a drowning woman.

Dearest D,

I love you more than I love myself... that's for sure and I will carry you with me for this journey at least... so that next life I have a chance to be with you each moment... cry not my dearest dear as I am with you in some silent corner of your being... touching you and feeling all the deep pain in you... I love you more than I can ever express...

S

Dearest S,

As each day goes by, becoming a part of my past, I try to blot out the grey and focus on the brighter hues of life. Sometimes I succeed and I can feel my spirits rise in celebration of all the wonderful moments that I have had the good fortune to experience. But when I fail, I am overcome by intense negative emotions that need a tremendous effort to get out of or else I will be submerged! As waves of depression and guilt attack me (the intensity is decreasing) I think of the faith you have in me... in my abilities to cope and rise above it all. And as

346

the feeling gradually subsides, to be replaced by a deep sense of gratitude, my longing for you increases in direct proportion! Complicated, aren't I? And then I just sit and write down whatever I feel and though it may seem trite (which often it is!) ... it comes straight from my heart! I must confess... every time I send you one of my 'poems' I feel like that bard, Cacophonix, in Asterix comics – ending up gagged and bound, all trussed up on a tree because he wants to sing and no one wants to listen! But it's just my way of expressing myself... I just write about my true feelings and thoughts and call them poems (for want of a better word!). And then, you are also to blame for encouraging me by saying that you love my poems!

D

My S,

What happens when your Guardian Angel becomes your lover??? You are blessed with a gift more precious than you can ever imagine. You feel lucky... the chosen one! And that's how I feel... even though it was born in the darkest hour of my life, its light is bright enough to illuminate a thousand lifetimes. It was as if God realised the depth of my depression and desperation. He sent you to pluck me out of the abyss I was free-falling into... no, maybe not to pluck me out but to act as a parachute, to hold my hand and help me glide fearlessly to safety and cushion me if I fell. I know for a fact that God – that supreme, nameless, faceless power – watches over me. I often wonder whether you were sent as a test of my strength (that I finally failed!) or a gift (that I deserved). Whatever the reason may be, I do not wish to question it – just enjoy the wondrous healing beauty of your love and bask in its glory. I die a million deaths when we part not knowing when the next time will be... not wanting to let go... Yet, every meeting is a strengthening of our unique and rare bond which knows no limits, sets no rules and expects nothing in return. There are very few people who can honestly say that they have experienced an emotion like this where you want to give all that you have and get more than you give; where you cherish and yearn for togetherness and respect each other's space. A feeling that does not fade at the end of the day but becomes stronger with each new dawn. An emotion that you wrap around yourself, secure in its comfort and warmth. A feeling that reinforces your desire to live because life is beautiful and your existence matters to someone... somewhere.

So tell me...

What happens when you fall in love with your Guardian Angel? You transmogrify into this amazing being who feels beautiful and young... who feels powerful yet can lose control so easily, who is content yet never satisfied... full of positivism and hope because it is magical and mystical finding your soul mate... secure in the knowledge that he is in your heart as you are in his...

I love you

D

Dearest D,

Gosh... you sure are making this guardian angel feel like someone from another planet... crazy woman, don't you realise that he is the lucky guy... he is the one who is the recipient of unconditional love... he is the one who is basking in the warmth of her beauty, her desires, her overflowing emotions... he is the gainer, as everything is free and fancy for him in life... and his world is fuller and more complete with his pretty woman's emotions "wrapped around him, secure in comfort". It is incidental that he loves his D with the intensity and passion of a

lover (discarding the guardian angel garb with disdain!),
... yes, his pretty woman is very special to him and heaven
on earth cannot break him free from this craziness...
that's how this story unfolds mysteriously without much
theme and end, so much like the unfinished symphony,
ageless... Is this his definition of true love in form... or is
this one of the greatest living tragedies of our era ...??

> *yours & only yours*
>
> *S*

Divya had the unenviable task of juggling different roles and maintaining her sanity at the same time. Florence Nightingale, physiotherapist, counsellor, philosopher, wife, mother, daughter-in-law, daughter, sister, all rolled up in one schizophrenic tangle. She learnt how to clean Ravi's wounds and change the dressing, check his blood pressure, help him with the bedpan, sponge him and help him with his exercises. The prolonged intake of very strong antibiotics had not only killed his appetite but had also created an intense aversion to food. He stopped eating by himself and had to be fed. Often force-fed like a child.

"Guess who came to the institute today?" She distracted him with small talk and slipped in a spoon full of mushy food into his unsuspecting mouth. He had stopped eating solids and spat out anything that required him to chew. It was heart-wrenching to see him regress like this.

"You have to eat, Ravi. How are you going to get your strength back if you continue like this?" she cajoled and pleaded.

"You just want to poison me," he said angrily, his eyes wide and manic. "Just see that look on your face. You are enjoying my suffering." His accusations increased as his mental faculties began to get more and more affected.

"He doesn't know what he's saying. He doesn't mean it," Divya had to keep reminding herself as tears automatically filled her eyes. "This is not him speaking."

Often he would knock the spoon out of her hand, spilling food on himself and the bed. Mealtimes became a full-fledged battle.

"You feed him, Divya. He just doesn't listen to me." Ma ji was giving up too.

Not wanting him to stay hungry, she continued with her efforts, regardless of his curses and punches.

In his lucid moments Ravi would be filled with remorse.

"I didn't mean to hit you. But I hate being forced to eat. I don't want to eat. I hate the sight of food. I can't swallow."

She would try to pep him up and that was her biggest challenge. How could she possibly cheer him up and speak words of hope when tears of despair flooded her own heart?

Along with all this Divya had to be Tanya's buffer. Whenever she called from Delhi Divya would force some cheer to enter her voice.

"Hi, darling! What's up? How was college?"

As perceptive as ever, Tanya could see through her act and hear the deeper emotions in her superficial words of greeting.

"Mum, what's wrong? You don't have to put on an act with me. Is Papa giving you a tough time about eating again?" Her voice quivered with emotion.

Although distance increased her worries tenfold, Divya was glad she was far away. But she was weary of her continuous struggles. For how long could she put up this brave front? Was she wrong in wanting to protect Tanya? For how long could she continue to shield her from the realities of their life?

Thankfully Tanya had Buddhism to give her the strength to cope with the multitude of emotions that clouded her sun every morning. It was Buddhism that helped her put things into perspective and find answers to the questions that constantly plagued her. It helped her through the longest and darkest nights of their lives. In many ways she became stronger than Divya.

As for Divya... yes, it was Sanjay's unconditional love that she clutched on to for dear life to help her stay afloat.

My S
You have given me
memories
tinted with warm shades of love
coloured with bright streaks of
passion...
Memories
that hold me together
keep me from falling apart
strengthening me with
their silent energy
protecting me from
the world.
Memories
I thrive on seeking

sustenance and renewed pleasure
for though I believe in
the power of Now
I live
off those wonder moments
of yesterdays with you
and
for those tomorrows
in your arms...

So darling...I need nothing else
D

D... I admire you more than you can ever imagine... I love
you more passionately than anyone ever has or ever will...
I adore you for your sensitive mind and your vibrant self...
and I hate myself for not being able to give you all that
you need... I carry you in me 24 hours, 365 days...
luv u a million lives...
S

******

The phone rang. "Hello?" Divya said, impatiently brushing loose strands of prematurely greyed hair away from her eyes. Her nerves were frazzled. She had just finished trying to feed Ravi. He emerged victorious in this particular 'dinner war'. Keeping his mouth clenched tightly shut, he had refused even a drop of water. She was mentally and physically burnt out.

"Hey, Divi! It's me!" Jyoti's cheerful voice penetrated the thick miasma of depression and frustration.

"Oh hi, didi. How are things?"

Divya quickly put a lock on her emotions, scared that she would start crying on the phone. "Everything's okay here. Don't' worry about me, didi."

There was no point burdening Jyoti with her troubles. And anyway, there was nothing she could do from across the seven seas.

"You take care. Thanks for calling. Bye," Divya said prematurely ending their conversation and putting down the phone.

She knew it was completely out of character because both of them used to have long heart-to-heart chats whenever Jyoti called, in spite of the exorbitant international rates. But Divya also knew that she wouldn't have been able to handle Jyoti's usual questions about Ravi. She would have broken down. It was the shortest conversation Divya ever had with her sister. A couple of hours later Jyoti called again and wept into the phone… as Divya knew she would.

"Divs, what's wrong?" her voice heavy with sisterly concern. "Your voice was so dead this morning. I never want to hear you sound like that again. I can only imagine what you are going through. I wish I was there to give you a hug." There was nothing she could do. There was nothing anybody could do.

"I'm okay, didi." Divya had her emotions under control once again. She had to put Jyoti at ease. "Don't worry, I am okay." She repeated as if to convince herself. "Nothing I can't handle."

Divya hated what she was turning into – a bitter and cynical woman. Most of the time she was functioning on auto-control, not giving herself the luxury of expressing her feelings. She was turning into stone. Their financial situation was depressing. Ravi's medical treatment was exorbitant. For the first time in their lives they were in debt – a situation she'd never thought they'd ever be in. She decided to sell her jewellery to repay their relatives.

"I never wear all those necklaces and bangles anyway," she rationalised. "I don't go anywhere. What's the point of keeping them locked up in the bank when we need the money now?"

When they heard about her intentions, Tara and Varun were horrified. They refused to let her entertain the idea. They sent her some more money instead. For how long could she go on taking money from others like this? There was nothing Ravi could do for he was fighting his own silent battle as he lay there 24 X 7 on his bed, staring at the ceiling, a prisoner in his body. Bedridden and completely dependent on others, he prayed for release. But God was not listening.

Divya dreaded coming back from work, not knowing what state of mind she'd find him in when she got home. She searched for answers as she lay awake at night, wondering about the future. It would be so easy to succumb to the arms of sorrow. What would happen if she caved in? What would happen to Ravi? To Tanya? Clutching at straws for support, she prayed for the strength to carry on. Secure in the knowledge that Sanjay would understand, she wrote to him about her horrific fears and innermost feelings… emotions that otherwise would not have seen the light of day. His amazing love light shone through her tunnel, lighting up her path through the journey of her life.

"You can do it. You've done it for so long. Don't give up."

She needed a miracle to happen.

Dearest D,

I know exactly how you feel and there is really nothing I can do except:

wait quietly for another chance

another moment

to brace my arms around my angel

in soft comfort of completeness

till the breathing comes easy.

In a rhythm of a single heartbeat

and when the pulse of life

throbs violently often and

often quietly

and then slips in silent tones

till sleep in deep

we drape ourselves in silent warmth

a 1000 miles away...

till another morn...

Can I love you more each day... can I in my silent ways love you more???

Your S

Dearest S,

We meet

then part

clouds colliding

against mountains

raining down emotions.

You are the sun playing hide and seek...

gold against my greys.

We meet...

I am a firefly
incandescent
in the black night,
a butterfly
flitting in the gentle summer breeze...
ethereal.
Then you leave...
my glow dims
my wings grow heavy.
The vacuum inside expands
all consuming
driving out reason.
I feel clichéd
A silent cry is born deep within
imprisoned by my lips.
I must not cling.
You go away
again.
I love you
D

Dearest D,
I love your poems endless... you did inspire me to scribble
a few lines in the dead of the night staring onto the sea...
I love you for all that you are and for all that you seek my
love...
Yours S

Dearest S,

What would I do without words?? Even with them I feel so inept at expressing my deepest, innermost emotions...

Reaching out
for your words
suspended around me
I pluck out the ones
I long to hear...
words of love to make me feel beautiful
and young...
of care and concern
to pull me out
of this self-made abyss.
I glow –
a golden orb
in your evening sky.
Syllable by syllable
I roll these words in my mind
savouring their taste
making them linger
forever.

Your D

Opportunity Calls

Once again Divya's life took another strange turn. She visited Delhi to spend a few days with Tanya and take a much-needed break. During her stay she was offered a job that would pay her more than double the salary she was earning in Kolkata. She jumped at the offer. Not only would she earn more, she would also be able to shift to Delhi with Ravi and Ma ji. They would be with Tanya again as well as within driving distance of her parents. She would finally get the emotional support she was longing for. It seemed like a win-win situation.

Her earlier pleas of shifting to Delhi had fallen on deaf ears. The two things that had prevented this were her job and the flat. Now Ma ji and Ravi would definitely agree.

I will give in my resignation as soon as I got back to Kolkata, she thought excited at the prospect.

All she needed to do was try and sell the Kolkata flat and buy a place in Delhi. Rushing headlong, at breakneck speed, towards a nervous breakdown, she could not make it on her own anymore. She desperately needed emotional, physical and medical support. Under the circumstances, it seemed the most logical and rational thing to do. This was a Godsend. Her mind was made and she accepted the offer. Tanya was thrilled with the news.

"We will be together again," she said happily.

And so were Divya's parents.

"You can stay with us till you find a house," Varun offered.

It seemed as if now their life condition would finally improve.

But she was wrong.

She was in for an unexpected shock.

Ravi refused to entertain any ideas of relocation.

"This is my house and I don't want to shift to Delhi," he said stubbornly. "Delhi is terrible. The weather is awful and the distances are killing."

"How does all that affect you?" Divya argued. "You will be in a room in Delhi just like you are here in Kolkata. You'll be in air-conditioned comfort and you won't be commuting anywhere. Just think... at least you'll be with Tanya again. You know you miss her a lot."

She dangled the 'daughter carrot' as an irresistible temptation. But it didn't work. He refused. Not willing to give up she resigned from her job, hoping that seeing her determination, he would change his mind.

It was not an easy decision for Divya either. It was tough giving up a job that had educated and nurtured her for fifteen years. She loved everything about her work and about Kolkata. She would miss the wonderful friends she had been fortunate to make over the years. She would miss Sanjay.

But she was a woman desperately trying to hold on to her sanity. She had to look out for herself, just so that she would have the strength to take care of the significant others in her life. There was no one else who could make this decision for her. She had to rely on her own wisdom.

But if she was determined, so was Ravi. He steadfastly stuck to his resolution. Every evening they would argue about this issue, ending in a stalemate as neither of them was willing to give in. Divya spent sleepless nights tossing the future around in her head and turning in helpless frustration, waking up hopelessly tangled in her bedsheet of thoughts. She needed someone to take the rudder and guide her in the right direction so that she could sail along effortlessly. But there was nobody.

"You go ahead with your plan, Divya. We'll follow later," said Ma ji, taking charge, trying to find a way out of this deadlock. "Don't worry, Ravi, I will be here with you," she said as she stood next to Ravi's bed, running her hand over his head.

Divya was aghast and speechless. She couldn't believe this was happening to her. It was as if a fence had suddenly been erected with Ravi and Ma ji on one side and her on the other. She felt like an outsider – not part of the family. Why couldn't they try to step into her shoes and see things from her side for a change? After all it was just a house – bricks and cement – that they were hanging on to. What about peace of mind? Happiness? Emotional security?

"Why are you doing this, Ma ji?" Divya spoke to her mother-in-law that night, after Ravi had taken his sleeping pill and drifted off into a drug-induced sleep.

"It's okay. We'll manage. Ravi is in no condition to leave," Ma ji answered.

"We'll take him on a stretcher by plane. I've already spoken to the airlines and they've assured me it can be organised," Divya explained.

She knew that if Ma ji agreed to shift to Delhi, Ravi would have no choice but to come along as well. He couldn't possibly stay alone. But she couldn't convince

Ma ji to change her mind. Divya could see where Ravi's stubborn streak came from.

For twenty-three years she had put her feelings and dreams aside on the back burner, as she stoically stuck the pieces of her shattered rose-tinted glasses together, not willing to let go of her naïve romanticism. So what if she ended up living a stilted life? Bitter and angry at what she felt was the selfish unfairness of their attitude; Divya refused to change her plan. A part of her died a cynical death inside as she proceeded to make plans to leave.

Her friends supported her decision... and surprisingly, so did her parents. They could see her slowly but surely falling apart.

"After all, you are not leaving him... you want to take him with you."

"You have to think about yourself. It's high time now."

"If you are not mentally and physically fit how will you take care of anyone?"

"You have to think of your financial situation. Of Tanya."

Their voices of reason echoed in Divya's mind. Then why was her heart heavy and her steps leaden? She had never thought she would ever leave Kolkata! In fact, it was one of the toughest decisions of her life. She spent many sleepless nights praying for guidance and wisdom. Hoping for a sign that would show her the way. A star of Bethlehem, a streak of lightening, a voice in the night... anything.

Was she taking a step in the right direction?

Should she just forget about her life and carry on like she had done for the last twenty-three years? Being a crutch and a nursemaid?

As it is, half of my life is already over so why rock the boat now? she thought, her mind playing the devil's advocate.

Go with the flow. The job offer is a stroke of luck, it was meant to happen. It's a blessing in disguise that I shouldn't reject, another part of her argued.

Which part was wearing the halo and which one had the horns? Divya wished she had the insight to know.

Leaving Home

The farewell parties started. The days passed by in a hectic blur. Her little black book was full of appointments. There were days when she was invited out for all three meals – breakfast, lunch and dinner, and then a tea or a coffee thrown in! Her friends were amazing – they were her major source of strength. They knew what she had been through... they had seen her suffer. They stood behind her... her pillars, preventing her from crumbling and giving in. She hated the fact that she would be leaving them. She would miss each one of them terribly.

Sanjay was initially shocked and upset. This was completely unexpected. He tried to talk her out of her decision, hoping he'd make her change her mind.

"You just need to hang in there. You are strong. You can do it," he urged.

But Divya needed to do this for herself, even if it meant that this desperate act might end up being her swan song. She had cast the dice and was now ready and willing to pay the price. Soon he too gave in and wished her luck. As she packed her suitcases, she was full of regret. There was a strange emptiness inside. A vacuum that was sucking her in. A black hole of nothingness.

The day of her departure dawned.

"Have a good new life," Ravi said forlornly, as she kissed him goodbye.

"Why are you saying that?" she said tearfully hugging him, still not willing to give up hope. "You will be joining me soon. You promised me you would."

"We'll see," he replied as noncommittal as ever.

Ma ji hugged her, a sad look in her eyes. "Have a safe journey, beti."

Divya hated goodbyes and this was the mother of all farewells. Why did it have to end this way? Where was her happy ending? What happened to the "… and they lived happily ever after?"

She tried her best to dissuade her friends from coming to see her off, but they were adamant. They refused to let her go to the station alone in a taxi.

"You can't leave Kolkata just like that. All by yourself. We are going to give you a proper send off."

She was blessed to have such wonderful people as her friends. She wept unashamedly in the car… tears of frustration and despair chased each other down her cheeks in a steady flow. Her friends helped her on to the train and waved goodbye. Tears blurred their eyes. Powerful emotions clamoured inside her – raucous… heavy. She longed to release them. To free herself, for they pulled her down. Yet she hung on to them like a security blanket, desperately clasping them to her breast, afraid to let go. She was walking on the delicate tightrope dividing sanity and madness. Fragile… the bubble of emotions burst. Broken fragments of thoughts, dreams and desires hung in the air around her. Their jagged edges pierced her. She bled tears of confused despair as she felt her world disintegrate around her. She struggled to maintain the calm façade of her social image. Aware that the other co-passengers were giving her covert strange looks, she turned her face away and stared out of the window at the busy platform. At her group of friends dabbing their eyes.

She was facing a new tomorrow but she still carried the baggage of yesterday. She felt a boulder of guilt and grief settle solidly on her heart. It would stay with her for a long, long time. As the train left Kolkata, heading towards her uncharted future, her cell phone beeped. Sanjay.

"I can imagine the intensity of your emotions. I love you and admire your inner strength…"

Reluctantly
my fingers unfold
releasing
all that I cared for –
The carefree days of my youth
secure in my parents' love.
Clinging desperately to the last second
not wanting to leave
not ready to go
into the unknown future.
But I went.
I let go
as I did your hand
not wanting to hurt –
a part of me dying.
As each finger opens
I lose something
precious.

"Veg? Non-veg?"

The monotonous nasal voice of the train attendant cut through her disturbing cloud of thoughts. An anti-climax of sorts, bringing her back to her present.

"Veg? Non-veg?" he repeated asking her preference for dinner.

"Nothing" she was about to say. The thought of food seemed so mundane and unthinkable. But the rational part of her took over.

"Veg, please."

She needed the strength to face her future. She needed to put her emotions on hold till further notice. She tucked her tear sodden hanky away with a determined shove.

No more tears, she thought. *I will take one day at a time. I have always been good at that.*

The train was running late, as usual. The other passengers complained but for once Divya was thankful for the tardiness of the Indian railways. The delay of two hours would give her some more time to herself. Lying awake all night lulled by the gentle rocking of the train, she had calmly arranged her swirling thoughts into little mental boxes, to be opened, if ever, when she had the strength to face the contents. As the first rays of dawn slowly pulled the reluctant sun up into the lightening dark of the sky, she felt at peace. She watched the pale golden orb rise like a bubble and fill a corner of her horizon. She was filled with the kind of hope that only the birth of a new day can bring. She began counting her blessings... one by one. Tanya topped the list. She always would.

Divya was now confident and sure of herself and of what she had to do. She and Tanya would go house hunting and find a suitable house with a garden and big windows, to let the sun and fresh air in. A house with a view that would bring cheer to Ravi. Soon they would be able to shift him to Delhi. Before long they would all be together again. She was fortunate to have the support of her family and friends in, what most people would think was a drastic decision. And to top it all, she had a brand new job waiting for her – lucrative as well as challenging. Soon… things would fall in to place and all this would seem like a bad dream.

Then of course she had Sanjay. His love would stay with her forever whether they were together or not. It was a love that was beyond proximity… that would not dim with distance or fade with time. An ageless and divine love. As she went down the checklist, she welcomed each blessing with a warm mental tick of gratitude.

The train slowly chugged into New Delhi railway station. Coolies started running beside the moving compartments ready to jump in as soon as it slowed down. Divya looked around at what had been her neutral haven for twenty-four hours. This compartment had been her sanctuary, protecting her from the debris of her crumbling world. Twenty-four hours of solitude and introspection was what her weary soul needed to recover. She had not uttered a word, except for "Veg please". Keeping to herself, she had not made any attempt to communicate with her fellow travellers. She had used this precious time to pull herself together, and get out of the rut she was getting stuck in. She was back on track again. Strong and confidant.

There was an infectious air of excitement around her. Passengers started wearing their shoes and gathering their belongings, impatient to disembark. As the train moved in Divya eagerly scanned the waiting crowds from her window in search of Tanya. She soon spotted her. Tanya stood out in the melee… a perfect picture of vibrant youth. The little sequins on her turquoise blue kurta shone in the sunlight. Her chiffon scarf fluttered gaily in the breeze, like the delicate wings of a butterfly. Her dark hair framed her face in bouncy layers.

It's amazing how quickly she had blossomed into this young beautiful lady, Divya thought as maternal pride filled her being. Hidden behind the darkened one-way glass of her train window, she watched Tanya lovingly, unobserved. She saw her glancing expectantly at each carriage, checking the number as it went by. She was looking for 'A2'... her mother's carriage. Divya saw her eyes light up as they registered the number and settled on A2. She walked purposefully alongside the train, waiting for it to stop.

As the train screeched to a jerking halt, Divya's mobile phone beeped in a strangely coincidental, synchronised harmony. It's amazing how Sanjay's timing was always spot on! He was thinking of her.

"Your story unfolds mysteriously, so much like an unfinished symphony. I will love you silently, from afar as I always have. I will love you till I die..."

Blinking back tears, she gathered her courage and her bags, and hailed a coolie. Taking a determined deep breath, she prepared to leave the comforting shelter of the train. Following the coolie who was struggling with her heavy suitcases, she walked down the narrow aisle. She stepped out, onto the platform, into the warmth of the afternoon winter sun. She stepped into Tanya's tight embrace.

"Hi, Mum." Tanya hugged her. Her cheerful voice and happy smile filled her heart with its positive power.

"Hi, my darling," Divya said, holding her slim body tightly against hers.

"Everything's going to be okay," they spoke simultaneously, each one reading the other's anxious